THE

WATCHER

THE WATCHER

The Gifted Series

Book One

ENNIS STANLEY

Published by Francing Pages.

First Edition.

Copyright © 2025 Ennis Stanley.

Illustrations by Scarlett Alexandra, copyright Ennis Stanley.

All rights reserved. No part of this book may be reproduced or transmitted by any means, except as permitted by UK copyright law or the author. For licensing requests, please get in touch with the author at ennisstanleytheauthor@gmail.com.

Disclaimer:
This is a work of fiction. All characters and events are the product of the author's imagination. Any resemblance to actual persons, living or dead, or real events is purely coincidental.

ISBN: 9798262099290

DEDICATION

This book is dedicated to my two children, Scarlett and Braeden.

Acknowledgements

The author would like to thank her husband Kevin, her family, and her friends for their endless encouragement and support. To Jen, Anita and Shelagh for reading the early manuscripts and believing in her. And to her friend, Helen, without whom she never would have had the courage to publish.

Thank you all x

The Gifted Series - Book One - The Watcher

The Gifted Series - Book One - The Watcher

CHAPTER ONE

THE TARGET

A breeze circulated around his ankles as he sat on the leather corner couch he always occupied on a Saturday night when she was out. He didn't, however, shudder at the sudden chill or look irritated at the abrupt draft. He didn't feel the cold, and right now his mind was busy elsewhere. He'd been watching the same girl all evening; her posture becoming increasingly slumped the more she drank. He knew it had never been her intention to stay this late, but her best friend and other colleagues had persuaded her, and now he had to sit there and endure the shrieks of laughter and shouts from their table.

He watched as she stood pulling down her top, which had begun to rise while she slouched, and walked towards the bathrooms. Whilst she was gone, he relaxed slightly and took in the other customers frequenting this popular public house. Most people he saw were normal humans, sporadically clumped; them all enjoying their private rendezvous with those they cared about. Drinking and feasting on culinary delights whilst the winter weather played havoc outside.

Impatiently, he clicked his phone screen; she'd been gone for five minutes. If she were much longer, he'd risk the embarrassment of entering the wrong toilet to check if she was alright. He could never tell who or what might happen in this city, and he'd be damned if she went missing whilst he was watching. Putting his glass of whisky to his mouth, he inhaled the nutty vanilla essence, letting the liquid wet his lips as his tongue licked the excess, savouring the flavour. He'd been nursing the drink for some time now and realised that he might have to finish it and buy another if the girls were to stay any longer. He was already receiving irritated glances from passers-by who wanted his table. He was never one to linger unnecessarily, but he could only leave when she did - and right now, it looked as though she was staying put.

His eyes once again flowed over the other clientele: The supernaturals of this world. He focused on the three nightwalkers sitting in the dark and dingy far corner, their discussion centring on their potential victims. He didn't feel any concern or need to intervene; he knew the vampires from old, and their plotting did not cause him to worry. All the vampires of this city knew their limits, and if they ever became overly frivolous, the laws laid down by their leader, or indeed his community and Emperor, would punish them. He turned his attention to two witch lovers whose whisperings were so hushed even he had trouble hearing them, so he moved on to scrutinising the were-shifters occupying tables a few over from him. As he made eye contact with one of them, the whole group began to fidget, their conversation falling silent. The discreet scratching of their nose, the nervous sip of their beer, their eyes searching anywhere but at him – he noticed it all. He didn't want to make them uncomfortable, but nor did he want them to think he was submissive or weak. He was superior to all these beings and wouldn't let his reputation slide. His gaze momentarily shifted to four individuals who had just walked in. These boys were different to the were-shifters he'd just been watching. These were their superior relatives: mammal-shifters. The Watcher could sense the beasts prowling within their bodies, and as he caught the eye of one of them - a medium-height black guy with a head of tight curls and trimmed styled goatee - he felt the mammal's yellow eyes blaze menacingly at him. The Watcher raised his glass to acknowledge another supernatural before his vision was distracted by the young woman returning from the bathroom.

She had tidied herself up whilst in there, her hair had been brushed, her lips reapplied with lipstick, and her hands smelt of jasmine moisturising lotion. She staggered slightly as she entered the bar area, bumping into the counter, the hand of the black guy grabbing her shoulder to keep her steady.

"Oh, I'm so sorry," she said, her voice full of apology and a small giggle escaping her lips.

"Hey, no problem, Logan," the mammal-shifter said, ensuring she could stand straight.

"Oh, Quinn, I didn't see you there." She threw her arms around his neck, his coming around her waist as she fell into him again.

"I think you might have had enough," he said, pulling away to study her face.

"I know, but they keep buying me drinks. I never wanted to stay out this long; you know me." She smirked, taking his pint and gulping at it before returning it to his hand.

"Yes, I do know what Lexi is like," he said, sipping the beer, keeping it out of her reach.

"You said it. Just wish I was strong enough to say no to her. But you know how she gets. Sometimes you must pick your battles," she smiled. Quinn, too, knew Lexi from work and was aware of her persuasive nature. "And I've had a long week. I spent most of today on my laptop at home, so I couldn't resist the invite out."

"You work too hard, you know," he said, sipping his drink.

"It's always like this in the run-up to Christmas," she said exasperatedly, leaning into the bar, her shoulder rubbing his.

Over in the corner, The Watcher gripped his glass, his arms tense, his body straining not to advance and pull her away. He knew he shouldn't feel this way, but he would intervene if she rubbed shoulders with him again. She was too good for a mammal-shifter, even if Quinn was her work colleague. He felt his eyes cloud, the red mist rising through his body so strongly that he couldn't help but erupt a slight growl from his throat. Hearing the noise, the mammal-shifter looked over, and seeing the scrutiny in his stare, he retreated from her instantly.

"Where are you sitting?" Quinn asked, looking for somewhere to take her before The Watcher could react further.

"Over in the green booth." She indicated to the far side, and one of the girls waved at them as if on cue.

Quinn returned the gesture and assisted her over to them. He knew when he was being warned to keep his distance.

Once he returned to the bar, the mammal-shifter and The Watcher made no further acknowledgement of each other, and the evening continued to pass without incident. The supernaturals of this city were aware of The Gifted beings from the Hartvigsen estate, and all kept them at arm's length.

However, the small group of mortal girls knew nothing of these beings and ordered another bottle of wine, so The Watcher remained in his seat regarding them from a distance. He was not here to hurt them or, indeed, hurt anybody.

He was just here to subtly, watch.

It was eleven-fifty before he stirred from his perch, the girls were getting ready to leave, and he drained his glass, sucking in through his teeth at the taste, before pulling on his grey funnel neck coat and tightening his scarf. He didn't require the scarf, or the coat for that matter, but he knew he'd have unwanted attention if he wasn't dressed suitably for the weather. He strode purposefully towards the women heading for the door, one hand in his pocket, the other coming to rest on the arm that shot out in front of him, holding it in mid-air before it touched him.

"Please don't hurt her," the mammal-shifter said, his hand hot under The Watcher's grasp.

"Please do not touch me!" The Watcher stated, his smoky tone reverberating from his throat.

The mammal-shifter immediately lowered his arm as The Watcher let go, his ochre-brown eyes scanning the green-eyed stranger.

"I know your kind, and she doesn't deserve her fate."

"And what fate is that prey?" The Watcher asked, hearing the pub door shut as the women vacated.

"The fate you have in store for her."

"You know nothing of what she is to me or of who I am to her or what the fates have decided," he replied in an irritable tone. His quarry had vanished.

"Yes, but I know your kind," the mammal-shifter said, with evidence of a plea in his words. "I just don't want her harmed, or any of them."

The Watcher did not know why he even tolerated speaking to this creature. Mammal-shifters were beneath him, and he had been taught never to engage them unless it was of some benefit.

"I will not hurt her; that is not *my* nature. I want to make sure she is safe." He had no idea why he was explaining himself. It was none of his business what he was doing and why. And, if he wanted to, he could cause significant harm to him and all in this pub, so why was he bothering? Because it wasn't The Watcher's Gifted ability to hurt or to maim, he wasn't bloodthirsty. If anything, he was the opposite. That, however, wasn't to say he couldn't.

The mammal-shifter nodded at The Watcher's reply. He knew he would never stand a chance against a Gifted, but he couldn't help but say anything. It was not in *his* nature to watch hurt and not do anything to stop it.

"I hope you are sincere," Quinn said, stepping back to allow the man to continue.

"I am never anything but."

And, with that, he left the pub's warmth for the cold, icy weather that had started raging outside. Turning left towards the high street, he sniffed the air, inhaling Logan's scent. The jasmine had faded, yet the smell of sun-blushed skin, candy floss body wash and Sauvignon Blanc flowed over him, leading him towards the taxi rank. He watched the girls huddle under a bookstore canopy, their scarves pulled high up their necks, their hands enclosed in woollen gloves, and their shoes splattered with puddle water. Leaning against the clock pillar that stood centrally amongst the cobbles of the market square, he retrieved a cigarette packet from his pocket and placed a tab between his teeth. Enclosing the white stick with cupped hands, he lit it, the embers glowing subtly as his lungs relished the familiar burn.

"Xcuse me mate, you gotta light?" A woman had wandered over, her blonde hair slicked back against her head, her grey eyes highlighted by black eyeliner, and her coat was the colour of blood.

"What do you want, Portia?" he asked her, pocketing his lighter.

"Just wanted to see what you were up to," she smirked,

her long talons, tipped with scarlet nail polish, running lovingly up his upper arm and around to the nape of his neck. He knew her game and quickly moved from her reach. She was a stunning woman with an immaculate body shaped to perfection, whose curves would tempt any man. But she had never turned his head; he knew her secrets and didn't hold her in high regard. She also belonged to another, and that other, even he couldn't rival. His Master's lover was somewhere he would never venture, no matter how beautiful.

He was forever faithful to him.

"Oh, don't be like that, Jorn," she simpered, as he tilted his sights towards the bookstore, his ears pricking at the sound of the women who were now getting in a taxi. "Hey," she made him incline his chin to her, "she's gone now." Her lips moved to his as her hand delved under his coat.

"Please leave off me, Portia," he said calmly, moving further away, his eyes searching the street for a sign of his Master watching. Was he being tested? It would be just like his Master to send Portia out to try and tempt him.

"He's not here, Jorn; it's just me." He wanted to believe her. He wanted to believe that she was acting solely under her own fruition, but he suspected none of her actions were genuine. He'd not existed for centuries and had not honed his skills at avoiding manipulation to be taken in by her. He had his own agenda tonight, and her being here was just an irritant.

Her hands tried to encircle his neck again, yet his swift reflexes grabbed them and held them hard and straight behind her back.

"I said, get off me!" He began to walk away slowly, aware that people were looking at the interaction.

"I'll get you one day, Jorn Hartvigsen, one day I'll have you between my legs begging me for more," she called, laughing maliciously.

Some of the passers-by turned to see her yelling, muttering behind cupped hands in sympathy for the poor guy in the long coat as he strode away, shaking his head. Never would he lie between her legs. He was too good for her. She'd started her life as a whore, and even though now she had his Master's protection, she'd die a manipulative whore, and he'd have nothing to do with her.

Once out of sight of the crowds at the taxi rank and pubgoers, he ran through the back streets, his feet barely touching the paved walkways and tarmacked roads. His shoes skimming the waterlogged surfaces, as he made his way out of the main shopping area into the housing estate and beyond, into the countryside. Halting at the door of the mansion he and his brothers co-inhabited, he wiped his feet on the mat, the coarse fibres grating the soles of his brogues.

"Good evening, young Jorn," an elderly man with a cap said, looking up from his paper as Jorn entered the kitchen.

"Evening, Hadley. How are you?"

"Very well, thank you."

"Is The Master home?" Jorn asked, removing his scarf.

"Yes, sir, he's in the den."

Jorn did not doubt that Portia was already down there with him, so he made his way up the ornate staircase to his own quarters.

His suite was the third door to the right, and it was just the way he'd left it. The room looked hardly used. The sofa was central with its cushions plush and poofed, the whisky decanter was full, and his desk that housed four computer screens were all showing similar screensavers. He brushed the mouse while removing his coat, making live CCTV footage appear. The first camera shot was of a small, terraced dwelling, which zoomed in on a paved pathway and door. The second was in the front room with a matching settee and chair, an oval-shaped coffee table in front of a log-burning stove, a TV to its left and a stacked bookshelf to the right. The third was in a small kitchenette that led to the back door and to an enclosed courtyard, where he could see the girl from the pub attempting to unlock it. The silhouettes through the glass told him she was not alone. He knew it would be this Lexi the mammal-shifter had spoken about.

Both women fell through the door, laughter etched on their faces as they grabbed each other by the cuffs of their coats, pulling themselves up and adjusting to the tight alley between the kitchen cupboards. The girl with dark hair took her jacket off, flinging it onto a high-rise chair, where it instantly slipped off. Yet she did not care; she was more interested in making coffee. However, as she held the kettle under the spraying faucet, the lid shut, sprinkling her with icy water, which made her instantly drop the implement as though she'd been bitten by something. Zooming in on her face, he could see it was in hysteria, and for one moment, he envied her innocence and suddenly wished he was with her, enjoying the moment of fun and drunken giggles.

"Jorn?" His door opened inwards, revealing a long-haired man in rustic jeans and a black t-shirt.

"Yeah?" Jorn looked up at his eldest brother, whose hair was dripping down his face and smelling of chlorine.

"The Master wants to see you," the long-haired man said.

"Why?" said Jorn, exasperatedly. "There's nothing to report. If there was, that's where I would have gone first. It was just another boring night tracking her."

"I don't know. He just wants to see you." The brother ran his hand through his wet hair, scattering droplets over his shoulders.

Sighing, Jorn said, "If he wants to get to her and initiate the process of bringing her in, then he'll have to let the others play their hands. This pussyfooting around is now no good."

"Yes, I said you'd say that. Maybe that's why he wants to see you, to cancel your watch?"

Tutting, Jorn pushed back the chair he'd been sitting on, and with one last glance at the girl on the screen, he stood and left the room, allowing the door to swing shut behind him.

He'd have to marvel at her innocence another time.

CHAPTER TWO

THE TASK

He retraced his steps down the stairs and then to the archway that led to his Master's rooms below ground. The corridor was brightly lit, and the LED spotlights were evenly spaced along the classic white ceiling. It reminded Jorn of hospital corridors, pristinely clean, with a pale green dado rail running halfway around the wall. Even now, as he ran his finger along it, there wasn't one speck of dust. The flooring was venture porcelain, and so reflective that it was as though it was covered with water. It was so immaculate that there were no footprint marks on it, and if there ever were marks, they were soon eradicated by the robotic mop that continuously prowled the halls, whirring its blue tassels to collect every spot of dirt. Jorn stepped around it as it approached, its small electronic engine vibrating on its mission to try and clean the already flawless walkway.

His brother, Randin, walked a few steps ahead; he was shorter than Jorn and more thickset, his arms practically bursting from the sleeves of his top, and his hands were large and well-used. He was, for the most part, the engineer amongst his brothers. The architect. Designing and building anything from shelving units to apartment complexes, family homes and estates. He had numerous contractors who answered to him, yet his most important job was keeping the family unit going. The Master of the community was, in Jorn's mind, an eccentric narcissist, and it was Randin's role to try to keep him level. The name Randin meant 'beautiful advice giver', which was what Randin was. He was beautiful; there was no doubt about it. He had milk-white skin inherited from their mother, blonde hair in a messy bun on top of his head and a short-cut beard. His eyes were clear blue that rarely glowed the red of anger unless severely provoked, and that was infrequent. He was the community's trusted advisor, who could talk anyone out of any situation, no matter the issue. Only perhaps Kol, the youngest, who could get a rise out of anyone, knew which of Randin's buttons to push. But that, Jorn knew, was what a youngest brother was meant to do; torment his elders.

They stopped at a set of double chestnut oak doors, the black handles of cast iron such a contrast to the sleek white of the walls that Jorn had always thought Randin's design to be a little odd. Yet somehow, they blended with the house, and he never reproached his brother for it.

Jorn raised his eyebrows at him now, who smirked as they both clocked the sign hanging on one of the handles.

'Enter at your peril.'

No doubt Kol pranking them both.

Jorn lifted his hand to knock but needn't have bothered. Both doors opened simultaneously into a room that was such a contrast to the hallway that it was like they'd time-travelled. The room was high-ceilinged, with wooden beams and rich furnishings, segregated by two large black marble pillars with a thoroughfare that led to what Jorn called the 'comfort end'. It had a thick white rug that covered half the floor, on top of which stood two L-shaped pale blue sofas and assorted footrests of various greys and faded pinks. The fireplace was roaring, the flames licking the brickwork behind, the large screen above the mantle circulating with shapes that went in time with some music—a riot of colour against the dreary opaque walls. Jorn could see Portia leaning over the back of the couch, her exquisite body within an all-in-one jumpsuit, one leg lifted at an angle showing off her pert bottom as they walked in. She knew perfectly well they'd notice, and Jorn hated her for it.

Why was she so far up her own arse that she had to show it to all that entered? Ignoring her, he followed his brother to the left, the reflective flooring preceding them as they made their way to the 'cold end' of the room. In there was a large desk housing three computers, where Jorn could hear the endless sounds of whirring PC processors. Beyond the desk was a wall on which hung a large tapestry that Jorn knew was woven with gold and hid the secret passageway to his Master's private bedrooms.

His Master was sitting at the desk, with his silver-grey Great Dane, Seija, sentinel next to him on the floor. Her tail swished from side to side as she watched both men approach, her warm hazel eyes seeming to smile at them as they stood there waiting. Her Master ignored their entrance, his eyes flicking back and forth across the screens, his fingers nimble, tapping the keys, his hand swiftly moving on and off the mouse as required. He must have known they were there, but he kept them waiting, and both men stood patiently. After a few minutes, he looked up, his pointed chin and precision goatee enhancing his already beautiful features. His dark, almost black eyes seemed to bore into them, and Jorn could feel the intensity of his glare.

"Thank you, Randin. You will no longer be required," The Master said, his voice cutting the air like a knife.

Randin looked at Jorn and raised his eyebrows, shrugging. He wasn't worried about his brother's safety, but would have preferred to have stayed. However, he turned, nodded at his Master, and made his way past Jorn.

"Randin," he turned back, "take Portia with you."

Randin nodded again and walked purposefully to the comfort end, linked arms with Portia, and they both left, Portia, fingering Randin's arm suggestively; she just couldn't help herself.

Jorn stood there, able to see the screens reflected in his Master's eyes. He made out that one screen displayed an email of congratulations, another was showing a pornographic film involving two women at that present moment, and the third displayed the screen that was playing above the fireplace.

"Right... Jorn." He pushed back his seat and swiftly stood opposite him, his arms folded and ankles crossed. "How was your evening?"

Jorn knew he wanted to know about the girl's every move, but there really wasn't much to tell. He hadn't gotten close enough for it to be worth his time.

"There's nothing new to report, sir. She went out with friends, and I watched her in the public house. Nothing out of the ordinary."

"Yes, I was afraid it would be unproductive." He stroked his chin, leaning back to take his glass from the desk. "Come... sit with me." He moved effortlessly to the sofas and sat, one leg crossed over the other, sipping his drink. Jorn sat awkwardly on the edge of his seat. He knew better than to make himself comfortable.

"So, I've been thinking, Jorn, correct me if I'm wrong, but it may be time we moved in on this girl."

"That is perhaps appropriate, Master," Jorn agreed, nodding.

"Yes, I think it is the only way to get what I want from her, though it pains me to say it." He sipped his drink again. "I think I would like you to get to know her... personally."

Jorn furrowed his brow. Personally? "Er... what exactly do you mean, Master?" Surely, getting to know her personally was not his area of expertise. One of his other brothers might be better suited for that. Kol would be better than he was. Even his twin, Jorun, who could love anyone and get to know a person's entire life in an evening, would do a better job.

"Er... forgive me for speaking out of turn, but surely Jorun or Kol would be better for that task than I would be? I am The Watcher. It is what we have done with the other, erm... tasks you have set me. If it is personal interaction you want, they are more qualified."

His Master shook his head, "Do you think I would have asked you if I thought one of your brothers would be the better option?" he said, pursing his lips, as if Jorn was questioning his judgement.

"No, sir, I am not questioning you, I don't believe I am suitable for this task. I am The Watcher," he repeated. "I note emotions and feelings, log events. I can change memories if needed. I do not interact on a personal level." Jorn sat with his hands flat on his thighs, wishing he was back in his room, with his screens, watching... her.

"Oh, Jorn, you are not merely The Watcher, though, are you?" The Master said, draining his glass and smacking his lips at the taste of exquisite red wine. "You are the master of vigilance. I've seen you and your studying. You would be the best person, as you know exactly what she would like. You have studied her for years now."

It was true; Jorn did know her well. He'd watched her throughout her teenage and adult years, on his Master's orders. Her first serious boyfriend, losing her virginity, heartbreak, and job failures. If she'd done it, Jorn knew about it. He was the vigilant Watcher, the artist who could hide in plain sight. An expert in deception. Yet he knew he could never be personal with this particular woman. There was something unnatural about her that drew him to her, pulling, nudging and niggling at him constantly. His Master, surely, could not know how much getting to know her would affect Jorn. He knew he wouldn't be able to resist her. Just her scent made his insides burn with lust. It was why he watched her so intently. Her eyes made him feel different. They'd never spoken or even smiled at one another, yet there was an undeniable connection he could not ignore. He knew just one touch from her would cause him to burn like fire until he had her. How could he get to know her without touching her? That was certainly impossible.

"I can see this idea vexes you," his Master said, leaning back luxuriously into the cushions with his arm spread along the back of them.

"I am not vexed, Master." Like hell he wasn't. He could already feel an abnormal heat under his collar. "I just don't think I can do this as well as some of my brothers."

"Well, you have no choice. This task is from the top, and you know The Emperor will not allow you to decline his request."

"The Emperor?" Jorn could not believe it.

"Yes, Jorn, The Emperor," his Master said with exasperation. "He would like someone to get close to her, and he has requested that you do so."

The Emperor getting involved with the events of this part of the family was unheard of and had been so for some time. This was incomprehensible.

"How does he expect me to do this? I have no previous experience with this type of task, Master. How can he think I am the best?" Jorn got to his feet and walked to the mantelpiece, his hands gripping the marble surround.

"Yes, Jorn, but that is your advantage. You have no prior expectations. Jorun would jump in feet first as he always does, hence why he has an entourage of women on the go and Kol, well, he's too mysterious to pull it off without suspicion."

"I cannot do this." Jorn knew he couldn't. He was too close to her; the pull he felt was too strong. There was no way he could touch but not feel anything. For centuries, his heart had remained intact, and yet instinctively, he knew this woman could already be his downfall.

"Well, there is no negotiation here, Jorn. You will do as I ask, or as your Emperor asks, or you will be stripped of your abilities." His Master got to his feet swiftly and returned to his desk, refilling his glass.

Stripped of his abilities? Couldn't The Emperor think of a new threat? To strip a Gifted of their abilities was a death sentence. Jorn knew it was an agony no one had ever survived - not even The Emperor could survive a stripping, not that anyone had ever dared challenge him. He was the most powerful, Gifted supernatural in the world, at least as far as Jorn knew. The Emperor was the ruler of all in the world to which Jorn belonged. His strength and ingenuity were legendary. He'd apparently stripped his own father to get where he was today. He was the one who had given Jorn his watcher ability. He was the one who had given Randin the power of counsellor - to be the ultimate adviser, the negotiator. It was how Jorun could love all things and take any person and make them his. It was how Oska could sense maladies with one touch, how he had an affiliation with nature that no one could understand. It was how his brother Lamont knew his way around numbers like the genius he was, and how Kol was the dark, sultry son, the youngest and most mysterious. And yet, The Emperor had asked Jorn to bring this girl in. Why?

Why ask someone who had no skills at seduction to do this task? There had to be a bigger plan, a bigger picture.

"What is the end goal, sir?" Jorn asked, moving quickly back to his Master, who was clicking away at his computer again.

"I don't know the end goal, Jorn. You know The Emperor; he is a man of many secrets. She's most likely got some hidden ability that he wants, and he needs her to lower her barriers before he takes it away from her." Jorn could feel the anger boiling in his stomach at those words. "You know him; he always plays with his food before eating it." Jorn began to seethe under his skin, but skilled as he was at hiding his feelings, he pacified his face and merely looked bored.

"So," Jorn said, "he believes that if I get personal with her, it will make her more susceptible to him and his ability to strip her at will?"

"I think it's pertinent to think so," he said.

"But why?" Jorn shook his head.

"Don't ask me why he tells us to do things. We do them when he requests it, and we... succeed."

Jorn nodded, allowing his fate to wash over him.

"I shall start tomorrow then," he said, taking a few steps backwards, careful not to turn his back on his Master.

"Yes, you will; I have all your credentials here." He pulled out a dark blue lanyard, an ID badge, and a file of papers from the desk drawer. Taken aback, Jorn stepped up, glancing at the badge.

'Jorn Hartvigsen, Sales Director'

"Sales Director? Where?" Jorn questioned, beginning to feel hot again, the sheer vastness of his Master's orders unsettling him.

"The company the girl works for, you'll be her new Sales Director, they've been after one for months. Your office will be near hers, so you will have ample, unquestioned access to her."

Jorn had never wanted to run from his missions before and always stepped up to the challenge. It was what The Gifted did. But this? This was too much, even for him. How could he do this?

"But I have never managed anything before, nor been any type of Director, let alone worked in sales. How can I do this?"

"For fuck's sake, Jorn," his Master said angrily, "will you stop the whining and moaning. This is what is asked of you, and this is what you must do. I do not want to hear another word." He waved his hand in dismissal.

"Yes, sir." With that, Jorn turned, clutching the file and ID, and walked slowly from the room.

"Oh, and Jorn." He retreated slightly, his eyes locking on his Master's. "There is no room for failure. You must do whatever it takes. Plant fake memories if you must." Jorn raised his eyebrows. His Master knew that he hated doing that. Giving someone fake memories meant providing an individual with a false history, and that was something

Jorn had never been proud of. "I will not have one of my sons stripped of his abilities, by my brother, just because *he* wants to turn a human into a plaything."

"Yes, Master," Jorn said, and, knowing there was no point in arguing, he left the office, closing the door silently and walking down the pristine corridor back to his room - his heart the heaviest it had ever felt.

How was he ever going to do this?

CHAPTER THREE

THE DIRECTOR

Logan's head pounded as she woke in the early morning, her mouth parched, her tongue so stiff that she had to lick around her lips and gums to loosen it. Stumbling out of bed, she made her way to her en-suite and sat down, the alcohol draining from her, tinkling into the toilet pan, seeming to go on forever. Holding her head in her hands, she tried to remember getting home. How had she got here? Did Lexi bring her? Did they get a cab? Sheesh! She really needed to be more careful and not allow the girls to ply her with more drinks than necessary.

"Hurry up, Loge, I'm bursting out here."

"Lexi?" Logan shrieked, feeling abashed.

"Of course it is," Lexi laughed as Logan got up and opened the door for her.

"How the hell did we get home, Lex? Did we get a taxi?"

"Don't you remember?" Lexi said, nipping past her to the toilet. "You kept wanting to leave as you said that creepy man in the corner kept staring at you."

Logan tried to think back to her night out with the girls. "Creepy man?"

"You know the one that's always in there, sitting on the corner sofa. You said every time you looked over at him, he was watching you." Logan stared uneasily around her room, a shiver emanating from her. It was as if he was watching her now, though that was impossible. She was safe at home.

"Really? Was he sitting watching that much?" she asked as Lexi ran back into the room and got into the bed, goosebumps covering her body.

"Well, whenever I looked over, he wasn't looking at anyone or anything but his phone. Yet you've always said he was a bit weird, so we left after the third bottle," Lexi said, puffing up her pillows before lying down.

Logan thought for a while. She *had* found that man creepy, but not as Lexi had thought or as she had portrayed it to her friends. He was creepy in that Logan thought she knew him, more than just recognising him from being around her part of the city, as if she knew him... intimately. She was sure they'd never seen each other outside of the pub. They'd certainly never spoken, yet she felt affiliated with him. He was an extremely good-looking guy with a chiselled face, which was, in her eyes, completely flawless. His sideburns were slightly excessive, but his rounded chin made his five-o'clock shadow extremely sensual. She imagined running her fingers over it, the roughness stimulating her touch so much that she blushed into the duvet. Every time she saw him, she felt the same way. His clothes wore him as though he'd stepped off the catwalk of some famous designer, every time in something new and expensive. The coat he'd worn last night had sat so shapely around his broad shoulders that it had to have been tailor-made, and when he'd removed it, he'd been wearing a loose shirt, its top few buttons undone, showing the beginning of a carved, toned chest and a bristle of dark hair. She'd glanced at him every few seconds on her way to the toilet, wondering what the hair would feel like as she ran her fingers through it. She'd fantasised about what his large hands would feel like on her breasts or his fingers on her inner thigh, working their way to her. His tongue inside her mouth...

"Jeez, my head is bad," Logan said as she pottered about the kitchen after their extensive lie-in later that day.

"Mine too," Lexi said, snuggling under the sofa blanket, awaiting her egg and bacon sandwich.

"How much did I even have last night?" Logan asked, flipping the egg.

"Too much," her friend replied, flicking through the TV channels and settling on an old Christmas movie about elves making wooden toys and a man in red becoming Father Christmas.

"Here." Lexi got up and took Logan's proffered sandwich through the old-fashioned hatch that led to the kitchen.

Logan's house was a mid-terrace, one-bedroomed home with a lounge and courtyard garden. Logan was a garden enthusiast and had transformed her bland, patioed area into a haven for bees and butterflies. While waiting for her egg to cook, she looked out into the dreariness, the plants looking very bedraggled in the damp December weather. The garden bench, her father had made her, looked waterlogged and green from moss. If she hadn't felt so hungover, she might have gone out to it and brushed it down. The arbour in the corner looked longingly at her; it needed some TLC, and she couldn't wait for the spring when it would be brought back to life with new shoots and the bell-shaped flowers of the dancer creeper. Those were some of her favourite flowers, the blooms shaped like ballet skirts, flowing in the breeze. Her mind was suddenly filled with the image of wearing a flared skirt and dancing with the dark stranger. His hands pulled her into him, the smell of cologne on his skin and the touch of his lips on hers.

"Loge, your egg is smoking."

"Shit." She turned back to the cooker and flung the frying pan off the heat, shaking her hand as the hot handle burned her skin. "Damn it!" Holding her hand under the tap, she cooled the now-forming red patch, her face flushing with annoyance at herself and her thoughts.

"You weren't thinking about Neil, were you?" Lexi asked, bringing Logan back to earth with the mention of her ex-boyfriend.

"No, of course not. I was thinking of my garden and what I'm going to plant in the spring," she lied quickly. Well, it wasn't really a lie. She had been wondering about her foliage, but her mind had been distracted by a man she didn't know and who, irritatingly, she couldn't get out of her mind.

Ignoring the pain in her hand, she buttered her toast and smothered the bread with tomato sauce before adding the bacon and now crispy egg.

"What are we watching?" she asked, as she flopped down next to her friend, biting into her fried duo.

"Santa Claus: The Movie, it's called. I remember it from my childhood."

"Oh, I used to love this movie," Logan enthused.

"Yes, me too, but I don't really fancy it." Lexi clicked the remote again, and Logan concentrated on her food, resisting the urge to look at her hand as she felt it would worsen the pain. "What about this?" Logan looked up and saw a classroom with four delinquents, Judd Nelson smoking a cigarette, and Demi Moore's gravelly voice speaking.

"Sure," Logan said, slightly uninterested.

"Okay." Lexi switched off the TV and shuffled to look fully at Logan. "What's up?"

"What? Nothing," Logan said, looking away. "My hand just hurts," she fibbed again, holding it out for Lexi to look at.

"Sheesh!" Lexi said, holding it to her face. "You've had worse from gardening," she said, flinging it away. "I know you're lying. It's Neil, isn't it?" Seizing the notion, Logan nodded. "I've told you, Loge, he's not worth your pining. He was an idiot," she sighed heavily. "You're so much better off without him."

Logan knew she was right and was fully aware of that. Her mind and heart were in turmoil, but it definitely wasn't over her past boyfriend.

"You staying tonight?" Logan asked, changing the subject and switching the television back on to watch The Breakfast Club—anything to distract her friend from further probing.

"Yeah, I thought I might. I'll have to borrow some clothes for work tomorrow."

"You know you can," Logan said, putting her plate on the coffee table. Both women worked for the same company, though Logan was further up than Lexi. Eighteen months ago, she'd secured the PA post for the Managing Director. "I have to leave earlier than usual, though, as it's my turn to buy the pastries for the morning coffee trolley ritual." She rolled her eyes.

Since being at this company, Logan was used to the Monday morning ritual of the coffee trolley. Every Director had to provide the staff with a cake and a hot beverage to show their appreciation for their hard work. It was such a faff, as now Logan was her boss's PA, it was down to her to provide the cakes. He would never go himself; he'd message her Sunday evenings to remind her to buy them on her way when it was his turn. Logan, of course, was dutiful and did as he bid, but she never enjoyed it. She'd have to go around the open-plan office and dish out the drinks while thinking about the workload she'd have to deal with back upstairs.

"What's on the menu for tomorrow?" Lexi asked, slurping her tea.

"Well, as it's Christmas, I thought I'd get some of those individual Christmas cakes you can get, as well as the usual chocolate croissants and brownies," she shrugged. "You know Adrian, he won't care."

"And are you wearing that new suit you bought?" Lexi asked, wiping the last of her toast around her plate, soaking up the yolk.

"Yes," Logan rolled her eyes again. "The new Sales Director is starting tomorrow, so I have to be smarter than usual. I don't know what is wrong with my normal pencil skirt and shirt, but Adrian said in his message." Clicking her phone screen, she scrolled to the message. "*L*. Ugh, hate it when he calls me L." Glancing back at her phone, she continued. "*L. Don't forget cakes for tomorrow, and can you look smart as I want to make a good impression on the new Sales Director. Adrian.* He makes it out as if I'm not ever smart," she said with a tut, throwing down her phone.

"You can't complain, though, can you? Got your Christmas bonus yet?"

"No, that won't go in until the twenty-first." She smiled, feeling that she'd like to book a spa day or a mini break in the sun with it.

"How much is it? A thousand?" Lexi said in awe.

"Two thousand this year, as the business is doing well. And Adrian said there's an extra five hundred for putting up with him for the past year. Apparently, his last PA didn't last the three-month probation."

"Well, you must be doing something right, even if you

don't look smart," Lexi laughed.

"I bloody deserve that money. I work my arse off for that man and do all his errands for him. It was his idea to do this coffee trolley thing, and I'm the one who has to look like an idiot doing it. I'm sure Quinn tripped me up purposefully last time, so I spilt hot tea down my top."

"That sounds like Quinn," she said, smiling. "Always a joker, mind you, he was quite serious last night."

"Last night? Wait, what? He was there?" And like that, the memory of her bumping into him hit her. "Shit, I totally knocked into him on the way back from the bathroom." She smacked her forehead, face burning, and she turned away from Lexi, so the flush wasn't so noticeable. She'd fallen into Quinn because she'd been staring at the stranger and tripped on the uneven floor tiles.

"Yes, you did, quite spectacularly," Lexi smirked.

Logan held her head in her hands, embarrassed. "Jesus, I'm an idiot. He's never going to let me live it down."

"Don't be daft, it's Quinn. He's always had the hots for you."

Logan shook her head. It wasn't her he liked; it was Lexi. Yet she was too stupid to notice him look at her. Lexi had recently divorced after only ten months of marriage, and now she was back on the market, she'd wasted no time sleeping with any man who would have her. Quinn, however, wasn't one for just sleeping with someone. Logan knew he was biding his time for Lexi to get the missed sex out of her system before he made his move. Logan knew he'd always been a one-girl type of man.

Logan did not sleep well that night; her mind buzzed with mysterious men dressed in dark suits, and she was already running late when she parked outside the supermarket the following morning. Grabbing the cakes she had planned and some cheap, thinning tinsel, she ran back to the car, trying to avoid any puddles so as not to splash her new trousers. The suit she'd bought online, and when it had arrived, it looked better than it had on the model in the picture. It was a classic navy-blue trouser suit with three-quarter length sleeves and no buttons. Under it, she wore a lace cream top that subtly showed enough skin, but with enough sophistication to be professional. She'd finished the look off with stiletto-heeled cream court shoes, a chunky bashed silver bracelet, and her black waves held back in a side ponytail.

"Suit still immaculate?" Lexi asked as they reversed out of the space and revved up the road towards the city centre.

"Fuck knows, but if the traffic's bad, I'm going to be late, and he'll skin me alive."

"Look, don't worry, you'll make it. You always do."

Logan threw her jacket over the back of her chair and booted up her computer, tapping her polished nails on the keyboard. It would be okay, as long as it looked like she'd been in at least ten minutes before Adrian arrived. She heard the lift ping as she typed in her password, and glancing in her pocket mirror, she adjusted her hair so it didn't look so ruffled from her scarf when the door to the office opened.

Adrian didn't say anything. He just took the letters from her outstretched hand and walked towards his office.

Once he'd shut the door, Logan breathed a sigh of relief, and after fifteen minutes, she got up and made him an espresso before donning her jacket, straightening her top, and knocking gently on his door.

"Yes, L." Rolling her eyes, she walked in and placed the coffee on his desk before moving over to partially close his blinds to stop the sun that had started breaking through. It wasn't until she turned around that she looked back at him. "I see you took my request seriously," he said, looking at her formal attire.

"Of course I did," she said. "I'm proud of our work here, and I want people to feel that this company is worth their time."

"Well, thank you, L," he said, getting into his chair and sipping his coffee.

"What time will the new Sales Director be here?" she asked.

"I told him to come about eleven-thirty, I want everyone settled and busy. I can't bear the rush of Monday mornings, and there won't be much for us to do today, just usual introductions, et cetera. It's not the best time to start, a week or so before Christmas, but needs must." Coughing, he then added, "What's on the agenda until then?"

Whilst Logan told him of the day's events, she busied herself around his office. She straightened the plant pot, she ensured there were working pens on the coffee table and that he had a printout of the contract to hand. "Did you get the cakes?" he asked once she'd finished telling him about his day.

"Yes, and I bought some tinsel to liven up the trolley. This is our last time before the new year."

"You are too good to me, L," he beamed at her appreciatively.

"Not really, sir. I only want to make a good impression." She knew he'd been looking for a new Sales Director for months, so now that he'd secured one, she wanted it to be a success, and it might even ease her workload.

After decorating the trolley with silver and red tinsel, she ladened it with the cakes and pots of refreshments and took the lift down to the open-plan office that was buzzing with phones ringing and people chatting. She spotted Lexi over by the printer with a guy called Ralph, whom she'd slept with last weekend.

"Ah! Logan."

"Hey, Quinn," she said, the now regular heat of embarrassment creeping up her neck.

"Glad to see you're here."

"Why would I not be?" she smiled.

"Well, after the skinful you had on Saturday, I'm surprised you made it home in one piece." Quinn seemed overly relieved to see her, and she suddenly felt Lexi may have been right about Quinn and that she'd got it wrong about his intentions.

"Well, I did feel a little fragile yesterday, but I'm alright now." She pointed at her trolley, "Do you want anything?"

"Yeah, please, I'll have a coffee and a Christmas delight." He grinned, taking a cake and stuffing it, whole, into his mouth. Logan couldn't help but laugh at him.

"Excuse me, everyone, can I have your attention, please?" A voice shouted over the hubbub in the room, and just like that, all was quiet. Quinn looked as if he was going to choke as their boss walked into the room. Logan, however, continued pouring his drink and, knowing he took two sugars, opened the sachets and stirred the milky beverage.

"I'd like to introduce you all to the new Sales Director." Shit. Logan's head shot up. He wasn't meant to be here until eleven-thirty. Why was he early? She should have been there to meet him. She moved to the side to get a better look, holding Quinn's coffee out to him as she went, but before he took it, she saw the man standing next to Adrian. Her throat abruptly constricted; it was like her lungs had collapsed. Her heart might have even stopped. She suddenly felt faint, her head becoming fuzzy, and her vision blurred. She felt the mug she was holding slip from her hand, it falling slowly towards the linoleum flooring, the liquid sloshing over the rim. It was going to smash over her feet. She was never going to save it. Starting to bend over, her fingers brushed the handle, but she was going to be too late - it was going to hit the ground. But then a large hand cupped itself under it, the mug settling snugly in the palm, the liquid remaining almost motionless—only a single drop running down the outer edge of the china.

She gasped as she looked up at the owner of the hand,

straight into the dark green eyes of the man who had been haunting her dreams.

CHAPTER FOUR

THE CATCH

Jorn slammed his bedroom door, flinging himself onto the bed. He couldn't understand what he'd done to deserve this. Jorn had no idea how to be a Sales Director, let alone seduce a woman he cared about, without involving his feelings. He'd had women; of course, he had. But never had he ever thought of them any more than that. They had just been service providers and nothing else. Now he was to go to a job, he had no clue how to do, show that he was more than capable and then get to know her personally. What was the actual point of it all? The Emperor wanted her for his games, so why should he become part of her life?

"What the fuck are you going to do, Jorn?" he whispered into his pillow. "What a fucking mess you've got yourself into." He'd always wanted to get closer to her; that was a feeling that wasn't new to him, but he never would have instigated it. He was a Gifted supernatural. Relationships with mortals were unheard of, or in the least, extremely rare. What was The Emperor up to? The job part he could understand, as The Master said, it would mean he was near her without causing suspicion. But making her like him enough to bring her into the fold of the community's dynamics was surely impossible. Also, how was he to get her to like him but not want her in return? Well, he'd failed that. He already liked this woman.

He sat up abruptly, trying to clear his mind, and moved back to his sitting room and computer screens, the slightly grainy black and white images from his quarry's house showing no movement. Both women, it transpired, had got ready for bed and were now sleeping. Logan, he could see, had practically buried herself in the duvet, only the top of her head visible, a mass of black hair spread out over the sheet. Her friend Lexi or Alexia was right over the other side of the bed, one leg out on top of the covers, her mouth slightly open, her overly large breasts heaving now and again. As Jorn watched Logan, he felt the need to be in that bed with her, and even though he knew it was wrong on any level, especially going against his ethics, he thought that maybe one day soon, he could be. He could be between those sheets, his arm thrown over her shoulders, his lips at her neck. Before he knew it, his hand was down his trousers, feeling himself, his arousal growing with his imaginings that it wasn't long before he was in the shower touching himself. Who had he been kidding? He was going to be able to pull this off.

He was going to make her love him.

"Yeah?" He swivelled in his chair with just a towel around his waist, one of his screens showing the sleeping girls and the other googling the company he would be working for.

Jorun swept in barefoot, wearing shorts and a t-shirt, his floppy, long hair over his eyes, and his hands holding two glasses of champagne.

"I hear a celebration is in order," he said jovially, handing Jorn the drink.

Jorn just shrugged, "Not much to celebrate, brother. I've got a job to go to tomorrow that I have no clue about and a girl to make fall in love with me, all for The Emperor's amusement." He sipped the drink, it frozen in the glass. "What the hell, Jorun? This drink is frozen."

"Well, I thought you needed a little cooling off after your little wank in the shower," Jorun smirked.

"Fuck you!" Jorn said, putting the glass on his desk and wiping his mouth.

"I'm sorry, brother, I couldn't help myself," Jorun grinned mischievously.

"Well, try. I've got enough on my plate," Jorn stated, looking sternly at his brother.

"Look, I don't know what you're so worried about," Jorun soothed. "You know everything about this girl. You know all her routines, all her likes and dislikes. You must use that to your advantage."

"Yeah, but how?" Jorn shrugged. "I've never been serious in any of my relationships. We never can, can we? I mean..."

"Look, brother, just because The Emperor says she has to feel seduced, fall in love, whatever." He brushed his hand in a blasé way. "Doesn't mean *you* actually have to. Mortal women find it quite easy to fall in love, especially with us Gifted. We have charisma that others don't. You'll find it piss easy."

"Yes, but what do I do if the... er..." Jorn couldn't think of the right word. Whatever he said, he knew Jorun would see right through him. "Connection goes both ways."

Jorun's eyes lit up, "I knew it. I knew you liked this woman."

"I don't like her, like her. I just," he smiled, "like her." He walked over to the decanter of whisky and poured himself a glass. Jorun's celebratory fizz was still an ice block.

"Maybe liking her will help you succeed in the task better."

"Yes, but what can The Emperor hope to achieve by making me get close to her? I don't understand him. Him and The Master give me these missions, make me watch these clients and then when all the information is gathered, they either kill or abandon them." Jorn raised his arms in surrender. "I mean, The Emperor feels she has hidden abilities. But I can't see it, and I can usually see everything. She just seems and feels like a normal mortal woman."

"I have no idea, Jorn, but they need her for something, or The Emperor thinks she's worth getting close to, so I suppose we have to comply or..."

"We get stripped. Yeah, I have already had that confirmed by The Master," he sighed. "All they do is threaten until the task is complete."

"When has it ever been our job to question The Emperor? We are just the lowly offspring of his younger brother. We have no say in the events of this family," Jorun said, downing some of his non-frozen champagne.

"I know, but maybe it should start being our job to ask questions," Jorn said, looking away from his brother. Yet both he and Jorun knew that would never happen. The Gifted were used to their way of life. They'd never forfeit it for anything. "Anyway, have you come to give me some tips? Because I know that's probably why you've stopped by."

"You don't need any tips, bro. You're an expert at this; you just don't know it. You may have all the talents of a Watcher, but underneath that hard exterior and the barriers you put around yourself, I know exactly how you really feel about this woman."

"Really?" Jorn whispered.

"Jorn, please, call yourself a Watcher. Maybe you should watch things closer to home once in a while." Jorun leant up against the back of the sofa. "I am your twin. We are brothers not just by immortality or Gifts that were bestowed upon us when we were born, but by actual blood. We shared everything in the womb. I know everything about you, and if you look carefully into yourself, you know everything about me."

Jorn side glanced his older brother by thirteen minutes.

"I might not have your stealth and abilities to disappear into non-existent holes in walls or to play hide and seek as well as you, or have your mental sense. But I know how to watch people and log everything like you do. Just like you know how to seduce a woman, how to make her feel good about herself without even trying, know what to say, how to act. Be the gentleman women love." Jorn stared at his brother. "You know you can do this. It's your conscience that's stopping you."

"What the hell do you know about my conscience?" Jorn asked, taking a top from his drawers.

"I know that you feel something strong for this woman, and you can't bear the idea of deceiving her. Or the fact that at the end of the day, once The Master or The Emperor have had enough, they'll most likely kill her and call themselves the conquerors."

Jorn rubbed his face with the palms of his hands.

"You do know me too well," he said quietly, slipping on some casual trousers. "What the fuck do I do? I cannot make her love me and then let them kill her. I just can't."

"I don't know the answer to that, little bro," he ruffled Jorn's hair, "but I know you can do the first part of this task. They will eventually take everything from us, Jorn, but that's part of the deal, right? You can have these abilities and immortality, but you must do everything we ask, or it'll all be taken away." Jorun downed his drink, grimacing. Champagne had never been one of his favourites; he wasn't even sure why he'd brought it in. He would have enjoyed Jorn's whisky much more.

Jorn just nodded, sinking into his chair and glancing at the screen of the sleeping women.

"Okay, so I can't stop her fate, but how can I be a Sales

Director overnight?"

"That, my brother, is another easily solved problem."

Jorn looked at him.

"Ask Randin. He's the negotiator and communicator. He'll be more than willing; you know he will, and so will Lay. They both deal with the mortal population daily."

His brother went to leave.

"Jorun?" Looking over at him, Jorn smiled at his twin. "Thanks." He knew he would be okay if he had his brothers by his side.

The mirror in the lift made Jorn's skin look darker than usual. The lighting was that sort of bluish-white that highlighted every dark shadow of his face, and Jorn wasn't sure if it improved his look or worsened it. He rubbed the contours of his chin, the skin there somewhat rough with a day's stubble. He always preferred himself with a dusting of hair rather than clean-shaven, and being an immortal, it took a while for things to grow, if ever, so he rarely thought about shaving. He had his man bag over his shoulder. He might be a new Sales Director, but he wouldn't be one of those sophisticated types with a briefcase or tie. He wanted to be stylish, and being an immortal, his powers of persuasion were second to none. His Managing Director wouldn't say anything.

He was early, which was his plan. He wanted to catch Logan as she did the coffee trolley round. To see her doing the part of the job he knew she hated. He wanted to see her blush, see that rouge to her skin; even thinking about it now made his stomach feel queasy with desire. He needed to keep his head in the game for today, and he didn't want to go in too early with the reeling in. Subtlety was the best way to approach this, at least at first.

Logan's desk was unoccupied as he sauntered past it. She was downstairs already, so he knocked purposefully on Adrian Kelly's door. The Managing Director was speechless at his early arrival,

"Yes, I'm sorry I've arrived here at this time. It was just that I was eager to meet you again and to see the routines of a Monday morning. I don't know about you, but I hate Mondays, so I had to get here early, or I might not have come." Jorn laughed, taking his offered hand and allowing a few fake memories to filtrate up the man's arm, so he thought they'd met before.

Yes, well... er... Jorn," Adrian said, feeling nervous in front of this incredibly handsome and well-groomed man. "Er... let me show you around," he said, indicating Jorn to follow him.

"This is your office." Adrian opened the door to a basic room, with a large writing desk to the far end, two well-used leather chairs facing the desk, and a shelf system housing a few books and mundane ornaments that companies used to make their rooms more inviting. "It's quite plain in here, so feel free to titivate it. I'm afraid you and I will have to share my PA, who is very efficient, and I know she can cope with the extra workload until we find you your own."

"Oh no, that won't be necessary. I can manage my own paperwork," Jorn said, nodding. He had no idea what paperwork he would need to complete, but was sure he could do it himself. Logan had enough going on.

"Well, if you want to leave your belongings here, I'll take you down to the open office and introduce you to the team. Logan, my PA, is down there already. It's my day for providing cakes and beverages to the workers for all their hard work. Next week it will be your turn."

Jorn already knew about Adrian's morale-booster idea of a cake and coffee trolley. He thought the idea was ludicrous, but now that he was part of the team, he would have to comply.

He could smell Logan's perfume before he saw her, and he was momentarily floored by how amazing she looked in the dark blue suit. He was so surprised that he almost missed her reaction to him being there, so much so that he only just caught the coffee cup that had slipped from her hand.

His eyes searched for hers as she looked up at him, and as quick as a breath, the whole room dissolved for him. It was just her. Her chest heaving, her lungs barely working, her face blushing. Her hands shaking as she put one to her breast, the other to the trolley handle, as her balance was lost.

"Are you okay there?" He couldn't help his other hand go to her upper arm, steadying her, the hot cup of coffee sitting resolutely in his fingers.

"Oh fuck!" she gasped, her breathing rate starting to normalise as her hand went for the cup. "Thank you."

"No problem," Jorn said, smiling at her, her eyes of a burnt umber brown staring into his, with a look of slight confusion to them.

"Er... you're early," she said, trying to steer the trolley away from him. "Mr Kelly said you wouldn't be here until eleven-thirty. I meant to meet you in the lobby. How come you're early? This isn't the way it should be done." She seemed flustered.

"Yes, I'm sorry about that. I arrived early, as I wanted to get a feel for the place." Jorn suddenly felt an overpowering feeling of guilt. He'd never meant to make her feel like this. Had he been selfish in wanting to see her doing her coffee trolley round when she was at her least professional? "It was never my intention to put you out. I apologise."

"Oh, don't be silly, Jorn. You are more than welcome to come early. We are pleased you could see us all working in the usual chaos that is a Monday morning," Adrian said joyously, looking poignantly at Logan. He thought she was making an unnecessary scene. Jorn had to make this right.

"No, she is right, Mr Kelly. I should have arrived at the time we discussed. I know what it is like to work in a busy company. Being a Personal Assistant to the boss, I imagine she has a difficult work schedule to deviate from." He tried to smile at her, but she was avoiding his gaze. "I can only apologise, Logan."

She nodded briefly at him. "If it's okay, Mr Kelly, I'll continue this round and bring you your mid-morning tea." She handed Quinn his mug and moved away from Jorn. He'd completely messed up. He was no good at this pretence. It would have been better to have spoken to her at the pub on Saturday; it would have been more natural, and now he would have to put more effort into breaking the ice between them.

"Right, Jorn. Let me introduce you to the rest of the staff," Adrian said, opening his hands in an offering of direction.

Nodding and wiping the coffee from his fingers on his handkerchief, Jorn followed him around the room, shaking hands with new colleagues and logging everyone's names. He tried to avoid searching for Logan. He was angry with himself and felt the start of his new job could not have gone worse. He'd already got her back up.

The rest of the day went without any further significant events. He only saw Logan once more when she brought in tea at eleven-ten. She avoided all eye contact and only spoke when Adrian addressed her. Yet Jorn couldn't help but stare at her as she walked from the office. Her figure looked so sleek in that suit that Jorn marvelled at the fact he'd not made a pass at her before. However, that question could be answered before he'd even thought it. It wasn't in the job description of a Watcher to approach their clients; all they were there to do was watch, wait, and report.

He'd always seen his life as being a superior PI. He could float about like a wisp on the wind and gather intel on all the supernatural and natural communities. He could sneak into the nightwalker's den and hear their plans. He could listen in on a witch's séance and understand their mediums. He could even outwit a mammal-shifter in a fight, learning their styles instantly with the first punch. He was able to see through the eyes of any person and know their thoughts and feelings. He could sense a person's emotion with one look, one touch, with one word. He was an invaluable member of his community, and yet, with Logan, he couldn't get much on her at all. She was like a book with the most interesting, embossed cover, which had a thrilling synopsis on the back to entice everyone and anyone, yet he couldn't open her up and have a look. He could usually understand everyone. Mortals were meant to be the easiest, as they were the worst at keeping their emotions in check. Then it was nightwalkers as they barely thought of anything but their thirst. Witches were harder as they could use magic to hide, though he rarely had trouble getting through their barriers as a Watcher. Were-shifters that only came out at a full moon were secretive creatures, but were mortal most of the month, so they were pretty simple. He'd never met any of the woodland or mountain dwellers known as The Fae, he had no idea whether they would be easy. With a mammal-shifter, he had to get through the creature and the human part, so they were somewhat tricky. The Gifted were the hardest, The Master and The Emperor being the hardest of all, although Jorn was sure that if he wanted to, he'd get behind their barriers if he tried.

Yet, with Logan. He found her arduous, and that was probably why he found her most intriguing, why he let himself be taken in by her. She was more of a mystery to him than anyone had ever been. Was that the reason The Emperor was interested in her? Maybe *he* couldn't get a read on her either, and he, Jorn, needed to know more. Jorn knew she was special, but he had no idea why. He had to find out; he had to know her before they took her. Before The Emperor had her in his grasp.

He sat in his office just after five, the computer powering

down. He'd spent the last few hours listening to Mr Kelly talking about stocks, shares, shareholders and the company's prospects in the current market. If Jorn was honest, he hadn't really listened, which was an oversight on his part. He needed to be good at this job, but he was distracted by Logan only on the other side of the wall. He could hear her typing away at the keyboard now; she always seemed to stay late on Mondays. Was that the coffee trolley's fault? Most likely. Mr Kelly thought it boosted the workers' morale, but for Logan, it put her behind. Hanging his bag over his shoulder, he left, pausing to chance a glance into her room. She was bending over her desk, her hair in a messy bun, one of her pens sticking in it. She was now wearing her glasses, which he knew she only wore when her head hurt, and he hoped he hadn't exasperated her headache.

He lifted his hand to knock,

"Come in," she called, not looking up from the screen, her hand moving swiftly to the mouse before she turned her chair so she could sit on it.

"Logan?" Her eyes seemed to gasp when she realised it was him, her head twisting towards the door.

"Shit!" she exclaimed, clearing her throat and standing, her chair rolling away behind her, bashing into the wall. "Sorry," she said, pulling her jacket down, "I thought you were Lexi. What can I do for you?" she asked, quickly grabbing her chair back.

"I just wanted to say goodnight and that I was sorry for disrupting your day this morning."

"Oh, don't be silly." She waved him away. "It's forgotten. I'm just a stickler for formality when it comes to being in the office, and your appearance caught me off guard." She sat forward, looking through the papers on her desk.

"I'm off now," he said, failing to find something to say.

"Well, goodnight." She went back to her work, trying to ignore him. He stood awkwardly for a moment, and then, as he turned, she said, "Er... can I just ask you something?"

He turned back immediately. "Sure."

"Is your name Jorn or Yorn? Because Mr Kelly said Jorn, but I'm sure that's not the right pronunciation, is it?" She blushed slightly. Maybe she'd got it completely wrong.

Jorn smiled at her, "Yes, it's pronounced Yorn, but spelt with a J. People often get confused, so I answer to both. You can call me Jorn if it's easier."

"Oh no, I'd hate to get it wrong." She looked back at her screen, clicking her keyboard to remove the screensaver.

"Not really wrong, just... English."

"What's that supposed to mean?" she asked, furrowing her brow.

He shook his head. Why did he find it so hard to find the right words in front of this woman?

"Nothing," he said, feeling stupid. "Er... have you still got work to do?" he asked, feeling now that the conversation had started, he'd try to continue.

"Yes, I always have lots to do on a Monday," she

grimaced, trying not to look at him.

"Can I help you with any of it?"

"Jeez!" Her hand went to her chest as she looked to see him standing right next to her desk, the smell of his aftershave so intoxicating that she felt a tightness in her stomach. "What? Oh no, I often work late after having the weekend off. I'm used to it."

"Are you sure?" Jorn wanted to help her; being in the same room in this proximity made him want her more than anything.

"Unless you're good at touch-typing, and have your own laptop here, not really." She tutted, leaning into her screen and decreasing the brightness.

"Well, it just so happens I can touch-type, but don't tell my brothers. They think touch-typing is just for women, and I do have my laptop with me," he said, patting his bag.

She looked blankly at him, taken aback, "You can?"

"Yes, as a student, I worked as a receptionist in a call centre. It was easy money, and I learnt to type," he said, lying easily. Making up backstories over the years had become second nature to him.

"Right, well, I have four letters to type up for Adrian and a few emails to send. So, if you mean it and want to help, you could start with the letters?" He set up his laptop opposite her, his knees slipping under the desk where they would now and again brush with hers. He could see her face flush every time he did it, her hand going to her neck like it always did when she was embarrassed.

"So, Loge, how'd you get on with Mr Creepy to...day?" Lexi suddenly appeared through the doorway, her hands holding two McDonald's milkshakes, "Oh, shit."

Logan sighed, feeling her day could not get any more ridiculous.

"Thanks, Lexi," she chimed, scooting over to her friend. "I've got so much to do, so if I give you the money, do you mind getting a taxi?" Logan returned to her desk and foraged for her bag, taking out a twenty-pound note.

"Call me," Lexi whispered, as Logan pushed the note into her hand and shut the door.

"Er... sorry about that," Logan said as he looked up from his typing, her mouth encircling the straw, hoping the ice cream would cool her insides.

"Mr Creepy?" he asked, perturbed.

"Oh, sorry," she said, taking her jacket off, feeling she should elaborate. "It's just a nickname we had for you from the pub on Saturday night."

"Why?" he asked, leaning back and surveying her.

"Well, I don't know, perhaps because you always sit in the corner, never speak to anyone and always stare at me. Like always." Her eyes widened, "My friends all think I'm making it up, as they say that whenever they look over, you're always on your phone. But whenever I do, you're just staring back at me."

Jorn sat amazed for a moment. He'd never noticed her staring at him, and they had never really made eye contact properly. Yet she'd seen him, a Watcher... watching. That was impossible. It was a known fact that a Watcher was never seen unless purposefully, and he certainly had never been caught seeing. Though it transpired, he had.

"I'm not sure whether to take your silence as an admission of guilt or that you think I'm mad." She shrugged, sitting back in her chair, her glasses in her mouth, making her smile crooked.

"I didn't think you'd seen me," Jorn openly admitted.

"So, you admit you were staring at me on Saturday night?" she asked, replacing her glasses and clicking her mouse.

"I wouldn't say I was staring persistently; that *would* be creepy. But I did look over at you a few times. You are a good-looking woman, Logan," he said, feeling honesty was the best policy.

"No, you were staring way too much. It made me feel so uncomfortable that we left." Jorn stared at her, unwilling to concede to himself that he had been caught. "And then, correct me if I am wrong because I was quite drunk. You even followed us to the taxi rank, and a woman dressed in red stuck her hand down your trousers."

He sat there shaking his head. Never had he been caught out like this. This woman was impossible. She shouldn't have been able to see him looking at her. He was an artist. He could always hide in plain sight.

"She did not put her hand down my trousers," he said, in his defence. "I know her from old and she's always trying it on. If you were watching closely, I pushed her away." He could fucking kill Portia.

"If you say so." Logan shrugged again, commencing a new email.

He remained quiet for a moment, before saying, "I'm sorry if I creeped you out. It was never my intention to make you feel uncomfortable."

"Tsk. Don't worry about it. I'd had enough to drink anyway that night," she said, typing quickly while looking at the papers to her left.

Jorn continued his own letter Logan had given him to copy, and after he'd finished, he asked, "Which printer is it? There are so many on this server."

"Oh, here." She went to him and leaned in, her fingertips rolling on his mouse pad, her arm brushing his shoulder. Her scent put Jorn in a daze, and he couldn't help but inhale her more. Her skin smelt like sweets, yet the collar of her top was imbued with a floral perfume he'd never smelt before, and for one moment, his hand teetered near her left hip as if to pull her to him.

"It's the one that ends in five six nine." She moved away, her face glowing red, having felt the heat between them. He could smell the arousal on her, and it was the most seductive scent he'd ever encountered.

He suddenly didn't care she'd caught him watching her. This woman was extraordinary, and he would do everything in his power to prove he was anything but creepy.

CHAPTER FIVE

THE ACCIDENT

Logan could sense he was still standing by her door, waiting for her to get her things together and go home. She wished he wouldn't. The feelings he gave her made her feel disconcerted. She wanted to be near him constantly, yet was so afraid of how she felt that she wanted nothing more than to be away from him. But she smiled, acknowledging him as she switched off the office light, and they walked in silence together to the lift.

"So... full day tomorrow," she said, pressing the down button.

"Yes, I'm looking forward to it; well, I think so," Jorn said, trying to avoid looking into her eyes.

"You should enjoy it here. Adrian is sometimes a hard taskmaster, but he is fair. I like working for him." The ping sounded, and Jorn, being the gentleman he was, allowed her to enter first.

"Yes, he seems very committed to his company," Jorn said, selecting the basement button to the underground car park. "Where are you going?" he asked, his finger poised.

"Same level."

To stop the awkwardness, Jorn asked, "So, is Lexi your housemate?" He knew perfectly who Lexi was, but Logan didn't know that, and it was a natural question.

"She's one of my close friends. I brought her in this morning with the proviso I'd give her a ride home," she sighed. "I didn't think I'd be staying this late."

The lift doors slid open into the cool concrete car park, the orange lights casting elongated shadows over the vehicles dotted around. Logan rummaged through her bag to locate her keys all the while aware of Jorn's presence. She didn't want to admit she couldn't, for the life of her, remember where she'd parked this morning; she'd been so late. So, her only choice was to click the key fob and hope it wasn't too far away. As luck would have it, her dark polo was only seven cars down from where they walked, and she was relieved to have found it easily.

"Well, thanks for your help tonight, Jorn, I'll see you tomorrow." She skirted around him and headed toward her car, thankful to be away from him.

"Yes, I'll see you then," Jorn said, moving purposely to his car.

She'd only just got in hers and switched on the ignition when she heard the engine of his car roar to life, that gravelly loud rev of a large engine and exhaust. His vehicle passed her, and she shook her head. He drove a chic Audi R8. Of course, he did. It was evident to Logan he'd only have the best, and she watched it purr out of the garage, its alloys looking as though trimmed with gold. She couldn't help but think that he was a poser, but she also knew she couldn't blame him. If she looked as well-groomed as him and could afford it, she'd have the best supercar going.

She plugged her phone into the dash and coasted quietly out of the space, her nice standard exhaust producing just the right amount of sound. Scrolling through the screen, she clicked on Lexi's number.

"Hey, sorry that I had to bail. I've only just got out," Logan said, turning onto the street.

"Never mind that, you lunatic. What happened between you and Mr Creepy, or should I call him Mr Hottie?" She heard Lexi giggle like a teenager at the other end, and Logan had to resist rolling her eyes again.

"What do you mean?" What had Lexi imagined they'd got up to after hours?

"Oh, come on, Loge, he's totally got it bad for you. Did you see the way he saved that mug of coffee this morning and how he stayed behind to help you? Jeez, I would have jumped his bones."

Logan scoffed at her friend's crassness.

"I just can't believe he now works with us. After all the avoiding on Saturday and over the past few months, he's suddenly at every turn I make," Logan said, indicating left at the roundabout, switching on her wipers.

"You noticed him a lot more than I did when we've been out, but I get that it is a bit weird. Did you see Quinn's face when he walked in?" Lexi almost shrieked, "I did. He looked daggers at the guy. I think there might be some history between them." Lexi was always one for gossip.

"Really? I can't imagine anything bad on Quinn's side. He's so lovely," Logan said, trying to get out of Lexi that she liked him.

"Yes, he's okay in a simple, boring kind of way."

"Oh, come on, Lexi, Quinn is so cute; I've seen how he looks at you." Logan couldn't believe how blind her best friend was.

"Really? Quinn? No, I'm too much of a flirt for him."

"That is probably true, but even he could put up with your flirty ways, and you never know; he could tame you a little bit."

"I like being a bit wild, and anyway, I don't want to become the office slag, you know."

"Well, Lex, you've stooped as low as Ralph, so you already are," Logan pointed out, stopping at a pedestrian crossing.

"I know. Did you see him today? Wouldn't leave me alone. Maybe I should just get with Quinn to get rid of Ralph."

"Don't you dare; I like Quinn. He doesn't deserve that sort of treatment," Logan replied, queuing up behind a four-by-four.

"No, I wouldn't do that, but I was thinking, with this new

Sales Director, aka Mr Hottie, maybe I could see if he needs a PA? Surely, he can't do all his paperwork?" Logan raised her eyebrows. She knew that Mr Kelly was thinking of getting Jorn a PA, as he hoped he'd also take on the Marketing Director role when his brother James retired, which would be soon, he thought.

"Maybe. I'll sow the seed if you like," Logan offered, moving a few metres forward. "What the hell is the hold-up?" she voiced aloud, edging over to the right in her seat to see that a car had stopped up ahead and put its hazard lights on. "Oh my God!" she exclaimed.

"What?" Lexi hollered.

"Your Mr Hottie. He's only just holding up the whole street of traffic. He's parked up, put his warning lights on, and nipped to the cash point. What a dick!" Logan couldn't believe the arrogance of him. Not only was he a show-off in his supercar, but he was a rude boy, also. Damn it, why the hell did she feel so attracted to him?

"Well, when you're as hot as him, you can get away with anything," Lexi commented as Logan turned the steering wheel to go around him.

"I feel like scratching his car just to be annoying," Logan laughed, continuing her journey.

"I dare you," she replied.

"Not likely. Anyway, Lex, I'll see you tomorrow."

"Sure, sure. Drive safely." Logan ended the call and enjoyed the rest of her journey home unimpeded.

Logan loved having her own house, it might be small and quaint, but she loved every inch of it. The heating was already on when she opened her back door, and she relished the heatwave that hit her after being out in the damp December evening. Switching on the kettle, Logan put her coat and scarf away and began getting some vegetables out for dinner. She had been dreaming all day of a vegetable broth her mum used to make in winter. So, after throwing on loose bottoms and a fluffy jumper, she danced about the kitchen, peeling the root vegetables and singing to her favourite music mix. She tried desperately not to think about Jorn but couldn't help, now and again, wish he was with her. To have his hands on her hips as she swung them from side to side to the beat, have his lips on her neck and how he would distract her from the cooking; that all would be abandoned, and he'd take her on the couch. Fuck! She needed to stop imagining things like that. He was Mr Creepy, not Mr Hottie.

She added the stock to the veg, allowing it to simmer whilst she got her hoover out to begin cleaning her front room. Monday evening was cleaning day for her. She'd found the older she got, the more routine meant something. Also, she tended to be a slob on the weekends, so Monday seemed a good day to clean. However, this Monday had taken its toll on her, and her brain ached behind her eyes somewhat more than usual. Fishing her glasses from her bag, she hoped they'd help. Returning to the kitchen, she stirred her broth, the smell making her stomach grumble. Just as she got a knife out to test if the potatoes were ready, her phone buzzed continually on the worktop.

Unknown number.

"Hello?" she said, cradling the device to her ear, betting it was a sales pitch.

"Hello, is this a Miss Hunter?"

"Yes," Logan said sceptically, "who is this?"

"I'm sorry to phone you, Miss, but do you know a Mr Adrian Kelly?"

"Oh God! What's happened?" Logan felt her heart drop into her stomach, knowing immediately that this was not the phone call she'd anticipated.

"I'm one of the nurses from St. Joseph's."

"Shit, is he alright?"

"He's been in an accident, and we are trying to get hold of his family."

"What do you mean accident? Is he dead?" Logan could feel her eyes clouding.

"No, Miss, but we need to inform his family. On the hospital records, he's put you down as next of kin."

"Yes, I know," she said, not meaning to sound gruff. "His wife, sadly, has early-onset Alzheimer's, so he asked me if I wouldn't mind. She's in a home in the southeast of the city." Logan turned her hob out and began getting her coat on, her executive brain kicking in. "Please, can you tell me what happened?"

"I can, Miss, but are there any children we should be informing?"

"No, they had no children. Please. Can you give me any more information? Can I at least come to the hospital and speak to someone in person? Should I be worried? I mean, is it fatal?"

"He's still in surgery now."

"Right. I can come right now. Can you tell me where I need to go?"

Logan could not believe this. Poor Adrian.

"Make your way to level six. That's the surgical unit where one of my colleagues will meet you."

"Thank you so much for calling. I won't be long."

After hanging up, she grabbed her keys and made her way to the car, not waiting for the door to click shut behind her.

She drove like mad through the streets, the rain splashing at her windscreen, the wipers working overtime, her heart hammering hard in her chest. She dialled Lexi again but was met with voicemail. What the hell had happened to him? Her moaning about him to Lexi last night made her stomach feel wretched. At least today, she'd been good to him and spoke highly of him to Jorn.

Swerving her car into the car park she slotted straight into a space before running up the stairs to level six, where there was a waiting area and a receptionist.

"Hello. My name is Logan Hunter; I'm Adrian Kelly's next of kin. Can you help me?" she said to the receptionist.

"Yes, of course. Please take a seat, and I'll get Johnny, who spoke to you on the phone."

Wringing her hands in apprehension, she moved towards a seat but found she couldn't sit down. She needed to know how he was, and she began to pace, getting strange looks from a man sitting in the corner, but she didn't care. She'd never been in this kind of situation before. What should she do? She tried Lexi again, no answer. Who else could she contact?

The woman reappeared and sat behind the desk. Where was this Johnny? She paced for a further ten minutes and then re-approached the receptionist.

"Listen, can someone please tell me what is happening?"

"I'm sorry, Miss, but we're extremely busy; I'm sure Johnny will be here soon. Erm..." She handed her a phone and a wallet. Adrian's belongings. "That's all he had on him," she said.

"What do you mean? Is he dead?" Logan couldn't hold it together any longer. "What the hell is going on? You tell me I can come, and then there's no one to tell me what's happening. You won't even tell me if he is dead or not. Please. Isn't there anyone who can help me?" She grabbed at her face, feeling lost and afraid.

"Please, Miss, calm down; I will find out what is going on." She left again.

Logan looked at Adrian's effects in her hands, feeling guilty for abusing the receptionist. Damn it! Clicking the phone screen, she saw it was password-protected. She should, perhaps, phone his brother.

"Right, Adrian, what is your password?" she whispered, pressing the buttons. "260967? Not his birthday." She thought again, "141069" the phone unlocked, making her eyes close with sadness. His password was his wife's birthdate. She scrolled through his stored numbers, coming to 'Jorn Hartvigsen.' She hovered over the green swipe button. Could she involve him? He was new to the company, but as she pondered, she knew she'd not want anyone else by her side bar him. She pressed the button, it ringing three times before he picked up.

"Good evening, sir." Logan was silent momentarily, not knowing whether she should say anything. She should probably hang up. "Hello, Adrian?"

"Jorn, it's Logan," she said after further deliberation.

"Logan? Are you okay?" She sobbed suddenly, feeling an unbearable need to cry continuously. "Logan, are you alright? What's going on?"

"Erm... It's Adrian," she heaved down the phone. "He's been in an accident." She couldn't get the words out.

"What? Where are you?" Jorn asked.

"At St. Joseph's, sixth floor."

"I'm coming; stay there." He hung up.

Logan held the phone to her forehead, her tears still coming. At that moment, she realised how alone she was, how vulnerable she felt, and how insecure she suddenly was. Surely, she should have tried Lexi again, or even her father, who would have dropped everything and come without batting an eyelid, but the only person she had wanted was him. The guy from the pub, the guy she barely knew, the guy she'd spent some solitary hours with typing emails. Why was there such a pull to him? What did he hold over her? He'd scared her on Saturday with his constant staring, yet now all she wanted was his eyes on her, watching her. Protecting her.

"I'm sorry, Miss Hunter?"

Logan shot up towards the desk to see a man dressed in green theatre scrubs and a mesh hat.

"Yes," she said, wiping her tears away.

"I'm sorry to keep you waiting." She felt her heart elevate slightly; he didn't look too grave. "Do you want to follow me to the visitors' room?"

"My friend is coming to be with me," she said, feeling Jorn had told her to stay where she was.

"That's okay; Claire will show them through." He looked at the receptionist, who nodded.

Logan followed Johnny through the security doors to a plainly decorated room with a few landscape paintings and a mixture of mismatched chairs and sofas.

"Please, sit down," Johnny indicated, sitting next to her so he could see her completely. "Right, so I understand you work for Mr Kelly?"

"Yes, I'm his PA. Please, is he okay?"

"I'm afraid it's not good news." Logan swallowed, her hand going to her mouth. "From what we understand, it was a hit and run along the main High Street, opposite The National Bank." Logan knew the street; it was notorious for accidents. "He's suffered a severe head injury, which has caused a bleed to the brain."

"Oh God!" Logan collapsed into her hands; this really wasn't happening. It just couldn't be.

Johnny waited for her to calm down, his hand rubbing her shoulder.

"Will he recover?" she gasped, trying to compose herself.

"At the moment, it is too early to tell. He's back from surgery, and now we wait. Unfortunately, bleeds on the brain can go one of two ways, and of course, we hope there will be no long-term damage. But it's too early to tell due to the amount of swelling. I'm afraid the first few days are the most critical. He's in an induced coma now, and we'll, of course, keep you updated."

Logan nodded, "Can I see him?" she asked, looking at the nurse earnestly. "I know he won't hear me, but I just want to tell him that I'll look after everything. I just want him to know I'm there."

"Of course, if you give me a moment, I'll see if the consultant's happy for you to see him, and if he's stable enough for you to sit with."

"Thank you." Logan sat with her head in her hands, feeling sick; her headache had returned with a vengeance, and she felt unattainably exhausted. It was one hell of a Monday she was having.

"Logan?" His voice washed over her like a warm heat

haze, allowing the feeling in her stomach to return, and she immediately hated herself for how she felt, but she couldn't help it.

"Jorn!" She got up, flinging her arms around his neck, falling into him, her sobs loud in his ear, snot running on his jacket. But she didn't care. As his arms enveloped her, she felt safe and protected, his scent relaxing her, her breathing stabilising; she wanted to stay in his arms forever.

Because if she was with him, she'd always be safe.

CHAPTER SIX

THE PIN

Jorn bloody hated traffic, he hated driving, and he hated rain. He hated this whole fucking day. He'd made such an idiot out of himself in front of Logan and then hadn't listened at all to Adrian's instructions on what his job entailed, so he was none the wiser on what he had to do. He hated his life right now. What happened to just being someone who watches others and reports back? This wasn't in his job description, although there never had been one for being a Watcher. You were given these abilities when born and grow into them until you reach adulthood, and that's where you stay—locked as a twenty-four-year-old until either killed or stripped. Jorn had been a Watcher coming on three hundred and thirty-two years now, and this had been one of the most difficult days of his existence.

He pulled into the mansion's parking garage, entered his room, and, in an instant, flung himself face-first onto his bed. He felt shattered. He wasn't sure why. Was it because he hadn't used his brain this much for years and was mentally exhausted?

"For fuck's sake, just give me five minutes," he called into his pillow as he heard his sitting room door open.

"Jorn?"

"Sorry, sir." He jumped off his bed and moved into the lounge. "Sorry, Master. I thought you must be Jorun," he said, chancing a glance at his screens of Logan's house; she was in the kitchen.

"So... how was your day?" The Master asked, leaning against his couch with his ankles crossed.

"Productive. I have made contact, and I think I'm getting somewhere."

"Good. How long do you think it will take to succeed?" he said casually.

"Erm... I'm not sure. Depends on how personal you want it to get," Jorn said, feeling slightly deflated at his Master's words. Here it comes—the deadline.

"Oh, The Emperor wants it to get very personal," he replied, raising his eyebrows.

"Well, as I haven't got Jorun's skills, it might take me a while," he said honestly, looking back at the screens. "And I'm afraid I'm not one to rush things. It's not in my nature, sir."

"That's too bad, Jorn. He needs it done by New Year's Eve."

Jorn shook his head. "That's under three weeks, sir; I don't think anyone can fall in love that quickly, especially not her." Jorn knew she wouldn't be like that in three weeks. He knew this woman. She didn't give her heart out to just anyone, and really, did he want her to?

"Well, The Emperor is coming on New Year's Eve to claim her and I don't want him disappointed." He turned, but before departing, he left a small suit pin on his desk. "And I want you to wear this at all times; I need to see what you are up to. It's small so that it won't be noticed. Craig says the battery within it is rechargeable and will last up to twelve hours," he smirked. "Engineering is marvellous, isn't it?" He left, slamming the door in his wake.

"Argh!" Jorn screamed, grabbing his chair and throwing it at his door, it buckling slightly, making the entire room shudder. He pulled over his shelving unit, his books and old texts crashing onto the floor. He yanked out the drawers from his wooden chest, chucking them at the walls, smashing into the plaster, creating dents in the wall, and chipping the paintwork. "Argh!" he shouted again, taking his sitting room lamp and hurling it at his window, it crashing against the double-paned glass.

"Jorn! Jorn!" Randin's arms came around his chest, holding him by his side, Jorn struggling to escape the hold. "Stop this!" Kol and Jorun ran into the room, followed by Jorn's other brothers, Lamont and Oska.

"I CAN'T. I WANT TO FUCKING HIT SOMETHING!" Jorn shouted, kicking out at his brother, but Randin stood fast, holding him tightly.

'Jorn, stop this', Jorun called to him, trying to mind-link

him as all twins of their kind could.

'I don't care and don't want to feel like this.' But after a few more minutes of struggling, Jorn slowed his rebellion and finally, with the nod from Jorun, Randin let go of him. Jorn didn't look at any of them. He just walked to his bathroom and banged the door closed.

"What was that all about?" Kol asked, "I've never seen him lose control like that."

"No, something has upset him," Randin said. "Maybe this task The Master has got him doing is one step too far for him." Randin looked at Jorun for confirmation.

Jorun nodded. He knew what was troubling Jorn, he could feel it in his heart. Jorn was in love with this mortal, and there was nothing Jorun or his brothers could do to help him. He either had to do as The Master bid him or be stripped of his abilities.

"You stay here and make sure he behaves; I'll go smooth things over with The Master," Randin said, leaving immediately.

Jorn stood seething in the shower, allowing the hot water to roll over him. He couldn't do this. Yesterday, his job had been so clear. Now, it was a jumble of emotions he didn't like or know how to deal with. He needed to get out of the shower to watch her, be near her, and see her every movement. And yet he didn't want just to watch. He wanted to be with her.

Pulling open the bathroom door, he clocked Jorun sitting on his sofa reading a magazine, Lamont was busy putting the last of his clothes back in the drawers, and Oska was attempting to pull the lamp back into an okayish, upright position. He ignored them and moved to his desk, his eyes flicking along each screen searching, but he needn't have bothered. She was back in the kitchen again, cooking, her other favourite pastime besides gardening. He watched for a while and then saw her pick up her phone. What was she doing? Was she crying? It had better not be that ex-boyfriend again. He saw her switch off the hob and put her coat on. Was she going out again? This was totally out of character for her on a Monday evening.

He ran to his drawers and began getting dressed, before brushing his teeth and spraying cologne on his skin. On returning, the boys hadn't really moved, and he continued to ignore them, looking again at the screens; she had left, but her front door wasn't closed properly.

"What on earth is she doing?" he said, under his breath to no one, as he watched the car pull out onto the road.

"So?" Jorun said, throwing away the magazine.

"Just don't, Jorun, please. Not right now." Jorn shook his head. Where was she going? He looked at other surveillance cameras along the streets, searching for her vehicle.

"What are you looking at, Jorn?" Lamont asked, coming over to the desk.

"Logan... she's gone out again, and I don't know where." His eyes darted to the next screen.

"Jorn!" Randin had come into the room. "Why, Jorn, why did you do that? I don't understand. You know The Master has no tolerance for that type of behaviour." He grabbed

Jorn by the shoulder, spinning him round to face him. "I've sorted things with him, but Jorn, you must hold it together. You can't just fly off the handle like that." Randin shook his brother, "Are you listening to me?"

"Yes, Randin, I am listening. For fuck's sake, it won't happen again," Jorn said, exasperatedly. Why didn't they all just leave him alone?

"What happened, my brother? I've never seen you so angry; your eyes were blood red," Kol said, caringly.

"Kol, leave it," said Jorun. He knew that Kol could press Jorn's buttons, and they didn't need another scene.

"Yes, Kol, leave it," Randin said.

"What? You're not. You're still goading him, so why should I stop?" He folded his arms. "I'm just showing I care."

"Shut up, Kol," Lamont added. They all knew Kol's ways of winding up.

"Yes, Kol, you..." Jorn stopped as he heard his phone vibrating in his jacket. Taking it out, he saw it was Mr Kelly, "Hush, all of you." His brothers immediately desisted. "Good evening, sir." Jorn listened to the person at the other end and couldn't believe it was her phoning him. She'd phoned him out of all the other numbers in her boss's contacts.

"I'm coming; stay there." Hanging up, he turned to Randin and asked, "Can you go to this address and shut the front door for me?" He scrawled Logan's street number down and got his coat and scarf.

"Jorn, where are you going?"

"Logan, she needs me." He left the room.

"Oh, I do hope it's something dreadful, so she throws herself into your arms, Jorn." His Master was leaning against the wall outside his room. "A damsel in distress is just what you need." Jorn stopped, closing his eyes to gain composure. "Oh, and don't forget your pin, Jorn. I'd hate you to disobey me." As he turned, his Master threw him the small brooch he'd swiftly fetched from his room. "Now make sure you put it on, and don't be a child about it."

God, Jorn hated him!

Once in the car, he sped towards St. Joseph's, the pin in his pocket like a thorn in his side. He couldn't wear it; he just couldn't. He wouldn't do it to her. If her death was impending, then he wouldn't have her final days on display for him or The Emperor or, in fact, anyone to watch. He knew his brothers would respect his privacy and not even contemplate watching anything broadcast. But, his Master? Nothing seemed beneath him.

He sped through the waterlogged streets, driving erratically, yet he wasn't afraid of losing control. His abilities enabled him to predict other people's actions, and he managed to swerve and slam the brakes in plenty of time; all road users were predictable to a Watcher as skilled as Jorn. Once parked, he moved swiftly to the sixth floor, all the while smelling her perfume in the air. The receptionist showed him through the doors into the visitor's room, and there she was, in sweatpants and a fluffy jumper, the slippers on her feet soaked. She'd not even changed her shoes.

"Jorn!" With her arms around his neck, he felt utter relief and contentment, yet he couldn't stop the anger from creeping in. His Master was right. She was a damsel, and he'd answered her distress call. He couldn't help but stroke her hair as she cried into his shoulder, her body trembling under his hands, her scent rinsing over him like sunshine.

"I'm sorry I called you," she said, into his shoulder. "I couldn't think of anyone else. Lexi didn't answer her phone, so I scrolled through his contacts, and your number was just there. I'm so sorry."

He pulled her to a chair briskly, "Logan, you don't have to apologise. I'm glad you called me."

"I didn't know what else to do." She took a tissue from the box on the table, wiping away her smudged make-up. "Did I ruin your evening?"

"No, don't be silly. I wasn't doing anything," he said honestly. "Have they said anything about what happened?"

"They said it was a hit and run, that he's got a brain injury, and they can't be sure whether he'll recover." She screwed her eyes shut, more tears falling. "Why is this happening, Jorn? I was just with him not four hours ago."

"Were there any witnesses?" Jorn asked, beginning to pace.

"I don't know, I didn't even ask," she replied, feeling stupid.

"I'll speak to the police. I'll pay for an investigation," he said earnestly, seeing her distress.

"Surely there'll be an investigation anyway. It was a hit and run."

"You'd be surprised what people get away with these days, Logan," Jorn said, looking at her.

They were silent a while, and then she said, "I saw you earlier, parked up with your hazard lights on. That's how accidents happen, Jorn, when people like you think they own the right to stop where they like."

He looked at her, "This has nothing to do with me, Logan."

She furrowed her brow, "I wasn't saying that. I was only making a point. I..."

The door opened, and the nurse entered, "Miss Hunter?" Logan jumped up.

"Yes."

"The surgeons have said you may sit with Mr Kelly if you would like to."

Logan walked out into the foyer, Jorn following. "No, Jorn, I'm sorry; I want to see him alone." She put her hand to his chest as he nodded, "But don't go."

"Of course not." He stood back, feeling the retribution of his earlier misdemeanour.

He allowed the nurse to show her down the corridor, and once she was gone, he moved stealthily, his feet making no noise and his body seeming to blend in with the wall. Lamont called it his chameleon talent, yet he didn't change colour; he just melted in so well with his surroundings that people would walk straight past him. An expert spy. He crept towards the nurse's station, where two women sat in scrubs. One was on the phone checking through the computer as she spoke, searching for what Jorn saw were blood results, and the other was documenting in a folder.

"So, did you hear?" the one on the phone had finished making the other look up. "That Mr Kelly, who's just come out of theatre." They both turned to the private room just to the left of them. "Was, apparently, hit by a black Range Rover. Eyewitnesses said it looked like the car was aiming for him; the vehicle mounted the pavement, missing everyone else but him. Poor guy, he didn't have a chance."

Jorn turned his face into the wall, a primal growl edging up his throat as he rolled his hands into fists. It had been a targeted hit. Of course, it had been. His Master would stop at nothing to get what The Emperor wanted. He'd known that Logan wouldn't have been able to resist falling into his arms after this type of shock. He just knew it. Was that why he'd given him the hidden camera so that he could see Logan's reaction and his own? Could he really stoop that low?

"I'm going to fucking kill him!" Jorn cursed through gritted teeth. "He's got no right."

He turned and edged back towards the exit. That's what he'd do; he'd kill him. Stab him in the back, shoot him with a gun, or bloody poke his eyes out with a fork if he had to. But he wanted to give him pain, pain beyond what he'd ever felt and when The Master was left bleeding on the floor, he'd start on The Emperor.

He threw open the double doors that led out into the lift system. Logan would understand why he had to leave. He felt the red haze filter in his eyes, the fury coursing through his arm muscles and into his hands. He was going to kill them all.

"Jorn?" His red eyes focused,

"Lay?" His brother stood there in a suit, holding his briefcase. "What are you doing here? If Randin sent you to change my mind, then he should have sent you all," he seethed, pushing past him towards the lifts.

"No one has sent me. I'm here on official business." Jorn squinted at him. "I'm Mr. Kelly's lawyer."

"Wait? What?" He returned to stand in front of his brother.

"I've come to speak to Miss Hunter." Jorn didn't like this. Were they all in on this concocted plan of The Emperor's?

"You know Logan?" Jorn asked, his hand out to halt Lamont.

"Miss Hunter? No, I have never met her. And before your crazy mind thinks up anything, I'm on your side, brother." Lamont's hand went to Jorn's shoulder. "I have been Mr. Kelly's lawyer for years. I did not know you had been sent to work for him until Randin told me before I left."

Jorn was wary of his brother's allegiance. Lamont had always been the sensible one of the six and had rarely gone against his Master's wishes or, indeed, said anything against him. Could he trust him?

"She's sitting with Mr Kelly now. Do you know what happened?" Jorn nodded at the receptionist, who allowed them back to the visitors' waiting room.

"The police report is still coming in. Apparently, a vehicle matching the description of a Range Rover mounted the pavement and hit Mr Kelly as he waited to cross Carnival Lane. According to sources, no one else was injured or hurt, and the vehicle took off through a red light."

"Plates?"

Lamont shook his head, "No, dead end, they were fake."

"You know it was a *black* Range Rover," Jorn insinuated, looking poignantly at his brother.

"No, Jorn, I know what you're thinking," he said, with a grimace. "Portia was in The Master's private chamber when the incident occurred, I know, I could hear them." He rolled his eyes.

"Doesn't mean it wasn't her car."

"Yes, but it doesn't make it hers either," Lamont said, raising his eyebrows.

Jorn knew he spoke truths. Black was a common colour, and Range Rovers were popular with rich mothers and celebrity couples.

"What do you want with Logan, then?" Jorn asked, still feeling that his Master was knee-deep in this despite his brother's reasoning.

"That's confidential between me and her." Jorn tutted. His brother was always a professional.

There was a knock; the nurse had returned.

"Er... Miss Hunter would like you to go to her," he said, looking at Jorn.

And, without even looking at his brother, Jorn got up. He couldn't think of anywhere he'd rather be right now.

The killing of his Master would have to wait.

CHAPTER SEVEN

THE HOSPITAL

Logan followed Johnny down the bleach-smelling corridor, her feet slipping slightly in damp slippers. It had been very unlike her to leave the house in them, but then this situation was not normal; all she'd thought of was getting to the hospital quickly. She stood in the doorway of the ward side room for a while, her hand at her mouth as she looked at her boss. He looked so ashen-faced, his features suddenly gaunt, his head covered in a bandage. His arms were resolutely by his side under the blankets with machines on either side of him. The sound of a heartbeat was all that could be heard over the wheeze of the breathing apparatus.

"Thank you." Johnny nodded at her as she went to the bedside, pulling up a chair, her hand feeling under the covers for his. It was warm and smooth, and she held it gently.

"Adrian?" She felt slightly stupid talking to him. She'd

often seen it in films where the loving family member spoke to the person in the bed. But in the films, they would suddenly twitch their fingers like some miracle, or there would be some indication that they could hear the speaker. Yet Adrian lay motionless.

"Adrian, it's Logan." She took his hand and placed it on her face, her skin feeling cool in comparison. "I'm not sure you can hear me, you probably can't, but I want to tell you anyway. I want you to know you'll be okay and back to work soon. But in the meantime." She heaved, not allowing the tears to come again. "You can rely on me to keep the business going. I'll keep everything under control, and I've not got long until the Christmas break, so I'm sure the helm won't be in my hands for long." She sighed, "I've got Mr Hartvigsen here with me, er... Jorn. I feel he will be great for the company, and I know he'll assist me in any way he can. I wasn't sure of him initially; he seemed arrogant, crass, and a bit of a know-it-all. But, well, after spending time with him this afternoon, I feel I can trust him. Call me stupid or a girl who likes her new co-worker more than perhaps she should." She half laughed at the look Adrian would have given her if he could, "I know you'll think that, but I can't help it. There is something about him that I don't understand, but I know he has our best interests at heart, and I'm afraid I must believe there are decent young men who grow up to be like you or my dad in this world. Who treat women well and respect their elders, as he has shown you tonight. Oh! I don't know." She lifted her arms up in surrender, "I'm waffling, I suppose. But I want you to know I will rally the troops, and we'll keep it all going for you." She felt her phone vibrating in her pocket, but she ignored it. It was most likely Lexi. "I don't want you to worry about Julia either. I will go to her tomorrow and sit with her on pizza date night, and, of course, I won't forget the Amaryllis bouquet I know you were going to buy her. I know they are her favourite at this time of year."

She gazed around the room at the machines and, allowing the tears to fall freely, she opened a packet of wipes she had in her bag and began cleansing his face. His cheek had a graze, and a bruise had started to form on his jaw. "I'm so sorry this happened to you, Adrian; you don't deserve it; you don't deserve any of it."

She thought about his wife, who'd been diagnosed with early-onset Alzheimer's two years ago. Initially, he'd tried to manage her at home, but he started being late for work and disappearing at lunchtime because she couldn't be alone for too long. Logan had made him get some home help, but even that hadn't assisted him for long. Julia was often up during the night and soon lost her ability to use the bathroom unaided, and once she fell down the stairs when he was out, Logan insisted he got some proper help. She now stays in specialist accommodation with twenty-four-hour nurse care. Logan had visited her a few times with Adrian, as, at first, the guilt he felt nearly broke him. She'd often find him in his office in tears, so soon after she'd begun treating him like you would a father. She thought he looked at her as you would a daughter, having not had any children of his own, and Logan, though she loved her own father with all her heart, loved him like one. He annoyed her as all parents do, and bossed her around, telling her to do things she hated. Yet now, as he lay in front of her, she'd have that man any day.

"Miss Hunter, is everything alright?" Johnny stuck his head in.

"Yes, er... is my friend still here?"

"Yes, he's in the waiting room. Would you like me to get him?"

"Do you mind? I'm not quite ready to leave yet, but I feel guilty he came, and I kind of shunned him away."

She looked back at the bed, "I think you've chosen well, Adrian. Jorn will be an asset to the company." She knew she was repeating herself, but she didn't want him to feel alone. "And I'll tell you a little secret," she bit her lip, smiling. "Did you know he can touch-type? I can imagine you raising your eyebrows at me right now. Do you believe it? He helped me type all those letters you had... me do..." She wiped her tears away, smiling to herself.

"Hey, are you telling him all my secrets?" She smirked, looking up at Jorn as he stood framed in the doorway, his ankle crossed and leaning to one side, one hand in his pocket.

"No, just that one. It's the only one I know," she sniffed.

"Here." He handed her a tissue.

"Thanks." She held her head in her hand, the pain over her eyes suddenly sharp.

"You, okay?" Jorn was at her side, crouching down.

"Yes, my head, it just pounds continuously. I'm tired, and crying doesn't help."

"Come on, let me take you home." As if on cue, her stomach rumbled. "And you're hungry."

"Yes, I was cooking my dinner when the call came through." She fingered unnecessarily with the green blanket, "I feel bad leaving him. I know he hates the quiet. After Julia moved into the home, he used to play audiobooks through his smart speaker to keep his mind busy."

"Hang on." He returned shortly with an old CD player. "The nurses said he could borrow it overnight. It's no smart speaker, but it's background noise. What station do you think he'd like? Radio four?"

Logan giggled, "Most likely."

He plugged it in behind the bed and tuned it roughly to radio four, the static occasionally crackling, but it was better than the silence of hospital machines.

Logan took Jorn's hand and placed her lips on his cheek, lingering for longer than she should have, but she couldn't help her impulsive move. His skin smelt so masculine, and the stubble there, though short, was so soft that she could have stayed there for hours.

"Thank you, Jorn."

"Anything to help your pain," he said, feeling a surge of something totally inappropriate.

She walked ahead of him as they left the ward, her face flushed, her head throbbing with unease, and her headache worsening. What she really wanted was a bath and bed, but she knew she had many things to do now that this had happened. As she held the door for Jorn, a man stepped up to her, holding a briefcase.

"Ah, Miss Hunter?"

"Yes," Logan said, looking confusedly at the man in the straight tie and suit.

"Oh yes, Logan, I'm sorry; this is one of my elder brothers, Lamont," Logan looked weirdly at Jorn, "he's strangely Mr Kelly's lawyer."

"Right?" Great! More headache.

"I'm sorry to trouble you, Miss Hunter, as I know you've had a traumatic evening, but I have been sanctioned by my firm and by the request of Mr Kelly to inform you of the plans for Mr Kelly's company should anything ever happen to him."

"Right," Logan said again, feeling her head worsen. "Is it going to be quick? I want to get home and go to bed."

"Well, I will try to be as quick as I can, but as you can imagine, due to Mr Kelly's accident, the running of his company, immediate finances, and household…"

"Just get to the point, Lamont, please," Jorn said, rolling his eyes. "Can't you see that she's exhausted?"

"Sure, sure, well Mr Kelly has directed my company that should anything happen to him, his mental capacity be brought into question or on his demise, you should take over as Managing Director and endeavour to run the company as you seem fit until his return and/or death."

"Okay," she repeated, feeling slightly faint. "Is there any chance we can do this at my home? I don't feel up to doing it here."

"If you would permit me."

"For fuck's sake, Lamont, stop being all professional, just say it how it is." How irritating could his brother be?

"Yes, Jorn, but things are delicate." Jorn scoffed. "But if Miss Hunter wishes so, I can, of course, come to her house, and she can sign the necessary paperwork."

"That would be great," Logan said, pressing the lift button and rubbing her temples. She'd have to take some paracetamol when she got back.

"Logan? Why doesn't Lamont take your car, and I'll take you home in mine?"

She nodded, her stomach starting to churn; her head was so bad. As she leaned into the wall of the lift to cool the burn behind her eyes, she groped in her bag for her glasses again. They just needed to see her home, then she could put a cold compress to her forehead.

Her head was so bad that she didn't have the energy to marvel at Jorn's interior upholstery or question the speed he was going. All she knew was that the seats were super comfortable, and she may have slept if the journey had been any longer.

"Have you ever had your headaches investigated?" Jorn asked, as she opened her back gate. Why she used her back door most of the time, he'll never know.

"Yes, the GP said they're most likely migraines caused by stress levels and constantly looking at screens." She opened the door, and he waited for her to invite him in. "Come through." She led him into the house, showing him the lounge where he could sit and wait for his brother. Turning the hob on, she started to heat up her broth, before opening her medicine box and downing some paracetamol and adding a cold pad to her head.

"Shit," her vision suddenly went black, and petrol-coloured spots burst in front of her eyes. Was she going to faint? She jumped instinctively as a voice spoke within her mind,

'Logan, you must fulfil your duty. Do not resist.'

There was a blade in her back, and she yelped before her kitchen came into full view again, and she was standing over by the stove stirring the saucepan.

It wasn't the first time Logan had blacked out during one of her headaches, yet it was the first time she'd heard and felt something. She had no idea what the voice meant or what the pain was, but after the blackouts, the headaches would completely disappear. She was never sure if it was circumstantial, having had paracetamol, or if they went because she blacked out, but she was relieved that the pain had gone.

"You okay?" Jorn asked, walking in.

"Yes, I just touched the edge of the pan." She smiled at him, feeling she could show him yesterday's burn if he asked. "It was hotter than I thought."

"Lamont is at the door if you're ready."

"Sure, I'll be there in a minute."

Jorn seemed to stand awkwardly, and it wasn't until Logan

vacated the kitchen with a bowl of broth that she understood why. Lamont was still on her doorstep.

"Why didn't you ask him in?" she joked, motioning Lamont to step over the threshold.

"Well, it's your house," he smiled apologetically, as Lamont entered and sat on the edge of the sofa cushion, getting out his laptop.

Lamont was thorough and spelt out all the paperwork, so Logan didn't have to read it. She would be in sole charge, and if she required help with the management of the company, there were agencies that would help, which Mr Kelly had previously solicited. She was to understand that the status within the hierarchy would be revoked should Mr Kelly return or if he passed away.

"Right, and if you just sign there, we're all done." Logan dutifully signed the official-looking paper Lamont offered her.

"Tomorrow is going to be horrendous," she said, wistfully, to no one in particular.

"No, it won't. It will be fine. The team knows what they're working on," Jorn said encouragingly.

"You say that like it's easy being a Managing Director," Logan snorted, walking into the kitchen to wash up her bowl.

"I meant it won't be as bad as you think. You have a good relationship with your co-workers, which I saw today. Have some faith in yourself."

"I didn't want this, Jorn," she grimaced, downing some water.

"Yes, I know you didn't, and I wish I could take it away, but I can't. And anyway, from what I've seen, you practically run the place. Mr Kelly couldn't have picked a better substitute."

"That's powerful praise from someone I've only just met," she said, draining the sink and placing the leftover broth in the fridge.

"Yes, but... well, look, I'll be honest with you, Logan, I like you... a lot. You caught my eye some weeks ago at the bar, and I see now, after today, that my somewhat perhaps 'creepy' staring didn't do you justice. You're so much more lovely than I thought you were."

Logan stared at him, "Are you always this forward with women?"

He avoided her eyes a moment as he moved nearer to her, then turning, he locked her umber eyes with his green ones, "No." And with that, he moved his lips in line with hers and waited; if she wanted to resist, she had time. His lips were warm and gentle as he touched hers, slowly coaxing her mouth to embrace his, his tongue savouring her taste in case she pushed him away. Yet she yearned for him. Heat flooded her body. His touch to her face with his hand sent a shiver of lust up her arm towards her neck, her gasp never escaping as she held the edge of the worktop to keep her balance. His hand went to the back of her head, pulling her in closer, wishing he had the courage to touch her further. But he couldn't. What he was doing wasn't right. He wasn't doing this for himself;

He was doing it for him, The Emperor. He was lining her up for her own demise, but he couldn't help it. Her hand was moving down his back, under the rim of his jeans, her fingers slipping towards the top of his butt cheek, pulling him into her. Would he be able to stop her if her hand moved round to the front? God, he wanted her, yet there was a wetness on his face, and pulling away, he saw the tears in her eyes.

"Logan?"

"I'm sorry, it's just that I can't do this, not now. Not with Adrian the way he is. The guilt I feel is overwhelming." She bit her bottom lip, knowing she was acting stupidly, but she couldn't help it. Jorn fell forward, resting his head on her shoulder.

"Yes, I'm sorry," he said, standing back and adjusting his jeans. "Wrong moment."

"It wasn't not great though." Logan felt out of breath and wished she could continue, but her heart felt riddled with guilt, and she couldn't enjoy it as much as she wanted to.

"I should go," Jorn said, looking back at her.

"Yes, I should shower and go to bed. I have a new job to go to in the morning."

"Yes, er... me too. Right." He turned to leave, tapping his pocket to see if his keys were there.

"Jorn?" He looked at her. "Thanks for that. It was... nice."

He just nodded and left the room.

CHAPTER EIGHT

THE FIGHT

Lamont waited patiently in the car. He had a feeling he might be waiting a while, but that was okay with him as he had lots of filing to do and emails to send. However, he'd just got his laptop booted back up when Jorn threw open the car door and got in. He sat slightly stunned for a moment, watching his brother start the engine and swerve out of the space before thinking he should perhaps say something.

"So..."

"Just don't say anything," Jorn said, feeling embarrassed. Logan had totally rebuked his advances, and he was finding that difficult to swallow.

"Hey, look, Jorn, taking things slowly in a relationship is okay. You don't have to bed people on the first date or even kiss, for that matter."

Jorn just nodded, flashing someone to go ahead of him.

"I don't know what The Master or The Emperor has you doing. But if you like this girl, you must tell them and make sure you can do things at your own pace; to hell with what they say."

"It's not that simple, though, Lay, is it?"

"Well, it should be. When you love someone, it should be treasured, nurtured."

"You speak from experience?" Jorn looked over at his brother. If he was honest, Lamont was probably the sibling he spent the least amount of time with.

"Maybe I am, or I think I am. I know what it's like to like someone so much that every time you are apart, you feel as though your soul has been torn from you, and the only cure is to be together. When you feel that way. Really feel that way. You'll know what love is."

Jorn had never felt like that about anyone, and he wasn't sure if he could ever feel like that with Logan. At the moment, it was just pure desire. To have her succumb to him, to have her melt under his tongue, for him to induce goosebumps on her skin with just his voice.

"Do you think Jorun feels like that about everyone?" Jorn asked, running a hand through his hair, the scent of Logan on his clothes.

"I know that in the beginning, Jorun used to find it hard to conceal his feelings from others. He has the biggest heart, and I know he finds being who he is exhausting." Lamont shrugged, "With my ability, I can kind of switch it off. My brain is my weapon, and when I don't need it, I can relax and chill. With Jorun, his emotions are always at one hundred percent."

"I know what it feels like to be working at a hundred percent, all the time," Jorn sighed, slowing at the crossing.

"Yes, being a Watcher, you are always on the go, no matter how many people you are watching or the intensity. With Logan, it seems to have been intense for some time, and now you've made contact, you've got to be The Watcher and a normal human. It is difficult to be two people within the same person."

Jorn knew what his brother was getting at. Being a Watcher, he had to be on the ball constantly, with eyes in the back of his head, but he also needed to be a vault of secrets. He'd seen things and logged them since he was born. Even as a baby in the crib, he would watch. He knew the secrets of his Master. He knew the secrets of his mother. He knew the secrets of his brothers. Though over the years, like Jorun, he'd learnt to compartmentalise and, in a way, forget. He didn't want to be a know-it-all or make his family feel vulnerable in his presence. If you can't relax at home, where could you? And yet, since this new assignment, he felt vulnerable in his sanctuary. He knew his Master was not a man to be trusted, and now even more so. He knew someone from his Master's employees had something to do with Mr Kelly's accident, but did it go higher than his Master? Was it The Emperor who was calling the shots? He knew his Master could be manipulative and do anything for personal gain. But run down a man in cold blood? He just wasn't convinced he was like that.

He clicked the fob, locking the car once they'd pulled up. The house was quiet; his brothers having retired for the night. That was good for Jorn; he could stealthily approach his Master without Randin or Jorun's interference. However, his thoughts of stealth were quickly defused when he heard voices in his room.

"Hell, do you think he will do as your Emperor commands? Do you think she is..."

Jorn kicked open his door to find his Master and one of his mammal-shifter bodyguards watching his screens.

"Get the fuck out of my chamber!" he roared, grabbing the mammal-shifter and chucking him through the opened door where he crunched into the opposite wall, his arm twisted awkwardly, his eyes burning yellow as his creature stirred, yet Jorn had eyes only for his Master.

"AND YOU? WHO THE HELL DO YOU THINK YOU ARE?" All the willpower to not attack or engage had vanished entirely from Jorn's mind as he drew back his fist to get the first punch in, but his leader didn't get his status as Master from being weak. He twisted out of the way, smashing the side of Jorn's face down onto the desk, his cheekbones shattering, before yanking him up and throwing him over the other side of the room, his body crumbling into a heap. Jorn, however, wasn't done with him. With blood pouring from his hairline, he allowed his anger to filter through his body, his veins almost bursting through the skin, bulging out as he leapt at his Master, his fist smacking into his face, knocking him into the sideboard, all the photo frames collapsing.

"HOW FUCKING DARE YOU? YOU CANNOT DO THIS TO ME!" He took hold of one of his ankles and threw him over his shoulder onto the floor, the floorboards under the plush cream carpet cracking, making a human-sized bow in the wood. "I will not fall in line anymore and take it on the chin. You will allow me to do this task my way, or so help me God, you can get The Emperor to strip me now and be done with it."

His Master almost flew out the divot he had made and punched Jorn across his other cheek, his ring splitting the skin and sending him sailing into the TV cabinet, the corner catching the side of Jorn's head, partially clouding his vision. Staggering to his feet and using the cabinet as a launch point, he pushed off it, colliding with his Master, them both falling to the floor. Blood dripped from his nose onto his Master's face as he pummelled his fists into his jaw. His Master, however, seized Jorn's rolled knuckles, crushing the bones in his hands with one strong grasp, forcing Jorn to cry out. His Master then got his leg under him and kicked out, shoving Jorn back into the desk, causing the screens to cascade like dominoes onto the desktop, the glass shattering over the worktop. The back of Jorn's head smashed into the wood, making lights pop in front of his eyes. His breathing was suddenly laboured, and he was convinced some of his ribs had splintered. Glancing up, he glimpsed his Master rolling up his sleeves, preparing to lay him out. Falling onto all fours, he attempted to get upright to prepare himself for the onslaught, blood running into his eyes.

"I know you instigated... Mr Kelly's accident," he said, as he hung his head, his concentration beginning to wane; the hits to the skull slowly taking their toll on his body. "...So don't tell me you didn't. You knew...she'd need a shoulder to cry on." His knees buckled as he tried to remain focused on the conniving bastard that was in front of him. "See, you can't even deny it, can you?" He fell forward again onto his hands, gasping and spitting blood onto the floor.

"Why would I wish to deny it?" his Master scathed.

"You're unbelievable." Leaning back, Jorn slowly slipped down the wooden cupboard, blinking profusely, trying to keep his mind from going blank. "Why are you so full of hate? Can you not see what you are doing to me... to us? Why do you do this for him?" Jorn wiped his mouth, smearing blood onto his hand, "What are you so afraid of?"

The room was unexpectedly filled with shouts and curses from his brothers. Jorun had run in, wearing only his boxers, his chest smudged with lipstick marks.

"You cannot intervene again." Jorn fumbled in his pocket and threw the pin at his Master's feet. "And take this. I refuse to wear it. I will be doing... this task my way... or not at all." Every breath ravaged his lungs. He pointed at his Master, "You will... not... come in here and watch my computers." He turned to the side and tried to get up, but his head swam like he'd been on the drink, and his neck couldn't hold it up much longer. "You will not let anyone, not a guard or co-worker, see the things that I see. You cannot tell me... *what* to do... or give..." He held his head up. He must stay focused, "Me a deadline." He had to get these last words out before it went dark, "Remember... *I've* been... watching you since... I was born..." He put his hand gingerly to his head, his skull feeling broken, "I know things, Master, things you won't want people to know. Remember... I know... you." His head fell back, his arm falling to his side.

"Shit... Jorn?" Oska ran to his side, gingerly feeling the pulse in his neck. The others stood looking at their Master, unsure if they dared to move towards their fallen brother.

"Oska, sort him out," The Master instructed, whilst wiping blood from his nose. "Make sure he's comfortable." And with that, he swept from the room.

Randin and Jorun knelt at Jorn's side whilst Kol and Lamont stood back, allowing space, both smirking at each other. None of them had ever stood up to The Master, let alone picked a fight with him and even though Jorn seemed so completely broken, they stood in amazement. Jorn, the placid and quiet Watcher, had been the one to do it first. After over three hundred years of being told what to do and complying no matter what, it was Jorn who had taken the first step.

Jorn coughed suddenly, making them all jump. "I'm gonna puke." Oska grabbed Jorn's wastepaper basket, emptied its contents over the floor and held it for him. He dry-heaved into it, unable to get his head up off the shelf housing his television. Squinting, he looked up at Oska and was mesmerised at how oval his brother's face shape was and how, like Randin, he had inherited his mother's milk-white skin. He blearily glanced at them all staring down at him, his hand shaking slightly as he reached up to his head, yet before it got there, he lost his momentum and flopped back to his side again. His breathing was harsh. It was as though he'd inhaled some of his blood as his lungs felt sticky, elevating his breathing rate. His breaths short and shallow. Managing to open his eyes again, he spotted his twin. "Jorun? Put on some clothes."

They all laughed as Oska tentatively examined his head.

"What do you think, Oska?" Randin asked, watching his healing brother. Sighing heavily, Oska placed his hands on Jorn's upper arm, and closing his eyes, he searched Jorn's body with his ability for his physical injuries.

"Skull is cracked in two places, four broken ribs, crushed right hand, splintered cheekbone, black eye, not to mention scratch marks and gashes here and there." Oska attempted to brush Jorn's hair to one side to take a closer look.

"Are you sure... it's just four... broken ribs?" Jorn gasped, his head lolling to the side again. "Bin." He tilted his head to vomit, but still, nothing came up.

"Yes, and definitely concussion," Oska confirmed, getting up and leaving the room, only to return with a cold compress placing it over Jorn's right eye.

"Is he going to be okay?" Jorun had re-entered fully dressed.

"He will. But he's been severely beaten, particularly in the head. He is, however, still talking and is aware of what is happening... Jorn? Jorn?" Oska rubbed Jorn's arm.

"Yes, brother," Jorn replied, briefly opening his eyes again.

"It's okay. I just wanted to make sure you can still hear me and that your hearing has not been affected, which may account for the nausea. It's your head that's the likely cause of the vertigo."

"I do feel... very off balance," he whispered, allowing his head to slump.

"I bet you fucking do," Kol exclaimed, joyously. "But bloody hell, Jorn, I didn't think you had it in you."

"Stop it, Kol, this isn't an ideal situation," Randin said sternly. "The Master is not happy."

"Come on, Randin. We've all wanted to punch The Master at least once," Kol chimed, jumping around and fighting an imaginary opponent.

Swallowing, Jorn looked up at his youngest brother, "Kol, stop that. You're... making me feel like I'm on a ship, the floorboards are moving that much."

Kol desisted, and Jorun crouched down to his twin. "Who's the lover tonight? Freya?" Jorn asked, knowing full well it was.

"How did you know?" Jorun asked, amazed even after all these years at his brother.

"You must know... all of you... that I know everything around here." His breathing was beginning to become slightly easier, his body was healing, but breakages were hard to mend quickly, even for a Gifted of his calibre.

"You say that, Jorn, but do you know something about The Master that we don't know?" Randin asked, moving to be nearer him.

"Jorn? Jorn?" Oska shook his brother slightly, he knew that sleep would help him, but he, like Randin, couldn't let him sleep.

"Yes, Oska," Jorn sighed, shifting slightly to get more comfortable. "This floor is so hard."

"Come, brother, let's get you to the bed," Randin said, cupping him under his arm.

"No, not yet. Just let me be a while." Jorn gasped, moving his hand to his eldest brother's face. "Do you remember our mother?" Randin blinked at him. No one ever spoke of her. "Your face now is the picture it was when Jorun and I were born. You were so worried about her that day." He managed to reach Randin's face, his beard soft under his touch. "You'd heard her screaming in labour for hours, and you were so pale when pappa eventually let you in their bedroom to meet us."

"Jorn?" Randin gushed.

"You won't recall it, Jorun," he said, glancing at his twin. "But when we were named and our abilities came to us, we were only minutes old. I remember lying on mother's chest, with you next to me, and I remember watching her. She was so happy. Her dark hair stuck to her face with sweat, her cheeks rouge with the heat of labour. She had a heartbeat that was so fast in my ear, and her voice was like that of an angel. It's a cliché to say it, but it was. It was the most loving, beautiful voice I had ever heard. I can recall it like she was here now." He looked wistfully at Jorun, "And pappa, he was so elated at having twin boys, you would not believe it. His face has not been that serene for centuries since."

"How do you recall all this, Jorn? You were just an infant," Oska asked, lying his head against the cabinet.

"I am a Watcher, and it is my job to see all, to know all, to be the spy in the dark, the fly on the wall. The one who sees but is not seen." His head fell back again.

"It's like he's drunk," Lamont said.

"That is how I feel, but I'm not." He groped again for the bin and, this time, vomited into it. "The nauseated feeling is the same, too." Wiping his mouth on his sleeve, he said, "But this is not like being drunk, my body feels absolutely shattered to pieces."

"Well, it looks it," Kol said.

"I need to get on the bed so I can heal effectively," Jorn said, trying to move from his sitting position.

"Here, buddy." Randin picked up his brother easily, and with Oska's help of pulling the covers back, they laid him gently into the sheets. Once comfortable, Jorun asked,

"Jorn, please, can you continue? Tell us more about mother. What else did you see?" he asked, sitting on the bed sheets.

"You would not believe the memories I have of her and pappa. For he loved her unconditionally, and she him. When we were born, and we both lay there on her chest getting her body heat, Randin, Lamont and Oska were allowed in, and Randin was so pale and so scared. He, of course, had been told to look after the others whilst mother was in labour. In those days, it wasn't customary for the father to be in the birthing room, especially not in the society we were born into, but pappa never would have left her. He sent for our older brothers, and they came in. Randin was very relieved that mother was safe. Being five years old, Lamont wanted to keep mother all to himself and tried to push us off her. How she laughed at your incredulity." He looked at Lamont, remembering his mother's laugh and wry smile. "As for you, Oska, you were amazed. You, of course, have the ability to see nature for what it is. You marvelled at how two babies could come out of their mother, and she still be all right. Even then, your interest in the human body was apparent." Jorn shut his eyes, his head sinking into the pillow. "Our pappa loved us then, and there was so much laughter in him. Now he has lost his way, and I cannot... see... him ever being... that man again." Jorn couldn't stay awake any longer. His body was healing him at a rate that required sleep, and soon, all his brothers but Oska left. He would keep vigil to ensure there were no lasting effects from Jorn's fight with The Master.

Oska would watch his brother as his brother had watched him all his life.

CHAPTER NINE

THE PLANT

Logan couldn't sleep. No matter her position, her bed tonight wasn't comfortable. She tried to kid herself that it was the mattress. It was old, and the springs were poking through. Or that it was her feet that were cold, which made it hard to get snuggled, or that her pillows weren't puffed up enough, but it wasn't even that. It wasn't even the fact she had become temporary Managing Director of Kelly's Kustom Kitchens. It was the fact she'd let Jorn go home. Why had she been so stupid? Even if she hadn't wanted sex, she could have asked him to stay, just to have him there. His warm, soft hands over her shoulder, his breath tickling her neck, his legs entwined with hers.

"Argh!" It was no use. She got up and took some milk from the fridge, put it onto the gas, and then dissolved some chocolate powder into her favourite mug. Whilst she waited for the milk to heat, she looked over at the space where Jorn had kissed her, right up against that worktop. Jeez, it had been intense, so intense, she didn't think she'd drawn breath again until he'd gone. He'd smelt so utterly delectable that if she closed her eyes now, she could still smell him. Damn it! She had it bad for him. Was seeing him today going to be awkward? Sure, it would be, it always was. She didn't know how Lexi did it. Just waltz into the office, having had sex with one of the design technicians and think nothing of it. Oh, to be confident in your abilities to provide good sex must be amazing. Logan didn't think she was bad at it, but she wasn't adventurous. She loved to try new things but could never instigate it, and when she was encouraged to, she always felt self-conscious and silly.

Sighing, she stirred the hot milk into the powder and went to the lounge, switching on her small fibre-optic Christmas tree, illuminating the room with an ambient glow. Snuggling under her blanket, she scrolled through the TV catch-up page, found a rerun of an old series, and began watching it, hoping it would switch her mind off. After five episodes, she gave up, and despite having had one before bed, she got in the shower.

Taking out a dry-cleaning bag from her wardrobe, her hair still wet, she held the pinstripe trouser suit up to her. Could she wear this today? It was, perhaps, a little too much, hence why she hadn't worn it yesterday. The suit had been one of those impulse buys just as she started at Kelly's, and had worn it only once. Slipping on the trousers, however, she remembered why she'd bought it. The material was 100% virgin wool that slid over her skin like silk. Instead of the matching jacket, however, she wore a cream bib-necked woollen top and a kimono wrap cardigan.

She entered the hospital a little after seven-thirty; she

wasn't sure if they'd let her in this early, as it was most likely some kind of medicine round. But they buzzed her through, and she clicked up the corridor in her heels, feeling ready for the day even though she'd had near zero sleep. On arrival at the ward, she noticed the stereo was back at the nurse's desk,

"Er... I thought that your colleagues said Mr Kelly could have this overnight?"

"Oh yes, don't worry, he did, but then your friend brought in a digital speaker, so that's in there now playing an audiobook," said a nurse with tired, bloodshot eyes.

"My friend?" queried Logan.

"Yes," she yawned, "excuse me. Yes, Mr Hartvigsen, who was here with you last evening, brought it in. You've only just missed him."

"You know Jorn?" Logan said. Perhaps she was a past lover.

"Are you kidding? The Hartvigsens are like royalty around here. They donate so much to this hospital. The entire new cancer wing was built due to their donations."

Logan frowned, "Really?"

"Haven't you ever heard of them?" She sat there aghast, stifling another yawn.

"No..." Logan said, abashed.

"His father is in Hello and OK! at least three or four times a year," she said, startled at Logan's ineptitude at following celebrities.

Despite herself, Logan couldn't help her heart rate elevate, and her breathing shudder at the words the nurse spoke. Jorn had been here, with a speaker, already? His family were famous and in magazines. Surely, the nurse had got the wrong family. Why would someone as prestigious as Jorn possibly come to work for a company such as Kelly's?

"Are you sure you've got the right family?" she couldn't help but ask.

The nurse laughed, "Of course I have. Everyone was talking about him when you left. The one that came with you, though, is perhaps one of the quieter ones. I've never seen him in the news, but the youngest is notorious, and one of the brothers made millions from an online agency he sold."

"Really?" Logan said, feeling more stupid by the minute.

The phone next to the girl rang, and as she answered it, Logan walked into Mr Kelly's room, baffled at the nurse's words.

"Where has this man been all my life, Adrian?" she asked him stupidly, as she sat down next to her boss. She wasn't expecting a response, nor got one, but she had never spoken truer words to herself. "Did you know who he was when you employed him?" She smiled; she knew Mr Kelly would have done his research thoroughly, but it would have been nice of him to warn her of who he was.

After being assured the staff would contact her if there was any change to Mr Kelly's condition, she drove to the basement car park and to her new role. The car park was empty but for a white Astra that Logan knew belonged to a fellow trader on the bottom floor.

"Thank God I'm here before he is," she mumbled, as she exited the car and reached for her bag. Once in the lift, she adjusted her top and checked her make-up in the mirror. "You can do this, Loge." And with a sigh, she walked out onto the fifth-floor landing.

It was silent; the only lights on were the halogen ones dotted all over the building. Unlocking her office door, she found everything as she had left it and began switching on the additional lamps and firing up her PC. She unlocked Adrian's office. She wasn't going to sit in there; that felt too much like he was already gone, but she opened the door wide just in case she needed to get any papers from it or go through his filing cabinet.

"Just treat it like any other Tuesday morning," she told herself. "Everyone knows what they're meant to be doing today."

After making herself a coffee, she sat scrolling through her emails and seeing if anyone had replied to her ones from yesterday. Only Stephen's Supplies had returned her query on chrome taps, saying they would investigate. Well, she supposed she'd only sent the email after five yesterday.

Her mobile rang abruptly on her desk.

"Hey, Lex."

"Oh my God, Loge, why didn't you pick up when I called you last night? Is it true about Mr Kelly?"

Logan grimaced, "Yes, I'm afraid so." Logan stuck a mint in her mouth and leaned back comfortably.

"Why didn't you answer my call?"

"I could say the same for you," she said, slightly annoyed at her friend. There was silence. "Lexi?"

"I was with Quinn," she suddenly blurted.

"You bitch!" Logan cursed, "You totally let me waffle on about him yesterday, and you were seeing him all the time."

"I know, I know, I just didn't want you to say I told you so."

"Well, thank God. He's been after you for months," Logan said, clicking her computer screen again as an email came through.

"Yes, I know."

"So, what did you do?" she enquired.

"Oh, he just took me to dinner, we had a snog in the car park, I went home, and he went home. It was very civilised," Lexi said, hoping Logan realised how reserved she'd been.

Logan was astounded there'd been no sex.

"I've always known he would not jump in bed with a girl on the first date," she said, beginning to type a response on her keyboard.

"No, and I like that." Lexi paused, "I think I like him."

"Thank goodness; he's definitely a good catch, babe." She sent the email, "Listen, Lex, I've got a plateful today. Shall we try to meet in the canteen for lunch?"

"Deffo. I'll see you later." She hung up.

Logan continued scrolling through her emails, which were now coming through, and without thinking, she put her glasses on. Maybe she could avoid headaches today.

"You're in early."

Logan yelped, her hand going to her chest.

"Jesus, can you make more noise when you come in? You scared me half to death." Jorn smiled at her from the doorway, and she instantly felt a rush of warmth to her body.

"Sorry if I made you jump." He strolled in, carrying a plant and placing it on her desk.

"Er..."

"Sorry, my brother Oska said that every desk at this time of year should have one of these on it, so I bought you one."

It was a Christmas poinsettia in a golden pot.

"Your brother?" Logan asked, maybe she should get herself a copy of the Hello! magazine to bring herself up to speed. She stroked the plant leaves; it truly was stunning for this time of year.

"Yes, he's a bit of a horticulturalist. You'd get on with him," Jorn said, feeling embarrassed.

"Why do you say that?" she asked, glancing at her screen again as another email came through.

"You like gardening, don't you? Well, your bookshelves are full of gardening books, and your back courtyard looks as though you care for it in the warmer months." He shrugged.

Logan didn't know why, but she couldn't help herself. She didn't care who he was. To her, he was just a normal guy. She walked around her desk, placed her hands on his shoulders and went to kiss his cheek.

"What's happened to your eye?" She withdrew quickly, scanning his face.

"Oh, I had a spot of bother last night with one of my brothers, but I'm fine, just a little sore." He took her hand, not wanting her to leave, "Were you going to kiss me?"

Logan shook her head, "Just to say thank you for taking your speaker to Mr Kelly this morning. You really listened to my rambling yesterday."

She reached for his head and made him bend down; there was definite yellowing around the eye.

"What happened?" she asked again.

"Nothing. It's just a disagreement between family members, like I said." He moved away from her. "Yes, I took it earlier this morning. I never use it, and it meant the nurses could have their radio back." He started taking off his jacket, the waft of aftershave swamping Logan so much that she held her breath, trying not to breathe it in, as every time she did, the tumbling sensation in her stomach made her heart elevate.

"You seem to mention your brothers a lot," she surmised, returning to the safety of her chair and desk.

"Well, I... er...," he looked embarrassed, "still live with them."

"What? Really?" I bet that wasn't in OK! magazine.

"Yes, I have my own home, but it's currently rented. I find living alone kinda... ha... lonely and pointless. I moved out thinking I'd like to be independent, but I found I was around there so much that there wasn't any point in living away from them."

"Ah! Yes, I wish sometimes I still lived at home, although my sister and I used to fight like crazy." She sat down as her phone started ringing, "Kelly's Kustom Kitchens, Logan speaking, how may I help you?" She listened to the voice at the other end, nodding her head.

"I'll be in my office." She waved quickly at Jorn before clicking her computer, trying to find the invoice the guy was talking about on the other end.

The morning went by swiftly. The phone didn't seem to stop ringing, and Logan's head was already beginning to ache when Lexi knocked on her door frame.

"Here, Loge, I brought you a sandwich."

"Hey, I thought we were meeting for lunch," Logan said, sipping some cold tea.

"We were at twelve-thirty," Lexi said, looking at her

watch. "It's now a quarter-to-four."

Logan gasped, looking at the clock on her screen. "Shit, sorry, babe."

"No, it's fine. I didn't really expect you to turn up anyway, so I took Quinn."

Logan raised her eyebrows, "Did you now?"

"Yep. He's so sweet, you know."

Logan grinned, "You seeing him tonight?"

"Yes, he's coming to mine for dinner. I thought I'd do that beef thing that you do with red wine." Lexi looked poignantly at her friend.

"Oh, the braised beef?" Logan asked, looking through some more paperwork.

"Yep, that." Lexi looked hopefully at her again.

Logan sighed, "You want me to send you the recipe?"

"Can you? That would be amazing, as would step-by-step instructions."

"Oh, Lex, I'm not sure I can manage that. I've got so much to do, and I've got to see Adrian's wife at five-thirty. Shit, I need to think about leaving." She took her phone, setting an alarm so she wouldn't work too long.

"Please, Loge, please..." Lexi begged, practically getting on the floor and praying.

"Why can't you just get a takeaway?" Logan said briskly.

"Oh, because I told him I could cook."

"And he believed you?" Logan laughed, picking up her phone and pressing number five. "Jorn, do you have the figures for last week's profits? I can't seem to find them."

"Please, Logan," Lexi begged. "You wouldn't want me to look stupid in front of him, would you?"

"You forget that you're the one who has dug herself this hole," Logan gestured, walking to the filing cabinet.

"I know, but you could help me get out of it." She pouted her lips.

"Get out of what?" Jorn asked, walking in holding the papers Logan had asked for.

"Jorn, tell Logan she has to help me." Lexi looked imploringly at him.

"I cannot think that Logan wouldn't help you. She must have her reasons," Jorn said, placing the papers on her desk.

"Lexi has told the guy she's seeing that she'll cook for him, but she has no idea how to cook the thing she has said she'll cook, and now she wants me to give her a step-by-step account of how to do it, when I'm already snowed under," Logan explained, picking up her phone again and dialling a number,

"Hey, Luce, it's Logan. I've got some figures here from last week that are not adding up. Can you look into them again for me?"

"Maybe I can help?" Jorn said, looking at Lexi, "I can cook."

Logan rolled her eyes. Of course, he could cook. He could probably clean, garden, and fix cars, too. Was there anything he couldn't do?

"I bet you can't cook beef like Logan can," Lexi said, pointing at him.

"Well, I don't know, I've never tasted Logan's beef," Jorn smirked.

"Oh God! Right, here's a list." She started jotting down some ingredients, "And then meet me at mine at five, and I'll get you started. But you owe me, Lex." Logan cradled the phone and waited for Luce to come back to her.

"I love you, babe," Lexi chimed, exiting the room.

"Of course you do," Logan said. "Yes, yes, I'm still here," she replied down the phone. "Oh, Lexi?"

Lexi returned. "Can you get me an Amaryllis when you're out? I'll send you the money."

Looking startled, Lexi said, "A what?"

"Oh, never mind. Yes, Luce, hi there." Logan brushed her away, going back to her call.

"Hey, I'll come with you and show you," Jorn said helpfully, motioning Lexi to exit the room first. "Let's leave Logan to it."

Logan collapsed into her car when she finally left the office at four-fifty. Her head throbbed like crazy, and she still had to go and see Julia, cook for Lexi and phone her mum. Tuesdays were always phone call nights for Logan, and she was a stickler for routine.

Lexi was on her doorstep when Logan arrived, and she hurried past to her kitchen, where she went through the ins and outs of how to cook beef.

"Unfortunately, you're meant to do it over four hours, but you've not got that long. Here's the method. I recorded myself saying it on my way home. Just listen to me, and you'll get it done." She forwarded the recording before dashing upstairs to change. Slipping on a pair of skinny jeans and a woollen grey jumper, she took her hair out of its tight ponytail and instantly felt her head relax. Downing two paracetamols with a long drink, she checked on Lexi's cooking.

"Right, so you can borrow my oven pan, but please bring it back and tidy the kitchen when you're done."

"Thanks, babe." Logan wrapped her scarf around her neck,

"Er... did you know that Jorn was related to the Hartvigsens of the large estate outside the city?" she suddenly blurted out.

"Of course I did, didn't you?" Lexi said exasperatedly at her friend.

Logan shook her head; how did she not know this?

"I only know about the youngest brother. He's always in the papers for misdemeanours and of the father who donates lots of his money to different charities. I'd never really heard of Jorn," Lexi said, cutting up some peppers. "Though I don't know why. He's definitely the best-looking one out of them all."

"I feel such an idiot not knowing who he was," Logan said, putting her coat back on.

"Loge, it's best not to know him that way. You should just get to know him like you would any normal person. Going in with preconceived ideas isn't good for any relationship, business or pleasure." Lexi laughed, stirring the pot.

"And we all know what preconceived ideas we both had: Mr Creepy versus Mr Hottie," Logan laughed.

"Well, he's definitely not Mr Creepy anymore, that's for sure," Lexi said. "I can't believe I didn't recognise him when we were in the pub. All the Hartvigsens have that smoky, beautiful look about them."

Logan smiled tiredly at her friend. She, too, was sure he would not be known as Mr. Creepy anymore.

"Did you get me the plant?" she asked, looking around the kitchen and getting her keys from the hook.

"Oh yes, Jorn's got it; he said he'd pick you up at five-twenty."

"Say what now?" Logan said, taken aback, "Jorn... he's taking me to see Julia?"

"Sorry, my bad," Lexi said, sucking in through her teeth. "I couldn't help myself. He's so got the hots for you, and I just wanted to give him that extra push. Believe me, he didn't take much persuading to come with you." Lexi bit her lip. Had she pushed her prudish friend too far?

"Jeez, Lex, I just wanted to go alone," she said. Could her friend be any more incorrigible? "Too many different people will confuse her."

"Oh, it will be fine. You worry too much," Lexi said, pouring in the wine.

"Or you worry too little," Logan huffed. It wasn't that she didn't appreciate Jorn coming with her. It would be nice for the company. But she just knew she'd want him to come on to her, and now knowing who he was, did she really need all that in her life?

CHAPTER TEN

THE HOME

Jorn allowed Lexi to talk all the way to the supermarket and back again; she barely drew breath, and he smiled to himself, thinking of her and Quinn. The mammal-shifter wouldn't get a word in with her around, but that was perhaps what he liked. He supposed having a talkative companion was better than one that doesn't talk. He'd met a few girls who didn't speak much, and they were so dull. He couldn't imagine life with Lexi would ever be dull. After dropping Lexi at Logan's, he sped home. His suit felt like a straitjacket, and if he was going out again, he needed to be more comfortable.

He passed his Master in the corridor and said nothing. Silence was better than fighting; he didn't have time to apologise right now. He knew he'd have to, as his Master could hold a grudge for decades, and he didn't fancy living like that, but right now wasn't the time. His room was a mess when he entered; there was his blood on the carpet and bed sheets, and the contents of his bin strewn over the floor. His body had healed reasonably well as he'd slept last night; like most of his kind, the healing properties of their blood were good, but it wasn't instantaneous. His head still throbbed, and his eye had felt like it was blown out of its socket, though now it was just irritable with occasional twitching. His ribs had not yet completely mended, and as he bent over to get his shoes, his intake of breath was sharp, making him apply pressure to the wounds that couldn't be seen.

"I knew it was too good to be true that you would leave me alone today," he said, as he approached the front door, his Master standing at the foot of the stairs.

"Please, Jorn, I do not want another fight," his Master said quietly.

"And you think I do?" Jorn said, putting his wine-coloured bomber jacket on.

"Well, I don't think you'd want another beating, though I see you've healed well." Jorn couldn't even muster a retort. "I can also see you're going out, and I'm sure it's to see that lovely girl with the amount of cologne you've slapped on yourself."

Jorn rolled his eyes, walking to the door. He didn't have time for this.

"I just wanted to say I'm sorry for yesterday, Jorn."

"Excuse me?" Jorn stood back, utterly amazed.

"Yes, I'm saying sorry," his Master said, and Jorn was surprised that the apology reached his eyes.

"What's brought all this on?" He continued walking away; otherwise, he would be late.

"I can see that being in your room and watching your computer screens was slightly below the mark, and the spy pin perhaps not my best moment," he openly admitted.

"Right," Jorn said, standing on the doorstep.

"But..."

"Here it comes; there's always a but."

"There has to be when there are tasks to complete," his Master said flatly.

Jorn just nodded, feeling the apology would only go so far.

"The deadline is still New Year's Eve."

"I knew your apology was too good to be true," he said, moving away from the house and towards the car in the driveway.

His Master nodded, "You know I mean it, Jorn."

"Yes, of course I do. When have you ever joked about anything like this?" He slammed the car door and revved it from the parking space, scattering the pebbles of the drive. He hated him right now.

Logan seemed distracted when she got in, her eyes diverted to the outside of the car.

"You're quiet," Jorn said, changing gear.

She smiled, "I would think you'd be pleased with the peace after shopping with Lexi."

"Man, she can talk," he said, in agreement.

"She talks a lot when she's nervous."

"Nervous? She doesn't seem like the kind of woman who gets nervous."

"Oh, she does, pretty badly. She was the same at school. Got her into heaps of trouble."

"Really?" Jorn wasn't surprised. Even as an adult, Lexi seemed able to talk herself into mischief.

"Yes, talking always got her in deeper water than actually getting out of it."

She was silent again, and then Jorn asked, "You don't mind me coming with you tonight, do you?"

She sighed, "If I'm honest, Jorn, I kind of wanted to do this alone."

"Right... shit!" He felt his heart sink slightly. He was not getting any further with her at all.

"No, you misunderstand me. It's not because I don't want you to come; it's just... how do I say it?" She turned to look at him, "It's just... it's not good for me."

"What do you mean?" he asked, pulling up in the care home car park, relieved.

"It's not good for me to be in close proximity to you. Every time I'm near you, I get this feeling inside me, and all I want to do is rip your clothes off. Even now, speaking to you about it is making me hot and... I don't like it." She turned away, embarrassed at her honesty, "I've never been like this with anyone, especially as we've only known each other for like... a day and especially who you are and who your father is." She threw her hands up in surrender.

"My father just has money, and he likes to give it away to look good in the media. I'm not like him. I make my own way in the world," he said firmly, making Logan feel that he didn't really get on with his dad.

She smiled, "I'm not taking that away from you, Jorn, it's just weird, and I don't like how you make me feel."

He turned fully in his seat to look at her, "I'm sorry if I make you feel uncomfortable, but... if it's any consolation." He stared at her a moment, "You make me feel the same."

"No, that doesn't help." She smirked, "It, in fact, makes it worse."

"Why worse?"

"Because I'm not one for spontaneity. I like to be in control, and when I'm around you, I'm not in control of myself."

Jorn thought for a moment and wondered if he'd have felt like this if they'd come together of their own volition, not at his Master's command. But, in all seriousness, he knew deep down that he'd have felt this way whether he'd been allowed to make contact or not.

"Perhaps you can't control everything," he said, leaning

over to move her hair from her face.

"Yes, but where does that leave us if I can't control myself?"

"Free to do this." He reached around her neck and pulled her to him, her lips tasting of orange lip balm. She sighed longingly in her throat as his warm hand reached under the rim of her jumper, his fingers tingling her skin, the scent of her intoxicating him.

"You have no idea... how much I've been wanting you to do that today?" she said breathlessly, as they pulled apart.

"Really?" he said, looking into her eyes again, their colour mesmerising him.

"Yeah... I thought last night I might have put you off."

"It would take a lot more for me to be put off," he said, coaxing her mouth to open to him again.

"I thought you'd think," she said, pulling away, "I was irrational."

"No, you weren't irrational," he replied, looking back at her, "you were honest, and that's a good thing."

"It is?" she asked, turning away so as not to be tempted by him again.

"Of course. I'd much rather you were honest than letting me continue and you not enjoy it."

"Yes, I suppose so." She glanced at the building they were about to enter. "Right, we'd better go, or we'll be late."

They both exited the car, and Jorn handed her the plant he had bought at the supermarket. He refrained from taking her hand or touching her in any way. He knew she liked her independence and wanted her to see that he expected nothing from her until she gave it freely.

They entered the reception area, where Logan signed them both in.

"Hello, Logan, haven't seen you for a few months. Is everything all right with Mr Kelly?" the auxiliary nurse asked as Logan led Jorn into the large day room, which had only a few stragglers late for their dinner.

"No, I'm afraid not, Olivia. He's been in an accident and, therefore, cannot make his date tonight," Logan said gravely.

"Oh gosh, is he okay?"

"No, not really," Logan grimaced, "he was hit by a car."

"Damn, it was him yesterday that was hit? I heard it on the local news."

Jorn shifted uncomfortably. His Master, one day, was going to pay for what he'd done. As Logan explained what had happened, Jorn looked around. He hated the smell of these places. There was always that scent of mustiness mixed with stale urine and sweaty bodies. He could sense death on some of the people walking near him, and for the first time in a while, he felt glad that his life had been unnaturally extended. To end your life in a place like this must be the worst thing for a loved one to watch, and he felt for Mr Kelly.

"Hey, are you okay?" Logan's hand was cool in his as she got his attention.

"Yes, of course." He grasped her hand, yet as quickly as he noticed it in there, she took it away.

"Let's go."

They found Mrs Kelly sitting at a table with her napkin on her lap, her hands were busy twiddling it in circles and ripping it, causing small fibres to float into the air.

"Hello, Julia."

The woman looked up at Logan, her eyes wide at the interruption.

"Amaryllis, such a beautiful flower. My Adrian always buys them for me. Did he send you?" she asked.

Logan smiled, "Yes, he did, he's running late at work and didn't want you to be alone on date night."

"Are you my daughter?" Julia asked, squinting at Logan.

"No, but I work with Adrian. I'm Logan." Logan looked at Jorn, and he pulled the chair out so she could sit down.

"Who's this good-looking chap? Are you my son?" Julia asked.

Jorn looked at her, "No, ma'am, I'm not, but I also work with your husband."

"Who, Adrian? Where is he? He's always here for date night," she repeated.

Logan grimaced, "Yes, I know he is, Julia, but he can't make it tonight because he's working, so I've come instead."

"Did you? Do you like pizza? It's one of my favourites." She looked beyond where Logan sat to see if the nurses were serving the food. "Amaryllis," she said again, looking at the flowers Logan had. "My Adrian always brings me one. Have you seen him? He always comes on date night." Logan looked sadly at her.

"No, he's not coming tonight, Julia, but I love pizza. Would you mind if I shared some with you?" Logan asked, trying a new tactic.

"Yes, you can, dear, but when my Adrian comes, you must let him sit with me. He never misses date night."

The care assistants brought in the pizza, and Julia had three slices with potato wedges, while Logan and Jorn only nit-picked theirs. Neither of them had an appetite. Julia gave them both a big hug when they went to leave,

"Oh, it's such a shame you are going; Adrian will be coming soon. He never misses date night."

"Yes, we would have liked to have seen him," Logan said, holding her hand. "We shall try and pop in again during the week."

"Please do. Maybe we can go for a picnic. Adrian loves picnicking on the lawns."

"That sounds great. Goodbye, Julia."

They walked silently to the car; even Jorn, who wanted

nothing more than to talk to Logan, couldn't find the words. He couldn't believe that someone as young as Mrs Kelly could have such an early-onset of the disease and have it taken hold so rapidly. He heard Logan sob slightly and placed his hand on her leg, which she took in hers and squeezed.

"Thank you," she whispered, continuing to look out the window.

"What for?" he coughed.

She sniffed, "For coming with me."

"I'm sorry, Logan, but I've never seen anything so utterly heart-breaking. How long has she been like that?" Jorn knew that Logan had helped Mr Kelly with his wife, but only watching things from afar hadn't given him the insight this meeting had. He felt wretched.

"Oh, it's been gradual over two years, but in the last seven or eight months, it's got so bad that I helped Adrian find her a good place to go to. He couldn't cope with her anymore."

"Poor Mr Kelly," he said honestly.

"Yes, poor Adrian. It has broken his heart."

They were silent the rest of the journey, each alone with their thoughts.

"I'll see you in the morning, then?" he said; he wouldn't even attempt to be invited in, as he pulled up to the kerb. He knew she needed her space and was more than happy to give it to her.

"You certainly will." She opened the door, "Let me go and see what sort of a mess Lexi has left."

It was on the tip of his tongue to ask if she wanted help, but he just laughed.

"Good night, Logan."

"Bye, Jorn." She left the vehicle, and he pulled away, not looking back.

The games room was booming when he passed it on the way to his quarters, and without even looking in, he knew Kol and Oska were having a pool competition. He knew Lamont was in his room on a conference call, Jorun wasn't home, and Randin was with The Master, going over plans regarding refurbishing the ballroom. Jorn wondered what that was about, but his brain ached, and for the first time in years, he closed his bedroom door, fell on the bed in his clothes and slept.

CHAPTER ELEVEN

THE DATE

The next few days were a blur, and Logan wondered how her week had suddenly got to Friday. It had been one of the most trying weeks of her working life. She had found every night more difficult to sleep, and by the time it got to Friday, she was working on four hours of broken sleep and fuelling it with excessive amounts of caffeine. Despite his office being next to hers, she'd hardly seen Jorn. She regularly heard him on the phone, but he never came to see her; perhaps he, too, was feeling the pressure of the job, and when she thought about it, she probably worked a lot better without him distracting her.

Looking back over the week, she thought she'd done a good job keeping the company going. She'd managed to secure a new contract doing the bathrooms and kitchens, for a local firm building sixty new houses over the far side of the city, which was likely to bring in some decent profits. She smiled smugly down the phone once they'd confirmed the final details, and they said they'd send an email for her and the Sales Director to sign. Once Jorn had sent a copy back with his computerised signature on it, she sent it back to them and finally switched off the computer for the weekend. She would try not to open her laptop over the two-day period, or at least only check her email through her phone. She didn't want to miss anything important.

Lexi messaged her to say she and Quinn had moved on to the next level, and Logan grinned stupidly at it. Logan's next level and Lexi's were completely different. Lexi's would most definitely be full-blown sex, but Logan's would be a bit of fumbling or foreplay. She'd always been a little bit prudish. She couldn't help it. She put it down to the fact that she liked to be in control, and taking it slow was how she'd always done things. Glancing at the clock, she saw it was six-forty. It was later than she thought. Pulling on her jacket and switching off the desk light, she closed her office door. Walking to Jorn's, she saw the light was on, but the door was shut. Teetering slightly, she knocked tentatively. Maybe he'd avoided her this week because he was no longer interested.

"Yeah?" She smiled at the sound of his voice and pushed open the door.

"Oh, sorry, I didn't realise you had company." A man was sitting in the chair opposite Jorn, but even before she took one step in, he stood up, a bottle of beer in his hand.

"Ah! You must be Logan." Logan was taken aback by the sheer size of the guy. Built like a brick shithouse, with a well-trimmed beard and mid-long blonde hair tied up in a half ponytail. He had chalk-white skin, and his crystal blue eyes were so striking that Logan couldn't help but stare.

Modestly composing herself, she walked in, holding her hand out. "That's me and you are?"

"Logan, this is Randin, my eldest brother," Jorn said, swigging at his beer.

"Jesus, just how many brothers do you have?" she asked, realising she knew nothing about Jorn's personal life, whether it was in magazines or not.

"Five," Randin said, bending down to kiss her hand.

"Wow, the testosterone in your house growing up must have been immense," she surmised.

"It still is," Randin laughed, draining his bottle. "Well, little bro, I'd best be going." He moved to clap Jorn on the shoulder.

"Please don't leave on my account," Logan said, feeling guilty for interrupting.

"It's okay, I was just leaving anyway. See you later, Jorn." Randin left, and Logan looked over at him.

"Five brothers? Wow. I didn't realise you had that many."

"Yes, five brothers, one of them my twin." She raised her eyebrows.

"Twin brother? Sheesh, are you identical?" She couldn't imagine anyone being as good-looking as Jorn was.

"In looks, maybe, well, we would be to the untrained eye, but we're very different people," he said, pushing his chair in under his desk. "You off home?"

"Yes, thought I'd just pop in and see you before I went," she sighed. "Did you get my message about Mr Kelly?"

"Yes, sorry I didn't reply. It's good he's off the ventilator. Hopefully, they'll be able to reduce the sedation even more now."

"I hope so. I just want to know he'll be alright," she said, her fingers brushing along Randin's vacated chair.

Jorn nodded, "Got any plans for the weekend?" he asked, moving around as if to leave.

"No, not really. Sleep, I think. I've not been sleeping well this week."

"Really? Why? Worrying?" he asked, shutting his office door and following her to the lift.

"I'm not sure. It's most likely playing a big part in it. I can't seem to switch off." She smiled, standing back, allowing the lift doors to open.

"You know what you need?" he said, allowing her to go in first.

"What?" she said, looking at his reflection in the mirror.

"Some alcohol. Fancy grabbing some dinner?" He arched one of his eyebrows.

Logan laughed, "Okay, so how does having some alcohol equate to, let's get some dinner?"

He just shrugged, pressing the basement number. "Well, I'm starving, and I've already had two beers with Randin, so I'm in the mood for more."

Logan thought about it. She could do with sitting and eating a decent meal. Despite cooking this week and heating up leftover broth, she'd not sat down and savoured any of it.

"Sure, I'm up for some dinner and alcohol."

"Great." He moved out into the cool car park. "I fancy Turkish. There's a new place I've heard is quite good on Juniper Street."

"Okay, why not?"

Logan changed bags in the car. "You have a going-out bag already in your car?"

"I know I'm ridiculous, but I like to be organised."

"I've never got that impression," he said sarcastically, holding his arm out for her as he locked his vehicle.

She took his arm, feeling the oh-so-familiar feeling of need filtering between them, which she tried to ignore, smiling to herself. She needed to forget about her week, her work and her routine. She had to chill, be herself. Relax. She could totally do this.

"Table for two, please." Jorn indicated to the corner table slightly out of the way and pulled a chair out for her.

"Drinks?" asked the waiter, whose hand was trembling, the distinct scent of shifter to him. Was he nervous? Perhaps it was his first night.

"Erm... do you want wine?" Jorn asked her, taking the wine menu.

"Yes, I'll have a..."

"Oh, you have the Spanish Rioja Alta Gran. We'll take a bottle of that unless you wanted something different?" Jorn said, looking over the list at her.

"Er... no, that sounds great," she said, glancing down the list. "Shit, Jorn, that's fifty-two pounds a bottle."

He just shrugged, "When I drink wine, it must be good. I'd rather have gone for the top one, but that's a little extravagant." She laughed at his cheeky smile. "We'll take a bottle of the Rioja Alta Gran, please, kind sir." The waiter nodded at him and walked away briskly to fetch the preferred wine.

She shook her head, "You are crazy to waste money on alcohol. It all tastes the same."

"Does it? One day, you should come to my house and see my father's extensive wine cellar; you'll be able to taste the difference then." He smirked, enjoying, for one fleeting moment, the concept of Logan coming to the mansion one day.

"Do you still live with your dad, too?" she asked, biting her lip at her slight reprimand. "Sorry, I didn't mean for that to sound accusatory." She didn't know anything about this man.

"No, don't be; we live in quite a large estate outside of the city, so we don't see each other daily. I have my own quarters. It's easy. Like I said before, I tried living alone but found I hated it." He shrugged, and Logan was surprised he didn't seem abashed by it. She started to unwind, and after they ordered, she asked him about his family and what his brothers did.

"Well, you know about Lamont, although he's not always done soliciting. He's a crazy good mathematician and used to do financial consulting, but he's easily bored, so he turned his hand to be a barrister. Oska is the medical genius in the family, but prefers wildlife and nature; he's currently putting his hands to landscape gardening. He did that gardener's programme a few years ago, you know, when you go to someone's house and do up their garden whilst they're away?" Logan blushed, knowing the programme she'd watched it religiously, trying to get ideas. Looking at Jorn now, she could see his resemblance to the head gardener. "Randin, he's a man of many talents." Logan raised her eyebrows. "Not like that. Firstly, he's an excellent architect, designing many properties and extensions. He just has an eye for things. He designed and built The Regal Hotel; you know, the one that's entrance is entirely made from glass?" Logan nodded. She'd never set foot in it because the rooms were way out of her price range, but she'd looked at the website. "His real passion, however, is counselling, so he does a lot for charities, especially those involved in childhood trauma programmes. Some of the stories he has make you ashamed to be human."

"I know the world can sometimes be a very cruel place," Logan agreed, thinking of some of the stories she'd read in the papers.

"Indeed. Jorun, he's..."

"I'm sorry, but Jorun?" Logan laughed at the similarity of the names.

"Yes, Jorun, he's my twin."

She shook her head, "What were your parents thinking when they named you? That must have been such a tongue twister when you were growing up."

"I suppose so." He grinned. "We both would just answer to either name."

"Do you know," she sipped again at her glass, "this is a good wine."

"I told you you'd like it," he said, moving his hands back so the waiter could put down their starters.

"So, what does Jorun do?"

"Jorun, he's... well, I don't really know what he is." He laughed. He couldn't think what Jorun was. "He's a bit of a dreamer. He loves life and women, so he doesn't hold a job down for too long. He started running a dating agency about five years ago and then sold it recently for a reasonable profit, so now he's just living off the interest."

"So, quite a successful family," Logan surmised, refilling their glasses. Jorun must have been the brother Lexi spoke of.

"Yes, my older brothers are and then Kol," he grimaced.

"Shit, there's another one?" She giggled at her inability to count.

"Kol. He's my youngest brother by seven years, and he's just a bum living off my father's money."

She laughed, thinking this must be the naughty brother

known for being notorious about the city. She wondered, however, if he ever felt overshadowed by his elders.

Jorn smiled, "I know what you're thinking. Isn't he bothered by his over-talented brothers?" She grinned at his ability to read her face. "The answer is... absolutely not. Kol is the black sheep. He has no cares, ambitions, or qualities except being annoyingly likeable and getting away with murder. He's probably the one the papers know the most," he blushed.

"Isn't that true of youngest siblings?" she asked, dipping some pitta in the tzatziki, trying not to dwell on the mischievous younger brother.

He laughed, "It is of mine."

Sitting back in her chair, she surveyed the man opposite her and momentarily forgot the conversation. She couldn't help but imagine what he'd look like with his shirt unbuttoned. Would he have muscles like his brother had? He wasn't too broad-shouldered, which Logan thought she preferred; she'd never been one for big men. She already knew he had some chest hair from Saturday night, which she smirked about. That was one of her fetishes; she just loved running her hands through it, and she betted that if he had chest hair, he'd have that bit of hair that showed slightly above the bikini line.

"What are you thinking about?" Jorn asked, looking at her all-knowing facial expression. Smiling, she said,

"Nothing, just how amazing it must be to have five brothers. To grow up in such a big family must have been fun." She flushed, cursing her wayward brain.

"Fun? It was, but we were always competing for our father's attention."

"Not your mum's?" she asked, moving her hands to the table, inches from his.

"I suppose we did to some extent, but mamma always gave us her attention until she passed away when I was twenty-four."

"Oh, shit, Jorn. I am so sorry. Me and my big, slightly alcoholic mouth," she said sympathetically.

"Hey, it's okay; it was long ago," he said, shifting in his seat uncomfortably.

"Your father, did he ever remarry?" She was desperate to know what had happened to his mother, but perhaps when she was sober would be better.

"No, he's had a few partners, but he was never the same after she went. He went into himself, really. I don't think he ever really forgave her." He was quiet and then said, "He has Portia now, who you saw the other night."

"What, that woman in red?" Logan couldn't believe it.

"Yes, I think he misses my mother so much that he just goes for anyone who is completely different. Portia is nothing like my mother."

"I can quite believe it." She knew it was customary for a son not to like a potential step-mum, but from what she glimpsed the other night, it seemed Portia had her eye on the sons as well as the father.

The waiter took away their starter plates, and Logan sat forward, her hand closer to Jorn's, casually resting on the table.

Taking his wrist in her hand, she fiddled with the silver linked bracelet he had, it held together with a woven leather clasp. "You don't find many men who wear jewellery," she said, holding his hand longer than was necessary.

"I don't wear much, but I like this bracelet, and I think it looks okay on me."

"Are you kidding? You'd look good in anything." She withdrew her hand quickly, feeling she'd said too much. "Damn my mouth."

He smiled, taking back her hand and feeling her palm, "You have very..."

"Rough hands?" Logan laughed, sipping her wine as he stroked her lifelines. "Yes, too much digging in the garden." She needed to stop saying ridiculous things, but couldn't help it. "I try many moisturisers, but none remove the wear and tear." She examined her hands at their dryness. "I get my nails done, but can't seem to shift the cracked look." She bit her lip. She was epically failing at being cool.

"You should try Hydroboost gel. My brother uses it and says it's the best he's used," he said.

"Maybe I'll try that." She laughed at their topic of conversation.

"Though, of course, there isn't anything wrong with your

hands," he said, taking it back in his hand and tracing his fingers over it again.

As the meal progressed, Logan felt more and more at ease with him, so much so that she even slipped off her shoe under the table and started rubbing his ankle. He smiled knowingly at her. She knew she shouldn't do it; it was evident that she'd had too much to drink, but she just wanted to touch him.

"Do you want another bottle of wine?" the waiter asked, whisking away their empty one and holding it behind his back.

"What do you think?" Jorn looked at her. "I think we should; we've had a hard week... you have anyway." He nodded to the waiter, who dutifully went off to get it.

"If I didn't know better, I'd think you are getting me purposely drunk, Jorn."

"Well, maybe, but it's not as if I'm not drinking with you," he said, sinking back into the couch he was on. "As we've finished, do you want to come and sit here?" he indicated the spare space on the sofa beside him.

"In a minute, I'm just off to break the seal." As she stood, Logan could feel the effects of the alcohol more, and despite how particular she was in her day-to-day life, she enjoyed the feeling of Jorn having slightly unwound her.

CHAPTER TWELVE

THE WINE

He watched her walk away from him as he sat at the table, his skin feeling hot under his collar, that he undid his second top button. Just her smile had him on the edge of his seat. Usually, at this point in any evening, he'd get the woman back to the car and have a quicky, but he knew with Logan it would be different. He wasn't going to take advantage of her whilst she was tipsy; she deserved better. He also had this nagging voice in his head that happened to be his Master saying, 'New Year's Eve, New Year's Eve.' He didn't bloody care how long he had left; he wasn't rushing it for his Master or himself. And he didn't want to do as he was told. He wanted to do it for Logan. She deserved none of this. Jorn's task had been set out to make her entirely under his spell, yet he'd fallen completely under hers. He knew there was nothing he wouldn't do for her.

"What are you thinking about?" she asked, slotting in next to him on the couch with one leg curled under her and her body turned to his.

"Honestly?" he smirked.

"Honestly," she said, watching the waiter pour them more wine.

"You."

"What about me?" she sipped the wine, tracing the seam of his trousers with her finger.

"How this evening has turned out better than I anticipated."

"Really? In what way?" Her other hand made its way round his shoulders and stroked the nape of his neck.

"Well, before you entered my office, I thought I'd be going home to five brothers who would all be drinking in the games room and shouting at the PlayStation. But instead, I'm here and getting slowly more drunk with much better and much more beautiful company."

"Tell me more about your family, Jorn, I find you fascinating. So, your name is Scandinavian, yes?"

"Yes, my parents are from north Norway, the town of Alta, right on the Altafjord. You ever been?"

"No, is it beautiful there?"

"Beautiful isn't the word, Logan. It's the most picturesque place in the world. The aurora up there about the end of February is just stunning. Of course, as a young boy, it got tedious, but I've been back a few times since we moved to England, and I must say, it's breathtaking." He looked cautiously at her, "Why do you smile at me like that?"

"Like what? I like to hear you talk about your family life. It sounds idyllic."

"It wasn't idyllic; no family is idyllic, but there were outstanding views and ice skating on frozen lakes in winter." He moved in to touch her thigh; his breathing increased, the tension between them so palpable it was a wonder the whole room wasn't getting it on with one another. "Lamont is very good at skating... not that he looks it." He drained his glass and refilled it to divert his need to kiss her.

"Okay," she took the glass from him. "So, I'm going to make the first move if that's alright because I can't bear this tension anymore, so stop me if you don't want me to."

She waited a few moments, a smile creeping up on her face.

"Are you expecting me to turn you down?" he asked, wiping his mouth.

Beaming, she smashed her lips onto his, inviting his tongue into her mouth with her own, it warm and tasting of garlic and wine. Jorn wasn't used to public displays of affection, but right now, all he could think about was her. Her heartbeat loud in his ears, her hand at the back of his neck rubbing his hairline, the pressure of her breasts on his chest. As she pulled away, he said,

"Er... shall we get the rest of the bottle corked and... go?"

Biting her lip, Logan suddenly realised what she'd just

done. She'd definitely had too much.

"I think we should before I embarrass myself even more."

"How are you embarrassing yourself? You really should stop caring what people think." He smiled as he notified the waiter and asked for the bill.

"Can we split the bill, please?" Logan asked as she returned to her seat and retrieved her purse.

"If you think I'm letting you pay, you've got another think coming," Jorn said, slotting his bank card into the machine.

"Normally, I'd argue, but that requires effort, and you did order some of the most expensive wine." She chortled, fumbling slightly at her jacket sleeve.

They exited the restaurant together, Jorn taking her hand in his as she snuggled into him, shielding herself from the wintry breeze.

"Jorn?" she whispered in his ear, giggling.

"Yep."

"I'm a bit drunk." She bit her lip again, feeling her face blush.

"Me too." Jorn wasn't intoxicated; it, of course, would take a lot to get him that drunk. With his fast metabolism, his body processed alcohol quickly, but he did feel slightly lightheaded. However, he wasn't sure if that was because Logan's scent was crushing his willpower to remain abstinent from whisking her home and to bed. They walked a while, not concentrating on where they were going, and once in a sheltered spot, Logan pulled him into a doorway of an estate agent. Her hand went behind his head, pulling him into her, his hands warm against her back as he caressed her, their tongues busy in each other's mouths, them both groaning as the passion increased, her hand wandering along his trouser seam.

"I'm sorry alcohol always makes me loose," she exclaimed, coming up for air.

He just smiled and yanked her from the doorway, continuing their walk past the closed shopfronts and open cafes.

They entered the gardens of one of the colleges; the fountains lit up for Christmas. The individual spurts were shooting out the colours of red, green and white. The pools bathed in shimmering colourful glows, the foam bursting with vibrancy. Logan let go of his hand and jumped onto the old, chipped concrete surround, walking with her coat open like a bird, her heels clicking heavily on the solid brick. Jorn watched her, the lights illuminating her hair, each colour highlighting her natural beauty, her skin glittering with a pearlescent sheen.

"Did you know a scholar of astronomy built these fountains? Each fountain mirrors the location of the three stars of Orion's belt. Zeta, Epsilon and Delta." She pointed to each fountain in the slightly wide 'V' shape. "And did you also know that on Orion's belt, the last star points to the brightest star in the sky, Sirius or some call it the dog star?" She looked up into the sky, and between the rolling clouds of winter, Jorn could also see the twinkle of the constellation Orion.

"Are you interested in astronomy, then?" he asked, grinning at her as she twisted around, looking skyward.

"Yes, my dad bought me a telescope when I was fourteen years old; it is still set up in my room back home. We'd sit for hours during the summer months stargazing."

She laid down on the fountain's wall, the water rushing beside her, her gaze upward at the heavens. Jorn's face suddenly appeared in her line of vision, and she smiled at him. Lying down next to her, his head alongside hers, he too looked upwards. He wanted to relish this moment. It was a moment of beauty to him—Logan as a girl who, in her slightly drunken state, had no cares or worries. The alcohol had lowered her barriers, and she was the girl who he watched through his screens. The one that danced around the kitchen singing to songs, who ran her bath and wallowed in it until the bubbles had all but dispersed. She was the woman who tended her garden so lovingly, who pondered for ages at the garden centre on which type of plant to buy. She was the young woman who stargazed with her father for hours at a time, sometimes staying up all night with him to see the sun rise over the horizon. He couldn't help the pang of jealousy he felt at the relationship she had with her father. His relationship with his father hadn't been like that for centuries.

"Jorn?" He tilted his head to look at her, stuffing away any thoughts of his father into the well-used vault in his brain. "Thank you for tonight. I've had a lovely time."

"Me too," he said, truthfully.

"And... I really want you to come home with me..."

"But?" he wrinkled his forehead.

"But I don't want to rush this thing we have, whatever it is, if it is even a thing."

He smiled. It seemed he and Logan were on the same page about their relationship, and he was mercifully relieved. "Yes, I would like this to not be rushed," he said, honestly. "Although I do very much want to come back to yours."

She smirked, "Me too, but I'm drunk and a drunken fumble, or whatever, is not quite what I want... right now." She sat up, stabilising her instability with her hand, "So I'm going to get a cab, and I'll see you on Monday?"

"Of course, but let me escort you to the taxi rank," he said, linking his arm with hers again and directing them both back towards the high street.

"It doesn't really seem like Christmas yet, does it?" Logan said as they stopped by an awaiting taxi.

"No, it never does in this country; there's never any snow." He opened the car door for her.

"Thanks, Jorn." She leaned in to kiss him on the cheek, but he turned, so she got his mouth. "That was naughty," she grinned.

"There's more where that came from."

"I hope so," she whispered naughtily, before getting in the taxi and driving away.

Jorn was suitably tipsy by the time he walked in the door

of the mansion. He had finished the wine on his journey and threw the empty bottle in the wheelie bin before entering the kitchen and heading to the cellar for more. Taking a glass from the cabinet, he sat at the table, glugging down the first pour. He hated his life; it was suddenly not his own, and he detested being out of control of this. Before Saturday night, he'd always known what life had in store for him; he had always been good at what he'd done and had recognition for it. But now, it was nothing like he wanted. He wanted to return to sitting in corners, hiding in the shadows, and following at a distance. He didn't like this new way of watching. Well, it wasn't even watching, was it? It was looking, touching, working, familiarising. For fuck's sake, it was falling for the target, and he hated that insecurity. He didn't like how she made him feel, yet he loved it. She made him feel so different; it was extraordinary. She gave him a sense of invincibility. Like the fight with his Master the other evening. He would never have seen that coming a week ago. He'd seen him in action many times before, and the opponent always came off worse. Jorn certainly had come off worse, but Christ, he'd enjoyed it. Just getting in a few punches was enough to quench the rage he'd had.

Stumbling from his chair, he walked down the hallway and staggered slightly up the staircase to his chamber's corridor, accidentally spilling his wine on the last step. He waited for another of the motorised mops to come out from its little charger pad and clean it up. Jorn was certain it had a sixth sense, and sure enough, out it beeped, making him laugh as he imagined it, saying, "Motor mop on its way, don't worry and don't dismay, I am here to save the day." He grinned at his idiocy.

"Stupid fucking machine." He fell, slightly, into the wall as he held the glass to his mouth.

"Are you drunk?" It was Jorun coming up the stairs behind him, eating a bowl of cereal.

Jorn took a while to answer and then said, "A little, yes."

"How much have you had?" he asked, munching noisily.

"Not enough," Jorn replied, throwing open his chamber door and almost falling into the room. He placed the wine on the side and removed his coat and scarf, missing the chair he flung it to.

"It's unlike you to drink this much, Jorn."

"Who gives a fuck how much I've had?" Jorn said, moving in and switching on the lights.

"What's happened?" Jorun asked, closing the door behind them both.

Jorn just laughed, slouching at his desk and draining his glass.

"How can you bear it?" he asked, suddenly seeming sober.

"What?"

'Feeling intimacy for someone so bad, it makes your chest ache!' He mind-linked his twin, sounding so anguished that Jorun put down his cereal.

'Feeling like that is rare, Jorn. I've never truly had it,' Jorun replied.

'I cannot bear it', he linked, flicking through the screen in search of her.

'What?' Jorun asked, aghast at his twin's distress.

'The fact that The Emperor will come and take her away, and there's absolutely nothing.' He stopped, the anguish so bad within his mind that all he saw was fire. *'Absolutely nothing I can do to stop him.'*

"Perhaps you can talk to The Master about it," Jorun said, out loud. Mind-linking his brother whilst he was in this state of mind proved too tricky. His brain was firing at a million miles an hour.

"That's a joke, isn't it? Can you imagine?" Jorn said, *'Oh, Master, you know the task you set me on, well I've actually fallen for the girl, so The Emperor can't have her.'* He couldn't let his Master hear his words aloud.

"It might be the only way," Jorun said, finishing his cereal.

"Fuck that shit!" Jorn scathed. *'There is no other way, my twin. No other way at all.'*

CHAPTER THIRTEEN

THE FAMILY

The last thing Logan wanted to do was hit the city on the last Saturday before Christmas to do her shopping, but she had no choice. She usually did late-night shopping on the Thursday before, but this year, she'd been working and missed the boat. To top it all off, she was hungover, yet it had been worth it. She'd had the most erotic evening with Jorn, even though they'd done nothing more than a little bit of kissing. He could practically undress her with his eyes. And his smell? Sheesh! She lowered her head to her scarf, almost tasting him, giving her the feeling of complete serenity.

Smiling broadly, she entered the small boutique and looked through the silver jewellery. It seemed to have become a Christmas tradition between her and her sister that they would buy each other something silver, and Logan was looking for earrings this year. On observing the different displays, she inhaled her scarf again, the masculine essence rinsing over her. She had it so bad for this guy; his scent stopped her thinking straight, which was very unlike her. She was always one for compartmentalising, but with Jorn, she couldn't. Everything she looked at, she wondered if *he* would like it, not if her sister would like it. Rolling her eyes to the ceiling, she selected a pair of Mantra-style earrings that the assistant kindly gift-wrapped. Well, that was one less thing for her to wrap when she got home. She left the shop for the now howling winds and rain that had started. It was such a contrast to yesterday that Logan wondered stupidly if last night had happened. Had she kissed the new Sales Director in that doorway?

Her bag started vibrating and extracting her phone, she swiped the green button,

"Hey Mum, are you okay?" she asked, going into another shop full to the brim of people. It was a wonder anyone could get to anything on the racks.

"Oh, Logan, are you out shopping?"

"Yeah, why?" Logan gasped, squeezing through the crowd.

"Could you grab me some socks for your father? I completely forgot when I was out yesterday," her mum pleaded.

"Yes, of course." She scanned the walls for directions to the men's department.

"Not jokey ones, just plain ones, you know, ones he can wear for work," she expressed.

"I'm sure he can wear jokey ones for work, Mum. No one's

going to see them." Her father worked in banking, and she couldn't see how wearing cartoon socks was really a problem.

"Yes, but then he'll know you got them," she chuckled.

"Okay, Mum, no problem."

"Oh, and are you coming for lunch tomorrow? Your sister and Ethan are?"

"Yes, Mum, I told you I could." Logan refrained from rolling her eyes as she picked up a pack of five plain socks.

"I just wanted to check. You never know, you might have another date or something." She could almost see her mum's smile through the phone as she returned to the women's clothing.

Gasping, she said, "How do you know I've been out on a date?" She took down a cashmere jumper that she thought her mum might like, and then, noticing a bottle green-coloured shirt, she held it against herself.

"Oh, Laurie from next door said she'd seen you in that new restaurant up Juniper Street."

"I bet she couldn't wait to tell you," Logan surmised. Laurie was the gossip monger from Logan's home village.

"What a coincidence that she was out the same night," her mum chimed, "so who is he?"

Logan wished she could think of an excuse not to tell her, but she couldn't. "He's the new Sales Director at work," she answered, moving forward to get in what looked like a five-mile queue for the till.

"Well, I expect to hear everything about him tomorrow."

Logan betted she did. "Okay, Mum. I'll see you then," she hung up and moved closer to the cashier.

Her car was still in the underground car park, and when she threw her shopping in the back seat, she noticed that Jorn's had gone. In a way, she felt slightly disappointed they hadn't met coincidentally, but that would have stretched her sobriety to the limit. She'd only just managed it last night. She'd so wanted him to come home with her, but sex was quite a big thing in her world, and she wanted it to be special if it was going to happen.

The drive to her parents' the next day was hazardous. The sleet had worsened overnight, so the roads were awash with floodwater. Jorn was right; it never snowed when it needed to in this country. The village where she grew up was a stone's throw away from the city she now lived in, but it was so quaint, and with it covered in snow, it would have been beautiful, but today, it was rain-washed and slushy. She pulled into the drive, and her sister's car was already there. Her mum seemed a little too excited when she entered through the front door, and Logan was under no illusion as to why; it was all down to the fact she'd been spotted on a night out with someone dark and mysterious who wasn't her ex-boyfriend.

"So, Loge, Mum tells me you've got a new man?" her sister, Tyler, said, dipping her broccoli into the gravy pool she had on her plate.

"Wow! I cannot believe it's taken almost an hour and a

half for you to ask about him," Logan said, forking her lamb. "You've lost your touch, Ty."

"I wanted to show you I am more reserved these days." Logan laughed at her sister, who lovingly rubbed her fiancé Ethan's thigh under the table. "It's true, isn't it, Ethan?"

"Oh, of course," he joked back, sipping his wine. "But yes, Logan, a guy from work?" Ethan couldn't help it now her sister had started.

"Yes, he's the new Sales Director," Logan replied, smiling at her soon-to-be brother-in-law.

"Name?" her sister asked.

"Jorn."

"Age?"

"Not sure, bit older than me, I think."

"Hair colour?" Logan chucked her napkin at her sister.

"Stop it."

"Sorry, Loge, I'm just pleased for you," Tyler said with a smile. "Is he good in bed?"

"Tyler May Hunter!" Logan's mum cooed, "No crudeness, please."

"Actually, we've not slept together," Logan said proudly, sticking her tongue out.

"What?" her mother exclaimed before clamping her hand

over her mouth and looking at Logan's father.

"Ethan, let's do the dishes and let the ladies talk." Her dad quickly vacated the table and took away the plates, allowing her mum to move a few chairs closer.

"Why haven't you slept with him, Loge?" Tyler asked, wiping her mouth on Logan's thrown napkin.

"Well, I've only known him a week, and well, you know me. I want to take things slowly. Neil and I only broke up a few months back. Don't want to rush into things," Logan said honestly.

"Oh well, that explains it; a week's not that long," her mum said, getting up as though the conversation was over. "Custard or ice cream?"

"Custard, for me, Mum," Logan said, smiling at her.

"Is that really why you haven't?" Tyler asked, quietly.

"Yes and no, I really wanted to, Ty. It's just that I'm not very good at spontaneity, and I don't want to jump in headfirst with this guy." She smiled, "I like him, like really like him, a lot more than I should at this stage, plus I work with him. How awkward would it be if it didn't work out?"

"Yes, I can see what you mean. But if you don't try, you'll never know," Tyler said, finishing her glass of wine.

"Oh, don't get me wrong, I'm pretty sure we'll go there. But I don't want to rush things. Also, I've had a hefty week. Mum must have told you about my boss?" she said, raising her eyebrows.

"Yes, how dreadful, but good experience for you, though. Could it be a permanent step up?" Tyler asked interestedly.

"Only if Mr Kelly wakes and gives me the post. I'm hoping the hospital will phone soon to update me. They've reduced his sedation, so fingers crossed." Logan moved aside for the apple crumble and custard her mum put in front of her. The smell of the apples reminded her of Sunday roasts as a child, when her grandma was alive.

"Hey, Dad, is my telescope still set up in my room?" she turned to her father.

"Of course it is, why?" he asked, taking his place at the head of the table.

"I was telling Jorn about it last night and just wanted to ask."

"Jorn? That's a funny name. Is he Scandinavian?" he asked, dipping into his dessert.

"Yes, Norwegian, but he hasn't really got an accent."

"Whereabouts in Norway?" Ethan asked, resting his arm along the chair behind Tyler.

"Alta, I think he said. He said the aurora up there is astounding," Logan said, thinking of him.

"Ooooh, Loge, you're blushing," her mum exclaimed, with a smirk.

"What? Oh, shut up." She spooned the crumble into her mouth.

"Is he good-looking?"

Logan didn't know how to describe Jorn. He was good-looking, beautiful in her eyes, but how to explain him?

"He has quite a chiselled face, always seems to have a day or two's worth of stubble on his chin, and his hair is kinda longish but messy. I'm sure he makes it messy on purpose, though. He's not overly broad-shouldered, but he's got some good definition to his arms. You should see his brother; now, he is broad-shouldered," Logan said, scraping her bowl.

"Sounds handsome!" her mum surmised.

"You'd like him, Mum. He's quite charming, and he would definitely know how to impress you."

"You know what? Why don't you invite him over Christmas Day, you know, in the evening for games night?" her mum said, enthusiastically.

"Oh yes, like that's going to make him want to date Logan more," Tyler scoffed at her mother.

"Does he have family?" her mum asked, ignoring her sister.

Logan told them as much as she felt she could about Jorn without giving too much away. She didn't want them to know about his family and their status; she didn't want to get their hopes up. Her mother always talked about biological clocks, grandchildren, and her daughters making good matches with wealthy men.

"You going to stay the night, Loge?" her father asked later

when Logan had wandered up to her room.

"No, I can't, Dad, got an early start tomorrow. Was just wondering if there were any stars out tonight, but it is too cloudy," she shrugged.

"Yes, there's definitely too much cloud cover. Maybe Thursday will be better," he said, his hand on her shoulder.

"Miss you, Dad," she said, winding her hands around his waist and hugging him.

"Miss you too, Loge," he said, hugging her even more. "I'm so proud of you, you know. For what you've been up to this week, taking on the Managing Director role, it's a huge deal for Mum and I."

"Thanks, Dad."

"And I hope this new man, this Jorn, treats you right."

"Well, it's early days, Dad, but so far he does," she grinned.

"Er... is he part of the Hartvigsen lot from the estate outta town?" he asked sceptically.

Grimacing, she looked up at him, "Yes, I'm afraid so. Is that an issue?"

He shook his head hesitantly. "No, but I want you to be careful. I know the old man is someone I would never trust," he tilted his head at her, "more money than they know what to do with."

"Well, Jorn obviously likes to earn his own money," she

said, moving downstairs to get her coat. "Please don't tell Mum; you know how she'll get."

Her father smiled, "Why do you think I asked you when you were alone? I sincerely know what my wife is like."

Grinning, she put her coat on. "See if Jorn wants to come on Christmas Day, Loge; it would be good to have another man around," her mum said as she kissed her goodnight.

"What, because there's so many ladies in the house?" Logan asked, hiding her face with her hood as she pulled it up.

"Safety in numbers," her dad said, the previous conversation forgotten.

"I'll ask him," Logan promised.

"He can come for lunch if he wants too, but I suppose he'll be with his family," her mum surmised, placing her arm around her husband's waist.

"I don't know, I'll see."

Logan wasn't sure how she felt about asking him over for Christmas Day. That seemed like a big deal, and she wasn't sure their short relationship was ready for it. But by the time she'd got home and found a bouquet of flowers on her doorstep, with a card in them signed,

J x

Her mind was made up. There was no harm in asking.

CHAPTER FOURTEEN

THE INVITATIONS

Jorn knew Logan was at her parents' house when he dropped the flowers off on her back doorstep; he had wanted to see her but thought it better to keep it simple. He wanted her to know he was thinking about her, but he liked the idea of being subtle. His chat with Jorun on Friday had been enlightening, and even now, he felt extremely lucky to have such a close relationship with him and all his other brothers. Jorun was totally on his side regarding Logan and was already trying to sow the seed with The Master to give Jorn more time. Jorn and Jorun knew it was futile, but he was happy his brother was trying. Their Master had never changed his mind about anything, and if The Emperor was involved, it was even more unlikely. But it gave Jorn a tiny wave of hope, and he would ride it as long as possible.

He studied his screens as Logan walked in her back door, holding the flowers. Her face glowing as she unwrapped them and placed them in a vase. He had purposefully chosen winter colours of vibrant reds, pastel greens and subtle oranges. Once arranged, she got her phone from her bag and seemed to deliberate on it. What was she doing? Just then, his phone buzzed. Grabbing it, he swiped the screen to see it was his Master, not Logan.

"You called for me, sir," Jorn said, approaching the comfortable end of his Master's quarters. Portia was there wearing nothing but a see-through night slip; him in nothing but a bathrobe.

"Ah, Jorn, I wanted to give you this." He handed Jorn a green and gold embossed envelope addressed to Miss L Hunter. "It's an invitation for your lovely damsel in distress to come to the masquerade ball on New Year's Eve."

"A ball?" Jorn asked, slightly confused. "On New Year's Eve?" he gulped.

"Yes. Portia has persuaded me to give a party and thought it would be good to have it in the old ballroom."

"Right, but Master. We've not had any type of ball since..."

"Yes, and it's about time we started having them again. We will be entertaining royalty." Portia clambered on the sofa, her hand wandering under The Master's robe, making Jorn look away. Was she trying to rub it in?

"Okay. I'll make sure Logan gets it," Jorn said, turning, feeling nauseated at his Master's exhibition with Portia.

"And Jorn?" Jorn stopped. He had to get the last word again. "Tell your brothers to stop trying to change my mind for you. It's not very manly to get others to do your dirty work, and I'm afraid she is too valuable to The

Emperor to let you have any longer with her."

He didn't rise to the bait; he couldn't bear it. He just walked to his room, slamming the door. Morning couldn't come quickly enough so he could get out of this toxic hellhole.

His feet splashed in the slush as he ran to work, his suit in a backpack jostling about the faster he ran. He wanted to run away from it all, the hatred, the lies, the guilt, the hatred... wait, had he thought hatred twice? He changed speedily in the lift and was adjusting his trousers when the doors pinged open. Looking in on Logan on the way to his office, he saw she was on the phone, so he left her for the time being. He did, however, clock the green shirt she was wearing, it shimmering in the desk light. It was a classic cut and enhanced her skin tone and hair, making him guiltily wonder what it would feel like under his fingers if he slipped it off her.

His email inbox was disastrously empty when he booted the computer, irritation flooding him for not having anything to distract him from thinking of her in that shirt. He supposed that with Christmas coming, everything was starting to slow down, and although having only just started this job, he had ten days off in two days from now for the Christmas break. He'd not really thought much of Christmas; since his mother died and they moved to England, they didn't celebrate it.

"Hey," Logan appeared in his office just after lunch, her hands full of papers. Sidling up to his desk, he grabbed her hip and pulled her into him. "Shit!" she gasped, almost dropping the spreadsheets.

"Sorry, I just couldn't help touching you," he said, a mad glint in his eye.

"I can see that," she said, turning to put the documents on his desk, her breath catching as he stood and parted her legs, shoving her gently so she fell back onto his desk.

"Jorn?" she whispered, untucking his top and feeling up his back.

"Yeah?" he said, unbuttoning her shirt, his tongue moving down to the lace of her bra.

"We shouldn't do this," she said, groaning as he licked her nipple.

"I just cannot help myself," he moaned. "It's this shirt; it makes you look fucking amazing. Is it new?" His mouth was back at hers, and she responded longingly.

"Yeah... it's... shit! I can hear my phone." With a moan of defeatism, Jorn moved off her, and she quickly grabbed his phone, pressing hashtag one, "Kelly's Kustom Kitchens, Logan speaking, how may I help you?" She cradled the phone, buttoning up her shirt and straightening her hair. Jorn stood there, tucking himself back in properly, running a hand through his hair to make it semi-smart. "Yes, of course, I will come straight away. Thank you for letting me know." She put the phone down.

"All okay?" Jorn coughed.

"Yes, it's Adrian. He's awake, and he's asking for me." She smiled at Jorn, "Rain check?"

"Most definitely," he said, allowing her space to move

past him.

"I only came in to thank you for the flowers," she said, looking back at him abashed.

"No worries, thought you'd like them," he said, his phone ringing. After a morning of not much going on, why were they all ringing now? "Er... Logan, wait a sec." He answered the phone and watched her while she waited. "Yes, it is. Can you just give me a minute?" He held the phone to his shoulder, "Come back in here before you go; I need to give you something."

He didn't want to give her the invitation, he couldn't think of anything worse, so he had to give it to her now before he lost his nerve.

"I'll be sure to do that, and Merry Christmas to you, too." He put the phone down.

She returned, wrapped up for the cold outside, looking expectantly at him.

"Right." Getting his bag, he found the invitation, "I just wanted to give you this."

Taking the envelope carefully, she said, "Jesus, it weighs a tonne. To Miss L Hunter," she read aloud as she turned it over to see the addressee, "hmmm... that's formal."

"Oh, that's my father for you. No expense spared," he grimaced.

Slipping her finger under the wax seal, she read, "We, Ottar and Portia, cordially invite you, Miss L Hunter, to a masquerade ball on **Nyttarsaften.**"

She looked at Jorn,

"Er... It's Norwegian for New Year's Eve."

"Oh, a New Year's Eve ball? And masquerade? I've never been to a masquerade, well, anything, let alone a ball." She laughed, running her hand over the decorative paper, "Will I have to wear a ballgown?"

"It's traditional to wear one, but there is no need to," Jorn said, suddenly envisioning her in a green one like her shirt. "So, will you accept or have you other plans? We only need to show our faces, and then we can," he shrugged, "mysteriously disappear."

"Really? Where? Your bedroom?" she blushed, despite herself. Glossing over the notion of having sex on New Year's Eve, she continued. "I can't very well say no, can I, after such detail in the invite, but you must promise not to leave me alone for one second. I will be way out of my depth."

"Oh, don't worry, there is no way I'll leave you with my brothers around," he smirked. "Goodness knows what they'd tell you."

"I'm excited!" she laughed. "It will certainly make a change to the usual cheesy club Lexi always drags me to."

"If you'd rather do that, that would be fine. I just know I'll be expected to be there."

"Jorn, it's fine, I'd love to come. Of course, if you want me to." She stood back to survey him, his face giving her mixed messages.

"Yes, I would very much like you to come," he said, nodding.

"Right... I'm going to go before there's more awkwardness," she said, leaning in and kissing him on the cheek.

He stood a while even after she'd disappeared into the lift. When he eventually made his passage from this world to the shadowlands, he was sure to be going straight to hell. How could he live with himself after what his Master and Emperor had planned for her? How was he going to stand back and let them take her? Would she be a sacrifice to the goddess of something or other, and was she to be burnt at the stake like Jorn knew they had done in the past? Jorn knew that he would rather die than let them do that to her, but even with his death, they would still hurt her. His death would mean nothing to his Master. He would be collateral damage. Only his brothers would mourn him; he had meant nothing to his Master for centuries, and he was not going to start now.

His phone vibrated in his pocket,

Did she say yes?

Jorn couldn't even bring himself to reply. His Master knew she would never refuse such an invitation, so he wasn't going to give him the satisfaction of a response.

His desk phone rang, "Yeah?"

"Oh, Mr Hartvigsen? It's reception. There are a few boxes of cakes down here for you to collect."

"Oh, many thanks." Jorn had forgotten to pick up the

cakes for his morale booster elevens' this morning, so he thought he'd do an afternoon one instead.

He set up the trolley, feeling like an idiot, but he swallowed, and after answering a few more emails and the phone a few times, he moved the trolley down to the next floor and began the humiliation. Lexi was very enthusiastic to see him, and he wasn't sure if she knew about him and Logan, as Logan hadn't mentioned it, or if she was just happy to see him. However, Jorn could tell things between her and Quinn were going well. They'd certainly moved onto the last level as she smelt of intimacies as he handed her a cake and Christmas napkin. He could also scent the distinct smell of cardboard and dust. A quicky in the store cupboard? Offices were always the same - everyone having sex with a colleague, whether it was just lust, love or a full-blown affair, there was always someone doing it with somebody.

Quinn stood near him when he got to his desk and actually had the guts to sniff his outer clothing.

"Do you mind?" Jorn asked, stepping away, knowing full well that he would smell Logan on him.

"Please treat her right," he pleaded, "she's one of the good ones."

Quinn was correct about that. She was most definitely one of the good ones.

"Thanks for the advice, but when I need it from a mammal-shifter, I'll let you know," Jorn cussed.

"Listen, man, I don't want to get on the wrong side of you. I know what you Gifted ones are like. But I like her friend, and if anything were to happen to Logan, Lexi would be traumatised," he stated.

"Quinn," Jorn looked around to see if anyone was listening. Everyone, however, was trying to look busy as he was on their floor. "It may surprise you, but I care for Logan as much as you do, most likely more. My intentions towards her are honourable."

"Just as long as they are. I don't like it when my friends get hurt." He chose a cake from the selection.

"Neither do I," he looked poignantly at Lexi.

"I'm not planning on hurting her either," he said firmly.

"That's good then. Seems like we're both on the same page." Jorn moved on with the trolley.

He was packing up the rest of the cakes when Logan exited her office. She took his breath away as she walked towards him, her face looking determined. Lifting her arms, she encircled his neck and crashed into his mouth, pushing him up against the wall, his hands going immediately to her bum cheeks, bringing her further into him.

"What's this all for?" he gasped, as she moved to his neck, her breath warm on his skin.

"Now I've tasted you; I just want more," she said, slipping her hand down the front of his trousers, his breath catching in his chest.

"Shit!" he groaned against her mouth, "Logan, don't," he gripped her wrist to stop her hand.

"Why? I can't stop myself. It's like I'm possessed." She smiled, still touching him, her nails scraping the inside of his neck as she tried to undo his shirt.

"No... not here. It's not the way I want it." He pulled her hand out, holding it tightly so she wouldn't turn away. "Listen, I want you with every fibre of my body, but like we said on Friday, we want to take it slowly. I need to take this slowly. I want it to be right."

"Great, now I feel like an idiot," Logan said, suddenly shy.

"Hey, please don't feel like an idiot. It's taking all my willpower not to bend you over this trolley, and to hell with it if we get caught." Jorn couldn't believe himself. How he stopped her, he would never know.

"You're right, it's just earlier if the phone hadn't rung..." she bit her lip.

"Yes, I don't know if I would have stopped you. I'd like to think I would have, but it wouldn't have been because I didn't want to." He tilted her chin to him, kissing her again. "It just has to be right, and I," he shrugged, "I want to take my time." He raised his eyebrows slightly. He knew that it would have to be special for her.

"Okay," she nodded, turning to the trolley, "I thought you'd forgotten about coffee trolley morning."

"Well, I did kind of, so I did coffee trolley afternoon instead," he smirked, adjusting his trousers and taking his coat from the bottom of the trolley.

"You going out?"

"Yes, I just need to grab a few things. I might not be back before you go home." He put on his jacket, "Oh, how was Mr Kelly?"

"Good, really good. Adrian said thank you for the speaker, and he should be getting out in time for Christmas."

"That's such good news."

"Yes, and he also said thank you for helping to hold the fort whilst he was gone," she said, smiling.

"Anyone would have done it," Jorn said, doing up his scarf.

"Oh, here, before I forget." She handed him an envelope of pale pink paper. "It's an acceptance to your father's party," Logan said, answering his quizzical look.

"You didn't need to formally accept," Jorn said, putting it in his breast pocket.

"Oh, I think I did," she said, "and er... I don't have a formal invitation or anything, but what are your plans for Christmas Day?"

"Christmas Day?" Jorn shrugged, "Not much. We don't really celebrate Christmas. Well, not since my mother's been gone." He winced, "My brothers and I do a secret Santa thing with presents, but we don't do Christmas dinner or anything."

"Really?" Logan frowned, "That's sad, Jorn."

"Yep. Well, my father... it's... er, complicated." He looked ashamed.

"My mum was wondering if you'd like to come to ours, at

first, for just our traditional games evening on Christmas Day, but she did say that if you had no plans, you could come to Christmas dinner. Only if you want to; there's absolutely no pressure or anything. And you'd have to put up with my mum asking you loads of questions, and my dad will probably put you on the spot about our relationship, so if you'd rather not, I'd understand. I mean, you probably want to..." Jorn put his finger to her lips.

"Stop gibbering. I'd be honoured to come and spend some time with you and your family." She grinned under his finger.

"Really?" she said, her breathing laboured under his touch.

"Of course. Just name a time, and I'll be there."

"Oh, I have no idea of times," she said, sighing with relief, "I'll have to let you know." She turned to go to her office.

"I'll bring some good wine," Jorn smiled, continuing to the lift to do his own Christmas shopping.

"Oh, and Jorn?" He quickly blocked the door to the lift with his arm, "Jorun said I passed his test." She laughed as she continued to walk towards her office.

He shook his head as he got in the lift, "I'm going to kill him." And the doors shut, enclosing him in the aluminium box.

CHAPTER FIFTEEN

THE TEST

Logan felt excessively flushed after her kiss on Jorn's desk, but couldn't help but smile to herself as she fingered the embossed envelope in her hands. She'd never been to a ball, like a proper one. She, of course, had been to her end-of-school ball, but that had been in the school hall when the decorations had been paper streamers and balloons. She knew that if this invitation was anything to go by, the ball on New Year's Eve would be extravagant, and she couldn't help but feel a little stoked that Jorn's father had thought to invite her. But she was sceptical. The way Jorn spoke of his dad made her feel that he was a man who had to be in total control of his family, and could perhaps come across as a bully, even though he was the patriarch of the family. She saw none of that love in Jorn's eyes when he spoke of him, that she saw when he spoke of his mother. If she was honest, she saw a lot of hatred and a sense of grief within them. Perhaps Jorn was right. His mother's death had truly affected his father, so much so that there was no love in him to give any more.

Looking in the mirror now, she wondered briefly what she had to wear in her wardrobe. The answer was easy. Nothing. She had nothing suitable for a ball, well, not a ball of that status. Which meant she'd have to go shopping again. A nice halter-neck would be good. She always seemed to favour halter-neck tops, and a halter-neck dress sounded perfect. But where would she find something like that this late in the holiday season? Most things would surely be sold out; well, anything in her price range. Waiting for her taxi, she scrolled through potential dress shops in the nearby area, none showing her anything that stood out or was unique. Imagine turning up and wearing the same thing as someone else; that was the only problem with this type of party. She didn't know anyone, so any of the women going could have tastes similar to hers. She supposed that was why she enjoyed going out with only a select number of people, not just at New Year's but at any point in the year. Everyone told each other what they would be wearing, so no one would wear the same thing.

"Oh, here she is, the Managing Director of the best kitchen company north of London," Adrian chimed, as she kissed his cheek.

"Oh, Adrian." She gently hugged the older man in the bed, tears in her eyes to see him so well.

"Why are you crying?" he asked, wiping her face.

"I don't know, I'm just so happy you're alright," she sniffed, taking a tissue from the table.

"Yes, and thanks to you, my company still stands." He smiled genuinely at her, taking her hand. "Your hands are freezing." He squeezed them both together, trying to warm them.

"Oh, don't worry about me, I'm fine," she gushed.

"I know you are. You look amazing, by the way. Management suits you, my dear L." She just smiled, "Have you seen Julia?"

"Yes, of course. I've seen her a few times. Jorn and I went to date night, and then I briefly went Thursday after work."

"How was she?"

Logan tilted her head, "The same, but she now thinks I'm her daughter and Jorn is her son."

"Jorn? Mr Hartvigsen went with you to see Julia?" Adrian asked, astonished.

"Yes, he came the first time, I think, to support me more than anything."

"I can see by the look on your face that he is settling in well. Perhaps too well?" He grinned at her, making her blush.

"I took Julia the Amaryllis you wanted to give her. She was very pleased with it," she said, changing the subject.

"I know you are changing the subject, my dear, but I'll forgive you."

"Have the doctors said anything about you going home?" Logan asked, giving him some blueberries she'd picked up on the way.

"Ah! Logan, I feel you know me better than I know myself."

"I know blueberries are one of your favourites."

"Yes, they are," he said, helping himself to one. "They've said potentially tomorrow or perhaps Wednesday."

"And you'll come to my parents for Christmas Day? I cannot have you being on your own." Logan had no idea why she was inviting him; she just felt compelled to ensure he was cared for.

"Don't be silly. I cannot gatecrash your family festivities. I've already arranged it; I'm going to James' for the Christmas period to recuperate." Logan felt instantly relieved that he had a plan, not that she would have minded him coming, but with the potential of Jorn coming too, that could make it awkward.

"I'm not being silly, but I'm glad you're not going to be alone," she said, stealing a blueberry.

"So, how is the office? Everything all okay?"

"Yes, it's all good." She told him about the deal she and Jorn had secured and how the designers had sent her some new designs she wanted him to look at when he felt up to it.

"So... I asked you to come here because I have a proposition for you." She sat up straight like she'd been called to the Headmaster. "I was wondering if you would like to keep working as the Managing Director, you know, in the new year?" She raised her eyebrows. "Now, hear me out. I'm getting older, and the accident made me realise that life is short, and I haven't really lived it much outside of the company. I have made enough money to be very comfortable, and I want to spend more time with Julia. Maybe have her home with twenty-four-hour help. Of course, at least at first, I will stay on in an advisory role. But it seems you've been doing extremely well without me. I've been checking in on the stock market today, and they've already increased by six percent." She looked confused at him for a moment. "It seems that you and Jorn know what you're doing, and I'd be honoured to have you take my place."

Logan was speechless. This had not been what she had expected him to say, "You've been good to me, Logan, you've always picked up the slack and your support with Julia has been way more than I ever hoped for in an employee."

She sat back in her chair, the emotions she was feeling rushing over her, "I... I don't know what to say, Adrian," she said hesitantly, biting onto her thumb in puzzlement.

"You're meant to say yes." He clapped his hand on hers. "I've been thinking of this a while now, even before my accident, so don't think this is something I've only just thought about or because I've been knocked on the head. I know you would do very well at running the company, and you have proved it this week. My brother agrees with me. There's no one we'd rather see at the helm of our company."

"But surely James' sons are better candidates than me," Logan said, stealing another berry.

"They are not businessmen and have no idea how to run a

firm like ours."

"But won't they think I'm taking their inheritance or something?" Logan frowned.

"They will be well looked after, and, anyway, they make their own money." He brushed her comment aside, "At least think about it. You don't have to say yes straight away. Think it over during the Christmas break and let me know."

"I will think about it; it is an opportunity many would snatch up," she said, feeling overwhelmed.

"Yes, but I'm offering it to you," he said, putting the finished punnet of blueberries on the table.

"Well... thank you," she said, flustered.

"So enough of that." He clapped his hands together as a sign to move the conversation onward, "What have you organised for the office Christmas shindigs?"

Logan told him about the office party she'd organised at the local Pizza, Pasta and Pie restaurant on Christmas Eve at 1 p.m. She always organised it, but this year, she had left it slightly late, but managed to squeeze in the party of the twenty-four employees and support staff.

She was in a bit of a daze when she returned to work, and her mind was decidedly elsewhere when she walked into Jorn's office. She was already thinking about changing the layout of Adrian's office. She'd always thought that his desk should be to the side, where the sun shone less, to avoid having to close the blinds. She also felt that the black couch made it look too cold, and she would either like to have a few throws on it and some comfier cushions or perhaps a brand-new sofa, maybe pale green or ivory.

"You'll never guess what Adrian has asked me?" She had arrived at Jorn's desk, not even looking at him, yet when she got there, she was taken aback by the man who sat in the chair and by the suit he was wearing. "Er... you're not Jorn," she said, taking a few steps away.

"Damn it. I hoped you'd fail my test."

"Your test?" Logan looked at the man who resembled Jorn so closely it was uncanny, even down to the lip shape and sexy smile. "You must be Jorun?" She held her hand out to Jorn's twin.

"What was it? The suit, the chin, the hair?" He put her hand up to his lips and kissed it.

"Er, I just know you're not Jorn. You don't even smell like him," she said, pursing her lips together, embarrassed.

"I must congratulate you on your passing of the twin test." He bowed at her, "I really hoped he was wrong about you."

"What do you mean wrong?" she said, smiling.

"Because I know what liking someone a lot can do to a man," he vacated the seat, "and I'm jealous."

"Why jealous?" she asked, smirking, instantly liking this guy; she could tell he would be fun to be around.

"Because he's found someone special before me, and, believe me, I've tried."

"Special?" she asked. What was it about today? Surprise central.

"Yes, Logan, my brother's never spoken about a woman as much as he has done with you, and that's saying a lot. He never really talks about anyone or anything. He's more of a watcher than a talker," he said, raising his eyebrows.

"Well, he's certainly not a flirt like you."

"What do you expect, you're a beautiful woman and one who can tell the difference between identical twins. That's a talent not many have."

"But you are so different," she said, studying the man in front of her. "Even your eye colour and demeanour."

"Yes, but these are things not everyone would notice. And my demeanour is great, thank you," Jorun said, moving around the office, looking in the filing cabinets and cupboards.

"Yes, you're certainly cock sure of yourself," Logan laughed, watching him.

"Well," he grinned mischievously, "there is no fun in not being confident with one's own self."

She had to agree with him, though she had never felt that herself.

"Where is he, your brother, by the way?" she asked, changing the subject.

"Er, I think he's doing the coffee trolley round thing you guys do here, not that I've seen him. But I seem to remember him messaging to say he would be out of the office this afternoon if I was thinking of popping by."

"What, he's doing it now?" She looked at her phone. 16:00. "I suppose it's better than not doing it at all."

"Do you love him?" Logan stood there, shocked at Jorun's directness.

"Love is a strong word, you know," she said, composing herself.

"Yes, but it is just a word," Jorun said, examining a book from the shelf.

"I'm not sure it is to a couple who say it to each other," she said, smiling. "I think you are very lucky to find someone who you can love unconditionally."

She felt the heat rising in her chest and up towards her neck. Did she love Jorn? No. Of course, she didn't. You can't fall in love that quickly. Truth be told, she'd never loved Neil, so she didn't really know what love was. He'd told her once, but she hadn't reciprocated it, which had most likely been the downfall of their relationship. Did she love Jorn? She couldn't, not yet, although she could see it was a possibility. She did think about him more often than was appropriate and of things they could get up to together in the bedroom, although perhaps he'd have to instigate some of it. She wasn't sure she had the confidence to try that position or suggest things. With a guy as good-looking as him, she'd have to pull out all the stops with him in the sex department. He was bound to have had many lovers, and she most likely had much to compete with. Yet Jorun said he spoke of her more than others. Was that just because they'd not done the sex thing yet, and he was venting off at home about how she wanted to take things slowly?

She suddenly noticed Jorun staring at her, "What?"

"Got you thinking, haven't I?" he jested. "I've got you thinking that you could very easily love my brother." She frowned at his presumption. "Tsk!" he said, moving towards the door. "I'd better get going. If you see my twin, tell him I was here and that you passed the twin test." He moved in and kissed her cheek. "See you New Year's Eve?" A quizzical look came over his face as though he was trying to read her from the inside out.

"Yes, of course. I've done my acceptance card." She patted her bag.

"Oh, my father will love that. He's such a stickler for formality."

Jorun waltzed out of the office, and Logan returned to hers. She was suddenly looking forward to the ball even more.

It seemed she had a lot to learn from Jorn's brothers.

CHAPTER SIXTEEN

THE PARTY

Jorn stood looking at the green dress in front of him, trying to picture Logan in it, and he moved from one foot to the other, debating whether the three-hour journey to the boutique in London was worth it. It was a halter-neck, of which he knew she liked, but was it the kind of green he wanted? It was darker than her shirt had been, and he wasn't sure if it was too near to black for her. The sales assistant slowly approached him.

"Can I help you?" He looked over at her, his mind thinking quickly. She had dark hair and was quite tall.

"Do you think you could try this on for me?" he asked, gently. He knew that she recognised him from some of his father's publications. She would, he knew, do anything he asked.

"Certainly, sir." She located her size and walked into the changing rooms, and when she returned, he studied her. Yet he was not interested in her face but in the way the dress hugged her figure and at the way the slight train fanned out as she walked.

"Would you mind just walking over there and back for me?" Putting her heels back on, she walked as if on a catwalk.

"Is this for your wife?" she asked. She also knew perfectly well that he wasn't married; the instant he'd walked into the shop, she'd scanned his hand for a wedding ring.

"Fiancée," he said without batting an eyelid.

"She's one lucky lady if you buy it, sir," she smirked, twirling in front of him.

"And I'm one lucky man who gets to undress her from it." She blushed at his words, but he ignored her. It was a truly glorious and very well-made dress. "I'll take it in a size ten, please." She nodded and returned to the dressing room.

He walked around the shop whilst the assistant gift-wrapped it for him, tying it exuberantly with a rose gold ribbon. He wanted to get her some unique jewellery to go with it but was unsure of what. He usually had his jewellery custom made by an associate in Italy, but there was no time for that now.

He raked over the jewellery display cabinets for ideas. Ideally, he wanted earrings, she had bracelets, and a ring would perhaps say too much at this point in their relationship. He didn't even know why he was going to so much effort; her days were numbered. And his heart felt like lead in his stomach as he thanked the cashier and exited the shop. This time of year was meant for happiness, and he had much to be happy about right now.

He'd found a woman who he liked, more than he should, and he would be spending Christmas with her. He hadn't enjoyed Christmas for decades, and this one would be better than most, no matter what happens afterwards.

He flicked through his email whilst at the traffic lights on his way home; it was too late to return to the office now. There were many adverts and Merry Christmases from suppliers that he just skimmed through. He opened the one from Logan titled Christmas Shindigs, and he couldn't help but laugh aloud at her.

So usual place for Christmas party was fully booked - my fault as I've been slightly busy, she'd added an eye rolling emoji, *So this year I've booked a table at Pizza, Pasta and Pie on Florence Avenue on the 24th. Mr Kelly has given me a budget for the tab, so first few drinks are on him as per usual. The table is booked for 1 p.m. so office shut down will begin from 12 noon, informal dress for work this day is fine. I hope you'll all be there. Merry Christmas and thank you all for your support this year and, of course, this past week. Logan x*

He supposed he should have guessed there would be some sort of office party, but seeing as Logan hadn't mentioned it, he'd thought maybe it wouldn't happen due to Mr Kelly being hospitalised.

Jorn couldn't help but notice Logan's avoidance of him the day before Christmas Eve. He wondered if Jorun had scared her off, but when he approached her office on Christmas Eve morning before all the other staff had arrived, he could hear her humming carols.

"Hey, you," she said, looking up from her desk. Her hair

was down, it floating over her shoulder in waves.

Perching on her desk, he smiled at her, "You seem happy."

She shrugged, "It's the last office day of the year, and I can't wait to relax properly. I've done all my wrapping, packed my overnight bag for my parents and their presents. I've even put fuel in the car, so I haven't got to worry about that. I feel pretty organised."

"Are you trying to tell me you're not usually this organised each and every Christmas?" he smirked, knowing full well that she was.

"Yes, but it doesn't mean I'm any less pleased." She stood, and he took the hint from her, holding his hand out and pulling her into him.

"You know," he grinned, "we really need to stop pussyfooting around; we're either seeing each other or we're not. This halfway thing isn't really working for me."

"I know you're right. It's just I'm not sure I want the whole company to know we're seeing each other; maybe just keep it under wraps for now?" she queried, studying his face.

"Okay, but if I have a bit too much to drink later, I'm not promising I'm going to be able to keep my hands off you," he said truthfully. "I want you, Logan, and I'm not good at hiding it. Ask my brothers."

"Yes, Jorun said you'd spoken of me at home."

"Ha. Don't even get me started on him. He's incorrigible," Jorn joked.

"I like him," she said into his mouth, "he's so vibrant and... loud."

"Yes, he's definitely the more outgoing of the two of us," he smiled, kissing her again.

"I bet he can get a bit much." She pulled him back, smacking her lips into his, and all at once, there was that feeling of heat they were both so familiar with. It radiating from their core, filtering through their bodies to the tips of their fingers.

"Shit, Logan, this teasing has got to end. I don't have the willpower anymore," he gasped, biting her lip.

"I know," she said breathlessly, pushing one leg between his to get that little bit nearer, "me neither."

He rubbed his hand up her thigh and over the curvature of her bottom, his fingers nimbly fingering the edge of her jeans. He could feel her tense as he left her mouth, nuzzling into her neck, goosebumps popping under his lips as he grabbed the hem of her top and yanked it over her head. She stood there in her bra, her chest heaving as he licked down to her cleavage. Moving, he turned her and laid her on her desk, her hair brushing some papers to the floor. Nudging her legs open, he bent down, her thighs coming up to hold him between them. They kissed and explored each other on the outside of their clothing, their muffled moans encouraging them to continue. Logan arched her back as his hand rubbed between her legs, and it was evident to Jorn that she wanted him, and yet his internal fight continued. He needed her, wanted to feel her intimately in his mouth; he wanted to caress, touch, lick her all over, but he was ashamed. Ashamed of what he was doing and why he was doing it. He, however, couldn't help himself; the feeling of sheer need was too overpowering. Her hand began to feel him through his trousers, and he groaned into her mouth.

"Shit, Logan!" he gasped, out of breath as she clamped him even harder to her.

"I know," she whispered, as his mouth slipped down her bra strap.

"I just want you." He stood back, looking down at her. Her hair fanned out on the desk, her chest heaving, the pulse in her neck throbbing—the scent of her seducing him.

"But this is not the way to do it?" she smiled, crunching her stomach muscles to sit up, her face tilted to look at him.

"No, it is not." She took her jumper, turning it the right way round before donning it and hiding herself from him.

He sighed, "I'm not sure how long I can wait, though," moving away from temptation, adjusting his jeans. "I don't think I'm going to be able to resist you much longer," he said, feeling as though he might just explode with pure need for her.

"Well, we'll have to. We have stuff to do," she laughed at his puppy eyes. "But after twelve. Who knows what will happen?"

Jorn was one of the last to arrive at the restaurant; he hadn't planned on being so late. He had just gone to pick up some bits for Logan's family and got waylaid. He was also getting more concerned about his feelings for her and that he seemed to be craving her. His task was to have her as putty in *his* hands, not the other way around. Yet, he couldn't help it. He desired her with every throb of his pulse, and having had another close encounter this morning, he needed to have more.

Whether coincidentally or not, Logan had strategically left the seat adjacent to her vacant, and he slipped into it swiftly, helping himself to the table wine, whilst she sat talking to Lexi. He was quite happy to sit and chat to a guy from finance with whom he'd had a few meetings over the past week. The guy was married, and Jorn hitched onto the concept of his family, the man droning on about his wife and kids, which allowed Jorn to look busy and interested, although all he kept doing was side-glancing at Logan. It was like she was a bright light to which his eyes were constantly drawn towards. She had changed from her jumper to a red halter-neck, and he couldn't help but congratulate himself on his purchase at the boutique. She was going to look exquisite on New Year's Eve, and even though, in the end, he would have to forgo her to The Emperor, he meant to spoil her.

"Hey, you okay?" Logan's face swam into view, and he realised that the guy from finance had gone, leaving him without anyone.

"Yes, of course." He tried to make his smile genuine, squashing his thoughts to the back of his mind. It seemed to have worked as she sat down, slipping off one of her shoes, and teased him with her foot up his jeans cuff. "You know, if you carry on doing that, I'm not going to be able to keep my hands to myself," he smirked, reining in his anger and reaching under the table for her knee, edging his hand up her thigh.

"I'm beginning to think that I don't care," she said, rubbing her lips together.

He leant forward and stroked the back of her hand, which was holding her wine glass. "Well, it is after twelve," he grinned playfully at her. "Do we really have to go through with this whole gathering?"

She threw her head back, laughing, "Well, I do as I'm the money."

Jorn sat there next to Logan, unable to do anything but listen and watch. He supposed he should have been well used to watching, but right now, all he wanted to do was touch. He slightly regretted not going any further this morning. The memory of her around him made him yearn even more for her, and it seemed to be making this whole office party so painfully slow. He just wanted Logan all to himself, and right now, it didn't seem he would get it. Even after the meal, when everyone was harmlessly tipsy and Jorn thought everything was drawing to a close, Lexi said,

"Hey Loge, we're going to the pub, coming?" He could tell by Lexi's poignant facial expression that she wanted Logan to go.

Logan, who wasn't any good at saying no, said, "Sure, let's." Lexi linked arms with her and led the way to the pub, stragglers from the office following.

"Looks like we've been shafted," Quinn said to Jorn, as they followed the girls.

"Yes, I might call it a night," Jorn said, slightly fed up.

"Nah, don't do that. Lexi just wants to spend a little bit of time with her friend before Christmas. Give them an hour."

Jorn didn't say anything.

"Look, I know you're one of The Gifted and a Hartvigsen, but are you all this hard to crack?" Jorn smiled at him.

"No, I'm especially hard. My brothers are perhaps better at socialising than I am."

"Well, that's a relief," Quinn joked, opening the door for him.

"You seem to know a lot about my kind, Quinn."

"No, not really, I just know about the Hartvigsens and their abilities. Your father is well known among us shifters, and has lived long in this city like my pack, so there have been run-ins. Perhaps not so much in former years. Is it true he recruits witches and vampires to do his dirty work?" Jorn scowled at him. A Gifted using vampires and witches was unheard of. However, Jorn neither confirmed nor denied this, so Quinn said, "I'm just cautious and curious about you, that's all. It's interesting to meet one of you. The stories I've heard from my grandfather about your family are elementary. I'd perhaps say you're infamous."

"What stories have you heard?" Jorn asked, catching up with the girls at the bar.

"Well, let's just say you are notorious for getting your own way, even if it means hurting, maiming and perhaps killing. And that your leader, The Emperor, is it? Is a narcissistic maniac."

Well, that was one way to describe The Emperor.

"You shouldn't listen to rumours, Quinn," Jorn said firmly.

"Hey, hey, I'm not saying I have, I'm just wondering, that's all. It's purely intrigue." He gave Lexi his bank card for his round, "I've always been an open-minded guy, and I like you, Jorn. You're not what I expected of a Gifted."

Jorn just raised his eyebrows.

"What are you two talking about?" Lexi came over, holding a bottle of wine in a cooler.

"Work," they both chimed together. It seemed that their lives, when in mortal company, were based upon lies.

"Hey," Logan squeezed in. Jorn's hand automatically went around her waist, and even though she glanced subtly about to see who was watching, she allowed it to stay there. Maybe coming here wasn't such a bad idea.

"HEY BRO!" There was a shout from over his head, and Jorn couldn't help but roll his eyes to the ceiling as all at his table looked over at the person who shouted.

"Arseholes," Jorn whispered to Logan under his breath as four of his five brothers descended on them.

With all the Hartvigsens under one roof. Tonight was going to be messy.

CHAPTER SEVENTEEN

THE NIGHT

Logan watched as Jorn's brothers threw their arms around his shoulders, accidentally knocking Lexi's drink over her top, making her shriek with hysteria. Logan knew she wouldn't be bothered; she'd already had quite a bit, and Lexi loved attention from anyone, particularly infamous men such as the Hartvigsens. Only Quinn seemed irritated and couldn't help but erupt a small growl from his throat, making Jorun and Kol smirk at each other. Seeing the looks between the men, Logan thought it was a good time for her to nip to the bathroom and test her theory on how drunk she was. It was a trial she had started as a teenager and now, to this day, still used to see if she was nearing her limit. She sat on the toilet, waiting to pee, holding her head in her hands and closing her eyes. If her head spun and she had a loud buzzing in her ears, that meant she'd reached her maximum alcohol intake and would most likely vomit or get a hangover. That was something she didn't want on Christmas Day; she was okay if she did it, and the buzzing was relatively low-key and didn't get a full-blown head spin. Well, the buzzing was there, but the head spin wasn't so much. She was safe for the time being.

"Loge, you in here?" Lexi knocked loudly on the cubicle door, making the lock rattle.

"Yeah." She sat a bit longer.

"What the hell is going on between you and Mr Hottie? He cannot keep his hands or eyes off you."

Logan smiled at the excitement in Lexi's voice. She hated being kept in the dark.

"Nothing really, why?"

"Don't you lie to me. I see him brushing your fingers when you hold a wine glass, stroking your inner thigh, and putting his arm around you with his fingertips under your waistband. I see it all, babe," she screeched, enthusiastically.

Logan flushed the toilet and opened the door, leaning into the frame. "Well, we've kissed a few times and had dinner." She left out what happened this morning.

"You've had dinner?" Lexi shrieked, making some girls who'd just entered the bathroom look daggers at her.

"Yes." Logan washed her hands and rubbed some moisturising cream in.

"Why didn't you tell me?" Lexi said, looking hurt. "I told you about me and Quinn."

"I know you did, and I didn't keep it from you

purposefully," she said, reapplying her lip gloss. "And I've been so busy that I've hardly seen you to tell you."

"Yes, but I had to hear it from Quinn that he thought something was going on between you two. I feel like such an idiot."

"Look, Lex, I've had a really hard week. And he's the fucking Sales Director, and I'm the Managing Director. We have to be professional." She looked at her friend. "You know I have to be professional about things."

"Temporary Managing Director," Lexi corrected her.

"Well... maybe not," Logan said, smirking.

"What the actual... he's offered you the job permanently?" Lexi whacked her friend on the arm, "I cannot believe you've been holding out on me about so much."

"You're the first person I have told. I haven't even told Mr Hottie," she said, biting her lip.

"Oh My God!" Lexi squeezed her tightly, "Will you promote me?"

"Look, I haven't accepted yet. I said I'd think about it over Christmas."

"Oh, Logan, this is amazing. I always knew you'd be good at running a company. I think you could take this one far. I have some great ideas. I think you could expand from kitchens and bathrooms to proper interior design. You know I'm good at that." Logan laughed at her friend.

"I'll see. I can't promise anything, but I agree. I do think I could maybe take it to the next level." She gritted her teeth apprehensively as Lexi grabbed her again, holding her arms against her side in another big hug.

"Wait for me whilst I wee," and she dived into the cubicle.

Whilst Lexi peed, Logan got her phone out. It was only 19:39. Scrolling to Jorn's number, she typed,

Shall we get out of here? Her hand wavered over the send button. Was she ready to leave? Could she? Was she prepared for the inevitable if she took him home? She had a reasonably early start tomorrow, and the company drinks money was spent, so her colleagues were on their own. They *could* leave.

"Ready?" Lexi asked, drying her hands.

"Yes, but Lex..."

"You're totally going home to have sex, aren't you?" Lexi crowed over her friend.

"No," she yelled, scandalised, "but I am going to call it a night. I'm off to mum's tomorrow, so I can't be out too late or get too drunk."

"Still on for Boxing Day?" Lexi and Logan always saw each other on Boxing Day to exchange presents and walk Lexi's family dog.

"Most definitely," Logan replied, kissing her on the cheek. "Merry Christmas, Lex. I love you, you know."

"Me too, babe. Can't believe you're going to be a proper

Managing Director!" Lexi squealed.

"Hey, no one knows," Logan cussed, trying to hush her friend, "so keep it under wraps for now."

"Okay."

When they returned, Lexi put her arms around Quinn, and the relief in his face was evident. Jorn's brothers were making him uncomfortable, especially with all the female attention they were getting.

"Logan!" Jorun waved her over, "Would you like a drink?" He indicated the bottle of whisky he had in his hands. Raising her eyebrows at him, she smiled, her phone buzzing in her pocket. It was Jorn,

Behind you.

She couldn't help but feel the heat inside her stomach at Jorn's message. Without turning, she reached past Jorun for her coat,

"I can't; I've got a busy day tomorrow. But knock yourself out."

She turned to find he was already in his coat and the scarf she remembered so vividly from the other Saturday. She absolutely desired him. Walking slowly past, she reached for his hand and pulled him subtly along. She didn't care about her work colleagues anymore. She was officially on holiday and could do whatever she wanted. Once outside, she took his face in her hands and kissed him. He tasted of whisky, his tongue loose in her mouth, circulating hers, his hands gentle on her back.

"Let's get a taxi," she said.

The ride home was a blur to Logan. She didn't think she'd ever kissed anyone for that length of time without stopping in her life. The taxi driver must have felt severely uncomfortable, but she'd never desired anyone so harshly, and she wasn't about to stop.

"Keep the change," Jorn said, handing the cabbie a twenty-pound note as he clambered out.

"So, fancy a nightcap?" she giggled, opening her gate. "I've always wanted to say that to someone." She turned, looking at him smile. "Why do they always say that in films? It's such a stupid line, they'd be much better saying, fancy coming in for some fumbling?" Jorn laughed at her, "It would be so much more honest, would it not?" She opened the back door, the heat from the house hitting her cold cheeks.

"Yes, but it is a little bit presumptuous," he said thoughtfully. "Maybe they say it for suspense purposes."

"Are you saying you don't want to come in for a nightcap?" Logan teased, opening her top cupboard, and even though it wasn't really a drink they were after, she got out a bottle of brandy. Pouring them both a generous measure, she handed him the drink. "Hmmm, I love the smell of brandy; it's so Christmassy," she said, sipping it, "jeez, it does sting your throat." She coughed slightly before having another taste. Jorn just watched her leaning into the kitchen worktop, "Come here." She put her glass down and waited until he was in front of her.

Lifting her arms, she untangled him from his scarf and

begun undoing his coat, before slipping it off his shoulders and flinging it onto one of her high-rise chairs. Jorn ran his fingers through her hair before reaching for the knot behind her head, allowing the halter-neck to fall forward. Edging around the bottom seam, he lifted it up over her head. She stood there in a red and black strapless bra, her chest heaving in anticipation, her fingers slipping as she removed his t-shirt, revealing bronzed skin and a small patch of curly chest hair, which she immediately scraped her nails through, the softness making her tingle all over. His lips were on her neck, she ran her hand around the rim of his jeans, and he grabbed her and sat her on the worktop, parting her legs to facilitate him. He flicked the clasp on her bra, and it tumbled to her lap, her sigh of ecstasy at her breasts release enthralling him. Taking a small step back, he looked at her, his eyes revolving over her body, her lips smiling playfully at him.

Getting down from the worktop, she took his hand and led him upstairs to her room, where she lay on the bed, waiting for him. Falling onto her, her legs swiftly came up around his hips, her heels digging into the bed sheets. They lay kissing for a while, his mouth occasionally moving to her breasts, his hands teasing at the button of her jeans.

"Jorn?" Logan said, shifting her head slightly to look up at him.

"Yeah?"

"How'd you feel about not going to that final stage tonight?"

His eyes widened slightly, but he had expected Logan to

shy away from him once at home. Once she'd got her head back in the game, the need to be in control took over.

"Well, you did only ask me in for fumbling. The final stage can wait." He smiled, moving his lips to hers again, her heeled feet crossing around his back.

"It's not that I don't want to," she gasped, as he licked her nipple.

"I know that," he said, moving down to her belly button and noticing a small jewel glinting there for the first time.

Standing up, he kicked off his shoes and socks before undoing her heels, allowing them to slip from her ankles. She stood up against him, her hands popping his jeans buttons before shimmying him out of them. Pushing his shoulders down so he was sitting on the edge of the bed, her zip now at eye level, she begun to undo it, his hands coming up to take over, removing her trousers so he could have a perfect view of the satin she was wearing.

"God, you're beautiful!" Jorn exclaimed, pulling her onto him, her legs on either side of him, their underwear now the only barrier between them. She smiled as she lowered herself to him, their lips slow at first, tasting each other, teasing, savouring every moment.

"Have you had many lovers?" Logan asked, brushing a loose strand of hair around her ear.

Jorn laughed, grabbing and flipping her over, this time with him in control.

"What kind of question is that?" he asked, his hand slowly

moving up her thigh.

"It's just a question," she smiled, running her fingers down his spine, watching goosebumps appear on his skin.

"Well, in all honesty, I've had many, but none for a while. Just can't seem to find the right woman."

She laughed again, pushing him up and over so she was back in control.

"What, until you met me?" she joked.

"Why, of course," he said, propping himself on his elbows as she tilted back, her fingers running through the curls on his chest.

"Shit, running my fingers through your chest hair makes me shiver," she said, biting her lip like he'd seen her do many times before.

"Don't do that," he moaned, flopping back on the bed.

"What run my fingers through..."

"No," he said, pulling her to him, "bite your lip like that." And he grabbed her again, rolling onto her.

"Why not?" she giggled, as he raised her leg, his mouth on her inner thigh.

"Because it makes me want to destroy your virtue."

Biting her lip again, she said, "Well, I think I like the sound of that."

"Believe me, it's on my to-do list."

Logan was lost to Jorn in her bed; his care and attention were unprecedented, and his large, warm hands did things she didn't think possible. She'd had men before, shared their bed and enjoyed it, but with him, it was different. In the past, she'd always felt restricted by her own inhibitions, by her own body, and yet, Jorn didn't make her feel vulnerable or overly exposed. In fact, she smiled to herself at her own daring and realised that it wasn't her that had changed, but that it was him. He made her feel relaxed and carefree. They would laugh and smile at each other. When Jorn accidentally threw her hard on the bed, and she slipped off it, he grabbed her in a fireman's lift to rescue her from metaphorical carpet sharks.

She sighed in gratification, turning his face to hers and kissing him. "Hmmm, you taste of me," she grinned, feeling the heat flush in her cheeks.

"And you tasted amazing," he said, adjusting himself so she was more comfortable.

"I highly doubt that it ever tastes great down there, but I'll take the compliment," she said, honestly.

"You'd be surprised. I think men taste women differently than you think."

Smiling, she moved off the bed and went to the bathroom to wipe down her legs and ensure her make-up wasn't completely ruined, before flittering down the stairs and returning with their brandies.

He was on his phone when she handed him his.

"What's the time?"

He laughed, "Only nine-fifty."

"I'm kind of glad it's not late, means I won't feel like death tomorrow." She clambered into the bed next to him, sipping her drink.

"Do you really think I'm going to let you sleep much tonight?" he asked, shutting down his phone and draining his glass.

"I hope not," she said, as he tipped her glass into her mouth, so she had no choice but to finish it.

"Well, perhaps I'll let you have a few hours. Can't have you being worn out for games night."

CHAPTER EIGHTEEN

THE DAY

As he always did, Jorn woke at the crack of dawn when the night was still upon him and before his alarm was set to go off. Logan had rolled away from him during the night and had her back to him, her black hair fanned out behind her, the duvet having slipped and showing him the curve of her hip and the base of her spine. He reached out and touched her, just to make sure she was real. They'd had more intimacies throughout the night but never reached that ultimate stage. Logan had her reasons, of course she did, and he would never think it was because of him that she steadied his hand and asked to take it slowly. They'd been seeing each other for only a week, and she was not easily persuaded to forgo her virtue totally to anyone. She'd been with a few lovers that he knew of, and she'd always taken her time with them. He had to marvel at her willpower; he never said no to anyone, but overall, he was a guy who hadn't had relationships. He'd had women, yes, but nothing that was as intense or seemed as meaningful as what he had with the woman lying next to him. She seemed to thoroughly enjoy oral sex, which was surprising, most women he'd encountered never seemed to like it that much. Yet she seemed to revel in it and wanted him in her mouth, which he would never complain about.

Propping himself on his arm, he turned to look up at the ceiling, thinking about New Year's Eve. Maybe they could just run away together. He had acquaintances worldwide that would house them for a while. His cousin Lachlan, in Scotland, had a plane Jorn knew he'd charter for him if needed, as he could never use his own without The Emperor knowing. But how would he explain to her that they had to go into hiding, or the fact that he wasn't entirely human or the fact that his uncle was The Gifted leader of the supernatural world? Or the fact that he wasn't his passport age of thirty-six, but over three hundred years old? This was why the mortal and immortal should never mix. There were too many variables, too many factors, too many questions. Even if The Emperor didn't kill her and they were able to continue their relationship, she would grow old, and he wouldn't, and that he couldn't bear. Not the fact that she would grow old, but the fact he wouldn't and in the end, he would have to watch her die anyway. It had been so wrong of his Master to ask this of him, so utterly immoral that Jorn couldn't believe that he had agreed to it. Though he supposed when his Master had requested it of him, he hadn't been so closely involved with the subject, and now he felt like the biggest arsehole in existence. Even worse than that. There were no words to describe what he was. He thought of what secrets he could hold over his Master and wondered if they would be enough for him to change his mind, but even if they were, The Emperor would never alter his plans for a nephew, no matter the cost.

Logan started to stir next to him, and he couldn't help but smile as she stretched.

"Shit." She sat bolt upright, allowing the duvet to slip further off her. "What day is it?"

"Hey." He sat up to her, his hands on her shoulders, "It's Christmas Day."

She sighed heavily, "Jeez, I thought I'd forgotten to set my alarm." She flopped back down again before looking at him. "Morning." He grinned at her, "Is it time to get up?"

"No, it's only a little after six."

"Damn my body clock." She tugged the duvet up to her breasts before rolling over and laying her arm over his chest, playing with his chest hair.

"What is it about chest hair?" he laughed, stroking her arm.

"I have absolutely no idea, I just love it." She purred contentedly before reaching around, taking her phone and setting her alarm for nine. "Just a few more hours."

Jorn woke with a jolt and, for a moment, wondered where he was. He could hear running water and a radio playing softly. Turning, he noticed that Logan wasn't in the bed, but from the sounds coming from her bathroom, she was in the shower. Feeling suddenly awake, he walked to the bathroom; she smiled as she heard him enter, his hand coming to rest on the sponge she was using to rub soap suds over herself. She stood as he washed her skin, caressing her thighs and hips, moving around her front to her abdomen and breasts. She fell back into him, her hand around his neck as the sponge brushed over her nipples and up her arms. Rinsing it in the water, he wiped off the foam, their mouths finding each other's, their hands touching, their fingers slipping along one another's skin in the water. Turning, she took the cloth and added more gel to it before rubbing it over his shoulders, down his torso and between his legs. Their kisses became more frantic, and soon they were pleasuring one another, their moans of sheer bliss echoing throughout the bathroom, the steam from the water billowing up to the overhead spotlights, steaming up the full-length mirror.

"So, what time does your mum want me over?" he asked, as he slipped his jeans on.

"Any time you like, you've got the address, right?"

"Yes, you gave it to me on Monday," he smirked.

"I don't know, about twoish? Mum always has dinner done for about three," Logan said, putting on some eyeshadow.

"Okay, and are they red or white wine drinkers, or both, or beer?"

"Jorn?" She put her hand on his arm, "Are you nervous?"

"Any man would be silly not to be a little nervous at meeting his, well... what are you... girlfriend? Boss? Lover's family?"

She giggled, "Well, I think it's a good thing you're nervous. It means you care."

"Absolutely, I care."

Jorn ran up the staircase four at a time when he got home. He wanted to be happy today, and he wanted to enjoy this Christmas. He wanted it to be special. He wouldn't let anything upset him. As he showered again, this time with soap that didn't smell of sweets, he contemplated whether he should shave. Just take it all off. But as he looked in the mirror after washing, he decided against it; she seemed to have a thing about hair, so he left it.

"Why is it always my room you all come to?" he asked, putting on some cologne as he heard his chamber door bang open.

"Because you're the only one who has a life at the moment, so it's the only way we'll get to see you," Kol said, sitting on the back of the sofa.

Unable to think of anything in reply, he sat on the chair, tying up his boots, slipping the cuffs of his jeans over the top.

"Merry Christmas, big bro," Kol said, chucking him a small square package. "This will go with your outfit nicely."

Jorn unwrapped the parcel to find a Holzhern watch.

"Thanks, little bro." He ruffled Kol's hair, putting it on his wrist.

"Now, can I have your Rolex?" Kol asked, going into Jorn's drawers.

"You've got your own Rolex," Jorn replied.

"Here." He got up and threw a slightly smaller gift at Randin, who had just walked in. "It's not much, but I know you need them."

Randin smiled, opening the packet to a pair of new-generation wireless earbuds.

"You see, everything, don't you?" Randin said, admiring his brother. Jorn just nodded, putting his wallet in his back pocket.

"What did he see? What happened to the other pair?" Oska asked, lounging on Jorn's newly vacated computer chair.

"He forgot he had them in and showered the other day," Jorn laughed, putting his coat on.

"You idiot," Lamont said, smiling at his elder brother.

"Didn't you put them in rice?" Kol asked, looking at his own wrist at an Apple watch, forgetting about the Rolex.

"That only works so much," Randin said. "You off out again, Jorn?"

"Yes, to Christmas dinner," he said.

"Be careful, won't you," Randin said, his hand on his brother's shoulder.

"What do you mean?"

"What I mean is." He steeled himself before he said, "You know this relationship cannot go anywhere."

"Thanks, Randin. Just for one day, I wanted to feel it

could." Jorn walked out of the room, ignoring his brothers. He knew Randin meant well. He always did. But today, he could have done without hearing the truth out loud.

After taking a few bottles of wine from the cellar, he jumped in his car and floored it out the driveway, his boot laden with presents. He had gone a little over the top with gifts for Logan's family, but he wanted to make a good impression and, above all, he just couldn't help himself. As he drove through the country lanes, he glimpsed the large houses set far back from the road. Each house was different and with an array of Christmas lights on. Some were dangling from gables, some had reindeer on the flat roofs of porches, some had twinkling fairy lights right to the top of conifer trees, and Jorn wondered how on earth the owners got them up there. Outside Logan's parents' house, the bare apple trees had large silver and red baubles hanging from the branches, each twisting in the cool breeze. The porch was adorned with crystal white lights and a large homemade wreath on the door. He had just popped the boot when the front door opened, and Logan stood there,

"Nice slippers," he called, looking at the new fluffy slip-ons she had on her feet.

"Thanks, they're from my mum," she said, turning to the side to show him. "Hang on, I'll come and help you." Reappearing in pumps, she walked to Jorn's car, leaning into the boot, "Jeez! Is this all for us?"

"Yeah, I kind of overdid it," he said, sitting on the rim of the boot, pulling her into him.

"Don't, my dad will see," she said, laughing as he slipped

his hand down the back of her trousers.

"Can't help it," he said, kissing her.

"I thought you might not come," she said, inhaling his scent.

"Why would I not?"

She was embarrassed momentarily and suddenly wished she'd gone all the way with him this morning.

"Because I'm making you wait." She studied his eyes to see if there was any misgiving to them when he answered.

"Logan, listen. I like you, and I'm not about to rush you if it's not what you want. I'm happy to carry on as we are." He pushed a lock of hair around her ear, "As a matter of fact, I like it." He smiled, moving into her lips again.

"Hey, you two get a room!" her sister, Tyler, called from the front porch, her hands holding some cutlery.

Logan flipped her the bird and smiled at Jorn, "We'd best go in."

"Here, you take these," he said, handing her the wine holdall. "I'll get the rest."

Jorn walked slowly towards the front door, the pebble driveway crunching under his heavy footfalls, his stomach slightly anxious. Like most immortals, even The Gifted had to be invited into a mortal's home, and he couldn't help but hope he wasn't left like an idiot on the doorstep. To waste time, he stood a while, inhaling the scents of the house. It was rich with the smells of nutmeg and orange, the scents he associated with Christmas. He could see the heat haze shimmering above the radiators, and the laughter coming from the kitchen made his heart swell with pleasure. Banging his boots on the door frame with the pretence of shaking off any excess water on them, he wondered if he should take them off, killing more time in the hope that someone might come and invite him in.

"Don't worry about your shoes," a voice said, coming from the hallway. "I tried instigating that into my family many years ago, but it went out the window like most things do when your kids are young." A slender woman stood in front of him, her hair as dark as Logan's, her skin the bronze of summer sun and her eyes, though like her daughters, were slightly more orange. "You must be Jorn." She held out her hand to him, "I'm August, Logan's mum." Shifting the hamper he was holding, he took her hand in his, feeling the warmth only a mother could have. "Come in." She stood to the side, and with relief in his heart, Jorn crossed the threshold of Logan's family home.

"Er... this is for you. Merry Christmas," he said, indicating the hamper.

"Oh, you didn't need to do that, but thank you all the same. Merry Christmas to you, too. Come through to the kitchen; that's where all the fun is." She rolled her eyes, laughing.

"Thank you." He followed her along the hallway.

By the time Jorn got to the kitchen and was introduced to her family, he felt he already knew them. Many photographs lined the walls, all at different stages of the family's life together. The birth of babies, the walking of toddlers, the first day at school and school photos. Family holidays, picnics, birthdays, and other Christmases. He saw pottery done by children whose paintwork was faded by years of sitting on a windowsill. He saw trinkets brought home from abroad, shoes waiting to go to bedrooms on the stairs, coats on the bannister, and despite Logan's mum's assurances of 'shoes allowed', he saw discarded trainers and boots, most likely swapped for slippers.

The kitchen was indeed where the fun was. Jorn could see Logan's father carving a roasted turkey, her sister decanting vegetables into a pot for the table and her fiancé mashing potatoes. Logan was pouring champagne into red flutes, her hair pulled to one side, her cheeks flushed with the heat of the room and a little smirk on her lips. She knew he was watching her, and he enjoyed the notion that she, too, was thinking about their night together.

"Jorn?" Logan's father held his hand out to him, and for a moment, he was distracted from his thoughts.

"Yes, sir."

"I'm Ben." Logan's father was a reasonably tall man with a slightly receding hairline and a full beard. He wore glasses that had slipped to the end of his nose in the warm kitchen, behind which sat ocean-blue eyes, such a contrast to Logan's that Jorn was surprised they were related at all. It seemed that she had gotten all her attributes from her mother. "Nice of you to join us on this Christmas Day."

"The pleasure is all mine, sir. We don't really celebrate Christmas in my house," Jorn said, catching Logan's eye and smiling.

"Yes, Logan said," Ben stated, handing his wife the cut turkey. "Well, I hope you like food, August insists every year she won't do as much as the last, but she always seems to manage it." He grinned at his wife's scowl.

"Well, I haven't had any breakfast, so I'll try to eat as much of it as I can," Jorn replied.

"Good man," Ben said, getting the gravy boat out. "Any good at making gravy?"

"I can give it a try," Jorn laughed.

"It's easy, you just tip in some granules and add hot water," Ben said with an eye roll.

"I can do that," Jorn said, moving in to help. "I was always taught to make it with the meat juices and flour.

"My kids would never use it as it looked too pale, so we just do granules now," August said, laughing.

"Then they don't know what they're missing," Jorn agreed, tipping in the granules.

"Jorn does quite a bit of cooking, I think, Dad," Logan said, coming to Jorn's rescue and taking the granules from his hand.

"Really?" her dad said sceptically.

"Well, since my mother passed, my father became a bit of a recluse when it came to the kitchen, so my brothers and I were taught to cook by our housekeeper," Jorn said, accepting the champagne August offered him.

A slight awkwardness settled over the group, and Logan's dad, feeling he'd stumbled onto a delicate subject, vacated for the dining room.

"Sorry about him," Logan said, using the leftover stock to mix the gravy granules.

"What? He's fine. They don't need to feel awkward. My family's just nonconformist." Jorn smiled, sipping his drink. Like Jorun, he'd never really been one for champagne, but he would never have turned it down.

"Wait until he's seen the wine you've brought," Logan grinned, knowing her dad's affiliation with wine.

"It was chosen specially," he said, winking at her, rubbing his hand over her hip.

"Goodness me," a shout hollered from the dining room, "Querciabella 2003. That's expensive wine, that is." Logan beamed stupidly at Jorn.

"See." She laughed, took his hand and led him to the dining room.

"Did you bring this, Jorn?" her father asked, his glasses on the end of his nose again to read the back label.

"Yes, sir, my father has an extensive wine cellar, and that is one of my favourites."

"It's an extremely good wine," he enthused, his eyebrows raised, "he knows a lot about wines?"

"He likes to think he's a bit of a connoisseur, but most of the time, I'm sure people just tell him what's good." Jorn shrugged, not wanting to talk about his father.

"I remember this one at that wine-tasting session you got me for my birthday, Tyler."

"Well, we have plenty, so if you ever want any, please just ask," Jorn said, sitting in the chair Logan indicated. "Although my father always says you should open it to let it breathe for an hour before drinking."

"Yes, he is correct, Ethan, grab the bottle opener, please." Ethan dutifully left the room.

"I would have liked a wine cellar, but August said they were old-fashioned when we moved here, so we turned it into a playroom for the kids, though, of course, now it's a den for gaming and late-night television," Ben said, the look of envy in his eyes.

"Well, dear, you can change it back now if you wish; the girls left years ago," August said in her defence.

"Oh really?" Ben said, smiling at her.

August sighed heavily, "You can do what you like, dear," she said with scepticism.

"Can I?" Ben said, a smirk playing on his lips.

"Dad, stop winding her up," Logan said, sitting down next to Jorn, her hand going to his thigh, the feeling of need filtering up his leg. "Just ignore him."

Smiling at her, he put his arm across the back of her chair, and his fingers intermittently brushed her shoulder throughout the meal. The shiver of lust began to creep up her neck, and she was glad when the main meal finished so she could vacate to the kitchen to help clear up. Jorn sat at the table trying to make small talk with Ethan and Ben; he'd always found making conversation difficult. He had never been a talker, as his ability was to watch, and that was usually a silent affair. As Ethan and Ben began talking about the forthcoming wedding in April, Jorn busied himself by drinking the wine they had now started and savoured every sip. He might hate his Master at the moment, but he knew his wines and the Querciabella was going down well. He'd already elected Kol and Jorun to come and pick him up later so he could drink, and one of them could bring his car back. He knew Logan always stayed at her parents on Christmas Day, so he knew he'd be alone tonight, and that was something he was dreading. Not only would he be alone, but there were no cameras at her parents' house, so he wouldn't be able to watch her.

"You alright?" Logan sidled up to him, sinking into her chair, her body turned.

"Of course, just full, that's all."

"Well, I hope you've saved space for dessert, as my mum's Christmas pudding is to die for." She laughed, finishing her champagne.

"I'm sure I could fit a bit in," he said, his face moving to hers, their lips almost touching.

"Hey, hey, none of that at the table," Ben said, making Logan jump.

"Dad?" she turned to him, his face full of amusement.

"Sorry, I couldn't help it." He accepted the Christmas pudding August gave him, helping himself to the cream.

"Just ignore my husband, Jorn, if you want to kiss my daughter at the table, you go ahead. It's nice to see her happy."

"Oh my God! You lot are so embarrassing!" Logan exclaimed, her face blushing.

"Now you're feeling my pain of four years, Loge," Tyler said, laughing.

"Yes, Jorn, what are your intentions towards my daughter?" Ben asked, setting his glass down and looking seriously at him.

"What the F, Dad?" Logan hung her head in dismay.

But Jorn, being a man of years, just looked at her and then looked at her father, "Purely honourable, sir."

The table was quiet for a moment, everyone looking at Jorn for a second before moving on to Logan's father, waiting for his verdict on the reply. "You cannot say fairer than that," he said, smiling.

"Let's just eat the pudding before you make Jorn run from the house," August said, sitting down.

"I think it would take Jorn a lot more than dad to scare him off," Tyler said, spooning cream straight from the jug into her mouth.

"No, but your table manners might," August scolded.

The meal continued, and there were no further questions

to Jorn about his intentions for Logan, and he was relieved about it. Not only because he didn't have the answers, but also because he knew he couldn't have any. Logan was just a plaything for his uncle, and soon, she would be handed over to him like a lamb to slaughter, and Jorn hated himself for it. How could he be sitting here, making niceties with her family, celebrating Christmas, with all this hanging over his head? Randin had been right to warn him. He was in too deep; he was getting too attached, and there was nothing he could do to stop himself from falling further and further into the hole he was digging. He just couldn't seem to resist her. Even at the dinner table, even in front of her father, he couldn't help but imagine her naked and on him. On so many levels, it was wrong to imagine what he was seeing, but he couldn't help his mind.

"So, Jorn, Logan tells us that you've just started working for Kelly's?" Ben asked, topping up their wines as the women began to clear away the used bowls, and August brought in some after-dinner mints.

"Yes, sir," he replied, feeling flushed in the chest at his previous thoughts.

"Have you done this sort of work before?"

Jorn chatted with her dad about his previous jobs. He was well-practised at making up stories about his life. Once he got going, he was on a roll explaining about the interview he had with Mr Kelly, about how he was used to being in marketing, and Mr Kelly said that after his brother retired, Jorn could be a good fit for the position.

"Yes, Mr. Kelly did say he might amalgamate the roles if

he felt I was up to the challenge," Jorn nodded, suppressing a burp. He really had overeaten.

"And are you?"

"I think so. I think Kelly's has a lot of potential," Jorn said, in all honesty.

"And Logan must have told you already, she told us this morning, that he's asked her to stay on as Managing Director in the spring."

"Er... no, she hasn't, but I think he would do himself a favour by asking her to stay on. I believe she is an asset to the company, and this week, she has proved herself to him by taking on the role easily." He looked up at her as she came in from the kitchen, "Why didn't you tell me Adrian has offered you the Managing Director role in the spring?" He wasn't accusatory, in fact, he sounded proud.

"Oh, it was the day I went to see him, I meant to tell you. It was when Jorun was in your office, and I started telling him and then realised it wasn't you, so stopped and then never really thought about it again." She sat, helping herself to a mint chocolate, "I said I'd think about it over the Christmas break."

"And are you thinking about it?" Jorn asked, nodding to Ben to pour him the wine he was offering.

"Well, I'm not sure. It's a great opportunity, though."

"Logan, you must accept his offer, you'd be perfect for the role," Jorn said, encouraging her. "You'd be foolish to turn it down."

"Yeah, I know, but it's a big change from just acting up to actually being Managing Director."

"No, it's no different. You are ideally placed to take the post. You already know the company and the staff. He couldn't have picked a more ideal candidate."

"You think so?" she asked, stroking his leg again, her affection for him growing at his sincerity.

"Most definitely. I think you could take the firm far, perhaps internationally. You have the correct mindset for it, and you know you'll have the backing of all your colleagues."

"Yes, Lexi said something similar," Logan said, moving her chair closer to his.

"And she would be right," Jorn said. "Believe me, I've worked for some companies and left, as they had the same boring old-tired men in charge. Young blood is what a company like Kelly's needs."

Logan looked at her dad, who was sitting back in his seat, his eyes squinting at Jorn,

"Dad?" Logan questioned.

"See Logan, this is what your mum and I said to each other earlier. You'd be a fool to turn this down. Jorn is right. You're right for the job, you have the experience, and you'd be good for the people who work there."

"Absolutely," Jorn agreed. "You have the right character, you're strong, patient, extremely proactive and well organised," he squeezed her thigh, "not to mention dedicated."

"Wow, Jorn! That's quite a character reference," August said, hiccupping, making him smile.

"It's the truth," he shrugged. "And I've only known her less than two weeks."

"I still have a week or so to decide," Logan said, resting her head on his shoulder, his arm coming around her waist, feeling the curve of her hip.

"You should preliminarily accept him and then negotiate terms in the New Year," Jorn said, nodding. "If you hate it, you can always step down."

Jorn had no idea why he was encouraging her to take the job; he knew it was folly. She wouldn't be at the company in January, and he inwardly cursed himself for even discussing it.

CHAPTER NINETEEN

THE WALK

Logan tossed and turned that night at her parents. The single bed was uncomfortable and lonely, and for the first time, she hated it. It was tradition for her and her sister, Tyler, to sleep over Christmas night, yet now that Tyler had Ethan, her experience of sleeping there was not the same. Even though she'd only had one night with Jorn, she craved his closeness and touch. He'd stayed late into the evening, participated in a board game of her mother's choosing and played a few rounds of poker, with Ethan and her father, using nuts as chips. Her dad had got quite inebriated on the wine, so in the end her mum had put the TV on, sending him to sleep, allowing her and Jorn to have a bit of breathing space before his brothers came. Jorun and Kol were polite when they arrived, none of the loudmouth taunts she'd seen at the pub on Christmas Eve, and she bet it was because Jorn had told them to behave. Her mum had invited them in, and they'd stayed for an hour drinking tea and charming her.

She clicked her phone. 03.24. Turning, she opened her drawer and pulled out the earrings Jorn had bought her. She'd felt terrible when he got her present out of his pocket, as she had not bought him anything. Holding one of the earrings up to the shining moon coming in through her skylight, she allowed the green jewel that dangled from the intricate chain-linked silver to glint. They were beautiful. She would wear them on New Year's Eve. If she couldn't afford a new dress, at least the earrings would make her feel special.

"Merry Christmas, Logan." Lexi's mum called from the front room as Lexi opened the door to her the next day. Lexi's parents lived a stone's throw from Logan's mum and dad, and it had always been tradition with the girls to meet up on Boxing Day.

"Merry Christmas, Kate," Logan called, not wanting to enter as she was wearing wellies.

"You'll come in for a mulled wine when you're done?"

"Thank you, that sounds great. Hello, Nirvana." Lexi's dog came bounding out, his lead attached, licking Logan's face.

"Nirvana, down," Lexi's dad came out to grab him. "Have a good Christmas, Logan?"

"Yes, thank you, what about you?"

"Oh well, it's the same every year. Ate and drank too much."

"That's a sign of a good Christmas, I think," Logan said, smiling.

"Right, come on, let's go. Bye, Dad." Lexi kissed him, and they left for the fields beyond the village.

Logan was quiet at the start, allowing Lexi to jabber on about her and Quinn, how her parents had argued over the evening games they were to play, and how her younger brother had got her a voucher for some online shop Logan had never heard of. Once beyond the houses, Lexi allowed Nirvana off the lead, and he ran off chasing the scent of some animal.

"So...?" Logan just looked at her.

"So what?" Logan smirked, knowing what she was getting at.

"So, did you and Mr Hottie get it on after the Christmas party?" Logan just looked at her friend. "You did, didn't you?" Logan shook her head. "You didn't? What... why?" Lexi stopped to look at her head on.

"I don't know, Lex, we just didn't," Logan said, looking hopelessly at her friend.

"You telling me you did nothing? No kissing or anything?"

"Oh God no, we did stuff, and he stayed over, but not... you know, the final stage." Lexi looked exasperated at her bestie.

"And why not?" Lexi knew precisely why.

"Because I said I wasn't ready," Logan replied, feeling ridiculous.

Lexi tutted, "What are you like, Loge?" Logan hid her face

momentarily. "So, how'd he take it?" she asked, whistling for Nirvana, who was over the other side of the field.

"Like you'd expect," Logan grimaced, "as a gentleman. He basically said that when I was ready, I was to let him know and that he was quite happy with the other stuff." She slapped her forehead, "I'm such an idiot."

"Well..." Lexi surmised, "... Loge, if I'm honest, I think it's a good thing you didn't just jump right in there. In a way, I wish Quinn and I hadn't. Not that sex with him isn't great or anything. It's just, I don't know. I just wish I'd waited."

"What's this? Are you telling me that you might be falling for him?" Logan pushed her friend, but Lexi gave as good as she got and pushed her back.

"Maybe. He's sweet and funny and great in bed. He's so attentive and has such loyalty I've never seen, particularly when his family is involved. I never thought that a younger guy could satisfy my appetite, but he really can. I don't know," she shrugged. "I guess I just like him a lot, and it is starting to frighten me."

Logan couldn't believe it; after her friend had gone so off the rails after her marriage breakdown, declaring she would never love again or spend more than a few nights with a man, here she was now, almost saying that she was in love with her work colleague. Logan couldn't help but smile at the irony. You can spend years looking for a partner, a soul mate, a husband, and yet you'd been working with them the whole time.

"So, you think I did the right thing?" Logan asked, carrying on the previous conversation, "Waiting?"

"Yes, definitely, if he's willing to give you the space and time you need, then it's worth it," Lexi enthused. "He'll definitely be worth it."

Logan grinned. She had thought this walk with Lexi would be Lexi having a go at her or laughing at how much of a prude she was, but it seemed she had matured, and Logan should have given her more credit.

"So, did Quinn get you anything for Christmas?" Logan asked, feeling a guilty pang in her stomach.

"You see, this is where he is sweet and attentive. When we were out last week for dinner, we passed the boutique down the alley, you know the one with the headless mannequins in the window."

Logan knew the store; she'd often longed for a garment from that shop.

"Well, I said, just in passing, that I liked this necklace in there, and voilà, here it is." She opened her coat and showed Logan the jewellery. It was a hammered rose gold bar hanging from a delicate chain, the bar easily lost in her cleavage, which Logan was sure Quinn would love.

Logan fingered the jewel, "Wow, that's beautiful, Lex."

"Ah ha." She slipped it back under her top and did up her coat. "What about Jorn? Did he get you anything?"

Logan told her about the earrings and how she disastrously hadn't got him anything, so she thought she might buy him something to wear on New Year's Eve to go with his outfit for the ball. But what could she get him because he likely had everything? When Lexi offered no ideas, they both carried on talking about the ball and what Logan should wear. Lexi promised to look through her own wardrobe to see if she could find something to fit her, though she wasn't optimistic. She'd never been to a real ball before, either.

"So, you'll get to meet his father," Lexi said, keeping an eye on Nirvana.

"Yes, and I'm so nervous about that, too. What happens if the press is there, or OK! magazine and I must have my photo taken?" she said, through gritted teeth.

Lexi looked at her, "Well, I'd love to have my photo in one of those mags, but joking aside, I don't think the press will be there, Loge. Even though the Hartvigsens are well known, they don't advertise the fact in public often. You should just be yourself and worry about what Jorn's bedroom is like. Because I bet he has every mod con going." Trust Lexi to think of things like that.

"And it's not just that, Lex, his dad sounds scary, and his dad's girlfriend... sheesh!" Logan grimaced, "You remember that woman in the red coat when we were waiting for the taxi that night we went out, you know, the other Saturday?"

Lexi looked at her quizzically, "What woman?" Logan couldn't believe Lexi hadn't noticed her; her coat had been so vibrant that no one could have missed her.

"You know the woman that approached Jorn as he had a cigarette." Logan suddenly stopped. She'd not seen him have a cigarette the entire time they'd been out together, not at dinner last Friday or at her parents, or even popped out for one at work. Did he actually smoke?

"I'm sorry, Loge, I don't remember her," Lexi said honestly.

"She had her hands all over him, and he told me that she was his dad's girlfriend; her name is even on the invitation."

"And your point is?" Lexi questioned.

"I don't know. There's just something weird about the whole scenario. His dad's girlfriend touching up one of his sons, and Jorn's obvious hostility towards him." She held her hands up. "He came into work the other day with bruises to his face that hadn't been there the day before, and it was yellowing, meaning it must have been there for some time. He said it was his brothers, but from what I've seen of them together, they're so tight that I think it was possibly his dad, and what black eye heals that well overnight?"

Lexi gasped, "Well, I agree that is weird. Maybe you just missed it the day before," Logan looked sceptically at her, "and I also agree that he and his brothers seem very tight. They're more like best mates than brothers from what I saw at the pub on Christmas Eve."

"Exactly," Logan frowned. "Oh, I don't know, the way he talks about his dad, it's like he's not really his dad. More like a boss, or dictator or..." she sighed. "Maybe I'm reading too much into it. There's definitely no love between them, and I know that upsets Jorn, although he won't talk about it," Logan said, squelching through some mud. "I mean, his family haven't celebrated Christmas since they lost their mum, and that was maybe over ten years ago. Oh, hell! I don't know!" she sighed again. "And another thing, he always refers to his dad as father, it's never dad or even pappa, like they would use in Norway. It's always father. When he spoke of his mother at dinner on Friday, he called her mamma, but it's never pappa, and I just find that weird. Father is so old-fashioned. It's like if he used the word pappa it would show too much affection. Oh shit! I haven't got a clue what I'm going on about. Maybe I just find it hard to believe that a dad could have six sons and not give them the time of day, or maybe I am just reading too much into it. But it just feels so wrong."

"Have you talked to Jorn about it?" Lexi asked, turning to start the walk back.

"No way. Who am I to get involved? I've only known him like five minutes. I don't want to alienate him completely."

"Do you really think his dad could be beating him? I mean, look at him, he's pretty well structured," Lexi speculated.

"Yes, I agree, but it doesn't stop me worrying or showing concern," she said, exasperatedly. "And I'm worried about New Year's Eve. What if I don't make a good impression, or his dad doesn't like me, or I drink too much?"

"Logan, Logan." Lexi put her hand on Logan's arm. "You're being silly. Perhaps you *are* reading too much into this, or you're seeing things that aren't really there."

"Yeah, maybe. I just feel there's something, some secret family thing, that he's keeping from me. Don't ask me why or how I feel it, I just do, and I know its roots are with his dad."

"Well, you'll have a good opportunity on New Year's Eve to investigate. Maybe you'll learn more then. What about speaking to his brothers?" Lexi asked, putting Nirvana on the lead before approaching the road.

"No way. I know them less than Jorn. I think I'll just have to go to this ball and keep hold of his hand so I'm never alone."

"You never know, you might have it completely wrong, and it *was* his brothers he got in a fight with, and this step-mum person is actually a nice woman, you just misunderstood her motives that night."

"No way, Lexi, I know what I saw and what Jorn told me. She tried to get in his trousers," Logan shrieked, raising her eyebrows.

"They sound like an interesting family. I can't wait to hear about it on New Year's Day. You know it will be a party of no expense spared."

"Yes, and that too. What happens if he thinks I'm just a commoner and not good enough for his son?" she said dramatically.

Lexi tutted, "Now you're just being ridiculous, Logan. And besides, it sounds as if Jorn wouldn't care what his dad thinks. He likes you, and that's all that matters, isn't it?"

Logan stood exasperated a moment, "Yes, I suppose so. I just wish I had someone else going that I knew, that I could lean on if things don't go right or if Jorn has to leave my side."

"Listen, Loge, you are one of the most modest, confident women I have ever known. You can totally handle this, and Jorn totally adores you. I could see that on Christmas Eve. He won't let you out of his sight."

Logan smiled; maybe she was right. Surely, his dad couldn't be that bad, and then there were his brothers. Jorn always talked so highly of them that they would certainly look after her.

They trudged back to Lexi's parents and had a mulled wine before heading to Logan's to watch old movies.

"So, I've got St. Elmo's Fire, The Outsiders or The Goonies." As much as Logan loved The Outsiders, they decided on the humour of The Goonies and making themselves a snack plate of pâté and other Christmas delights Logan had bought, they sat down under the blanket and watched the film, play-acting the truffle shuffle and shouting, 'hey you guys' at the appropriate moment.

Lexi received a call from Quinn just before midnight, and whilst they talked, Logan vacated to the kitchen to clear up. She'd made no arrangements to be in contact with Jorn today, so she busied herself by putting things away and wiping down the work surfaces.

"Hey," Lexi said, coming in with their glasses.

"Hey, how was Quinn?"

"Ah, you know Quinn. Totally doting," Lexi smiled. Logan was pleased for her. She deserved happiness.

"Yes, I always knew he would be one of those kinds of

men. Heart on his sleeve," she said, filling the sink with warm water.

"Yes, he is, but Jorn will be too, Logan. Just give him space. He will message or ring you, I guarantee it."

"Oh, I wasn't even thinking of him," Logan lied.

"You are such a bullshitter, and before you say anything, he's not not contacting you because you said no to him."

Logan smiled at her friend. Lexi knew her too well.

"Do you think I scared him off by asking him to my mum and dad's for Christmas?" Logan said, switching off the kitchen light once they'd finished.

"Look, if he felt that way, he wouldn't have come, would he? He's an adult and old enough to make up his own mind. Believe me, Loge, he wouldn't have come if he wasn't into you," Lexi said, removing her top and bra as they got ready for bed.

"I know, but what kind of person asks their Sales Director for Christmas dinner?"

"The kind of person who loves people and will do anything to make them feel wanted," Lexi said, jumping into the bed. "And, Loge, he's not a Sales Director, is he? He's a guy you're seeing. You and him working together is irrelevant."

"Not really," Logan said, bemusedly.

"Yes, it is, because actually, he's the guy from the pub, aka Mr Creepy."

Logan laughed. Lexi was right. She shouldn't worry.

"Look, you say he and his brothers are close-knit. Maybe they had a heavy night last night, and he's sleeping it off," Lexi said, snuggling under the duvet.

"Yeah, maybe you're right."

Logan got in bed and switched out the bedside light. She was cross with herself. She'd never felt like this over a man before.

The hold he was beginning to have over her was something she didn't like at all.

CHAPTER TWENTY

THE BOYS

Jorn opened his alcohol cabinet, grabbing a bottle of Jameson when he got home. He hadn't wanted to leave Logan. Just being at her side seemed to soothe his raging mind. Being at home made him feel closer to losing it with his Master and getting himself stripped. He meandered along the halls, their pristine cleanliness winding him up the more he walked. It was so unnatural for a house as large as this to be so dreadfully clean. His precision eyesight zoomed over every corner and crevice, and all he saw were microscopic fibres from dusters and cleansing wipes. His Master had an array of cleaning staff that would visit every other day and robotic ones to keep on top of the dirt on their days off. Jorn knew managing a large house such as this one these days was no easy feat, and with about half of the rooms not in use, he wondered why The Master kept it so. He knew that many rooms this New Year's Eve would be occupied, but other than that, the rooms were vacant, yet he wasted his money on keeping them clean. Would he feel a failure to his family and community if a speck of dust was left on a mirror or on an expensive ornament? The way Jorn saw him, he was a complete failure to his family. He knew his Master was tormented, and he wanted to, in a way, help him, bring him to the light and show him that life didn't have to be this way. But after last Saturday night, Mr Kelly's accidental accident, the spy pin and then the flogging Jorn got, he didn't think he could ever give his Master anything.

He stopped outside the ballroom, the smell of cleaning products and polish so rife as he opened the doors; he felt almost cleansed by the scent. The round tables had already been set around the edge, reminding Jorn of wedding banquets. The large, gilded mirrors and other furnishings buffed, and the wall of glass doors that led out into the stunning landscaped garden, Oska had designed many years ago, were crystal clear with not a smear in sight. The courtyard beyond was paved, edged with grand statues and carved hedgerows that, in their turn, led to the house maze his brother had planted over a century ago. The flower beds, Jorn could see, even in the winter, looked tended to, and figurines made up of fairy lights shone brightly through the drizzle. Each flower bed had a different array of animals, each twinkling brightly; a deer and her babies, a fox and her cubs, angels blowing trumpets and penguins gazing skywards. At the start of the maze, the towering sycamore tree had lights trailing around the trunk and then branched off on individual arms, making it seem like it was covered in a million small stars. In the far corner, he could see a dozen or so gas heaters covered with tarpaulin to be placed intermittently around the patio, for those wishing to take the night air on the thirty-first. His Master was going for the no-expense-spared look, and Jorn knew no one would be disappointed.

He swigged at the bottle, the whisky searing his throat and filtering down, warming his stomach. His head swam lethargically, a sensation he loved as it made him feel he didn't have a care in the world. Returning to one of the tables, he pulled down a chair from the stack and, putting his feet up on the counter, retrieved a packet of cigarettes from his pocket. He rarely smoked these days, yet tonight, he craved the burn to his lungs only a cigarette could bring. Placing the end in his mouth, he lit it, the smoke spiralling above him towards a vast chandelier, the teardrop diamond glass tinkling as the doors behind him banged open. He didn't bother turning around, as in an instant, Jorun was sitting opposite him and helping himself to a smoking stick.

"Jorn?"

"Jorun," Jorn replied, taking another drag and swallowing a mouthful of drink.

"You know *he* won't be pleased you're in here."

Jorn nodded. What did he care right now what The Master thought?

"I see your mood hasn't improved since the journey from Logan's."

Jorn shook his head.

"It's worse. And this," Jorun grabbed the bottle of whisky, "isn't helping you."

Jorn shook his head again, irritated; it was usually Randin who came out with the obvious. Jorun took a glug and handed it back.

"This isn't you, you know."

Jorn shrugged, taking more drink.

"I haven't seen you drink like this in years."

Jorn just nodded again. It was true he didn't drink much these days, but right now, he needed to indulge. He'd had one of the best family days he'd ever had or that he could remember in former years, and yet, he felt so deflated his chest hurt.

"I know you're in pain, and I hate that."

Jorn hated it, too.

"And yet, here we are," Jorn finally said, taking a few more mouthfuls, the sting to his throat reduced. He was getting used to it.

"And yet, here we are," Jorun repeated his words. "What happened to the brother that left the house this morning? You seemed... happy." Jorn just stared at him. Was he happy this morning? "But now you seem... so angry."

Jorn didn't know what to say to him. He was right, though.

"I'm not angry, Jorun, I'm fucking livid!" He stood abruptly, pushing his chair back, and it crashed to the floor, the sound echoing throughout the room. "This morning, I had this stupid idea in my head that I could go to Logan's and have a good day. Which, of course, I did; I had a great day. For the first time in fucking years, I saw what it was like to have a family. Not just brothers who, believe me, I know what you all do for me." He looked at Jorun, he didn't want him to feel unrequited. "But there was a mother who cared and loved her children, a father who doted on his family and would sacrifice his own life for them. I saw what it was like to have a family unit first-hand, and I'm ashamed to say I was jealous. I was so envious it made my heart ache," he grasped at his chest.

"But do you know what kept going round in my head the entire time?" He looked questioningly at Jorun, who stared back knowingly.

"Randin's comment as you left?" Jorun knew his brother more than Jorn gave him credit for.

"Nothing can ever come of this, Jorn, he said, nothing can ever come of this," he repeated, downing a few more mouthfuls of amber liquid, trying to get the burn back in his throat. Sucking in through his teeth, he said, "And I know he's fucking right, and I totally get that. But it doesn't *make* it right. Why can't I have that, Jorun? Why? Why can't I have a family unit like that? We've been on this earth nearly four hundred years." He held his arms out in surrender, almost dropping the bottle, the cigarette hanging from his lips, "And what have we to show for it?" he said, putting the bottle down on the stage, where an orchestra would have played centuries ago.

"We've got fucking nothing!" he whispered, his voice almost breaking as he leaned his hands to the stage, barely holding it together. "I have nothing to show for it." He took another sip before gasping, his emotions so off-key that he felt his life was crumbling around him. "I have never really wanted for anything, just go about my day-to-day life watching and reporting. But what has that brought me over the years? Absolutely fucking nothing." He wiped his eyes, "We're empty shells of nothing, Jorun. Just vacant people who have so much life to live, yet live no life. Well, no life that's worth anything. We belong to existence, yet don't really exist. I mean, look at me. I have no friends outside you and the boys, and Lachlan, I suppose. I have acquaintances, sure, but no real friends. I mean fucking hell. The closest thing I have to a friend outside this family is a mammal-shifter, and he's not really a friend, more a colleague who I talk to outside the office because he's friends with..." He couldn't even say Logan's name; his despair was peaking, and if his brother didn't do something soon, he was going to go mad in the anguished hell he was slipping into.

He turned to Jorun and was taken aback to see Randin and Oska there with him. Shaking his head, he slipped down to the floor, leaning back into the stage panelling. "How long have you two been there?" he asked, hiccupping, the bottle in his hand almost dry.

"Long enough, Jorn, long enough," Randin said, pulling himself and Oska a seat down, not taking his eyes off his brother.

"I mean, shit." He placed the bottle down and held his hand out, Jorun chucking him the silver packet of cigarettes. "The past week or so," he sparked up, "working at a proper job, with a proper employer and proper work hours. I've felt... human. Like this is what I was meant to be, meant to do. I never asked for special abilities, I never asked to be immortal, or have enhanced senses, or have the capability of speed, or be able to follow people or melt into the shadows and go unnoticed to all or create fake memories for people. I mean, how fucked up is that? I can give people fake memories; make them think they've done things they never have. What's worse, I can make people forget, make them think they haven't done something, haven't learnt things. I've done that so many times for The Master, and most likely The Emperor, even I've forgotten whose memories are whose. How fucked up is that?" He was quiet, and then, "I never wanted any of it," he looked at Randin, "though I got it, and I should be grateful, right?"

He stared at Randin, waiting for him to come out with some expert words he'd say to one of his clients when they were in such despair. Yet he just stared at him. He didn't have the words either.

"Surely, you've felt like this before?" Jorn asked him, draining the bottle. "You've had immortality longer than any of us, you've had the body of a twenty-four-year-old so many more years than we have, and yet your mind is ancient. Surely you must have felt this before, Randin? Tell me that this isn't rare what I'm feeling. Please."

Randin gazed at him a moment, "Relationships are difficult, Jorn. I suppose I know there can never be any commitment for those with gifts," Randin said, looking at his hands. "Life is ongoing for us all. We must adapt. We can only share our life with The Gifted. It is the way it has always been."

"Are you telling me that you're okay with that?" Jorn asked. "You're okay with that existence? With that feeling of nothingness?" Randin looked away, defeated. "Well, I can't be okay with that anymore, I just can't. I want more,

Randin. I want to be free from all this shit. I want to be normal." He moved to try and get up, his body not quite in line with his brain, the alcohol making him feel unsteady and without coordination. "Maybe I should ask The Emperor to strip me; you never know I could survive. I could be just a normal human and be able to have the things I want."

"No one has ever survived a stripping, Jorn, you know that," Oska said.

"Oh, I know, but maybe then that's the answer. To die and be at peace. At least then the pain won't be felt any more." He moved onto all fours and, using the stage, stood up, his head swimming so much that he watched the floor come up to meet him, but Jorun grabbed him.

"Jorn!" His brother held him, shaking his body as if trying to knock some sense into him. "You cannot mean what you are saying."

"Why not?" Jorn said, falling forward, his head resting on Jorun's shoulder, feeling more drunk by the minute. "Why not Jorun? Why can I not, for once, have what *I* want? Why does it always have to be what *he* wants? What *they* want?"

"It just has to be, Jorn," Randin said, walking over to them. "It's just the way it is."

Jorn looked at Jorun and pushed him, "No, it isn't," he choked, "it doesn't have to be like this. Not anymore. I'm not doing it. I WON'T LET THEM RULE ME ANYMORE!" He kicked the bottle across the room, it flying straight into Oska's outstretched hand before hitting the glass doors.

"You see? Why'd you do that? Why'd you save it?" Oska stood aghast at his brother. "Because you're scared of The Master, you're scared of what he'd do if we mess up this clean and tidy room. I'm not scared anymore; I cannot be scared anymore. I want more to my life. I want more than this shite existence he's allowed us to live." He grasped his brother's t-shirt, "I want more, Jorun, I want *her*, Jorun, I want to grow old." Tears came easily to him now, "I need to save her, I just can't..." Jorun put his arms around his brother and held him, "I can't do this any longer," he gasped into his brother's shoulder.

"We have to, Jorn; it is the way it's been for millennia for our kind." Randin's hand went to Jorn's shoulder.

"NO!" He pushed Jorun and shoved Randin back. "NO! I don't want it. Look at us, we're just nothing, nobodies walking around this town, around this city. They feature our family in magazines and write articles, but we're still nobodies. We've got nothing to show for it but our name on a plaque at a hospital or at the opening of a new school. We're still nobodies. The mortal people envy the idea of immortality, and yet being immortal is so unbelievably cold and lonely. I'm sick of being cold and lonely." He looked at his empty hands, his cigarette butt on the floor. "If I have to give her to The Emperor, then I would rather be dead with her than continue this solitary life I have come to lead." He stumbled towards the door.

"Where are you going, Jorn? You're in no fit state to make it back to your room," Randin said, moving towards him.

Jorn laughed, "Oh no, Randin, I need more alcohol, and I mean to find it."

"I think you have had enough, my brother." Randin's hand rested on his upper arm, but Jorn lashed at it, grabbing it and flipping him over onto the floor, his eyes glowing red.

"Don't even begin to think you can tell me what to do, Randin. I was quite happy in here on my own, drinking myself into a coma. I asked none of you to join me." He swayed slightly, the tackle with his brother unbalancing him.

"Randin," Jorun said, helping him up from the floor. "Just leave him. He will be okay, shouting at him or telling him to stop is not the right way to bring him back."

"If The Master sees him like this, I don't know if I'll be able to talk him out of another beating," Randin whispered into Jorun's ear, as they watched Jorn swing open the door and almost bump into Lamont on the other side.

"Here, Jorn." Lamont entered the room, handing him a bottle of Jameson, "I've been saving this for you."

Jorn knew he was lying. Lamont loved Jameson just as Jorn did. There was no way he'd save him a bottle.

"I know you're lying, but I love the notion all the same. Come, brother, let us share it." Jorn put his arm around Lamont's shoulders, staggering back to the table. "Randin?" Jorn squinted up at him as Lamont helped him sit.

"It's okay, Jorn. I know." Jorn just nodded. He was sorry he'd injured Randin's pride. Randin was a big man, and to be thrown over by his intoxicated brother would have hurt him. "You must try and curb your emotions, though. Being like this is not healthy for any of us. This is just the way things are for our kind. Believe me, I have studied and read mostly everything there is to know about us. It is just the way things have to be." He put his hand out as if to stop Jorn's retaliation and then got his phone out.

"You messaging The Master to say you've got me under control?" Jorn scathed, chucking the cigarette packet down; he'd smoked them all.

"No, I'm messaging Kol to get his arse down here with some weed and cards."

"Like that's gonna help," Oska said.

"It will, trust me," Randin whispered.

"You think I can't hear you?" Jorn scoffed.

"No, I know you can hear me, Jorn. Stop being an arsehole." Randin stared at him.

Jorn knew he was being dramatic and an arsehole. But he hadn't asked them to join him, so it was their fault he was acting like this for them.

"Look, I was quite happy in here with my mate Jameson so don't give me any shit."

"Yes, and if we hadn't have come, you would have smashed a window, and The Master would have been down here and pummelled you to a pulp," Randin said, shaking his head.

"At least then I could have told him what I think."

"You think he doesn't already know?" Randin shot back.

"Well, if he does, he should do us all a favour and put me down," Jorn said. "And I know he doesn't know what I think."

"You think so? If you really think that, Jorn, then you don't know him at all."

"Okay, enlighten me then, brother. What does The Master think of me?"

Randin just looked at him.

"He doesn't think jack shit, because he doesn't know any of us anymore and hasn't since mamma went." They all gasped at the mention of their mother, and Jorn couldn't help but laugh out loud. They were all scared of The Master, even Randin.

The glass doors opened suddenly, and Jorn half expected it to be The Master coming to put him down, but Kol strolled in from the garden, having jumped from his balcony above the ballroom.

"Here, Jorn," he placed a joint in his mouth and lit it, "inhale deeply," Kol instructed.

Following a long intake, he blew the smoke up to the ceiling, "Fuck me," he coughed, "what is that?"

"That's pure girl scout cookie, that is," Kol replied, passing Randin a deck of cards and throwing a cloth bag on the table.

"Poker?" Jorn asked, recognising the chip bag.

"Of course," Kol said, pulling up a chair.

Jorn sat there watching Randin deal out the cards and set up the table. Randin was always the dealer. He always said that he wouldn't be a bad influence on his brothers and gamble, so would just watch them gamble away their own money instead.

"Slakes?" Jorn asked, taking another long drag, the rush calming his brain and making him feel unfocused.

"Sorry, Jorn, what was that?" Kol laughed, taking the bottle from Lamont.

"Fuck you, bro," Jorn laughed, "er... stakes?"

"Three thousand?" Lamont said.

"Sheesh! I'm going to be so broke," Jorn said, handing the joint to Jorun, tilting his head to the ceiling and watching the diamonds shimmer.

"You know you'll clear us out, Jorn, so be quiet," Oska said, laughing as he looked at his cards.

"Well, I can barely see the cards, so we'll see." He gulped another mouthful before the joint came back to him.

Randin laid out the three community cards, and Jorn increased his bet by four hundred pounds.

"Shit, I'm folding," Lamont said.

"You'd think you'd be good at this game, Lay, with your mathematical mind," Jorun said, meeting Jorn's bet and raising him another hundred.

"No, I just know when Jorn has a good hand," said Lamont.

"At least he's not shouting anymore," Oska added, folding his hand as well.

"But he can *still* hear you," Jorn said, feeling his head was getting too heavy on his neck.

Randin laid out the river, and Jorn showed his hand, "Four of a kind."

"Fucking hell," Jorun said, throwing his hand down, "bastard!" as Jorn swooped in to take the pot.

"I may be wasted, but I'm still king of poker."

Randin dealt out more cards, and they started again.

"I'll raise you a hundred," Jorn said, putting his chips out before resting his head on the table.

"You gonna puke?" Oska asked, touching Jorn's arm.

"What? No, my neck's just tired." He kept his head on the table, managing to look at his cards again as Randin laid out the flop.

"I'm out," Jorn said, downing more alcohol. "Roll another one, Kol. I can tell your hand is rubbish." Kol threw his cards down and rummaged in his pocket for his drugs.

Jorn watched his brother intricately roll the joint, at the way he rubbed the paper between his thumb and forefinger and how he licked one end and then the other before closing it up. He might not be good at anything other than being annoying. But he sure knew how to roll a good joint.

Sighing, Jorn stood up quickly, his chair crashing over

again.

"I need some air." He staggered to the doors, managing to unlock the top bolt Lamont had closed after Kol had entered.

"He's totally going to puke," Oska said again, sipping at his glass.

"And I can still hear you," Jorn said, leaning against one of the pillars, looking out into the darkness, the light-up creatures seeming to wink at him. He gazed up to see the rolling clouds over the moon, casting unnatural shadows on the ground, the rain now a fine mist. Sniffing the air, he sensed that some form of snow would soon be coming. Perhaps not the white fluffy stuff that seemed to fall with an abundance when he was younger, but something was coming. He stumbled slightly on the flagstones, smiling at his uncouthness.

"Jorn?" Kol stood there, offering him the joint.

"I'm so fucked, Kol!" he said, leaning onto his brother; he was not, however, bad enough to forgo the roll-up. Inhaling deeply, he blew the smoke into the frozen air, it billowing away, melting into nothingness.

"I know, but it's funny to watch. Not seen you like this for a while." Jorn smiled at his youngest brother, ruffling his hair, "Why does everyone do that?" Kol asked, flattening the ripples.

"Because that's what older brothers do," Jorun said, coming out and handing Jorn the bottle.

"I love the fact you said the alcohol wasn't helping me and

then keep giving it to me," Jorn said, taking it.

"Yes, but I know when and when not to stop you doing something."

"You're a good brother," Jorn said, clapping him on the shoulder.

"Here he goes," Randin said.

"Wait for it," Lamont grinned.

"I love you, you know," Jorn said to Jorun.

"Right on cue," Oska laughed, taking the drink.

"I know you do," Jorun replied, clapping his brother back and pulling him into a hug.

"But I do, and I know that I'm drunk, and I know that I rarely show it, but I do love you. All of you. Without any of you. I would... well!" He dragged at the joint. "I'm going to see mamma." He started walking towards the maze, "Don't follow. I'll be fine."

"You'll totally get lost," Jorun said, helping Jorn walk to the maze entrance.

"No, I won't," Jorn said, smiling, "but I will take that." He took the drink from Oska and walked into the evergreen tunnels.

Jorn had walked these leaf-strewn paths for decades, and he knew how to find the centre. Left, right, left and left again, keep going past one path on the right and then one on the left, then two rights. He saw the erected sculpture of his mother, her beauty captured so superbly by Oska that he stared up at her a while, sipping his drink. He wished she could help him get the answers he sought, answer his problems, and help him solve his heartbreak. But she couldn't. She just stood there, her face tilted towards the sky, her gaze looking endlessly at the heavens for all eternity.

Sinking to his knees, he hung his head in despair. "I'm sorry, Mamma, I'm so sorry," he spluttered, putting his hand out on the cold ground to stop himself from falling over. "You always told me to be true to myself, to be strong, to have patience and to keep father from imploding on himself. But I can't. He's stooped too low this time. He and his brother have pushed me to my limits, and I can't take any more." He inhaled the joint and blew smoke rings into the air, his head spinning so much he knew that he was probably going to vomit soon. His body was good at absorbing alcohol, but he'd drunk almost a bottle and a half of whisky to himself and had had many pulls on Kol's special cigarettes. He wouldn't be able to stomach much more.

"I don't have the strength to just hand her over," he inhaled again. "Do you think I have a chance? Do you think I can save her? Do I have enough strength to defy them both?" His hair was ruffled by the frozen air, causing him to glance over his shoulder, but he saw nothing, just the hedges rustling and the sound of his brothers approaching slowly. He knew they'd follow him stealthily to ensure he was all right. But you couldn't sneak up on a Watcher, albeit a very drunk one. He could smell Lamont's aftershave and Jorun's breath as he chewed on a mint. He could scent the weed in Kol's pocket and the plastic on Randin's fingers from the cards he'd been dealing. He could sense Oska's despair at the way his brothers were trampling along the newly raked paths, ready for New Year's Eve.

"They're coming, and I know I must find the strength to save him from himself, to save him from his brother, and to save her. But I don't know how, and I don't know if I can. It just seems so......" he stopped talking, fearing they would hear.

"I'm sorry, Mamma!" He got to his feet fluidly, walked over to the bench, grabbed hold of the armrest and vomited over the grass.

"Told you he'd puke," Oska said, laughing.

"Shut up, Oska," Jorn managed before bending over again. "I wish it tasted the same on the way up," he gulped, wiping his mouth before bending over again.

He moved to sit down, leaning his head on the backrest, the stars swimming in front of his eyes as he peered upwards. He could see The Plough or The Big Bear, his father used to call it, when they stargazed back in Norway. He could see Orion, and his heart seemed to bleed as he remembered Logan's face walking on that fountain.

"You have all you need, my son."

Jorn sat forward, staring at the statue of his mother, her face so serenely beautiful that he smiled at her, for even though he knew he'd just imagined her saying those words, he now knew he had the strength to go on and fight for what he believed in.

"Jorn?" Jorun stood in front of him, making Jorn focus on

him. "You okay?" he asked, giving him a mint.

"Yes, I think so..." Jorn stood up, grabbing his brother's arm for security. "Let's get some rum and play some more poker. I'm feeling lucky."

They left the maze, Jorn's heart feeling lighter than when he entered. He knew his journey was nowhere near complete, and the hardships that were to come, he knew, would stretch him as thinly as they could go. But he also knew he had the strength to fight for what he believed in because no one deserved her, not The Emperor or his Master. Perhaps not even himself.

CHAPTER TWENTY ONE

THE HEADACHE

Logan waited all day to hear from Jorn. Even after Lexi left at six the day after Boxing Day, he'd not been in touch. She didn't want to admit defeat, but she felt it. Defeated in their relationship before it had even begun. She knew he was special, and to not hear from him was like a kick in the teeth, especially after he had bought her the earrings. You didn't buy someone such an expensive gift and then not contact them again, did you? Surely. She switched on the telly, hoping it would be a distraction, but it wasn't. She channel-hopped constantly, only able to stick with something for ten minutes before switching to something else. At eleven, she decided it was best to go and have a bath. She ran the water to the right temperature and added a glitter-filled bath bomb. She had copious amounts of bath bombs on her top shelf. The boxes were covered in such a thick layer of dust that she made a mental note to discard them. That was what she'd do tomorrow. In between cooking for her family gathering on Monday, she'd clean and throw away the old stuff she never used.

She had just sunk beneath the bubbles when her phone buzzed.

"Aargh!" Drying her hands, she reached for the device.

Sorry, I've not been in touch. Heavy Christmas night with my brothers. It's taken me two days to get over it.

She almost dropped her phone.

You free for a phone call?

Blushing, she messaged back, *Er... I'm in the bath,* followed by a laughing emoji.

Are you? I can always video call?

Okay. Her stomach flipped with anticipation and dunking her head under the water so Jorn wouldn't see her fly-away hair, she waited for him to call. As his face appeared on her screen, she couldn't help but smile, and she strategically angled the screen on her bathroom stool.

"Hey, you," she said, feeling the well-tuned flush to her stomach when she saw him. He was sitting on a sofa, wearing a light-coloured t-shirt. "You look like you're still hanging?" She could tell he wasn't quite right.

"You could say that. I think the last time I was sick was about two o'clock."

"Really? How much did you have?" she said, rubbing soap between her hands.

"Too much to tell you about, plus I was up until midday

Boxing Day playing poker."

"Fucking hell, Jorn, you must have been wankered," Logan said, laughing.

"Let's just say I won't be testing my liver again until at least New Year's Eve. I think I concerned Randin at some point, but then the vomiting started, and he knew I'd be alright." He grinned, and despite Logan's slight concern for his drinking too much being a problem, she felt warmth at its sound.

"Did you lose much, or don't you play with real money?" she asked, lathering the soap up and down her leg, feeling his eyes on her, watching every move.

"Er... no, I came out on top actually, despite being intoxicated, eight hundred pounds to be exact."

"Fucking hell, Jorn!" she cursed again, slamming her leg back into the water. "Eight hundred pounds!"

"The stakes were three thousand," he said in a blasé tone.

Logan stopped what she was doing and sat wide-eyed at him, "Er... if you have that kind of money to burn, why do you even work?" She couldn't help feeling a little cross at his extravagance.

"Hey, don't worry, it was only chips, not real money," Jorn lied quickly. He had more than enough money to waste gambling, yet she didn't need to know that.

"Shit, I thought you really had the chance to lose three thousand." She continued washing.

"Ah, do you have to keep lifting your leg like that?" he asked, shifting in his seat.

"Why, does it make you uncomfortable?" she laughed, lifting it even more and rubbing it again.

"No, but it makes me... sweaty," he said breathlessly.

"Does it?" she smiled. "Well, maybe this will teach you not to leave it two days before contacting me." She put her leg back in the water.

"Yes, I apologise about that. I just wasn't in any state to call or even message. Jorun said you'd be pissed, especially after Christmas." He looked guiltily at the screen.

"Well, I did wonder if I had scared you off with my family-indulged Christmas," she said, blushing.

"Listen, Logan, like Tyler said, it would take a lot to scare me off, and I enjoyed meeting your family. It did perhaps make me feel a little jealous of what you have, but it certainly didn't scare me off," he said. "I must say I've missed you, and seeing you in the bath makes me want you, but that is probably all my body can take right now. Too much excitement might make me puke again, and that wouldn't be pleasant."

"No, I can safely say that would be a complete turn-off." She smiled, slipping under the water and wetting her hair again.

He laughed at her as she surfaced. "You look bloody gorgeous, you know," he said, holding the phone closer to see if he could get a better look.

"Well, in all honesty, even though you look a bit pale, I would still jump on you," she smirked, rubbing shampoo into her hair. "You're lucky you caught me. I only decided last minute to have a bath. If I had showered, I would have missed your call."

"I'm glad you had a bath then," he said, yawning.

"Me too," she said, getting the shower head from the taps.

"It looks like you're busy, Logan. Can I call you again tomorrow? I'll feel a bit more myself, I'm sure of it."

"Of course. I have a day of cooking ahead of me for my family gathering on Monday."

"Family gathering?" he questioned.

"Yes, my parents are hosting the annual family party. Want to come?" she asked sarcastically, not expecting him to say yes.

"As much as I liked your parents, I have many jobs to do for New Year's Eve that my father has given me." He rolled his eyes.

"Don't worry, I didn't really expect you to say yes anyway. It will be totally boring, and my aunt will just keep asking you if you're going to propose, and that will be mortifying for us both," she laughed, testing the shower head water temperature.

"Not that I don't want to meet your extended family, but the idea of having to stand for any length of time or make conversation isn't sitting right with me right now, either," he smiled. "But I will phone you tomorrow, though."

"Yes, please do," she said, starting to rinse her hair.

"Good night, Logan."

He hung up.

She sighed heavily, breathing out in relief, he was still as interested in her as she was in him.

Having already planned her day, Logan lazed in bed until ten the next morning; she knew she had lots to do, but couldn't quite get the motivation to do anything. Yet, her being her, she got up religiously at ten, and though she currently detested the idea of cooking and sorting out all the unwanted products in her bathroom, she began her chores. Putting on her marigold gloves, she scraped her fringe back with a black alice band, threw on some old jogging bottoms and got the bleach out. She always enjoyed cleaning when she had things on her mind, and right now, she had a lot to think about. Jorn, the Managing Director post, and his father revolved at length through her mind, and she began to get annoyed at herself. She knew she was most likely winding herself up about his dad more than she should, but she didn't get a good vibe from Jorn when he spoke of him. And she needed to know why. She wished they'd stayed longer at the pub on Christmas Eve; she could have learnt more about Jorn from his brothers and got to know them all as a family. As she cleaned, she made up her mind to phone Adrian later and accept the job; she was sure he'd have her on a six-month probation period, which suited her fine. She could quit and return to life as she knew it if she hated it. Though she also knew that she wasn't a quitter, and she'd do her damn best to bring that company up rather than let it fall at her feet. She had many ideas, and if Jorn was right in his encouragement, she would like to expand their products nationally, perhaps internationally, with the correct guidance. She, of course, would employ Lexi as Chief Interior Designer. Lexi had always had an excellent eye for décor and knew that she often worked on many ideas in her parents' garage. Logan was cross she'd not thought about it before her promotion. Lexi was talented, and though she was loudmouthed and overly confident, she never put herself forward to the right people. Now, Logan could be one of those people who could give her the push she needed.

She started on the bathroom. Switching on her phone, she put on some music and sang loudly as she scrubbed the shower, tiles and scoured the toilet bowl. She removed everything from the bathroom cupboard and threw a few things on the floor that she could bin. Finishing the bathroom, with a satisfied smell of bleach filling her nostrils, and a clearer mind, she moved onto the bedroom. She opened her wardrobe and grabbed all her clothes, laying them on the bed. She sorted things she never wore and put them in a plastic bag, ready for the women's refuge. She was hanging up her suits after tidying her wardrobe out, when the front doorbell rang. Looking out the window, she saw a black van on the pavement, poorly parked, with its hazard lights on. When will people learn that using hazard lights doesn't give them a licence to park where they like? Opening the window, she peered down.

"Can I help you?" The person on the doorstep looked up, making her gasp. It was Jorn; he was wearing a thin grey

V-necked jumper and dust-marked dark jeans.

"Yes, you can, I have a special delivery for a," Jorn looked down as though reading an address label. "Miss Logan Hunter." She blushed as she remembered what she was wearing, "Er... what are you doing?"

"Cleaning," she smiled, her face flushing.

"Thought you said you had cooking to do?" he smirked.

"I do, but I thought I'd clean first," she grinned, taking off her gloves.

"Well, come down, I've not got long."

"You know I don't like it when you park like that?" she said, looking again at the van.

He just shrugged innocently. "Hey, it's Jorun's parking."

"You're both as bad as each other," she said, rolling her eyes to the ceiling and shutting the window. With a glance in the mirror, she sauntered down the stairs, moved aside the recycling she needed to take out, and opened the door.

He stood there holding a single yellow rose tipped with red.

"Hey," she said, looking at him, feeling all she wanted to do was grab his face and kiss it.

"I'm sorry I can't stay, but I just wanted to bring you this." She took the rose, holding it to her nose.

"You know what this colouring signifies, don't you?" she

asked, innocently.

He grinned, "Yes, or I wouldn't have bought it." He moved up to her. "Look, if it's not okay, then I'm sorry, but I've had a lot of time to think yesterday and during my... er, inebriated state."

"He was bloody wasted, Logan," Jorun shouted from the front of the van, making her giggle.

"Yeah, yeah, all right," Jorn brushed his brother's comment away.

"Yes, he told me last night," she called, looking back at Jorn leaning into the frame, holding the rose to her nose again.

"Look, I'm not here to talk about that; I'm here to do this." He grabbed her hip and pulled her in, their lips meeting, his tongue in her mouth, and for a minute, there was nothing else but him; his taste, his smell, his hands at her back, his body against hers. "I bloody want you, Logan," he almost panted, kissing her again, his hand slipping down the back of her trousers. "Seeing you in the bath made me, well..." he flushed slightly.

"Glad to know I have the same effect on you as you have on me," she grinned into his mouth as she kissed him back, a heat so hot in her stomach that she groaned, only stopping when she heard Jorun whooping from the vehicle.

"He's an arse," Jorn said, pulling away.

"Why can't you stay?" she asked, her hand stroking his neck.

"We've just been to get some cask ale that needs to settle before Wednesday."

"Can't the others sort it?" she asked.

"No, unfortunately, Lay's got some work to do, so he's gone to the office, Randin's busy erecting a DJ booth, and Oska's getting the driveway sorted."

"Driveway?" she asked, confused.

"My father likes to make a good impression, so Oska's been tasked with adorning fairy lights over the trees and stuff." He rolled his eyes again, "No expense spared."

"What about Kol?"

"Ha, you're having a laugh, aren't you," he exclaimed, "he just lazes."

"And your dad lets him get away with it?" she asked, feeling that if Kol got away with it, Jorn could too.

"Well, he's good at pretending he's helping," Jorn said.

"Come on, Jorn," Jorun honked the horn.

"Listen, I'll call you later," he said, bending down swiftly, grabbing her recycling, and chucking it in her bin on the way to the van.

Once they'd gone, she closed the door, smelling the rose, its scent so radiant that she blushed at the thought of his mouth on hers. She had it so bad for this guy, and if she wasn't going to have much time with him until New Year's Eve. She'd have to make sure the wait was worth it.

After showering, she began making a cheesecake for tomorrow. She loved Christmas with all the family gatherings, but right now, she couldn't be bothered. However, she dutifully made the biscuit base and mixed the lemon into the condensed milk and cream before leaving it to set in the fridge. She then started on some rocky road for her cousins, and once that was setting, she started the bean salad she promised her father she would make. He always loved her bean salad, and even when it was cold outside, he said he'd love to have some with the hot and cold buffet her mum was going to prepare.

Adrian didn't answer when she called him, so she left a message asking him to return her call. She then rang the local curry house and ordered a takeaway. She fancied a curry, and even though she knew she could do a better job, she'd done enough cooking today. Getting in the car, she drove to the restaurant, tipped the staff, and left with her curry. She was just getting out of the car, back home, when her phone rang.

"Hello," she cradled it, edging into her kitchen.

"Logan? It's Adrian."

"Oh hey, thanks for calling back. How are you?"

She chatted to her boss for a while, asking him about his Christmas and if he was recovering well at his brother's.

"The reason why I phoned is because I wanted to discuss the prospect of my promotion and the preliminary aspects of it."

"You know, L, this is the news I've been waiting for." She grimaced at his use of her nickname but skated over it.

"Really?"

"Absolutely. I had Jorn on the phone this morning talking about something completely different, and he said that you'd be extremely beneficial to the company." She wondered briefly why he and Jorn had spoken.

"I think Jorn is perhaps a little biased," she laughed, serving up her curry.

"I take that as a hint things are good between you two." She could hear the smile in his voice.

"Well, we're taking things slowly," she said shyly, biting her lip.

"Well, it's good to not jump in with both feet." She laughed at him. "I'm pleased you're taking the offer, Logan, and of course, we'll need to meet face-to-face to discuss it."

"Yes, that would be great. When you're up to it."

After a few more niceties, she hung up and put her meal in the microwave to heat. At twenty to eleven, she got ready for bed. Maybe Jorn was too busy to call, she was brushing her teeth, however, when she heard her phone buzz from the bedroom. Spitting into the sink, she saw it was him.

"Hey, babe." She closed her eyes momentarily, feeling like an idiot. Babe? Where did that come from?

"Hey, sorry it's late."

"It's not that late." She wiped her mouth on the towel and

climbed into bed. "How was the beer?" she asked, looking at the rose she had next to her in a single-stem vase she thought she'd never use.

"We've got too much, I know that," he sighed. "But my father is a stickler for organisation, so you know. We must do as he wants." There it was again. His father called the shots, and his sons followed his instructions.

"Well, surely it's better to have too much than not enough."

"Logan, you don't understand. Half of the people won't be drinking beer, they'll be wine or Prosecco drinkers, and the younger people will be on the spirits. It's a waste of money if you ask me. But that's my father all over." She couldn't think of anything to say to that, so she said,

"Where are you right now?"

"I'm in my bedroom; my head, believe it or not, is still a little hazy, so I'm having a reasonably early one," he replied.

"Me too, but not for the same reason. I've had a mostly boring day, and feel to entertain myself, I should try and get an early night, too."

"I'm sorry I'm not there with you."

"Me too, I know you could entertain me," she smirked down the phone.

"Only if you wanted me to," he said.

"Just talking to you makes me tingle," she whispered,

hardly believing herself.

"Logan, don't; it'll make me get in my car and come over," he cussed.

"I'd gladly have you for a sleepover," she said, her breathing becoming heavier in anticipation.

"Let me call you back on video."

He hung up, and she waited for him to call, her breathing rapid, her breasts heaving, a fluttering in her stomach that resonated through her body when she saw his face on her phone. She'd never done anything like this before, and she'd never felt so nervous, but when she answered, he was lying on his bed, his top half already naked, making her already feel completely lost in him. Her hands began exploring her own body, as he whispered and encouraged her to feel herself as if he were there, and she only half watched him on her screen, his own hands touching himself, running his fingers through his chest hair that made her groan with need.

"Jeez!" she exclaimed, wiping her face.

"You, okay?" he asked, putting the phone nearer his face to see her better.

"Yes, it's just..."

"Never done anything like that before?" he grinned.

"No!" She suddenly felt embarrassed.

"Logan, neither have I. Not that intense anyway."

"Really?" she asked, snuggling into her duvet.

"Logan, what we have is very intense. Well, it certainly feels like that anyway." He got up and walked into his bathroom, Logan watching him as he washed his hands.

"Is that a good thing?" she asked as he splashed water onto his face, rubbing his hands over his stubble.

He smiled, "What happened to the confident girl I had dancing around a fountain?"

She blushed, "She has inhibitions she has to deal with, and that girl was drunk."

He shook his head, "Logan, never feel you have to hold back with me or be embarrassed. I like you, and I think that you like me. That's it."

"I do like you," she said honestly.

"That's good," he smiled, slipping into a pair of lounge trousers. "I have to say, I wasn't expecting that from tonight's phone call."

"Me neither," she whispered, pulling on a pyjama top, the heat from their encounter waning.

"We'll both sleep better now," he said, putting his arm up and behind his head.

"Most definitely, and you didn't puke," she laughed, puffing up her pillow.

"No, I'm definitely feeling better in that sense tonight."

"I'm glad, I was kind of worried about you. Have you been that drunk before?"

"Well, not for a long time." He looked at her expression. "Don't worry, Logan, I don't have a drinking problem. Only when we play poker, I tend to find drinking helps my thought processes," he said, "and we played for quite a few hours."

"I would have thought alcohol would hinder you," she smiled, turning onto her side.

"It certainly hinders Kol and Oska; they just start getting stupid and throwing their money around, but I seem to keep a cool head. Hence, I win," he said, grinning.

"I thought you only played with metaphorical money?"

"Er... we do, but they're still gutted if they lose."

Logan rushed out of the house the next morning, having forgotten to set her alarm after her phone call with Jorn. Balancing the bean salad and her puddings precariously on the back seat, she scraped the windscreen, feeling a chill run down her neck from her damp hair. It was so unlike her to be this disorganised.

"Damn men," she scowled, as she threw herself in the front seat and blasted the cool air from her heaters.

The drive to her parents was slow; the sleet was coming down thickly, and her wipers protested at prolonged usage. Upon arrival, she could see many cars in the driveway and had to admit defeat by parking on the roadside. Pulling up her hood, she crunched her way up the pebbled drive, longing for the warmth the house would give her and was relieved to see smoke rising from the chimney. Her dad had lit the log burner, so with all the relatives, it would be toasty, and she couldn't wait to get in there. Her mum opened the door, a look of knowing on her face.

"Logan, I thought you weren't coming." Logan frowned at her mum.

"Why would you think that?" she asked as her mum hushed her into the warmth.

"Well, you're late, and you're never late."

"Yes, I'm sorry, I forgot to set my alarm."

"Jorn not with you?" Logan shook her head.

"Mum, don't try and pry. Just ask me fully what question is on your mind." Logan knew her mum too well.

"Okay then. Did Jorn stay the night? Is that why you're late?"

"Actually, no, he didn't," Logan said, handing over her burdens before removing her coat. "We were just talking late on the phone, and I really did just forget to set my alarm."

"Things are going well then?"

"They are mostly yes."

"Ah, oh!" her mum exclaimed.

"Oh, it's just his dad has got him doing a lot over the next few days to prepare for New Year's Eve, so he's not got much time to see me."

"That's a shame. Can't he come over at least in the

evenings?" her mum asked, walking through to the dining room where the buffet was laid out.

"I suppose he could, but it's quite good to have a bit of space, isn't it?" Yet, who was she trying to kid? Absence was tedious.

"Yes, it is," said her dad, walking through, holding out a glass of wine to Logan.

"Hey, Dad." Logan bent in to kiss her father's cheek.

"I hope you're not badgering her for details, August?" he said to his wife.

"I just want to make sure they're okay. I like him." Logan couldn't help but smirk at her mother's bluntness.

"I like him too, but Logan is right; absence makes the heart grow fonder." Her father pulled Logan in for a hug and said, "Having too much too quickly may not be good for any relationship."

"Oh, don't pretend you understand relationships, Ben," August scoffed, uncovering the salad.

"See, Logan, no matter what I say, it's the wrong thing," he shrugged, walking back to the lounge.

Logan did the rounds with her family, speaking to her aunts and uncles and discussing their journeys up the motorways and the weather conditions in their part of the country. She updated her cousin Elsbeth about her new relationship, and she swooned over the notion of having a new man, asking Logan if Jorn had any unattached brothers. Logan just smiled. She had no idea whether any of Jorn's brothers were attached, and in fact, she didn't know much about them at all. And she wasn't going to enlighten her cousin on who Jorn was or his family; that would lead to more unwanted questions.

She managed to escape the sitting room and sat a while on the stairs, scrolling through social media. After liking a few posts, she edged upstairs to her room and lay on the bed. Even though she shouldn't be tired, she felt exhausted; just having to make conversation seemed to be draining her, and her head was beginning to pound. Closing her eyes, she snuggled into her cushions and couldn't help but fall asleep.

Waking suddenly, she noticed that the sky outside was now a dull grey, the sleet had stopped, and a few icicles had appeared on the gable outside her window. Her phone buzzed in her pocket,

Where the hell are you? I'm drowning here. It was Tyler.

My room. Logan messaged back, rolling onto her side, listening to her sister's heavy footfalls stomping up the stairs.

"You could have told me you were coming up here; I could have sneaked away with you," Tyler said, sitting on her bed.

"I wasn't planning on staying up here; I have a headache and just fell asleep," Logan said, sitting up and re-doing her hair.

"Well, I..." More footsteps were coming upstairs.

"Here you both are." Her mum sat on her desk chair,

looking exhausted.

"Sorry, Mum, we just needed five minutes to breathe," Tyler said.

"Well, the aunts are talking about going for a walk. Please, will you both come and keep me company? Your father is taking the men to the pub for a beer and cigar before puddings." She shook her head exasperatedly.

Both girls got up loyally and followed their mother downstairs. Logan didn't mind walking; she had her boots with her, and the fresh air was helping eradicate her headache. Yet when her sister caught up with her, she felt she'd have done better staying on the bed. She wittered on about her upcoming wedding and how Logan needed to help her decide on the colour scheme and menu options, as Ethan was terrible at making decisions. Logan loved her sister, of course. They were literal soul mates and rarely argued now that they were older, but when it came to her wedding, Tyler was practically a bridezilla, and she felt sorry for Ethan having to deal with her. As they walked, Logan couldn't help but think of Jorn and wondered what he was doing. She supposed he could come over later after he'd done what he needed to do, yet she wasn't sure she wanted him to. Not because she didn't want him. She certainly desired him, but there seemed to be something special about waiting until New Year's Eve to see him and to be able to move on to the next stage of their relationship, for surely that was where the night would end.

"Logan? Logan? Are you even listening to me?" her sister asked, as they removed their boots after the walk.

"Yes, Ty, I'm listening to you. I think pastel green is a lovely colour. You know I like green, so yes, that's a good colour to go for." She rummaged in her mum's medicine box for paracetamol and downed a couple of tablets with some ice-cold water.

"So, I'll come to you tomorrow and go through some magazines for ideas?"

Logan stood at the sink, closing her eyes, them starting to burn with the ache that hung there relentlessly.

"Loge?" Tyler's hand was cool on Logan's hot arm.

"Yes, Ty, come tomorrow," Logan gulped, beginning to feel nauseous.

"Are you still getting headaches, Logan?" her dad asked as he bent down to get some more paper plates from the cupboard.

"Not quite so much anymore, Dad. I think they're mainly brought on by stress," she said, trying to reassure him. "I might not stay much longer, if that's okay."

"You went to the doctor, though, didn't you?" he said, putting his palm against her forehead.

"Yes, Dad." She shied away from the heat of his hand. "I get them very sporadically, less when I'm not working." She shrugged, playing down the fact she suddenly felt so rough.

"Well, if they continue, I think you should have them investigated further."

"I'm fine, Dad. Paracetamol usually sorts them out."

The drive home was even more complicated than getting to her parents; not only had winter set in, making the roads sheen with black ice, but her headache was worsening. She had to pull over twice because she'd felt so nauseated, and the third time, she vomited onto the grass, only just stopping in time. By the time she was home, however, it seemed to have lessened, and she couldn't help but smirk as she saw a small, slightly damp package on the doorstep. Taking off her scarf and coat, she flicked the tag,

For New Year's Eve. Although you could never hide from me.

She opened the box, and there, set in dark grey tissue paper, was a masquerade mask. She ran her fingers over the flawlessly painted orbital ridges, the subtle grading of green around the eyes melting to black along the outside. The jewels shimmered delicately above one eye, and though the other was plain, it seemed to enhance the mystery. Placing it to her face, she turned to the mirror and immediately felt incredibly daring. All she needed now was a dress to go with it, and having seen the mask, it put her in mind of a long green A-line cut dress she had in her wardrobe. Turning to go upstairs and look for it, she felt her head swim, the thumping in her skull returning tenfold so that she grabbed the bannister, scared to move in case she was sick again. Swallowing hard and trying to steady her breathing, she climbed the stairs slowly before sipping at the water on her bedside cabinet and lying down on her bed.

Feeling her phone vibrate, she looked at the screen,

Did you find your parcel?

Squinting with one eye, she replied to him, *Yes, it's beautiful, but you really should stop buying me things. I feel guilty.*

The dots appeared; *I don't want you wasting money on stuff just for an extravagant party at my father's.*

I wouldn't have minded. Logan put the phone against her forehead before typing; *Just need a dress now.*

Don't worry about that. I've got that covered.

WTF? She wrote.

Please let me spoil you, he typed, followed by a praying emoji.

She lay back gingerly, feeling her migraine ramp up a further notch, the nausea undulating persistently. Lying for a moment, she tried to blank her whole mind of any thought, anything to stop the torturous pain she was feeling. Her hands pushed hard into her forehead, gripping her head as though to prevent it from exploding. She felt the bed start to vibrate, and then a monotonous buzz began to filter through her body, seeming to make her bones tremble. She knew it was her phone, but there was no way she could answer it; her hands had to keep her head from imploding on itself. Her swallow reflex was in overdrive, and bile seemed to slosh in her stomach, and any moment it was going to surface. Clutching her head with her entire arm, she tried to reach for the water again. Her fingertips raked over the wooden worktop, knocking the glass to the floor; the sound of glugging water streamed through her ears so loud that it echoed within her skull. An unnatural heat rose through her body, and sweat was pouring off her. If only she could take off her jumper. Struggling to remain conscious, she removed one arm and then the other, the garment saturated, her breathing so laboured her lungs felt stuck in her chest. She was going to pass out.

"Jorn!" Her strangled cry ricocheted around the room, as agony fired shots through the inside of her head. She tried to massage her temples, but her arms weren't connected to her body anymore, and she had no willpower left to fight. The heat, oh the heat, was unbearable; it felt like lava licking at her skin. She reached to undo her jeans and managed to get them off before curling into a ball, her body a fragile frame of tremors, her breathing so erratic that there was no pattern. Logan lost her rhythm in the excruciation her brain was putting her through, and she started hearing voices, voices all around, voices of comfort, of fear, of torture, of perhaps the devil laughing or God calling her.

'Your time of duty is nearly upon you.' One voice in her head overrode the others; it was crystal clear, blaring through her brain like it had cracked open, and all was clear. She couldn't help but cry out, her stomach rolling again. She was going to vomit soon, and there was no one to help her, no one that would hear her call. No one that could stop this from happening.

Abruptly, the bed tilted, and someone's cool, large hands pulled her into them; the scent of him was so vibrant that she instantly began to relax, her face flush against the softness of his top. Keeping her eyes closed, she felt her pants for air even out, her pounding heart slowing, the headache began to ebb away, and the sporadic trembles through her body ceased. The feeling of contentment fell over her, her head resting on his chest as she listened to the steady beat of his pulse and the even inhale and exhale of his lungs.

"Jorn?" she whispered, feeling him stroke her hair.

"It's okay, I've got you."

Logan could feel herself sink further into him; her body was shattered from an ordeal that had lasted perhaps just fifteen minutes, though, to her, it felt like hours. After a while, she began to feel more lucid, and blinking, she focused on the room. Her curtains were still open; the sky beyond was black, the orange glow of the streetlight causing a halo through the glass, with the occasional flash of car lights illuminating the plastic panes. Her room was softly lit, and she knew without turning that the bathroom light was on. Her head was no longer on Jorn's chest but on one of her pillows. Her body was no longer exposed to the air but was lying under her bed throw, and she could feel a warmth to her back, a heat that earlier on would have made her feel claustrophobic, but now it brought her nothing but comfort.

"How are you feeling?" His fingertips were gentle as he caressed her exposed arm.

"Thirsty," she croaked, her mouth dry.

The bed moved as he went down the stairs, returning with fresh water.

Moving gingerly, she sat, pulling her knees up to her chest and accepting the glass from him.

"How did you know to come?" she asked, putting the empty glass on the cabinet.

"I knew something was wrong when you didn't reply to my message; I know how meticulous you are about things like that, and then you didn't answer my call. So, I just got in the car and came over. Good job your back door was still unlocked." She raised her eyebrows; she never left that unlocked.

"Thank you for coming." She reached slowly for his hand, squeezing it.

"Logan, we need to get these headaches seen to. I don't ever want to see you like that again."

"I'm sorry if I scared you," she said, flopping back into the pillows, the tremors returning. "I've never had one last that long or been that bad before." She shivered intermittently.

"You were whimpering when I got here." He moved up the bed and folded her into his arms, her fragile body encased in his iron grip.

"I've never felt so relieved that I wasn't alone anymore," she said, remaining still a moment, then shivering again.

"You know I'll always be here for you." He looked down at her.

"I'm pleased you came," she said, as goosebumps erupted on her skin.

"Me too," he said, pulling her throw up and over her. "You cold?"

"No, I don't think so, but I wish these shakes would stop."

He moved to her chest of drawers and, finding a pair of pyjamas, helped her into them.

"If it's okay, I'm going to get Oska over to take a look at you," he said, pulling the duvet up. "Just precautionary. This type of thing is right up his street."

Logan grinned, "I thought he was a landscape gardener."

"He is at the moment, but he has certain abilities that I think can help you."

"Okay, but not tonight... please. I want to sleep." He nodded, extracting his phone from his pocket. "And I don't think these aches are sinister, Jorn; I think they're something else."

"What do you mean?"

She looked at him and then closed her eyes. She wasn't sure what she meant, and even if she did, he wouldn't understand.

"It's just a feeling I have." She could feel herself relaxing into the sheets. "Will you stay?" she asked, her tiredness enveloping her.

"You try and stop me," he said, swiping his fingertips across his screen, messaging his brother.

She smiled wistfully; at least, this was one way to get him to come over and stay.

CHAPTER TWENTY TWO

THE COUSIN

It was dawn when Oska stood in Logan's bedroom after she'd invited him in. He'd had to come early, as he'd a busy day scheduled, and he knew Jorn's impatience would only worsen the longer he left it. Jorn couldn't bear seeing her so vulnerable, so he vacated downstairs, allowing Oska to work unimpeded. He paced the room, stopping every so often to listen to what Oska was saying and what Logan was answering. On the dining table, he saw the mask he had left for her on the doorstep and smiled briefly at imagining her in it. She was going to look stunning tomorrow.

Leaving the box, he returned to the mantelpiece and looked at his reflection. He felt he'd aged a hundred years overnight. He'd found it very difficult to switch off, his mind going a million miles an hour. He'd lain with her all night just watching her sleep, listening to her breathing, seeing her facial expressions as she dreamed.

What the fuck was he doing?

Tilting his head, he watched his brother descend the staircase, his footfalls heavy. Whatever he was going to say, Jorn knew it wouldn't be good.

"So?" he turned to face him.

"I'm sorry, Jorn." Oska shook his head, Jorn immediately fearing the worst, "I can't find anything wrong with her."

"What?" Jorn stammered, not daring to believe him.

"I can't find anything. Her body has been through some kind of ordeal, but I can't find any cause," Oska said, putting his hands in his pockets.

"What does that mean?" Jorn asked, his brow furrowed.

"I can't find anything, because there's no way in. She's blocking me somehow, like an invisible barrier. I touched her, held her hand, placed my hands on her chest, you know, the usual stuff. But there's nothing—just an emptiness. I couldn't even sense a broken toe from childhood or even a chickenpox mark. I, literally, felt nothing." He sat on the sofa, his head in his hands.

"What the hell does that mean, Oska?" Jorn asked, sitting next to him.

"I don't know, brother, I really don't. It's like something is stopping me from seeing in. Like some sort of force field." He smiled, knowing he sounded ridiculous.

"What do I do now?" Jorn said, exasperatedly.

"Well, the only thing I can think of is to ask Lachlan. If it's the headaches you want investigating, then he has the correct ability for that. Maybe my ability is too broad. He specialises in the brain and the head, doesn't he? Maybe he'll be of more help." He shook his head again, "I feel such a failure."

"Do you think this is why The Emperor wants her? Do you think she's hiding something we don't know about?" Jorn asked, suddenly afraid, and yet he knew what he said was stupid. She wasn't hiding anything; even as a Watcher, he could see that.

"I don't know, brother," Oska said, rubbing his chin. "I really don't think she's hiding anything purposefully. She has no idea what's going on. I believe she is innocent in all this."

Jorn clapped his brother's knee, "Don't ever think you are a failure, my brother. This has nothing to do with your ability."

"I've never been met with this type of issue before. It's very disconcerting."

"You didn't see her last night, Oska. I thought she was dying," Jorn said, getting to his feet again.

"No, she's not dying. I don't get that type of sense from her at all; in fact, I feel that she is strong. Perhaps stronger than you or I. She is unique and whatever The Emperor wants with her. I'm afraid it will not be good." He looked sorrowfully, for he knew that this was not what Jorn needed to hear.

"Don't I know it. None of this is good."

Oska stood, hearing footsteps on the stairs as Logan came down.

"Hey," Jorn was at her side in seconds. "What are you doing up?"

"I'm not an invalid, Jorn," she smiled, moving towards the kitchen, "I wanted a cup of tea."

"I can do that," Jorn said.

"No, I want to do it. Oska, would you like one?"

"Er... no thank you, ma'am. I must get going... Jorn?"

Logan looked at them both, and then Jorn said, "I'm afraid I have to go, father is cracking his whip again, and Oska needs my help."

"That's fine, you go. I'm okay," she said, looking at him, "honestly, I'm alright. I'm just going to rest today; I have no plans. I'll just make a cup of tea and watch a movie."

"I don't like leaving you," Jorn said, following her.

"Stop being ridiculous. Just go, I'll be fine. You have a lot to prepare for," she said, perhaps half-heartedly, and Jorn knew she was putting on a brave face for him. "Please go. You need to get ready for tomorrow. Please do not worry about me."

"But I can't not worry," he said.

"I'll be better if you're not here. I won't feel pressured into entertaining you," she grinned.

Oska walked to the kitchen door, "Jorn? She's right, she

needs to rest, and you hovering around won't get her that."

Jorn knew that he was beaten. "Okay. I'll phone you later?"

"That would be great." Jorn could hear the strain in her voice and felt torn between wanting to stay and needing to go because she wanted him to.

As he drove home, he fast-dialled his cousin. He knew Oska was right; if anyone could fathom out what was going on with Logan, Lachlan could, and Jorn marvelled at the fact that he hadn't thought of him first.

"Well, if it isn't my favourite Gifted son of a Hartvigsen."

Jorn couldn't help but smile at the man at the other end of the phone.

"Hello, Lachlan, you well?"

"Absolutely, but then you knew that already." Jorn grinned. "What can I do for you at this most ungodly hour on a Tuesday morning?"

"I've got something I want you to look into," Jorn replied.

"Jorn, you know my abilities don't always tell truths over long distances."

"Yes, I know that, but I was wondering if you could maybe try, just to put my mind at rest. If you feel anything sinister, then I'll fly her up," he said earnestly.

"Look, mate, I'm coming down tomorrow anyway. Can it not wait?" Lachlan didn't know why he bothered asking;

he knew Jorn wouldn't have phoned if it could wait.

"No, it can't."

"Knew you'd say that. Who's the client?"

"She's... well, she's just someone I've been watching for a while now, but she keeps getting these headaches. They're so debilitating that she sometimes blacks out, and last night was the worst one yet," Jorn said, indicating left.

"Okay, but I can't promise you anything. You'd be better off waiting until tomorrow when I can take a real look at her."

"Yes, I know, but I'm impatient when it comes to her. I've already had Oska take a look, and the rabbit hole gets even deeper," he grimaced. "He couldn't get any read from her. Like absolutely nothing."

Lachlan was quiet for a moment.

"You mean he couldn't get anything at all from her? No past illnesses or childhood breaks?"

"Nothing," Jorn said bluntly, pulling up the estate's long drive, Oska just ahead of him in his truck.

"Hmmm, that is strange; I don't know how you think I'm going to be able to get a read on her from all the way up here in the Highlands if Oska couldn't by being with her."

"Yes, I know it's a long shot, but I need you to try," Jorn pleaded.

"She means a lot to you, this woman?" Lachlan asked.

"Well, yes, you could say that." Jorn waited, listening to Lachlan scrape at a lighter and inhale deeply. "You'll do it?"

"It will take me time. I'll have to call you back later," he exhaled.

"Thank you, Lachlan. I know I'm asking a lot," Jorn said, pulling alongside Oska, disconnecting his phone and putting it next to his ear, exiting the vehicle.

"Jorn, if it's not good news, I won't be able to sort it until the new year."

"That's okay. I just need to know." He hung up, feeling some relief that Lachlan was now on the case. If Lachlan couldn't find anything, he didn't know what he was going to do.

He only half listened to Oska as they started laying out shingle on the paths of the maze. The Master had decided they were too muddy for the four hundred guests he had coming tomorrow. Jorn hated every bit of the manual labour, not because he didn't want to do it, but because The Master had commanded it. He could have paid someone to do it, but like always, he was a tight-fisted git, so Oska and Jorn had drawn the short straw. Oska tried to get Jorn to break out of his solitary mind frame, but after a while, he just got on with the work in silence. Eventually, much to Jorn's surprise, Kol and Randin came and helped, and it wasn't until they'd been there for half an hour, and the conversation got going, that Jorn realised Oska must have messaged them to come, or he might do Jorn an injury.

"Jorn?" His Master stood at the end of the path they were all working on, his fringe blowing in the cold breeze as his dark eyes surveyed the progress.

"Yes," Jorn said, not feeling like giving him any time.

"Can I see you in my office, please?"

"Why? Surely whatever you have to say can be said here in front of these three," Jorn said, chucking down his spade.

His Master tilted his head, "I will pretend you didn't just say that and that you are going to follow me without incident."

The Master turned on his heel, his suit making him look even more dapper than usual, but instead of admiring him, Jorn just bent down and tried to grab the shovel back, but Randin, however, stuck his foot on it to stop Jorn's retaliation.

Sighing in defeat, Jorn left his brothers and, before long, was sitting in front of his Master's desk, waiting for him to say something.

After a minute or so, he got up and went to walk away. He didn't have time for this. "I understand you contacted Lachlan this morning?" He stopped and returned, leaning into the desk, his arms and ankles crossed. He was sick of formality.

"Who told you I had?" Jorn scathed, looking at the floor, suddenly feeling defeated. Was everyone in this family against him? Lachlan surely wouldn't have told The Master. But then, who had?

"The answer to that is irrelevant."

"Was it Oska?" Jorn asked, avoiding eye contact with him.

"Like I said, the answer is irrelevant," his Master retorted, looking up at him from his seat.

"It isn't if you want me to answer your questions," he replied, turning to look in his Master's eyes.

"Why must you always be so defiant, Jorn?"

"Why must you always be so insubordinate, sir?" For the first time in a while, Jorn saw his Master close his eyes, praying for patience.

"What have I ever done to you to make you treat me like this?" Was he actually serious?

"Oh, where do I begin?" Jorn said, walking away again.

"Look, I already apologised for the spy pin. That was a low point, I'll give you that."

"And you think that is all there is?" Jorn said, moving to the bookshelf to try and distract himself from lashing out.

"I know you feel I do you wrong all the time, but I don't, Jorn. I let you have free rein; I let you come and go as you please." Did he think he was being courteous?

"Yes, but I'm never allowed to stay away, am I? I tried that, didn't I? I tried to move out, but you kept calling me and calling me, and asking me to do this and asking me to do that, so in the end, it was all I could do but move back in to stop me from getting persistent whiplash."

"You make your life sound so harsh. Do you know what I have lost to give you the life you have now, Jorn? What people have given to allow you to have what you've got? Do you?" He was now on his feet, his hands splayed out on the desk.

"Yes, I know exactly what you lost, Master," he said, staring at him.

"No, you only think you do," he said sternly.

"I am The Watcher, aren't I? I see everything that goes on in this house, in this family. Even when you think I'm not watching, I'm there, Master. I have always been there. Even on that day." Jorn almost choked on his words, remembering the day they were both talking about and yet couldn't say it aloud.

"It might surprise you to know that I am well aware of how vast your abilities are, Jorn," he said assuredly. "I know you know things that even I don't, so don't presume you know me when quite clearly you don't."

"How can you say that? I was there that day. I know what you did."

"You do not know anything," he said firmly. "There actually was a choice, and it was not of my choosing."

"But you didn't stop it happening, did you? You did nothing," Jorn accused.

His Master was silent a moment, and then he said, "I would have done anything to change the course of that day, but it was taken out of my hands."

"No, it wasn't. You are a Gifted leader; you could have prevented it, you could have stopped... her," Jorn choked.

"Not a day goes by that I don't think that, Jorn," his Master said, averting his eyes from Jorn's accusatory gaze. "But nothing I would have done would have changed the events on that day."

"YOU DON'T KNOW THAT!" Jorn shouted.

"YES, I DO!" his Master hammered the desk with his fists, puckering the wood, his eyes glowing scarlet.

Jorn stumbled backwards, the sheer power of his Master suddenly overbearing him, like a shadow crushing his chest. He gripped his throat as it became constricted, and his eyes started running as he strained against his Master's strength. His Master looked away, and Jorn fell to his knees, spluttering.

"Never presume to know me, Jorn. You might be a Watcher and of exceptional quality, but I am your Master, and if you actually believe I didn't do everything I could before that day, and on that day, to prevent her from doing what she did, then you do not know me." He returned to his seat as Jorn climbed back to his feet using the chair as support. "I have been in eternal pain since that day, and I hope that you nor any of my community members will ever endure that same agony. For losing your kindred soulmate is a torture I would not wish on any."

Coughing, Jorn said, "Then why are you asking why I contacted Lachlan about Logan? If you understand my feelings, why are you questioning me?"

"Because I did not know you contacted him about Miss Hunter, and if she was the reason, then I am trying to help you. I do not want you to suffer my fate."

"How can asking Lachlan for help make me suffer your fate?"

"Because it means you care for her, Jorn, more than you should, and that was not the point of your task." He sighed heavily. "I'm trying to save you."

"Why?" Jorn asked, "Why would you try to save me? I've always been a disappointment to you."

His Master shook his head, pinching his nose as though to curb his emotions. "You thinking you are a disappointment to me is my failure as a leader, not you as a member of this community."

"Or perhaps it is your failure as a father and not me as a son?" Jorn said, watching him for his retaliation.

He stopped to look at Jorn, scrutinising his face.

"I'm afraid that man died when your mother walked out on the ice. You know this," he said curtly, before rubbing his hands over his chin and clicking his pen.

"I don't think he did, Pappa," Jorn said, with a plea in his voice.

His Master tutted, brushing off his remark, "Anyway, down to business. You contacted Lachlan this morning. Why?"

"Because Logan keeps getting headaches. I had Oska look

at her, but he came up empty, so I asked Lachlan for help."

His Master nodded, "You even want to help her, when you know her fate is already written?" he asked, jotting something on his pad of paper before moving the mouse to load up his screen.

"How do you know her fate is written, Master; it has not yet happened?" Jorn said, unwilling to allow his despair to tumble from him.

"The Emperor will come for her, Jorn, and you better be ready to give her up," he said absent-mindedly, typing. "Can you send Hadley in to me on your way out?"

Jorn strode slowly to the door, knowing he had been dismissed, but before leaving, he glanced back at his father. He suddenly seemed old, and momentarily, Jorn felt wretched for all the ill he'd ever thought about him. It was apparent to him now that he was in as much pain about his mother's fate as Jorn was about Logan's.

"Jorn?" He looked back into the empty eyes, and for a brief moment, he saw the tormented soul at face value. "I am sorry that this is happening to you, but you must give her up, my son. I cannot let my brother take another loved one from me."

Jorn lay in his room all that evening, just staring up at the ceiling. He'd sent Jorun to Logan's with her dress; he didn't have the stomach to go to her now. The voice he'd heard in the maze must have been his drunken mind telling him it was going to be okay and that he had all he needed to see this right. He had to hand her over, and that was the end of it. There was no get-out clause, no way around the inevitable. She was lost to him, and the chest pain was so bad that his sternum felt cracked. Even when Kol came in offering him a game of poker and a joint, Jorn sent him away. He knew Randin had asked Kol to come, and not that he didn't love his brothers; he just wanted to be alone right now. He'd even switched off the cameras in Logan's house. He didn't need to watch her to know she was safe, to know she was beginning to feel more herself. He could sense it with every beat of his heart, with every tick of his brain. With every inhale of his lungs. He loved her and always would love her, but tomorrow, he would have to say goodbye, and that... he couldn't stand. He turned his head and screamed into his pillow, his throat becoming raw with the strain. He felt Jorun try to mind link him, but even that, he blocked out. No one could help him. He was a powerful Watcher, his brothers were powerful beings of The Gifted, and yet none of them could do anything to prevent this future from unfolding. There was no way out for any of them.

Awoken in the early morning by his phone, seeing it was Lachlan, Jorn contemplated not answering. Would he really have anything worth speaking about?

"Yeah," he said, pressing the green icon.

"Jorn, my man!" Lachlan was quiet a moment, "You, okay?" Jorn sniffed, wiping his eyes. Had he been crying in his sleep?

"Yes, er... what have you got for me?"

"Well, it's more of a fact what I haven't got for you?" Jorn felt his spirits plummet even further; Lachlan couldn't assist him either. "I can't get a read on her, I'm afraid. There's a wall around her that even I can't penetrate. I waited for her to go to bed to see if it lowered when she slept, but even then, her defences were so high I couldn't get through. If she were a computer, she'd be firewalled up to the eyeballs."

"So, what do you think this means?"

"It doesn't mean anything; it just means I'll have to see her in person, perhaps touch her, to get any sense of what's going on. You'll have to wait until I fly down," he exhaled heavily. "She seems very extraordinary, Jorn. I've never had anyone with so many barriers."

"She is... she is... exceptional," Jorn whispered, the ache in his heart beginning to tremble.

"She feels it, mate." Jorn took a deep breath. "Oh yeah, sorry about Iona; she totally ratted you out to The Master as she overheard our conversation. She always has to stick her nose in."

"That's okay", Jorn said, rolling his eyes at the nerve of Lachlan's sister, "he called me to his office, and I... well, let's just say I learnt more about him than I already knew."

"Really? I thought you knew everything," Lachlan said, surprised.

"Clearly, I don't, and I think perhaps he, too, has barriers that I've never penetrated or felt inclined to," Jorn said.

"Yes, I'm not getting a very good vibe off you. Are you okay? Your aura is way off," Lachlan summed up, his concern for his cousin's mental state increasing.

"I'm okay, thanks, Lachlan, and I'm looking forward to seeing you. What time's your flight getting in?"

"About midday. This exceptional woman coming tonight?" He sounded so excited at the prospect of meeting Logan that Jorn couldn't help but smile despite his grief.

"Yes, she should be."

"Good. I want to meet her as soon as I can."

"I'll be sure to try and introduce you, before The Emperor takes her," Jorn heaved, rubbing his eyes with his free hand.

"Wait, what?" Was this why Jorn's mental state was so worrying?

"It's a long story, my cousin. Come earlier if you can, so we can have a whisky, and I'll tell you about her."

"Oh, I most definitely will try and Jorn?" He waited. "You know if *he's* got his eye on her, it cannot be good."

"Yes, I most definitely know that."

Jorn stood on the airstrip leaning against his Audi as he waited for Lachlan's private plane to land, having a cigarette. He liked his cousin. There were five years between them, Jorn being the older, but it never seemed to make any difference to their friendship. They had played together as boys, and Lachlan, being his mother's sister's son, made him feel closer to his mother. Jorn's Master never really had much to do with her side of the family since she died; whether it was guilt, grief or just pure arrogance, Jorn wasn't sure. But since last night, he'd begun to feel that perhaps it was because of the sadness that he'd severed all connections. The guilt of centuries past lay heavier on him than Jorn had ever realised.

He scrunched his butt into the tarmac as he saw the plane touch down, pulling his scarf around his neck that little bit tighter. He wasn't cold, but at the moment, he always felt an unnatural chill down his spine. Even though tightening the scarf wouldn't help, he did it anyway. New Year's Eve had arrived, and he was nervous about this evening's celebrations. Could he go ahead with it? Would he hand her over? She was going to come to the ball, and he would have to pretend that everything was normal. He was going to have to pretend to enjoy himself when really, he knew, he'd be screaming inside. In a way, he wanted her to feel too unwell to come. That might delay things somewhat, and it might give them more time. But he knew deep down that she would be well enough and that he would have to comply with his Emperor's requests. He knew the consequences of not complying, and they would be worse as it most likely would involve not just him and Logan but his brothers and his father.

Lachlan slipped slightly down the plane steps as he disembarked, making Jorn smile. He was already drunk and would need an afternoon nap before they talked. He waved jovially, catching himself, before staggering towards Jorn, pulling a small overnight case and a suit in a black bag over his shoulder.

"Ah, my favourite cousin." Lachlan yanked Jorn into a full-sized man hug, patting him harshly on his back.

"How was the flight?" Jorn asked, taking his case and popping the boot.

"Good," Lachlan turned round and waved at the pilot.

"Danny flying you?" Jorn knew Lachlan's personal pilot from many journeys he'd taken on it.

"Of course, he is my most trusted pilot." He got into the passenger seat and buckled his belt. "So, brother from another mother, how are things with you? Your aura still seems way off-key."

"I'm alright, my cousin," Jorn shrugged, sticking the car in reverse and then flooring it off the tarmac.

"Okay, you say that, but in all seriousness."

"Lachlan, I can't be serious with you so wasted," Jorn smiled, pulling onto the motorway.

"I'm not that bad," he said, feeling his pockets for a lighter and opening the window.

"You must be if you think you're lighting up in my car," Jorn said, ploughing down the outside lane.

"Ah, shit!" Lachlan said, holding the cigarette in his mouth. "I'll pretend then like I've seen wee kids do." He mouthed, puffing out air, making Jorn snigger.

"You are stupid."

"Yeah, I know, but you love me," he said, grinning broadly.

The drive continued, and Lachlan eventually dozed off, so by the time they pulled up at the mansion, he'd slept off a lot of the alcohol.

"What room you put me in?" he questioned, taking his

bag from the boot.

"The same one you're always in. As far away from The Master as possible. I know what you're like with women once you get some rum in you."

"Is that the only reason?" Lachlan said, smirking.

"Well, and you're the opposite end of the house to your sister." Lachlan and Iona had a love/hate relationship, more so when he drank, so it was always better to keep them apart.

"So, what time's the party getting started?" Lachlan put his arm around Jorn's shoulder as they walked around the back to the kitchen.

"Seven is kick-off, apparently," Jorn replied, leading the way through the house to the grand staircase and up to his wing.

"I hope you and your lady won't be keeping me from my beauty sleep later," Lachlan joked, walking to his bedroom's en-suite and taking a pee.

"I'm sure we won't be making as much noise as you, you bugger," Jorn said, leaning against the wall waiting for him to finish.

"You know me, cuz, I can't deny the English women of some Scottish loving." He gyrated the air, and Jorn smiled at just how ridiculous he was. He wished he lived nearer.

"Well, I'm not sure the English women are prepared for such an Adonis." Jorn smiled before remembering Logan, the sadness returning to his face.

"So," Lachlan opened a decanter of whisky that was on the dresser, "You going to tell me what's going on, or have I got to pry it out of you when you've had too much to drink?" He handed Jorn a generous measure.

"No, it's not really that bigger deal; it's just the same old shit that goes on in this community, and nothing's going to change." He sipped the whisky, it being the first drink he'd had since his drunken Christmas night. He hissed between his teeth, enjoying the burn more than he wanted to.

"Listen, Jorn, I've known you my whole life, and I've never had you phone me about anyone, and then yesterday morning, after hundreds of years, you asked about this girl. I know you too well to know that this is very much a massive deal," he said, suddenly serious.

"Hmmm." Jorn swirled the contents of his glass around, looking to drown himself in it.

"What does The Emperor want with her?"

"I have no idea," Jorn said, sitting on the dresser chair, putting his glass down and holding his head in his hands. "It's most likely something to do with all the barriers she's put up around herself, knowingly or unknowingly. Even I, as a Watcher, can't find anything extraordinary about her and yet she is the most extraordinary woman I have ever met." He sat upright, resting his head on the back wall, keeping his emotions in check.

"But what could she be hiding that The Emperor doesn't already have? He has every ability we know of, doesn't he?" Lachlan queried.

"Maybe he is not as powerful as we believe," Jorn said,

sitting forward and saying aloud some of his thoughts from his night-time brooding. "At first, The Master asked me to watch her, just tail her, see what she got up to, find out her likes and dislikes. You know, the basic Watcher shit. At the start, I thought it must be because she had some unknown ability or gift, but I kept coming up empty. She seemed like a perfectly normal human woman, and yet, after a while, I couldn't stop watching her. Like I'd make excuses to be where she was or log things she did so I could predict her movements. She became a magnet to me, and I couldn't resist trying to be near her." He patted his own pockets now for his cigarettes, "Shall we play some pool?"

"Sure."

They meandered to the games room, and Jorn started setting up the balls whilst Lachlan sparked up, looking out of the window at the courtyard festooned with garlands and lights.

"Does he always go all out for The Emperor?" he asked, handing Jorn a lit cigarette.

"You know him," Jorn grimaced. "Can't ever be outdone by his brother."

"But they hate each other, don't they? I mean, after your mother's death, they've rarely seen each other, so why does he care?"

Jorn shrugged, "The Emperor has not been to this house in over one hundred and fifty years, so his coming now is a big thing for my father. He has to show off."

"Why did he invite him anyway? Seems pointless to invite

someone you hate," Lachlan said, splitting the triangle of balls.

"This party wasn't The Master's idea, though; it was Portia's. She's the one who's been pouring poisonous words into his ear. I know she's working for The Emperor, and my father goes along with it," Jorn said, taking his turn.

"But your father is one of the strongest men I know, Jorn." Lachlan stood back as Jorn lined up another shot after potting a stripe.

"He might have been in former years, but since mamma," Jorn swallowed, "he's been so lost. I think he's been doing The Emperor's bidding a lot longer than I realised."

"So, you think that The Emperor has in some way been planning this, like from the beginning?" Lachlan didn't seem convinced.

"I don't know, Lachlan. I just think my father inviting his brother, who he hates, to a ball at our house is something that shouldn't be taken lightly. There's something underlying, I'm sure there is." He leaned heavily into the window, the glass cooling his heated mind. "I just wish my father could see it."

"So, who asked you originally to watch this woman?"

"My father put me onto her first, but now I feel it has been The Emperor all along. He made me get so involved that I..."

Jorn was silent as he looked outside, watching the staff setting up the gas heaters.

"Couldn't stop?" Lachlan surmised, taking his shot.

"Yes. I just kept having to watch Logan; I mean, for fuck's sake. I had Craig install cameras in her home so I could watch her. That's just crazy, right, damn right, unethical. But I couldn't not watch her. I enjoyed hearing her laugh and listening to her chat on the phone. You know, she has this sweet dimple on her forehead that appears when she cradles the receiver to her ear. You know, just stupid things like that," he inhaled on his cigarette. "Then, The Master asked me to get to know her, totally not in my remit, so I asked him to give the task to Jorun, but he said it had to be me." He potted another stripe, "I couldn't understand why he asked me to get so close; it was an order he'd never given before, and I'd been watching her a while and couldn't find anything out of the ordinary about her. It was then he let it drop that the order had come from The Emperor, and I immediately grew suspicious. But I couldn't help myself, Lachlan." Jorn stood back, looking at his cousin, "I couldn't not get involved."

"You fell in love with her?" Lachlan said, blowing smoke into the air before potting a spot and moving to the next ball, his cigarette hanging from his mouth.

"I know I did; I mean, I know I have, but..." He shook his head again, "Nothing that comes from The Emperor is going to end well... for anyone. Especially her." He scuffed the cigarette out in an ashtray, running his hand through his hair. "I can't help how I feel, Lachlan. And yet, there is no way to stop the inevitable. He's going to take her from me tonight, and there's nothing I can do to stop him."

"Did you try talking to The Master, to your father, about it?" he asked, missing the pocket and waiting for Jorn to take his turn.

"I tried," he said, shrugging, pocketing another ball, "but he says his hands are tied. Either I hand her over, or The Emperor will relinquish my abilities."

"Hmmm, I thought as much. Same old bribery tactics. Do as I say, or I'll strip you."

"But right now, Lachlan, I'm beginning to think that he can have my abilities." He rubbed his temples. "If it means she'll be saved, maybe I should allow him to take back what he bestowed upon me at my birth. Maybe my death is the answer. Maybe that is what he wants."

Lachlan looked at his cousin, the game of pool forgotten.

"Jorn... you cannot be serious?"

Jorn looked at his cousin. Lachlan didn't understand, and he hadn't expected him to. No one could know how he felt. The only person who probably understood was his father, and Jorn knew that. This could be what the voice in the maze had meant.

He, himself, was literally all he needed.

As Jorn prepared for the evening, he splashed cologne on his neck and chest, his fingers slipping on the shirt buttons. His afternoon with Lachlan had proved beneficial, though he knew Lachlan didn't think it had made any difference. He felt ready. Ready for the inevitable, prepared to face The Emperor. Ready to face Logan's fate and his own if required. He would treat her like she should be treated, show her a good time, and then hand her over should The Emperor ask.

"You've always looked good in a tux." Jorn glanced at his door, doing up one of his diamond cufflinks.

"Wish I could say that you look good in that dress, but then I'd be lying." Portia leaned against the frame, wearing a long fire-red dress with an unsightly slit in the leg that went right up to her knicker line. "Are you even wearing underwear?" he scathed, straightening his bow tie.

"No." He shook his head, downing his whisky. "Drinking an awful lot these days, Jorn."

"And?"

"The Master is worried about you." She walked in, clutching her glass of red wine.

"Yeah, well, I'm sorry about that," he said, not sounding sorry in the least.

"I can tell you're not sorry at all," Portia quipped.

"No, I'm not." Although deep down, he thought that perhaps he should be.

"I know you're hurting, Jorn, but after tonight, it will all be over, and this little charade will be brought to an end."

He rushed at her, pushing his arm into her throat, making her drop her wine glass, it smashing over his floor.

"Charade? Charade? Is that what life is to you, Portia? A FUCKING CHARADE?" he shouted.

"It is... until..." she choked, "until tonight is... over."

He could sense through her skin that she was afraid, her heart was pounding, and he could feel her sweat glands heightened.

"I know what you are, Portia. Don't pretend your little act is fooling me or my father. I can see your heart, and it is black." He pushed his arm further into her throat, her bones crunching on each other, her lungs unable to take any more breath.

"Now, now, Jorn, that is not any way to treat a lady."

Jorn felt ice slide around his body as goosebumps erupted on the skin under his jacket, his breath caught momentarily in his lungs. Turning slowly, he released Portia from his grasp, her hands instantly at her throat, gasping for breath.

He stared into the eyes of the man who tortured people for fun, who had killed Jorn's grandfather to gain his abilities, and who had sanctioned Jorn with the impossible task he was going to have to fulfil. The Emperor stood there in a suit of the deepest purple, his masquerade mask hanging loosely from his wrist, his dark hair pinned back in a ponytail, and his irises, which were usually stained red, glowed mauve with contact lenses.

He entered Jorn's room, his gloved hands touching every surface, checking for dust.

"I hear you have quite a beauty for me tonight, my nephew?" He revolved his eyes to Jorn, and Jorn stared right through him to the place where his heart would be, but he felt nothing, just fire and ash. "Well? Haven't you?"

Jorn blinked rapidly and replied, "She is the most stunning

woman I have ever seen, sire."

"Is she? Well, I will be the judge of that." He lifted Jorn's empty glass and sniffed at it, "Jameson? Bloody hell, my brother has fallen off the path if he's allowing you to drink that muck."

"I choose my own whisky, sire," Jorn said, through gritted teeth.

"Do you? Well, you should try Macallan 1926; then you'll know what whisky is."

It was taking all his willpower not to launch himself at his uncle. "I think perhaps it comes down to personal preference and taste, my lord."

"Hmmm. Does it?" The Emperor questioned with a sneer. "So, to business." Jorn just stared stony-faced at him, waiting for his demands. "I will watch you and the girl throughout the evening, and I will judge whether or not you have succeeded in the task I set you. If you have, then I will let the evening unfold as evenings do. But when I have had enough frivolity, I *will* send for her." He looked at him straight in the eye, "And you *will* deliver."

Swallowing, Jorn said, "I will bring her, sire, to where you wish."

"Oh, I know you will," he said, smiling maliciously.

Jorn just nodded curtly.

The Emperor clapped his hands together. "Right, Portia, shall I escort you to the ball?" He bowed jovially, linking arms with her, crushing the broken wine glass into the carpet with his shoes as they departed.

Jorn fell into the wall, sinking to the floor, with his head in his hands. He could feel his own eyes turn red with rage as he punched his chest of drawers that stood next to him, his whole fist splintering through the wood.

"I am so sorry," he whispered, feeling his phone buzz in his pocket.

I've got her, sir. ETA fifteen minutes. It was Hadley.

Thank you, Hadley.

I know it's not my place to say it, but she's lovely, he replied.

Jorn pinched the bridge of his nose, curbing his tears. He was going to give her a night to remember.

Fuck the consequences.

He allowed the door to close as he moved along the corridor, knocking on Lachlan's room. His cousin opened it in the most exuberant white suit Jorn had seen on a man. His silver-white top hat sat crookedly on his head, and with one hand, he held a glass of his favourite rum; in the other, he had a cane that he kept swinging enthusiastically. Could he be any more eccentric?

"Right... so, you know the drill, yes?" Jorn asked him quickly, checking his mask in the hallway mirror.

"Yes, she'll be wearing a green halter-neck dress and be the most beautiful woman I've ever seen," Lachlan said, smirking.

"No, not just that, but you'll check her over before she sees me?" Jorn asked desperately.

"Yes, I will take her hand and see if I can get through the firewalls she unknowingly puts up around herself," Lachlan joked, though Jorn could see nothing funny in his task.

"And you must tell me if you find anything," Jorn said, moving down the stairs towards the already booming ballroom.

"Listen, my cousin," Lachlan threw out his cane to stop Jorn from moving any further. "I don't want this evening to go down any other way than happily for everyone. Of course, I will tell you what I find."

Allowing Lachlan to go in first, Jorn adjusted his jacket and slunk into the background, making himself seem invisible, and he was pleased for the first time in a while of his abilities. He clocked Kol already on the dance floor; laughter etched on his drug-induced face. Randin was chatting to their cousin Louiza. Jorn had never gotten a good vibe from her, so he avoided them. Jorun was at the bar rolling a bottle of beer around, speaking to a man Jorn knew only by sight. He could tell Jorun was on tenterhooks, and when he sensed Jorn, he nodded at him. Jorun had his back. Lamont wasn't in sight, though if Jorn concentrated, he could hear him talking out in the courtyard. Oska, it seemed, was still in his room, trying to decide on what shoes to wear. Jorn smiled, thinking of his brother. He was always indecisive about shoes.

He continued among the crowds, looking at the women's dresses. Some had pulled out all the stops and were wearing traditional ballgowns, had elaborate hairdos and were holding fans. Others had been more subtle. He could see The Emperor's wife; her dress was almost see-through, the amount of lace and diamonds on it must have cost a fortune, and her manicured nails, he could see, were embedded with sparkling rubies. As she put her glass of champagne to her lips, his uncle leaned into her and whispered something, making her look over the crowd. They were searching for him, yet neither could find him. He knew it wouldn't take his uncle long to clock him, but he relished in the notion of being hidden for a while. He stared intensely towards the entrance as he'd heard the limo pull up and the gravel crunch under the enthusiastic feet of Lexi and the not-so-enthused Quinn, who was most likely apprehensive about entering the house of The Gifted. But he wasn't interested in them, and he listened to the delicate feet of his lover, inhaling deeply, scenting her perfume on his tongue. She was his Queen, and he was going to make sure he treated her like one, no matter what was to come.

CHAPTER TWENTY THREE

THE BALL

She hadn't wanted to worry Jorn, but her head felt even weirder than it had during the headache. It was empty, like her brain had no further space for any memory or any thought and had entirely blanked itself. She'd ended up putting some chocolate croissants in the oven but forgot to switch it on and boiled the kettle twice without filling it with water first. Once she'd managed to heat the pastries and make a cup of tea, she selected a movie, and the beginning credits had only just started rolling when her doorbell rang. Feeling exasperated, she got laboriously to her feet.

"Hey, sis." It was Tyler.

"Ty?" Logan said, moving aside to let her into the room.

"You didn't forget I was coming to talk about the wedding, did you?"

Logan rolled her eyes. Of course, she had forgotten; she was forgetting everything today. Though, that didn't stall Tyler with her epilogue of what ifs and what do you thinks. And shall we do that or have this? Chocolate fountain, or is that chavvy? What kind of favours? Do you think Jorn will come as your plus one, and if he is, she needed to know so she could re-think her seating arrangements?

"Ty, Ty?" Logan put up her hand to stop her entourage. "Look, I'm not feeling brilliant. Can we just do one thing at a time?" Logan padded slowly to the kitchen to make some more tea.

"Your head still bad?" Tyler asked, removing Logan's coat from the high-rise chair.

"No, it's not bad, it just feels weird," Logan said, getting more croissants out of the cupboard.

"Maybe you *should* go to the doctors again?" Tyler said, accepting the tea and taking a sip, "Did you put sweetener in this?"

"Oh shit, no, sorry." Logan clicked the sweetener packet and handed her sister a spoon.

"Yes, you're right, your head must be feeling weird. You should deffo see a doctor in the new year," she said, nodding.

"You sound like Jorn. He's worried about me. He's already had his brother round, who is some kind of medical genius," Logan surmised, moving back into the lounge and snuggling under her blanket.

"Good. I'm glad he's looking after you," Tyler said, getting out some magazines from the two carrier bags she'd brought. "They've never gone on for over twenty-four hours, have they?"

Logan sighed, "It's not really an ache now, more a fuzzy feeling." She shrugged, taking the magazines her sister passed her.

They spent a good few hours perusing the wedding books, circling things they both thought would be fitting for a wedding that involved Tyler and her ways, and then swapped them to see if they agreed on the other's opinion. Tyler seemed to want everything, and Logan couldn't help but think she'd prefer a smaller wedding and to have someone organise it for her. She could imagine Jorn in a suit standing on a wintry hillside, the mountains in the background, and couldn't resist wondering if he ever got married, would it be back home in Norway.

"I think I want you and Macey in pale green. You've always looked good in green, and it will be spring, though perhaps purple would be better. Maybe a dark mauve?" Logan rubbed her temples, the ache returning, so she headed to the kitchen for more paracetamol.

"Loge, there's someone at the door for you." Logan quickly racked her brain on what else she'd forgotten today to see Jorun standing there, his hair windswept and slicked with sleet.

"Jorun? Please come in," Logan said, indicating for him to shut the door. "To what do I owe this pleasure?"

Jorun smiled at her, "You still look pale, Logan. How are

you feeling?"

"Not too bad," Logan said, sitting on the arm of the sofa, looking at him. "Is that why you're here? To check up on me. I've already had a few messages from Jorn," she smiled.

"Of course not, but I was instructed to make sure you were looking after yourself." He eyed the magazines and then looked at Tyler.

"Oh, Jorun, you remember my sister Tyler from Christmas Day?" Logan said.

"Of course, good afternoon, Tyler. Busy wedding planning, I see," he said cheerfully.

"Yes, but don't worry, I'm not exhausting her," Tyler said, looking up from the coloured papers of her magazine. Logan rolled her eyes at Jorun, and he took the hint that she was fine but bored of wedding things.

"I've just come over to give you this." He lifted a box from the floor, "It's for tomorrow." Logan looked disappointedly at him. "He wanted to come, but Oska has been working him like a pack horse, and he thought you'd rather have it sooner than later."

She brushed her fingers over the shiny rose gold and white box, the letters of the name Willow and Scarlett embossed in the corner.

"Willow and Scarlett? Jesus!" Tyler exclaimed, examining the logo, "That's an expensive boutique in Knightsbridge, that is." Logan looked at Tyler and then at Jorun.

"Look, Logan, my brother likes you a lot. Don't do him any injustice by not accepting this item," Jorun said, reading her mind.

"I know, but he's bought me enough already."

"Here," he took her hand. "He's not had many women he's actually cared for; if he wants to spoil you, let him." He smiled, "I just hope he's chosen something that suits you."

"Well, I'm screwed if it doesn't, as I have nothing suitable for this lavish ball your father is hosting," she said, storing the box on the small dining room table.

"Believe me, you could wear anything, and he'd still not look at any other women," Jorun said, his hand on the door handle to leave. "But if I know Jorn. He would have spent a lot of time contemplating, and he is usually accurate in his choices."

Logan couldn't help but blush, "You want to stay for a cup of tea?" she asked, rubbing her temples again.

"No, I must go, but I will see you tomorrow. Make sure you rest." He left quickly, closing out the cold as he slammed the door.

Logan and her sister sat a while just looking at the extravagant box, the wedding talk forgotten.

"Will you let me do your hair for tomorrow, Loge?" her sister asked, as she watched Logan run her fingers over the box again.

"Would you? You are so much better than me."

"What the hell, Loge, you do your hair more often better than I do, but I think I have some delicate clips that would look lovely against your ebony locks and depending on what this dress looks like, will most likely go with any ballgown," she said enthusiastically.

They sat a while longer, and then Logan said, "Right." She slid a nail under the small gold sticker that sealed the box, and pulling off the ribbon, she lifted the lid. There, lying inside the white tissue paper, was the dark green dress Jorn had bought. The dress, made from a silk-like material with chiffon over the top, flowed under Logan's hand as she lifted it out and held it up to her figure. The V-shaped neckline was quite deep, and the rear was almost completely backless. She couldn't help but tear up as she and her sister stared at the garment, which now hung on the door frame, the train almost touching the carpet.

"Blimey, Logan!" her sister said, amazed. "If this hasn't helped me decide on the colour of my bridesmaids, nothing will. That dress is stunning!"

It was no surprise to Logan that she slept in on New Year's Eve morning. She'd kept waking up in cold sweats and, more than once, had to get a drink from the kitchen. Maybe her headaches were due to dehydration? Lethargically, she made herself some breakfast and checked her emails before deciding to go back to bed. Thankfully, by mid-afternoon, she started to feel much more herself and lavishly ladened the bath with the glitter bath bomb she'd kept and soaked for an hour, before completing a head-to-toe pre-party de-fuzzing, leaving her legs silky smooth.

"There." Ty turned her around to look in the mirror after

she'd back-combed her hair and put it into a high, messy bun littered with small jewels. "Let's just try the mask before I spray it, in case it's too high, and the ribbon doesn't sit right." Putting the mask on, Tyler said, "Take a few extra kirby grips to put over the ribbon just in case you feel it slip throughout the night."

"Thanks, Tyler," Logan gasped, seeing the updo. Tyler might be a bridezilla, but she certainly knew how to do hair.

"He's not going to be able to take his eyes off you," Tyler remarked, packing up her hair stuff.

"That's the idea," Logan said, taking one more look in the mirror before removing the mask and starting her make-up.

"I cannot believe he's not coming to get you, though. I'd hate to arrive at a place I don't know on my own."

"I didn't like the idea at first, but with everyone in masks, it adds to the mystery of the evening," Logan smiled.

"Well, if you say so," Tyler just shrugged, putting on her coat. "Have an amazing time, sis, I can't say I'm not envious of you having somewhere so lavish to go."

"I know. I wish you were coming," Logan said, dusting her eyelids gradually with jade-coloured eyeshadow, giving them a smoky look.

"Ha, it seems we've both got something to bring to the table for my wedding. I'll do the hair; you can do the make-up," Tyler said, admiring her sister in the glass. "You could always do that gradual thing; I can never do that."

"It has taken years of practice," Logan said, running the eyeliner along her eyelid. "You must go, Ty, or you'll be late for your own celebratory drinks."

"Love you, babe," she squeezed her sister's shoulder and left.

Logan tied the neck silk ribbon in a bow, ensuring it lay flat against her skin, before standing back and sighing. She had never been a vain person, but she could tell she looked beautiful. The dress fitted her superbly, and luckily, it wasn't so snug that it showed her underwear line.

Her overnight bag was waiting by the front door, and her mask hung on the bannister as she stood waiting nervously. She'd never been picked up by a car before and couldn't help wringing her hands that were enclosed in elbow-length gloves. At precisely seven forty-five, the doorbell rang, and she opened it to an older man in a black suit.

"Miss Hunter?"

"Yes, that's me," she said nervously, smiling.

"I am Hadley, your driver for this evening. Are you ready to go?" he asked, his hands resolutely clasped in front of him.

"Yes, please, thank you." He looked at her,

"Er, do you want to bring a coat? It's very cold out here," he asked kindly.

Shit. She felt like an idiot; of course, she wanted to bring a coat. She grabbed it from the stair cupboard.

"This coming too?" He bent to pick up her small rucksack.

"Yes, please." She walked to the door.

"Do you have a masquerade mask?"

"Damn it!" She was failing at every turn, "I'm so sorry, I'm a bit nervous," she said, taking the mask from the bannister.

"Don't be nervous, Miss. I have worked for the Hartvigsens my whole life; you don't need to be anxious. My Master can be a little brisk, perhaps coming across as angry, but he has never been anything but courteous to me." He smiled, "Deep down, he only has his family's interests at heart."

"That is generous of you. I'm afraid Jorn doesn't talk highly of him," she said, slipping her coat on.

"Fathers and sons, sometimes they clash, but he does his best, and Master Jorn will realise that soon."

"Thank you, Hadley." He assisted her with her coat and then held an umbrella over her as they walked to the car. "Oh God! I've never been in a limo before," she whispered, biting her lip.

"Well, Master Jorn was particular." He opened the door for her.

"LOGAN!" Logan almost fell back, "SURPRISE!"

"Lexi?"

"I really thought Jorn was going to tell you, but clearly, he didn't. He invited Quinn and I so you wouldn't be on your own," Lexi screeched, her hands already clutching a glass of champagne.

Logan couldn't help but feel relieved that she wasn't alone and scooted in next to Lexi.

"You look fucking stunning. Who did your hair?" Lexi jabbered on and on throughout the journey, whilst Logan smiled and laughed at her comments. She loved her best friend, but she always got a little over-excited, and Logan wondered if Jorn knew what he'd let himself in for by inviting her.

She downed the last of her champagne as the limo pulled up to the steps of the mansion. Jorn hadn't exaggerated about the no-expense-spared look his father had gone for. The amount of twinkling lights and decorations must have cost a fortune. Lexi walked quickly up the steps with Quinn, not even looking beyond the grand entrance hall, but Logan took her time. She marvelled at the vastness of the estate, at the wide, expansive driveway littered with stone vases housing shrubs covered with glimmering fairy lights. Around the corner of the main house, she could see many cars parked, noticing Jorn's Audi at the front. She instinctively put her hand to her stomach, the nerves setting in, the lust already brewing at the thought of seeing him.

"I think Master Jorn thought they'd stop you being so apprehensive, but maybe you'd have been better on your own," Hadley said, holding the umbrella again, looking up the steps to where Lexi and Quinn had gone.

"Yes, I love my best friend, but sometimes she can be a little crazy." She beamed at the older man.

"Would you like a hand up the steps?" he asked, holding out his arm.

"Firstly, is my mask straight?" she said, and he looked at her, seeing much admiration in his gaze.

"Yes. You look beautiful. Jorn is a fortunate man." He linked her arm, and they walked smoothly up the steps, her heart going a thousand beats a minute, her breathing shallow.

"Any tips on how to act in front of Mr Hartvigsen?" she asked, as she got nearer the doors.

"Don't worry about making a good impression, Miss, you do that without trying. Just be yourself and always refer to him as sir; he hates being known as Mr Hartvigsen," Hadley instructed kindly.

She laughed, "That's good to know." He held her hand before they parted at the door.

"If you'll permit me, Miss, before we go in." She turned to him on the steps. "I just want to say that if you have to leave tonight in a hurry, trust Master Jorn. You mean more to him than I know he'll let on."

"You sound worried," Logan said, feeling a twinge in her stomach.

"I just love the family I work for, and I hate to see them in pain."

"Are they in pain?" Logan asked, feeling Hadley's testimonial to Jorn's father had an underlying meaning.

"My Master and Master Jorn have been grieving for many years. Just trust in your instincts."

"I will. Thank you." Logan was unsure what the older man was getting at, but he seemed so sincere that she took him at his word.

They continued up the steps, "Well, Hadley, wish me luck."

"You do not need any luck," he assured her, "and I shall take your bag to Master Jorn's room."

"Oh, damn it, I forgot about that. Is that okay? Or if not, I'm sure I can just store it somewhere."

"Master Jorn told me to do anything for you. It would be my genuine pleasure," he said, bowing.

"Thank you so much." She kissed his cheek, "Is it wrong to feel like Cinderella?" she whispered.

"Absolutely not." He pushed her slightly with encouragement, "Happy New Year, Miss."

"And to you, Hadley." With that, she turned, the train sliding out behind her as she swept around and made her way to a small queue of people.

"May I take your coat, please, and your name?" the footman asked.

"Oh, thank you. Er... Miss Logan Hunter," she said rather confusedly. It was so very formal that she was pleased to have half her face hidden in the mask.

"Miss Logan Hunter," the footman announced, and a man

held out his hand to greet her.

"Ah, Miss Hunter." She knew exactly who this man was. He was an older version of Jorn with slightly more facial hair, though he was expertly groomed. His brushed-gold mask accentuated his face, and even though she wasn't expecting it, as he smiled at her, she saw a slight twinkle in his eyes.

"Good evening, sir," she said, wondering if she should curtsey.

"You look beautiful, my dear. My son has told me much about you."

"Has he?" she asked, blushing.

"All good, I assure you."

She moved onto the woman dressed in red next to him, her blonde hair slicked back, her breasts on show as much as was socially acceptable.

"Stunning dress, Logan. Is it Willow and Scarlett?"

"Uhm... yes," she replied, going even redder if possible.

"Must be the most expensive item of clothing you own," she scathed. "And the earrings, such beautifully cut emeralds. He really did spoil you, didn't he?"

"Now, now," Jorn's father said, "jealousy is not a redeeming quality, Portia, and if you think it is, then you are deluded."

"Apologies, Logan. You look amazing."

She turned immediately away, and Logan continued through the hallway, Portia's words circulating in her head, as well as the ones of Jorn's father. Had he just stuck up for her? Maybe she'd been entirely wrong about him and couldn't help but glance back at them. Maybe Hadley's honesty about him had some truth to it? His head was still tilted towards her, and if she wasn't wrong, she thought she saw him smile before his attention was drawn back to more arriving guests.

Logan followed the parquet flooring towards a vast staircase that led to the upper chambers, it cornered off by a stretch of velvet rope. As she looked up, she couldn't help but wonder which way was Jorn's bedroom. However, she was directed down the right of the stairs and found the double doors of the ballroom open and the party in full swing. The room was enormous, with a high ceiling and walls painted with authentic religious pictures. Casting her eyes about for Lexi over the sea of heads, she saw her by the bar talking enthusiastically to Randin and another woman she didn't know.

"Ah, good evening, Miss Hunter."

"Good evening, Master Jorun," she said, his address making her sigh with relief that she had someone to talk to.

"Damn it. You even recognise me with a mask on?" Jorun remarked, kissing her hand and pulling her to him in a friendly embrace.

"Why, of course, your smile, your walk and even your smell are totally different to your brothers," she replied bluntly. He'd never fool her.

"Well, let me be the first to say how utterly stunning you look this evening, and you seem much rested since I saw you yesterday."

"Yes, I am feeling much more myself today."

"And I can see my brother has indeed got an excellent eye for fashion." He looked her up and down, marvelling at his brother's intuition.

"He has certainly done well, Jorun," she flushed. "Don't tell him, but I absolutely love it."

He smirked, "You do, however, have a bemused look on your face; who's upset you? Let me beat them for you." She laughed at him.

"Well, tonight is already not what I thought it would be," she surmised.

"How so?" he asked, taking her arm with his own and walking her towards a waiter who offered them a tray filled with champagne.

"Well, Hadley had some confusing advice for me, and then your father was, well..." Jorun raised his eyebrows, "he surprised me, that was all."

"My father, surprising? Are you sure you are talking about the right person?" She laughed again.

"Portia said something a bit belittling to me, and he, well, he stuck up for me. He scolded her in front of me," she smirked, glancing past Jorun, her eyes searching endlessly for his brother.

"She does get a bit above her station at times. I am glad my father came to your aid in my brother's absence."

"Yes, well, it was not expected," she said, looking back at him.

"You seem to have a low opinion of my father," Jorun said, sipping at his glass.

"No, I mean... I didn't..." She could feel the heat returning to her cheeks.

"Don't worry, Logan, I am only playing with you. My father is a hard bastard, and you are right to be wary of him," he said, raising his glass to a man a few feet away in a welcoming hello. "My brother, I'm sure, has no restraints when it comes to talking to people about our father."

"Yes, I am afraid he might have swayed my opinion before I had any right to make a judgement," she openly admitted.

"Well, don't be fooled. He is as challenging as Jorn has undoubtedly made out." She grimaced and then said,

"Where is he, your twin?" she asked, casting her eyes about again.

"Ah, he will be admiring you from afar, I am sure." He said, "He always says that the loveliest things are always best viewed from far away."

"Why? Because close up, they are ugly?" she sipped her glass.

"You are so far from ugly it is unreal."

"Ah, thank you. Portia also said these earrings are emeralds. They're not, are they?" She raised her eyebrows, remembering Portia's snarky comments.

"I'm afraid my brother wouldn't buy gems that weren't authentic, Logan."

"He's an arse he is." She couldn't imagine how much he had spent.

"You are worth it to him, Logan."

"Thanks, Jorun."

"Now let me take you to your friend." He escorted her to Lexi, who screamed at her over the music that she couldn't believe how amazing this place was and how much she loved Logan for having such a charming and generous boyfriend. Logan smiled at her and watched Quinn's face as he watched Lexi practically throw herself at him before dragging him off to the dance floor.

Taking another drink, she looked around the room, her eyes searching. She was determined to find Jorn before he found her. She clocked a man dressed in what looked like purple silk and his bow tie, which, she was sure, was sewn with gold shards. He caught her eye, and he sneered at her before turning to his companion, and in turn, she looked over at her. Changing direction, she happened upon a man in a pure white suit. His mask was plain black, and he walked using a cane, yet he most definitely didn't need it. He turned to her and grinned mischievously, making his way over. Twisting around in a full circle, tipping his hat to her and bending down, he took her hand in his.

"Do I have the pleasure of addressing a Miss Logan Hunter?" he asked.

"You do, sir," she beamed at his exuberance.

"Well then, let me introduce myself. My name is Lachlan, and I am cousin to Master Jorn of this, the great house of Hartvigsen." He spread his arms out, indicating the vast room they were standing in, causing her to laugh out loud. "Too much?" he asked, grinning at her.

"Just a little bit," she laughed again, feeling instantly at ease. "Very good to meet you, Lachlan. Wild suit you're wearing."

"You like it? I think it suits me very well."

She grinned, "If you want people to notice you, then it definitely does that."

"Well, I really wanted to go for a suit with subtlety, but those ones were sold out."

"That is very lucky, as I cannot imagine you in anything else," she said, giving him a sideways glance.

"You are curious about me?" he remarked, watching her.

"Yes, you are not like most of the men here."

"In what way?" he asked, intrigued.

"You don't mind laughing at yourself. It is obvious to me that many men in this room feel they must be bigger than the next and overly try to make a good impression, whereas you, you couldn't care less what people think," she surmised easily.

"You are very observant, considering you have only been in the room for less than twenty minutes."

"I think it's because I enjoy reading people far more than talking to them." She blushed. "Some people might say I am boring and too quiet."

"Well, you don't seem boring to me, and we are talking very fluently to one another," he said knowledgeably. "I think perhaps you are just particular with whom you talk to."

"Perhaps," she shrugged.

"Which means you are an excellent judge of character."

"I don't know about that. I just enjoy people-watching."

"That is why you and Jorn get on so well then," he surmised. "He seems to study people intuitively."

"As do you." He looked at her weirdly. "You did not know me, and yet you guessed who I was, which means Jorn either told you or at least told you what I was wearing, which means you listen carefully to people. I bet you are in the medical profession or at least have a job which deals with the public, where you have to do a lot of listening?" she smirked, taking a mouthful of drink.

"You are extremely perceptive," he acknowledged. "I am a specialist in neurosurgery, amongst other things."

"Ah! I see. He is very clever, your cousin," she nodded knowingly. "He's asked you to check me over?"

"I surrender." It now his turn to blush, "He did call and ask my opinion."

"I don't know why he's worrying, there's nothing wrong with me. I just get headaches. Though I know the one I had yesterday did linger longer than most."

"Yes, you are correct, I don't think there is anything dangerously wrong with you, but if you'll permit me." He removed her glove and, holding her hand with both of his, stared at it a while before saying, "You have truly beautiful hands." He replaced the glove and, in turn, said, "Would you like another drink? I was just on my way to the bar."

"Ah? Ooookay." Shrugging off the strange feeling he'd just given her when he'd held her hand, she said, "I'll have a glass of Prosecco, please. This champagne is going to go straight to my head." He took the half-full glass, and Logan opened her small clutch bag, rubbing another drop of perfume on her skin before regaining her thoughts to continue her subtle search around the room. Before long, another man wandered over, his beard almost touching his bow tie, his eyes beetle black behind the mask.

"What is a lady like you..." She put her hand on his chest to stop him, her breathing rate suddenly increasing.

"Oh no, I am so sorry, but I am not alone, I'm afraid." She moved aside and began to walk through the crowd, noticing that many people looked and stared; even the guy in the purple watched her walk by. But there was only one man she sought, and he was standing by the pillar near the glass doors, his silver and black mask unable to hide anything from her.

"My lady," he said, bowing to her.

"My lord," she curtseyed, so pleased that she had found him.

"You take my breath away," he said, pulling her arms around his neck and meeting her lips, his scent enveloping her.

"You look and smell utterly divine," she whispered, feeling his hand come to rest at the base of her back. "Were you watching me for long before I managed to get away from your cousin?" she asked, rubbing his hairline at the back of his neck.

"I clocked you the moment you walked in the doors."

"Big head!" she smiled, looking at him. "Jeez, even with that mask on, I can tell you're doing that smouldering eye look, and it's making me sweat."

He whispered in her ear, "Can you blame me?"

"No, but you need to stop."

"Why?" he said playfully.

She leaned, blowing in his ear, her lips so soft at his earlobe as she whimpered, "It makes me want you."

He whispered, his lips brushing her neck this time, "We'll have to be patient. I have to be seen to mingle." She kissed him, the tension in her stomach increasing. Her lips moved from his neck to his jawline, and then her tongue was in his mouth. She didn't care if she was making those in the vicinity uncomfortable. She wanted him, and he needed to do something about it.

"You are very impatient tonight," he smiled, pulling away slightly.

"Can you blame *me* now? You look totally hot in that tux."

He smirked, "No, but good things come to those who wait."

She tutted, "You sound like my dad. And I'll have you know that I'm fine; you did not need to get Lachlan involved with my headache issue," she scathed.

"I'm just concerned, Logan, that is all." He moved in to kiss her again, the masks grating on each other, yet neither seemed to care. They were together, and the whole room felt as distant as the moon.

"Excuse me, love birds, but I have drinks." She felt Jorn smile as they withdrew again to see Lachlan standing there holding three glasses.

"Cousin," Jorn said, taking the whisky Lachlan offered.

"Well, my brother from another mother. You have struck rhodium," he said, handing Logan her wine as she pulled a decidedly confused face. "Rhodium is one of the rarest metals on Earth, young Logan. It means you are even rarer than gold."

"Yes, I most definitely have," Jorn said, pulling her into his hip.

"Have you got a girlfriend, Lachlan?" Logan asked.

"You are the one who is perceptive. What do you think?"

he smirked, watching her.

She squinted at him a moment, "If I'm honest, I'm not sure; perhaps you've recently come out of a relationship. Oh no, actually, you're happy being single and like to have fun with many women and perhaps men as well?" She felt Jorn cough next to her, making her grin.

"Yes, I enjoy my life too much to commit, I'm afraid," he nodded, sipping his beer. "And perhaps I have not found the right person to settle down with." He turned his head slightly to watch a girl with red hair as she walked past chatting with a friend.

"Is that the cask ale Jorn and Jorun went to get?" she giggled, trying to regain his attention.

"It is actually. If I'm not on the rum, I'm on the ale," he took another large gulp, still slightly distracted by the redhead, "It's pretty good. Soon, I would have had enough to cut a rug!" He laughed, "Well, if you two don't mind, I see Louiza with Randin. I shall go and see them. I bid you a pleasant evening, Jorn," he nodded, "my lady." He walked off to find his other cousins, twiddling his cane.

"You know, I like him a lot," Logan said, looking at Jorn. "He's very eccentric."

"Yes, he is, and I do get on with him very well." He nuzzled into her, their lips meeting again. "God, Logan, here's me saying we need to be patient, but I ache for you." He trailed his hand down her back, feeling her bare skin, "You're going to stay tonight, aren't you?"

"If your father will let me," she chuckled. He responded with more kissing, the mask starting to rub on her skin,

"These damn masks are a little irritating."

"Did you bring a coat with you?" he smirked.

"Eventually. Hadley had to remind me to bring one." She laughed, "I'm glad he did. Do you know how cold it is outside?"

He took her hand and led her out of the ballroom, "Come with me."

CHAPTER TWENTY FOUR

THE EVE

As Jorn enclosed her in her coat, pulling the fabric together at the front, the fur collar sitting snugly around her neck, he could feel his sexual need go up a notch. His skin felt on fire every time he touched her. All his imaginings of her in that dress had not done her justice, and yet all he wanted to do was remove it slowly and reveal her body underneath. Grasping her hand, he led her to the courtyard, their eyes never seeming to waver from each other's, even though many people tried to get his attention. As they approached the high hedges, Logan saw the entrance to the maze, and she turned to Jorn, knowing full well what he was doing.

"If you think I'm getting lost in there, you've got another think coming," she smiled, increasing her grip on his hand.

"I'm hoping we can get lost together," he smirked, handing her a hip flask.

"And this is?" she asked, opening the lid and smelling the

strong spirit.

"It's port and brandy mixed. To keep you warm on our trip through the maze," he said, taking a swig.

She held the spout to her lips, "Hmmm, I'm not sure," she said, disgusted.

"Trust me, you'll need it in there."

She followed him under the canopy of evergreen into a world of hidden turns and hedges dusted with fairy lights. Their feet crunched over the slate on the ground, and Logan asked him if that was what he'd been doing with his brother.

"Yes, my father was determined not to have too much mud trawled into the house," he said, pulling her to the right and down a darkened passage. At the end, she found he'd brought her to a dead end.

"Great, a dead..." she gasped, for he moved up behind her, starting to untie her mask, his fingers causing her to ripple with goosebumps, though neither her body nor her soul felt cold. She allowed her mask to slip off her face, his hand strategically placed to catch it. His hands then pulled down the collar of her coat gently to reveal her shoulders, his kisses hot as they caressed her skin. He could feel her heart pulsating under his lips, listening to her chest as it heaved in passion for him.

"God, you smell amazing," he groaned, as she began to turn round and face him, her eyes locking onto his, her hands at his cheek. She searched his face, now untainted by the mask, and momentarily memorised his features. The lust took over, and she pushed him back onto a bench. Their tongues licked the insides of each other's mouths, their voices saying incoherent words to one another, her hand busy at his trousers.

"Logan, wait," he steadied her hands, sucking at her lip.

"You're right, you're right." She pulled away, holding on to the bench for support, her heart hammering so hard it seemed to hurt her chest. "Shit!"

"It's not that... I don't..." He was out of breath.

"No, no, you're right. We've waited this long, and believe me, I don't want to be freezing my arse off whilst we..." Logan laughed, looking up at him.

"Come here, though." He yanked her to him, his mouth engaging hers, his warm hands edging inside her coat.

"How long do you think... we... have... to... mingle for?" she managed to ask, between the kisses.

She groaned at his answer, "Maybe a few hours." His lips tenderly touched her neck, his words making the burn within her intoxicating.

"I'm so ready for you, Jorn," she murmured, as his mouth was back on hers.

"Really? I don't want to......" There was laughter behind them, and a few people entered the dead end.

"Oh, sorry," said a man in a blue and white mask, his partner in a pale pink one.

"No, don't worry, we were just going," Jorn said, his movements quick behind Logan to replace her mask. Only he would see her face. She was his and only his.

Taking a sip of the hip flask, he led her through the maze. It had never been his intention to take her to the centre, but as she was here, he thought he should. A few guests were milling around, a young couple kissing in the far corner, a group of lads having a joint. They approached the centre piece, Logan staring at the silhouetted figure of his mother. She was softly lit from below by a haze of purple and green spotlights, it looking as though his mother was dancing under the stars.

"She's beautiful," Logan said, touching the statue. It was so smooth, like sculptured ice.

"Yes, she is," Jorn said, getting a cigarette out of his pocket and lighting up.

"I knew you smoked, yet this is the first time I've seen you smoke since that Saturday in the square," she said, walking around the statue again.

"Yes, I don't do it often, just sometimes I feel like it." He got the flask out of his pocket and downed a few mouthfuls, watching Logan as she walked around the monument, her hand brushing the marble.

"My beloved Karrianna. For you, my love shall last for all eternity. My days are dark without you in my life. Your Love, Ottar." Logan read the plaque out loud, "Oh, Jorn." A tear fell as she read it, her heart heaving for Jorn's mother.

"Hey," he put his arm around her, blowing his smoke away.

"I wish I could have met her," she said, looking up at him.

"You and she are very similar in some ways. She had a big heart and would have enjoyed your company."

They emerged from the maze to find the ballroom pumping out dance music, and through the glass doors, Logan spotted Quinn and Lexi living it up on the dance floor. Jorn could smell the distinct scent of weed as they approached, and he wondered if he should tell his brother to curb his habits with his father around, yet Kol was old enough to look after himself.

"Jorn? Logan?" They both looked up to his balcony to see him sitting there as bold as brass, smoking a giant joint with two other men in masks. Logan waved up at him.

"He looks half-cut already," Logan observed, shivering slightly.

"He is beyond that, I think," Jorn said, putting his arm around her waist. "Come on, let's get back in the warmth."

"These masks aren't very good if he could tell it was us straight away," she said.

"No, it's just Kol, he's very observant, even when drunk, apparently."

As they entered the ballroom, Jorn sensed the watchful eye of his uncle, who was sitting at one of the tables with his father and Portia. The Emperor's eyes bored into him, and Jorn distinctly heard him sniff, inhaling their scent. He would know about their moment in the maze, and as Logan moved her hand to his shoulder, he saw his uncle nod a few times. Jorn knew he was giving him his seal of approval. He'd succeeded in his task.

Now, it was a countdown to the final curtain.

It took a lot to get Jorn back in the party mood again. The Emperor and his community had, all in all, sucked the life from him already. It seemed that Jorun and Lachlan hadn't missed the non-verbal exchange between them, and Lachlan stepped up to the mark by whisking Logan off to the dance floor, and Jorun took Jorn to Kol's bedroom for a smoke. He wished he could have had a clear head for the rest of the night. He didn't want his most intimate act with Logan to be in a haze of weed-induced fuzz, but he also knew that if he weren't under the influence of something, he'd never be able to continue the night. When Jorun eventually let him return to the ballroom, Logan was dancing enthusiastically with Kol, their bodies rubbing up against each other, her face beaming as she enjoyed the music. Jorn quite happily stood back with Lachlan and Randin, sipping his whisky. He knew Logan enjoyed a good dance once she had a drink and admired her from a distance.

"Jorn?" It was Quinn.

"Hey," Jorn said, his head still a little mushy.

"Can I talk to you for a minute?"

"Sure." They vacated outside, where Jorn sparked up, allowing Quinn one of his cigarettes.

"Thanks for inviting us." Jorn just shrugged, keeping an eye through the doors for Logan. "Er... this is slightly awkward."

"Just spit it out, Quinn," Jorn said, slightly irritated by the mammal-shifter.

"It's just, who is that man in the purple silk suit?"

"Hmmm, noticed him, have you?" Jorn said, admiring Quinn's resourcefulness. "That, my friend, is my uncle and overall ruler of The Gifted community."

"Yes, I thought he must be The Emperor. He seems to look at you and Logan a lot and..." he hesitated. "I don't like it."

"And you think I do?" Jorn scathed, noticing Oska strolling nearby.

"Hey, I'm just looking out for my friends, and I know you wouldn't do anything to put Logan in harm's way, but I'm concerned."

"Your observance does you credit, Quinn. But know this," he squared up to him, "I will not let anything happen to Logan."

Quinn backed off silently, "I know that. I just want you to know that if anything does go down, I'll have your back. There's just something I don't trust about him."

Jorn caught himself before he said anything that could offend. He knew Quinn was only being protective, and really, if Jorn needed help, he could use all he could get.

"I thank you for your kind words, Quinn. Logan is lucky to have such a man watch out for her." Before turning back to go inside, he said, "But if things do go down, please just get Lexi to safety. I will look after Logan."

Quinn furrowed his brow under his mask, "You think something will?" Quinn asked, looking from Jorn to Oska, who now stood with his brother.

"Things always go down when a load of us get together, and there's alcohol and women involved," Oska said, his hand on Jorn's shoulder. "But we're prepared for it, my friend. Please come in and enjoy the rest of the night." Oska put his arm around Quinn's shoulder and steered him in.

"I just wanted Jorn to know that I'll have his back," Quinn said, looking at Oska.

"And he knows it, Quinn, don't worry. We've all got Jorn's back."

Jorn stood a moment, watching Oska lead Quinn away. He knew Quinn meant well, but he sincerely hoped that he and Lexi would have left by the time The Emperor came for Logan, as Jorn didn't need any more collateral damage than was necessary.

His eyes scanned the dance floor for Logan as he returned, but she wasn't there. Looking at Lexi, she mouthed 'drinking' and glancing at the bar, he felt his heart fall to his stomach and the rage rise within him. His uncle was lifting his hand as though to touch her.

"I do hope you're not trying it on with Logan, uncle," Jorn asked, grabbing his uncle's wrist and throwing his arm down by his side.

"Of course not, my nephew; I was just saying how beautiful she looks this evening. The clips in her hair look like snowflakes. So, I asked her if it was snowing out," he smirked. He knew perfectly well it wasn't and that she had not been outside for some time.

"Were you?" Jorn scorned, almost standing between them.

"Why, of course. Well, it was lovely to meet you, Logan, maybe we'll meet again later."

He turned away from them both, and Jorn heard him laugh as he wandered towards the outside.

"Sorry about him; he's well known for his poor chat-up lines and wandering hands," he lied, noticing the goosebumps on Logan's arms. "You cold?"

"No, not at all, it's just." She shivered as she watched him walk away, "His touch just made me feel weird." She rubbed her upper arm, and Jorn could already see an imprint of his hand. He'd fucking touched her. "Do you see him often?"

"No, haven't seen him for many years," Jorn replied, trying to compose his face. "He and my father don't get on that well, but we had to invite him."

"Is that his wife?" His wife looked younger than her.

"Yes, that's Ellika; I think she's perhaps his fifth wife in so many years."

"Figures," she said, trying to avoid watching him anymore by looking into her glass and finishing her wine.

"Hey?" he touched her bare skin, the pimples disappearing, his hand instantly warming her.

"I'm okay. I just got strange feelings from him. Does that make me a bad person?"

"What?" Jorn laughed at her innocence, "Absolutely no way. If anything, it makes you the intuitive person Lachlan thinks you are." He looked over her shoulder at his cousin, his white suit still impeccable, his arm around the waist of a red-haired woman Jorn knew by the name of Ayla, his mouth whispering something in her ear, making her laugh.

"Looks as though Lachlan has pulled," Jorn said, trying to distract Logan from his uncle.

"Yes, I saw him cutting some rug with her just now," Logan laughed, quoting his words from earlier.

"Oh, I bet he was flashing some moves at her." Jorn knew his cousin's dance routines.

"Let's just say he was very exuberant," she smiled, looking in her empty glass.

Jorn tilted his wrist. It was ten to eleven. "So, I think perhaps..." he stroked her arm, feeling it would be impertinent to remove Logan from the room with his uncle on the prowl. Slipping his fingers up her neck and to her chin, he held her there whilst he moved in on her mouth. "I think that perhaps we've mingled... enough."

"Well, Master Jorn, in that case, we'd better make ourselves scarce," she beamed, allowing him to lead her subtly from the room.

CHAPTER TWENTY FIVE

THE DEVOTION

There were very few people in the entrance hall as they walked through. The loyal footman stood resolutely by the door, and Logan thought it was unfair to have him standing there in the cold, yet she followed Jorn up the grand staircase, marvelling at the features of this old mansion. The balustrade was made from both marble and iron, and the ironwork between the bannisters was intricately woven steel, portraying the idea of trailing creepers and flowers. Her hand slipped over the marble as her gloves slid up it towards the north side, the click of her heels muffled by the thick, well-worn, though highly cared-for carpet. The carpet stopped at the top of the stairs and turned into wooden flooring, intermittently covered in red Persian style rugs. They passed many shut doors, each one labelled with a different suite or other designation. As they passed a room called The Carpathian Suite, they could hear shouting.

"Kol," Jorn smirked, knocking on the door and opening it

inwards, Logan saw that he was wearing a virtual reality headset, and five girls were sitting on his floor watching him play.

"Jorn, Logan, come in and play Saber. I'm caning everyone," he laughed, taking the device off his head.

"No, it's alright, buddy, enjoy," Jorn said.

Logan chuckled as they shut the door, "He's so going to regret the amount he's done in the morning."

Jorn just grinned at her, knowing his brother too well for him to have overdone it by eleven o'clock; there was still plenty of time. He clicked open his door and pushed it, allowing Logan to go in first. She stood a while drinking in the features of his part of the house. He'd always liked his chamber, yet they were perhaps a little more battered in the most recent days.

"Hmmm, so you don't just have a bedroom, you have a flat inside a house?" Logan giggled, moving to the right-side door and turning on the light, seeing his grand four-poster bed. She thought she had rather have seen Jorn's quarters a little messy; it would have made her feel that her own house wasn't inadequate, but his room was immaculate, right down to the dresser being tidy.

"Don't get too awestruck," Jorn said, moving to the cabinet and pouring himself a large whisky. "I think Hadley, or someone, has tidied for me." He shrugged, slightly perturbed that someone had been in here without him knowing, and at the same time, was pleased someone had cleared up Portia's trashed glass.

"Even if it were messy, I'd still be awestruck. No wonder

you found it hard to leave," Logan said, honestly. Moving to the next door, she looked in his bathroom, the scent of him so rife in this room that she could have stayed there for hours. "I'll have one of those," she said, turning back to him watching her.

"Will you now?" he grinned, pouring her one and holding out the glass.

She took it, beaming back before returning to his bedroom, "Jorn?" He entered his room, her back to him, facing the bed, her hand already untying her mask, the glass of whisky forgotten on the nightstand. He watched as she allowed the mask to slip from her face to the bed, her hand returning to the bow she'd so skilfully tied before leaving her own home. Her hand fingered the material, pulling the cords until they were completely undone, allowing the halter to fall forward and expose her backless bra. She grinned, hearing him groan behind her.

"When I bought that dress, I knew the best thing about it would be to see it removed."

"Don't touch me yet," she whispered over her shoulder, her breasts heaving, her pulse throbbing within her. She eased the lower zip down and let go, the material sinking to the floor, her underwear now exposed, the French knickers enhancing the shape of her, that he couldn't help but react. He was behind her, his warm hands moving up the curve of her hips to her waist.

"Jesus fucking Christ," he gasped into her ear, continuing his caress.

"Thought I told you to wait," she murmured, moaning as

his hands touched her.

"I can't resist you anymore."

She turned slowly, undoing his shirt and exposing his chest, her fingers running along the contours of muscle, her nails gently teasing through his chest hair. Abruptly, he grabbed her hips, the need overtaking them both, their feet mismatched as they fell onto the bed, her hand soon unclipping his trousers, allowing him to escape. She almost ripped off his underwear, and yet when they were both naked, even her shoes had made it to the floor somehow, they stopped. They regarded each other with such respect that there was a moment when they both seemed nervous to continue. There would never be a time like this again in their relationship. Whether it lasted just another hour, a month or even a lifetime, they would never get this back. They would never get back that minute when they truly hadn't tasted each other fully, and for a second, they were both on the cusp of no return. Each thought that no matter what happened, there would be no going back.

Her lips found his, and then they were again lost to each other. Their hands exploring, touching, memorising each curve, each dimple, each mole. His tongue flicked at her nipples, goosebumps exploding on her skin the further he went, his mouth at her navel, enjoying the reaction of her tensing stomach muscles the lower he got. The room seemed to dissolve around them, and all there was in the world was the two of them. Two people entirely absorbed in one another; it was hard to see where one person ended and the other began. Their bodies were so in tune that all else was forgotten. Jorn had managed to block out the image of The Emperor touching her and of her fate. Of the fact that she was never going to be his forever, or that her death could be impending. There was just her, right now, with him, making him feel so utterly content that his mind was clear of any rational thoughts. Every time he touched her, she moaned in his ear, her skin so soft under his hands that, to him, she was sheer perfection.

Logan was glad she'd had a few drinks in her before they'd got to Jorn's bed. She was nervous. She'd known all day, all week even, that tonight would be the night she succumbed to him, that she would be entirely at his mercy. And even though her body trembled with anticipation, she couldn't have thought of anywhere she would rather be. She forgot she was in a house full of people, one of them being Jorn's father. She forgot about her vulnerability, of her self-doubt, of her shyness. She was no longer reticent or hesitant; she was self-assured, and that was primarily due to him and how he made her feel. He was tender, passionate, selfless, and so aware of her needs that she felt guilty if he was unfulfilled. Yet, with just one look, he reassured her that he was getting as much out of her as she was getting out of him.

He laid over her awhile, gasping into her shoulder, their breathing erratic, their bodies glowing in the aftermath of their intimacies. Her hands rolled down his spine, a satisfied murmur in her throat as she waited for him to surface. Shuffling slightly, she turned her head to him, a smirk on her lips as her own heart settled to a regular beat.

"You, okay?" she asked, stroking his arm, following her finger over his skin with her eyes.

Lifting his head, he cupped her head with his elbows, his

lips still hot as they kissed her. The passion, though spent, was already reigniting.

"Am I okay?" he sighed, searching her face. "I'm..." He felt her jump under him as fireworks banged overhead, the shower of dynamite rain echoing throughout the garden, as golden and green sprinkles thundered throughout the dark sky beyond the bedroom window. Smiling, he said,

"Happy New Year, Logan."

"Happy New Year, Jorn."

She searched his eyes, her mouth reaching for his again, her hands pulling him to her. Their kisses were inaccurate and messy, their breathing so laboured that Logan's chest hurt, yet she felt so euphoric she couldn't have cared less. All there was, was him with her, in his bed on New Year's Eve.

Shifting out from under him, she got off the bed and peeked through the lightweight curtains he had at his balcony door. She stood a moment, watching the bright colours shoot through the vast starry night, the cheers of those standing in the driveway subtle compared to the whistles and screams of rockets and showering red fountains. Jorn's arms, shrouded in a bed throw, were soon around her neck from behind. His body was so warm at her back that she sunk into him, the sheet wrapping them both together. Brushing aside the curtain, they stood a while watching the show Jorn's father had put on to ring in the new beginnings. They could hear singing and laughter coming from the mob downstairs, the crowd bellowing the traditional song Auld Lang Syne.

"For goodness' sake, can you hear Kol? He's so out of tune," Jorn said, laughing at his brother.

"We should be down there, shouldn't we?" Logan said, looking up at him.

"Logan, there is no other place I would rather be than naked with you at midnight on New Year's Eve."

He bent in to kiss her, the throw dropping from their bodies, them soon forgetting the crowd outside. Sinking to their knees, they began to explore one another again, both seeing if there was any spot they had yet to touch, yet to kiss. And even though they found no new bits to touch, they caressed every part again. Their bodies together, sweat beading on their backs, their mouths at each other's necks, the goosebumps awry on their skin. Their muscles screamed from extended use, and yet they couldn't stop.

They lay a while on the soft carpet of Jorn's floor, a slight breeze flowing over them from under the balcony door, making the gossamer curtains flutter lightly. He rubbed her arm as it hung lazily over his chest, their legs still entwined, the cover Jorn had brought over in a heap on the floor. Adjusting herself, Logan propped herself on her elbow, her head aching from her elaborate hairdo.

"You alright?" Jorn asked, turning to her.

She smirked, "Yes, of course, just my hair makes lying on the floor quite uncomfortable."

"Yet, there doesn't seem to be any out of place, despite our escapades."

"That's because my sister sprayed my hair with about half a bottle of hair spray," she said, touching it.

"And your make-up is still completely flawless, not any smudging."

Smiling at his observance, "That's because I primed my face with this kind of make-up glue that ensures a smudge-less and slide-less look," she said, reeling off the advertisement slogan.

"Well, it definitely works."

"It does, but my hair feels like a load of wire, and my face feels almost stuck to itself."

"You still look absolutely stunning, whereas I must look like a sweaty wreck," he smirked, standing, pulling her to her feet.

"You are far from a sweaty wreck," she said, feeling hunger for him again as he wandered naked to get their drinks.

They drank silently for a while, and then Logan said,

"Do you think people are going home?"

"Some, maybe, but most will be staying a bit longer. When my father hosts a party, they always go on into the early morning. They're probably all doing shots now, I imagine."

Jorn lay next to her, propping his head up, his fingers delicately touching her side, sliding down to the dip of her hip and onto her thigh. He watched the individual goosebumps burst on her skin, and he saw her tense the closer he got to her bikini line. Reaching up, Logan placed her glass down, allowing him full rein of her, his lips grazing her skin, his tongue licking her stomach, making his way up to her face. Jorn's gentleness was both a source of frustration and complete satisfaction. Neither had had enough of the other.

"Logan?" He'd reached her face, their eyes aligning, his expression pulsing with serenity as they searched each other's gaze. "I'm going to tell you something, and I'm not sure how you're going to feel about it."

"Don't say anything you don't mean, Jorn," Logan replied, her hands rolling up and down his back, feeling every rise and fall of his spine.

"I would never say anything I did not mean, Logan, least of all this and least of all to you."

Her chest heaved as the words she knew he was going to say hung in the balance, and for one second, she wished he wouldn't.

"I love you," he whispered. "You don't need to feel the same way or reciprocate my confession. I want you to know that no matter what happens between us, I love you and have done so since you dropped that coffee cup in the open office that morning."

She stared deeply into his eyes, wishing she knew how to respond, wishing she felt strongly enough to return his exclamation, wishing she had enough courage to forgo her inhibitions. But she couldn't; she just bit her lip, not knowing what to say.

"Now I've said it, I'm going to take another sip of my drink and then devour you again. Is that alright?" He went to move off her.

"Jorn." She held him on her with her legs, his hands barely able to reach his glass. "I've never told anyone those three words before, and you might find me slightly reserved for not doing so now, but it doesn't mean that I am not totally and utterly devoted to you." She smashed her lips into his, and neither of them noticed the glass as it slipped from his otherwise engaged hand to the floor, enabling the amber liquid to seep into the carpet.

CHAPTER TWENTY SIX

THE EMPEROR

"You enjoy watching me, don't you?" Logan said, looking down at him, her hands poised in her hair, removing the clips she'd let her sister so arduously put in the night before.

"Of course, who wouldn't?" It was twenty-past-four in the morning, and Jorn knew his time in this bubble of ecstasy was almost over. He wanted her just one more time before the inevitable handover to The Emperor. But he also knew that she was tender and sore and that it was wrong to ask it of her. So, he lay across the bed, stroking her outer thigh as she sat there naked, her breasts on view, the curve of her hips so tantalisingly near him that he couldn't help but touch her. He loved the shape of her body, the dip of her spine, the dimple above her sacrum. The way her arms stretched up, feeling for more accessories, the sight of her ribs, how they arced to the centre above her navel. The muscle tone of her abdomen and the sweetness between her legs made his pulse throb.

"You're doing that thing again," she laughed, putting out a hand to stop him running his fingers over her.

"What thing?" he smirked.

"That smoky-eyed look that makes me melt inside."

"I can't help it, I just love looking at you and imagining what we could do together, what we have been doing together."

She regarded him, almost sadly. She wanted him again, so absolutely, but she was sure that any more intimacy would make her sore, and she could not bear to feel like that. What they'd had had been amazing, and she wasn't sure any more would be as enjoyable as it had been.

"Hey." He sat up and pushed aside some of the hair she'd undone. On the back of her neck, at the top of her spine, was a small tattoo of two angel wings on either side of the bone. "I've never noticed that before."

Logan laughed as she felt around her neck to where she knew her tattoo was. "It was one of those spur-of-the-moment things you do when you're eighteen." She turned her head to the side to look at him over her shoulder. "I hide it with my hair or a halter neck ribbon most of the time.

"Why? It's very intricately done." He ran his fingers over the lines that were so thin and precise that it looked as though drawn with a pencil.

"I forget it's there," she said, smiling at him as he began to kiss her shoulder. "Do you mind if I take a quick shower?" She got off the bed and walked to his en-suite, his body falling loosely to the sheets in defeat.

After lying there a few minutes, he got up and, throwing some clothes on, made his way onto the balcony. There were vacant spaces in the drive now. Guests were leaving, indicating the party was ending and the inevitable was approaching. Sparking up a cigarette, he listened to the running water in the bathroom. He wanted to go to her, and he knew she would welcome him, but she needed her space, as did he. He needed to contemplate what he was going to do once they came for her because now, after their intimacy, he knew he'd never let her go willingly, no matter how much he tried to convince himself he would do. They'd shared too much, been together too much, and said too much to each other. He'd told her he loved her, and even though she'd not returned it, he knew she did. It had never been in Logan's vocabulary to say those three words. He knew that. He'd witnessed that throughout the years. She came from a genuinely loving family where emotions were so easily read, and yet she'd never professed it to anyone. He couldn't blame her; they'd only been seeing each other for just a few weeks, if that. He, of course, had known her a lot longer than she had him, and this grieved him. Yet he was not one to rush her, but when The Emperor came for her, he had wanted her to know that no matter what they said to her, she'd know that he loved her. For even though he had left it quite a few hours, Jorn knew The Emperor would come, as sure as he meant to catch her at the bar alone earlier. As sure as he meant to touch her before Jorn had returned. He'd felt the cool patch of skin on Logan's upper arm as he had touched her so tenderly. The Emperor had already marked her, and now Jorn would be powerless to stop any interaction.

Sniffing the air, he could scent the remnants of gunpowder still lingering, though the fireworks had finished hours ago. He heard laughter from Lachlan's room and smiled to himself. It seemed they were both lucky men to have found someone to share New Year's Eve with. However, Lachlan never had trouble finding anyone to have sex with. He was not picky, and yet he hoped his cousin would find someone to spend his life with soon. Even though he was younger than Jorn, their extended lives deserved to be shared with someone special, and he wished that for Lachlan as he did for all his brothers.

"Jorn?" Logan called him back to the bedroom, and he put his cigarette out. She was wearing black lace knickers, her hair hanging on either side of her face, a few droplets running down her chest. He stood there by the bathroom after washing his hands, just admiring her as she teased a brush through her hair. She was beautiful.

"Feeling better?" he asked, putting his hands in his jeans.

"Yeah. Your shower is amazing; I could have stayed there for hours." She smiled, patting the bed, "Come here."

"Let me brush my teeth first." He was quick at cleansing and felt slightly bad that he hadn't showered, yet he needed to grab every moment with her.

He walked to her, and she flung him on the bed, putting her leg over him, kissing his mouth as she'd never kissed him before, her heartbeat elevating, her hands running through his hair. Her urgency was tangible.

"What's all this?" he panted, accepting her advances.

"I don't know; I just had a weird feeling in the shower that we might not get these moments back."

She rubbed herself on him, feeling the sexual tension increase again. He pushed her up, and she wrapped her legs around him, tilting her pelvis upwards. Even though he still had jeans on, he could feel the straining in his groin. This was it, he told himself. It was their last chance to experience the closeness they both seemed to crave. They had already devoured one another, and yet they still wanted more. Maybe it was desperation on his side. If he kept her closely intimate, The Emperor wouldn't be able to have or take her. But Jorn knew that was folly. He could keep her going all night, but eventually, she would tire, and then his dreams of holding her would come to an end. Even now, as their last embrace began to peter out and their heart rates fell to a usual pattern, he could feel her finally relax into the bed. Her body was now exhausted and giving way to sleep and, in Jorn's mind, to the end of their relationship.

Managing to extract himself, he scooped her up and placed her in the bed properly. Her hair was mainly dry now, and as he ran his fingers through it, he was suddenly met with an undeniable urge to divulge everything. He wanted to tell her who he was, who his father was, and who his uncle was. But he knew she'd never understand, and right now, it didn't matter. He'd managed to steal some hours with her, being the most intimate he'd been with anyone in decades, and he'd never forget how she made him feel.

He became aware of noises in the corridor beyond his door, the quickening of footsteps, and instinctively, he knew the time had come and that he'd have to say goodbye, forever.

"I love you," he whispered in her ear, as he heard a knock upon his chamber door. "Whatever happens, don't forget that." He moved swiftly about the room, put his jeans back on and pulling a black tee over his head, he went to answer it.

It was a great surprise to find Hadley standing there, his chauffeur suit still on, his hat sitting on his head.

"Hadley?" Jorn questioned, moving out into the corridor.

"Master Jorn." He grabbed Jorn's hand and placed some car keys in it, "Please, Master Jorn, you must hurry. The Emperor's people are on their way, and they must not find you." Hadley reopened the sitting room door, pushing Jorn through it, shutting it and twisting the lock. "Your car is waiting for you. There's a bag in there that I packed for you, so I apologise if you felt someone had been in your room." The realisation began to fall over Jorn. "And most of Miss Logan's belongings that she brought with her from her house. Master Lachlan's plane is fuelled and ready with Danny in the cockpit."

"What?" Jorn stood there like a fool.

"Your father sent me. Please, you must go," Hadley said, shoving Jorn into the bedroom. "He cannot lose you, as well as your mother, for he knows you, Jorn. He knows what's in your heart." He ushered Jorn again, "He knows your uncle's plan."

"My father?" Jorn's father didn't know him at all, and yet, here was Hadley telling him to go on his father's orders. He glanced at the bed; Logan was now sitting up, watching both men.

Her being awake sent Jorn into automatic pilot. He most likely had just a few minutes to persuade her to come with him, to dress and to leave. Yet she got up and started to dress before he'd even said anything.

"I knew you were trouble when I first met you, Jorn Hartvigsen," she huffed, putting on her heels and accepting the jumper he gave her. "I just knew it, the stares across the room on that Saturday night, the glances down at your phone when I looked up, and yet I knew you'd been watching me. I saw you eyeing me in the market square and in the workroom when I was doing the coffee. I knew you were trouble, and muggings here fell utterly and completely for you."

"You're okay with leaving?"

"I didn't like your uncle when I met him; his hand has left a cold feeling on my arm, and I can see the fear in your eyes. Now, I think that running is unlikely to be the answer to whatever is going on. But if we must run, then we must run," she said, tying up her hair.

Jorn stood there mesmerised by her before there was another knock at his door, a more frantic knocking that told him they had to leave.

"You're not even going to ask why?" Jorn asked, taking her hand and leading her to the balcony.

"Well, I'm expecting you to tell me everything once we are

on that plane," she said, beaming up at him as he climbed over the rail. "But I know Hadley, he told me earlier that if we had to leave in a hurry, then I was to trust you, and I know enough about him just from my journey here that you and your father are his world, and so, I trust his instincts."

Jorn looked at her, astonished, "I should have told you at the very beginning."

"Yes, but sometimes, there just isn't the right moment." She smiled, moving in to kiss him before he jumped solidly to the ground. He turned to look up at her. The wind caught her hair, and her face grinned down at him as she climbed over the balustrade.

"This, I hadn't bargained for," she joked, leaning forward to jump. "If you don't catch me, I'm going to break something."

"I will catch you," he beamed, feeling that this could work. That he could run and live with Logan without having to worry about his uncle's wrath. "Come on, one, two..."

Before he got to three, he saw a delicate hand encased in a black glove reach around her chest and yank her back over the rail, her legs flying up, a scream lost in her throat as she disappeared.

"LOUIZA!" Jorn shouted, knowing his cousin's hand anywhere.

He heard glass shattering, doors slamming, and sprinting footsteps, followed by mind-numbing silence. He gazed for a moment in complete despair. He'd been so close to getting her away, and now she'd been taken straight from his outstretched arms. Snow began to fall, the delicate flakes melting instantly on his boiling hot skin, the anger building up through his body like a volcano about to erupt. He moved backwards, passed his Audi that Hadley had parked so kindly under his window for their getaway and then, taking a clear breath, he ran. He ran towards the house, leapt high, springing from the car bonnet, buckling the metal work and landing on the concrete of the higher platform. He was wary as he straightened up, edging into the room. It was just as he and Logan had left it. The chest of drawers was open in various stages of recent rummaging, and the bathroom door was ajar. The bed sheets were in a messy tangle, and Logan's dress lay abandoned on the floor. The sitting room was a different story; the whisky decanter was dripping over the side of the cabinet, a puddle of liquid soaking his rug. The large mirror above the unused fireplace had plummeted to the floor, and the glass had shattered, sprinkling the ground with shards of diamond. The sofa had been shoved, the scuff marks noticeable, and the sitting room door stood wide open, allowing Jorn a perfect view of the landing.

He felt the heat begin to burn, working its way up his legs, fermenting in his stomach before penetrating his upper arms and chest, the mist creeping in behind his eyes, turning his irises red. A primal scream fell from his mouth, reverberating throughout his room. The glasses burst out of the side cabinet; the photo frames fell from the walls. The ground around him trembled as he sunk to his knees, his desperation running through the house like blood through veins. He sensed his brothers feel his pain, their heads snapping up from whatever they were doing. Jorun physically clutched his chest, falling to one knee, the pain he felt so acutely. Even Lachlan jumped up from his bed, noticing the tremors through his room.

Jorn got up, his extremities shaking and yet his mind was suddenly clear, so clear. The clearest it had been since the beginning of this so-called charade. He now knew his uncle's intent and what was expected of him. He could hear the movement of people, but he wanted to find his uncle first, and he wanted to be alone.

Leaving his room, he edged down the corridor, seeing two mammal-shifters at the foot of the ornate staircase. Noticing Lachlan's cane leaning casually outside his room, he grabbed it; if he knew his cousin, it wouldn't just be a simple wooden walking stick. The head of it was that of a horned deer with metal antlers like a pitchfork. He twisted it in his hands, swirling it around like a dancer would a ribbon, bringing it up, smashing it through one guy's chin, the antlers sailing through the bone, knocking him up and over, his head crashing into the ironworks between the bannisters. The other started to transform, shredding its clothes and jumping out from the material as a big cat, its shoulder blades rippling as it stalked its prey. Jorn stood patiently, watching its tail swish from side to side, its bright yellow eyes attempting to stare him down. It pounced, and Jorn swung down the rod in his hand, it coursing through the spinal cord, breaking the creature, it crumbling to the wooden flooring, blood seeping from the gash he had made. Stepping over the fallen, he moved towards the archway that led to the basement and his Master's quarters. For a moment, he halted, becoming acutely aware of his heartbeat, it pumping rhythmically in his chest, his respirations subtle, his lungs expanding and deflating. Inhaling, he could smell Logan's skin, and even though she'd showered, he could taste her perfume and scent himself on her. As his hand went to the railing, he could see a few lone black hairs stuck to the rail eyelets. Reining in any emotions he was feeling, he ascended the pathway, his trainers squeaking on the incline, the grit from the driveway grating the sheened surface. The familiar sound of the robotic cleaner started as his feet touched the ground floor, and it took all his willpower not to kick it.

Rounding the corner, four more mammal-shifters stood there, their hands holding up automatic weapons, fingers poised. Jorn jumped up the wall, unhooking an ancient shield that garlanded the walkway. Holding it up, bullet after bullet rung home upon it, the metal punched with individual dents. Yet nothing got through, their ammunition ricocheting off it, echoing around the walls, the plaster pinging off every few inches. Lowering the shield as they reloaded, he rung the metal rod home through the first's chest, blood spurting out into Jorn's face, the man grabbing the cane with his hands as though willing Jorn to push it in further. Withdrawing it, the man collapsed, his fellows now shifting, one into a lynx, the others into two lions.

"You'd have been better staying human," Jorn said, twiddling the baton in his hands, slicing it through the air, smashing through the jaws of the lynx as it ran at him, the deer head sticking through the roof of its mouth as he twisted it in mid-air over his head, throwing it back along the corridor. The lions stood side by side, the tufts on their tails twitching as they surveyed their quarry.

"You know you can walk away? I will let you pass," Jorn said, standing aside so they could leave. "But if you attack me, I will retaliate."

He watched their eyes flash as the lamps that littered the ceiling reflected in their stare. The left started running first, it ducking under Jorn's first swipe with the rod, yet he brought down the shield onto its skull, the bones cracking under the blow, the beast crying out as it skidded on the shiny floor, colliding with the sideboard, coming to an abrupt halt. The other lay close to the floor, waiting as Jorn approached; it then scuttled around him and out of sight.

Breathing heavily, he stood in front of the oak doors. Those same doors, in front of which he and Randin had stood that Saturday night, he'd been called to the study to give his Master an update. He stood, feeling the blood of the mammal-shifters drip from his face, feeling his skin ache from the scratches and punches inflicted on him on his mission to get to this door. He could hear murmurings on the other side, hear a whimpering, someone pleading. Hear a girl crying. Lifting his arms to give him leverage, he went to kick open the door.

"What does she have that I haven't?" Jorn lowered his foot, his eyes scanning the hallway, them falling on a woman dressed in black. Her long legs were encased in dark, skinny jeans, and her top half was clad in a charcoal charmeuse silk shirt; the diamonds in her ears glimmering in the LED glare.

"Where do you want me to start?" Jorn said, looking at his cousin, her dark hair was pinned back tightly, "Anyway, you've always liked Randin."

"You are a fool to think that I would ever look at any of my cousins but you."

"That reasoning is precisely why I've never been interested in you, Louiza. You are too egotistical," he said bluntly.

"Aww, Jorn! Egotistical, that's a big word, even for you," she mocked.

"Narcissist, masochist."

"No, they're not so big."

"You are mistaken, Louiza," he said, not even looking at her. "These are other qualities you have that don't carry favour with me."

"My father knew it, but I just couldn't understand why you never indulged in my company. And then I realised." She began to walk towards him, making her way through the destruction he had caused, not even noticing it. As she stood in front of him a metre away, her perfume filling his nostrils, her skin perspiring, chest heaving, she said, "You only go for mortals."

She swung her weapon up, it ringing loud on Jorn's shield as he held it up to defend himself. He knew her game. A woman of prestige, such as Louiza, being The Emperor's daughter, would be enough distraction for any man. Her precision skill with any instrument was second to none, but to Jorn, it was mere child's play.

"You knew I had it?" she sneered.

"Of course," he said, moving nearer her, the sound of metal on metal still reverberating through the halls.

"Nothing slips past you, does it... Watcher?"

"Not much, but I can always be surprised." She stepped back before lashing out at him again, the glint of her blade slicing through the air and meeting his steel rod.

"You fight with such makeshift weapons, my cousin," she leered.

"I have to take what I can find. It is not normal for the residents of this house to have to fight their way through the corridors," he scathed.

Their weapons clashed again and again, a majestic dance between two partners, each trying to outwit the other, and yet it seemed they were very equally matched.

"You forget I have watched you fight since you were born," Jorn said.

"I have not forgotten, cousin, which is why I've brought back up."

Jorn felt it before he heard it, the blaze of fire on his skin, a piercing agony that vibrated through his body from the base of his spine. His knees buckled as the bullet crushed the nerves in his back; the pain that at first had felt like lava now burned with the cold of ice. Swivelling, he saw Portia standing there, her ballgown still on, her red-taloned hands holding the 9-millimetre pistol. Managing to hold the cane above his head, he launched it at her, it sticking like a dart through her thigh, her body crumbling, before he fell onto his hands.

"You see, cousin?" Louiza bent to talk in his ear, her breath cool. "I've learnt a few new moves you've never seen."

She hoicked him up, tying his hands behind his back, a groan issuing from his throat as she curved his back awkwardly.

He lay a while healing himself, waiting for the cold to subside and for his skin to push out the bullet that had wedged itself so accurately within him. He heard Portia curse loudly as Louiza pulled the rod from her leg,

"Fucking Watcher," she hissed, holding her breath against the pain.

"Stop whining, Portia, you've had worse," Louiza mocked, grabbing hold of the binds that held Jorn and dragging him along the floor towards the study again. Opening the doors, Portia limped through, allowing Louiza space to present Jorn to the awaiting audience.

She pulled him into a kneeling position on the white rug in front of the roaring fire. Breathing heavily, attempting to appear in less pain than he was, he looked to his left. Logan was there, her mouth gagged, her face streaming with tears, her cheek raw from being hit. Her lip was bleeding, and her hair was matted from being hauled off the balcony and dragged. The jumper he had put on her earlier was ripped almost in two, resembling more a jacket; her breasts looked mutilated with what seemed like bite marks and her belly ring torn out, the slow dribble of blood staining the rim of her trousers.

"Ah! You got him, Louiza," The Emperor said, accepting a kiss on his hand.

"He was already here, Pappa."

"Hmmm, that's interesting. Why were you coming here,

my nephew? Did you want to watch her demise at my hand?"

"You knew I would come for her, uncle," Jorn said, unwittingly studying his uncle's naked body, which was wrapped in strips of purple silk, bar his chest that showed an intricately drawn tattoo of his rib cage with a demonic hand grabbing hold of his sternum from the inside.

"Yes, I thought you would come, but I was never one hundred percent sure. Did you kill all my guards on your way?"

"No, not all of them and if you wanted them alive, then you should have chosen better shifters," he said gruffly.

He felt Logan look over at him, her eyes expressing such agony that he didn't return the stare. There was no way she'd ever forgive him for this, and he didn't want to see that in her facial expression.

"Well, anyway, it means nothing to me that you were on your way here. I sent Louiza to get you, as this bitch you are so keen on will not show me any of her abilities, no matter what I do." He lifted his hand and slapped Logan's face, the smack resonating through Jorn's ears, making his blood run cold.

"Well, hitting her isn't going to make her show her gifts, is it?"

"As you have watched her for so long and know her so... er... intimately, I thought you might know what the key is to unlock her?" he said, his voice dripping with venom.

Jorn now chanced a glance at her, his heart swelling with

love for this woman who was in such pain both emotionally and physically that he just wanted to hold her.

"The key, uncle, is the fact that there is no key." Jorn sneered at The Emperor, his riddles infuriating him.

"Just tell me plainly, Jorn. I have no time for games."

"Games?" Jorn scorned, "I do not play games with you, uncle. You sent me to watch this woman, to gain any insight into her that I possibly could, and yet I found nothing."

"I assure you, you did, my nephew. I can feel her power. I felt it when I branded her skin with my touch earlier. Her skin trembled under my hand and look there." He yanked her top to reveal the frozen handprint he'd left.

"No, uncle, you only felt what you thought you would. She is not special; she has no hidden gifts, no extraordinary abilities. There is nothing there but what you see in front of you."

"And what is that prey?" his uncle laughed.

"A beautiful, talented, caring, dedicated, loyal human. Plain and simple."

"No, Jorn. I have never been mistaken." He slapped her again, splashing Jorn with her blood as her cheek split.

"STOP THIS, UNCLE! SHE IS NOTHING TO YOU!" Jorn shouted, shifting in his kneeling position, trying to get to her.

"Oh, and I suppose she is to you?"

Jorn tilted his head to her, staring into her eyes that swam with a fresh wave of tears, her breathing heavy as she struggled to remain upright.

"Yes." He wanted to touch her so badly that he twisted his hands in the bonds Louiza had tied, "I love her."

The Emperor was still for a moment and then exploded with laughter, clapping his hands gleefully before resting them on his thighs to try to compose his hysteria.

"No, no, no, Jorn!" he smirked, "She was meant to fall in love with you. That was what I asked for."

"Life is sometimes surprising, uncle, it's..."

"JORN!" There was a sudden commotion behind him as his brothers, Lachlan and Quinn, piled into the room.

"Oh, look, it's the rescue team," Louiza cussed, pouring herself a drink.

"Do not mock what you don't understand, Louiza," Jorn's father whispered, sipping his red wine.

"What is this, Ottar?" The Emperor asked. "An influx of the country's most idiotic Gifted family members."

"Don't speak ill of my family, Ragnar. Jealousy has always been your downfall," Jorn's father said, his lips twitching slightly as he regarded his sons.

"Of which you have suffered most greatly," Ragnar retorted, his hand resting on Logan's shoulder.

"You are mistaken, brother. I have never been jealous of you," Ottar replied.

"You have always been jealous of what I have," Ragnar hit back, as though it was a fight.

"Ragnar, you have never had anything that I wanted; stop deluding yourself otherwise. You do not know me," he said sadly.

"I know you very well, Ottar."

"You, like everyone else, always presume to know me, and yet you don't know me at all and haven't done so since we were boys."

Ragnar stared at his brother, "I don't really need to know you, Ottar; what you feel and what you say is irrelevant. I have not come here to argue with you."

Ottar tutted, "What have you come to do then, Ragnar?"

"To see her for what she is." He looked at Logan, his eyes blazing with malice, "And if she does not show me her true colours when I beat her, then I'll have to move on to greater measures."

Abruptly, from behind his back, he pulled a gun and, turning to his left, he squeezed the trigger.

Hadley crumbled to the ground, grasping his chest, blood seeping through his shirt as his knees folded, his face smashing to the floor. Jorn's father ran to him, cradling him in his arms. Oska pushed aside some of his brothers and ran to their aid, but all in the room knew they could do nothing to save the older man. Jorn's father held him as Oska laid his hands on the wound the gunshot had left, attempting to heal him, saying words only Oska knew. Ottar spoke whispers in Hadley's ear; he spoke of promises to look after his family, to see that they were comfortable, that he would ensure their father did not die in vain. But he did not hear his words of kindness, did not see the anguish on his Master's face or feel the sadness in his words. His eyes were vacant and not seeing, his hand loose in Ottar's grip. He was gone.

Logan began writhing in her bounds, her mouth trying to say things that no one could understand, her face screwed up and red with anger. The Emperor knelt in front of her, slipping a cold finger between the gag and her cheek, pulling it down to around her neck.

"What the fuck is wrong with you?" she heaved. "Why are you so cruel? What has that man ever done to you?" She sobbed, her eyes flaring with sheer hatred for Jorn's uncle. "I have no abilities, no special powers. There's nothing to me but what you see, and now you've killed an innocent man, for nothing." She squeezed her eyes shut, "For nothing," she whispered, the despair etched in every syllable. "For fucking nothing," she repeated, looking at Hadley, held reverently in Ottar's arms as he hugged the fallen man who had tried to help his family.

"Well, my dear, it won't be for nothing if you show me what I want," The Emperor sneered. "If you show me what you've got, then his death will not be in vain."

"I've already told you a hundred times," she said, hiccupping, trying to blink her tears away. "I have nothing to show you."

"Really, uncle, this is ridiculous," Randin said, stepping forward, his negotiator abilities kicking in. Randin was the only one with a chance of diffusing this situation.

"Don't even think about it, my eldest nephew. Your ability won't work on me. You must remember I gave you that power, and I am, therefore, the stronger."

"I know I cannot beat you, uncle, but as Jorn says, Logan is a mortal woman and cannot give you what you seek." Randin shook his head, "I think perhaps this time you are wrong."

"Ottar, rein in your sons; they are speaking out of turn." The Emperor turned to Jorn's father, who was still slumped on the floor with his friend.

"No, Ragnar, they are not speaking out of turn. You are." Ottar got up off the floor, his shoulders broad, his fists balled, and his eyes rouge. "You cannot bear to be wrong, can you? Did it ever occur to you that this woman isn't what you think? That she isn't one of them. That she is just a normal girl who loves a boy?" he said exasperatedly. "You've been searching for centuries for one of these beings. If it has taken you this long, maybe you *are* wrong."

"Oh, Ottar, you are such a disappointment to me," Ragnar said, waving his brother off as though he was an irksome fly. "This is why I am who I am, and you are who you are. You have always been too submissive."

Jorn's father shook his head again, casting his eye over the dead chauffeur, his heart heavy in his chest.

"You are deluded, uncle," Jorn said, looking up at The

Emperor. Logan was special, but not in the way his uncle thought. She was special to Jorn in every way a woman could be.

"Deluded, am I?" The Emperor scathed. "Can you not see this on her skin?" He nodded at Louiza, who swooped, shoving Logan's head down to reveal the back of her neck. He moved up to her, his long-fingered hand stroking her right arm, her skin immediately feeling cold, tracing up it to the intricately drawn tattoo just below her hairline. "Can you not all see this mark imprinted here? She is one of them. I KNOW SHE IS!"

His face grew rather demented, his shoulders hunched as he grabbed her upper arms, her face crumbling under his touch as though breaking it.

"Stop this, sire. You are hurting her." Oska had come forward now, his blood-stained hand holding onto The Emperor's to stop him. "You will break her arms." Jorn knew his brother would never tolerate the abuse he was seeing; his caring, healing ability would have taken over, and Jorn thought that their delay in finding him and Logan was because Oska had stopped to try and heal the shifters. "She is a mortal woman, sire. You have not found what you are looking for."

"YES, I HAVE!" He chucked off Oska's hand so harshly that Oska almost lost his balance, Lachlan coming to his assistance.

"I know she is one, she bears the mark, and I know she's been having severe headaches. I know it all." He held his arms up in triumph. "I know you are having headaches, my sweet girl." He looked over at Lachlan. "Mind-numbing headaches that make you black out, that make you feel back pain. That make you... hear voices." Logan felt a new wave of tears start, for she knew that most people in this room were aware of her bad one the other day. Oska had tried to help, and Jorn had spoken to Lachlan about it.

"Ha!" The Emperor made her jump, clapping his hands again, "You see, I know it all." His lips touched her ear as he spoke. "I know everything." She shied away from him, shaking her head solemnly. "Lachlan?" Lachlan stirred from holding Oska; his face was pale in his plain jogging bottoms and long-sleeved top. His exuberance from the ballroom vanished.

"Yes, sire," he nodded briefly.

"What do you see when you look at her? Because I know Jorn instructed you to 'see' her, to look into her brain." He sketched the air with quotation marks.

With a cough, Lachlan replied, "I do not see anything debilitating about Miss Hunter, sire."

"And why is that?" The Emperor almost purred.

"Because..." He looked at Jorn with sorrow in his eyes. "Because, my Lord, I cannot see through the shield she has around herself." He looked to the floor, not meeting the looks of all his cousins.

"Thank you, Lachlan. You have been the most honest with me this night."

There was silence for a moment, and then Jorn said, "This is all bullshit, uncle."

"Is it Jorn? Well, when I want your opinion, I'll ask for it." He turned his back to the audience, his hands gripping the fire mantel, a pondering look in his eye. "So, how best to get what I want?"

The brothers just watched each other, each wondering what the next was thinking or what the plan was. Could they all take him on? Could they win? Did they stand a chance? Even Quinn stood waiting for instructions from the brothers he now treated as friends.

"You already know what you're going to do, Ragnar," Ellika said, sighing.

"Yes, I suppose I do. It's just I don't know if I want it anymore."

Ellika moved swiftly to her husband, her talon-fingered hand of rubies massaging his shoulders. "The instructions were to take both, so let us take them and be done. I am bored with this night."

He smiled at her as he pulled the blade from the mantel. The long unsheathed metal that was made of tungsten steel glinted in the firelight. The sheen embossed red with flame before he twisted round and plunged it through Logan's chest down to the hilt.

CHAPTER TWENTY SEVEN

THE NATURAL

The breeze from his uncle moving past him ruffled his hair, and he was briefly taken back to that Saturday night in the pub when Quinn and his friends had entered the building. And yet now he seemed to watch in slow motion the blade twist into Logan's chest, her eyes widening as it sliced through her skin. She bucked forward, hunching over the sword, before losing her balance and tumbling back into Lachlan's outstretched arms, before she hit the floor. The Emperor stood still, holding the handle, the blade getting longer the further she fell and before Lachlan had her completely, the metal dripped with blood as it hung from his uncle's hand. Oska was there, skidding on his knees, his hands putting pressure on the wound that poured blood from her chest, her skin already saturated. It already pooling on the floor. There were shouts and curses all around; Jorn's father had whipped off his shirt and bundled it against the wound, and Randin was hollering at Kol to get something else to curb the flow. But Jorn just knelt there, watching. Watching the scene unfold in front of him. It was as though his eyes seemed not to be working correctly. His eyelids were blinking too slowly, too slowly to be natural, and yet all he could do was look, not at Logan but at his uncle. His uncle stood straight, a sentinel being of great power, and it was as if a halo of golden light shone around him. The Emperor, whose eyes were now the brilliant red Jorn remembered from his nightmares, surveyed Jorn, and for a minute, they stared at one another. Each investigated the other, searching each other's souls for the answer to the conundrum in front of them. How could The Emperor get what he wanted, and how could Jorn get what he wanted?

Steadily, Jorn pulled apart the bonds from behind his back, his strength now fully returned, the ties biting into his wrist causing them to bleed, and yet he felt no pain. He couldn't feel pain when he knew that his Queen was dead. Despite Oska's ability to heal, despite the quick work of his brother and of his cousin, Jorn knew that no one, not even a Gifted, could come back from a stab in the heart. And yet...

"Remember, my son, she is your strength. The usurper must fall, and a true Gifted shall rise."

Exploring the depths of his uncle's soul, he could see the answer he needed, but how could this help him? Yet he knew the resolution before he even knew he had. There was no other way; he had to save her, and he was the only one who could, because he understood now. He understood his uncle's obsession with Logan, and he understood his obsession with him and why it had to be him and no one else to have her love. It was because of what *he* was. What Jorn had been born to be. What he had had all his life and only his uncle had known.

Not even Jorn's father.

Holding his arms out in front of him, his body in surrender to his uncle's powers, he said,

"I know what it is you want, sire." Everything in the room stilled. The shouting suddenly ceased, and the pleading for her to live stopped. Even the blood seemed to stop dripping from her now pale chest.

"JORN, NO!" his father called, trying to get to him before he said the words that he had most feared.

"If you save her, sire, you can take what it is you seek." He bowed his head, his hands outstretched, "I offer it to you freely."

The Emperor smirked, a malicious grin of total triumph shown all over his face.

Jorn's father suddenly collided with him, pulling him in, his arms about his neck, his sobs shocking the room as he begged his son.

"Please, please, do not do this."

Jorn hugged his father. The man whom he had hated for centuries, who had made him do things he didn't want to, and who had not shown love to any of his sons since his mother had walked upon the ice, wept into his shoulder.

"Please don't!" Ottar said, his body trembling under Jorn's hold.

Lifting his father off his shoulder, Jorn looked into his

eyes, and for the first time, he saw the man who had loved his family. Who had played with him in the snow as a boy.

Who had adored them all.

Who had loved his mother for all eternity.

"I must, Pappa," Jorn whispered, wiping the tears from his father's face. "You would have done it for mamma."

Ottar closed his eyes, knowing that his son spoke truths. He would have traded places with her in a heartbeat if it meant she would still be with them today.

"Not a day passes when I do not wish it so," he said, nodding.

"What does he mean, Jorn?" Lamont asked regarding the embrace between his father and brother with wonder.

"Yes, brother, what are you speaking of?" Jorun asked, his hands still holding the shirt to Logan's chest, though all knew it was pointless now.

Jorn looked over at each brother, them in turn searching him for some explanation.

"Oska does not have the power to save her," Jorn said, seeing the sadness in Oska's eyes as he confirmed the truth. "But he does."

They all followed Jorn's gaze, all eyes focusing on The Emperor, who was standing by the fireplace, looking in on the family united in front of him.

"NO!" Randin shouted, "No, my brother, you cannot do

this."

"Do not be mistaken, Randin. He can, and he already has," The Emperor smirked, burning off Logan's blood from the blade in the fire.

"Can someone please tell me what the hell is going on?" Kol said, his cheeks damp with tears for Logan, his shirt off and placed now half-heartedly at her chest.

"How long have you known, Jorn?" Randin asked, his face contorted with pain for his brother.

Jorn smiled, "I think I have always known my eldest brother; it's just taken this event to bring it to the forefront of my mind." He moved to kneel next to Logan, pushing her hair from her face, feeling her still-warm skin under his fingertips.

"What?" Kol repeated, "What have you always known?"

"For fuck's sake, Ottar, are your family Gifted beings or just stupid humans?" Ragnar snorted, holding the now-heated blade out in front of him.

"My sons are a whole unit, Ragnar; they have something you and I never had. They have something you would never understand." He looked at his sons individually. "I have watched them grow into the most amazing men I have ever seen, and I will be forever proud of them."

"Well, from where I am standing, there is nothing but weakness. It seeps from them."

"It is not weakness, Ragnar. It is love, compassion, loyalty, friendship, hope, goodness. It is all that you are not. We were always opposites, you and I, which is why I have them, and you have that." He nodded to Louiza, who sat nonplussed on the couch.

"There is nothing wrong with my Louiza," The Emperor pondered, looking at his daughter.

"That is a matter of opinion," Ottar voiced, looking down at Logan, her broken body still lying on Lachlan's lap.

"So, uncle," Jorn turned to The Emperor, his eyes focused on him now. He did not want to see Logan's blood on the floor; he did not want to smell her sweet perfume rife on her skin. He did not want to see the face, which had had so much flush to it only hours ago as he made love to her, now lost of all colour. He did not want to remember her smile as she'd looked down on him from the balcony or her serene beauty hidden by a masquerade mask. How her skin had shimmered in the lights from the maze, how her hair had sparkled. How her eyes had mesmerised him as she'd walked across the room to him. He did not want to remember, but neither did he want to forget. He wanted her to be his last memory.

"Will you take what I offer in exchange for her life?" Jorn asked. "Will you take the one thing I know you crave above all things? Will you give her back her life in exchange for my ability?"

"WHAT?" Jorun shouted, moving to his brother, but his father stood and barred Jorun from touching his twin. "Jorn, you cannot do this to me. You are me, and I am you. We are linked. Your death will kill me!" Jorun exclaimed, his father's hand on his arm stopping him from advancing.

"You will not die, my brother. For eternal life is forever long."

"I cannot live without you by my side. We have always been together, always," Jorun said, attempting to push his father away.

"I know, but I cannot let her die. One day, you will understand."

"But I don't understand now," Jorun said, trying to get to Jorn, yet his father's hand was strong.

"But you will." Jorn turned away from his brothers. He did not want them to see his grief.

"I do not get it. Why does The Emperor want your ability, Jorn? He gave it to you when you were born; he already has that ability," Kol said, taking a wet cloth and wiping Logan's chest of dry blood.

"Don't you understand it, Kol?" Randin said, his inability to keep things quiet made him speak up. "He...he... he is a naturally Gifted being."

Randin's brothers stood there in disbelief. A natural was unheard of, so rare that it had not been seen for millennia and yet...

"Yes, you are right, Randin. I was born with my abilities. The Emperor did not bestow them upon me as mother and father thought. As soon as he touched me, he knew that I was a powerful being. Perhaps as powerful as him. So, he has been biding his time, waiting for me to be at my weakest, giving me missions so I may, in time, sacrifice myself for someone at his mercy." Jorn looked at his uncle, who only nodded.

"And you did not know, Pappa?" Jorun asked, almost shaking his father as though to knock some sense into him.

"I have always suspected Jorn's abilities were elemental, but I was never going to ask about him to my brother. It would have only endangered him further." Ottar slumped his shoulders in defeat. His brother, The Emperor, had won again. "My brother has never helped me. He has never done anything for us unless there was something in it for him." He looked maliciously at The Emperor, and for a moment, the two brothers stared at each other, the conversation of silence mesmerising the boys as they tried to understand the revelations within the room. "His conniving plans regarding Jorn and Logan have only ever been for his own personal gain."

"Why should I not do things for personal gain, Ottar? I am The Emperor, after all."

"You have always been the same, Ragnar. Helped nobody but yourself," Ottar stated firmly.

"I have always helped you when you asked for it," Ragnar said, shrugging. "Sometimes, Ottar, things are out of my hands."

"You could have assisted me more in former years, Ragnar. You know this. But your selfishness has always got in the way."

"It wasn't my selfishness that forced her to walk away, Ottar. It wasn't my selfishness that made her go out onto the ice that day," Ragnar sneered.

"You are an unimaginable bastard," Ottar said, shaking his head. "You said you'd help me with her, and you didn't. You took advantage of a family in need and have since reaped the reward. And now, you take my son. All for your advantage."

Ragnar smirked, "Whether for personal gain or not, it matters not, my brother."

"I gave you everything you wanted, Ragnar. None of it was lawfully yours," Ottar said quietly, the shame of what he'd done years ago reverberating through his heart.

Ragnar sighed, "You allowed me to take everything, Ottar. So, I can now take what should belong to me."

"JORN'S ABILITY IS NOT RIGHTFULLY YOURS, RAGNAR!" Ottar bellowed at his brother.

"I AM THE EMPEROR, OTTAR. I CAN DO WHAT I LIKE!" Ragnar shouted, his superior authority making all those in the vicinity cower under his presence.

He turned to Jorn, his leadership hovering over the people like a cloud, forcing them to look down at the floor. His entire family were beneath him.

"You will save her uncle, and then you will leave her alone. You will not touch her family or have any connection with her whatsoever," Jorn said, his uncle's authority having no power over him suddenly. "You shall leave this house and never return. You will leave my family alone. There is to be no more tormenting. The contract between our families will be null and void. I cannot have you hurting them any more than you already have."

"There has never been any contract, nephew. I am The Emperor of The Gifted community, and I will do what I like," Ragnar hissed.

"No, uncle, you will not. I will not relinquish my ability to you unless you do this," Jorn said.

"No, Jorn, for you have already offered it to me freely. I will save her as I feel her death at this moment is unnecessary. But you cannot stop the future from unfolding."

"You have no right to be in your position of power, uncle. You cannot treat people the way you do!" Jorn said, his hands pulled behind him by Louiza as The Emperor approached Logan. "May you rot in the fires of hell."

His uncle tutted, "Be careful, Jorn, for I may change my mind."

He walked over to Lachlan, and Lachlan surrendered Logan's frail body to The Emperor.

Despite his harshness, he laid her flat against the floor, her arms down by her sides, the pool of blood next to her clotted like liver. With one hand, he scooped up her head and with the other, he hovered it over her heart. His body shook as he said words none of them could understand, his lips quivering, barely making a sound. A wind rustled his robes, and the flames stuttered momentarily in the grate. The sound of rushing could be heard, like water over a cliff, and a tremor shook the earth as he continued his incantation. Jorn watched her as the vigour returned slowly to her body. The tone increasing, the colour to her hair brightening, the flush to her cheeks regaining. Soon, the sound of breathing could be heard; the distinct rise and fall seen.

She sat up quickly, her chest heaving with a need to expand her lungs as an infant would as it took its first breath. Turning, she gazed over at Jorn, her face melting into a beautiful smile. It was the smile he loved and would love now for all eternity.

For wherever he was going, that memory would never ever be lost. It would last forever.

CHAPTER TWENTY EIGHT

THE DARK ANGEL

The air that filled Logan's lungs was cold. A coldness like she'd never felt. It was as if she were out in the snow, the air biting at her chest, making her extremities tremble. She could feel the blood rushing through her veins, the individual pulse as it circulated her. She could feel her cheeks heat, her fingers tingle, her toes twitch, and her stomach gurgle. She could hear the intermittent breath of Lachlan as he leaned up to her, scanning her body for any sign of illness or fatigue. She felt them all staring at her as Oska removed his shirt and pulled it around her. She saw sorrow in Randin's eyes as he observed her. She noted the tears on Kol's cheeks, the single stream of water running down, making a path through the minute hairs on his face. Lamont sat on the sofa, his head in his hands, Quinn's hand on his shoulder, his face drained of any colour. She saw Jorun and his father locked together in an embrace that was so full of pain that her heart throbbed violently. She wanted to ease all their grief.

Lifting her eyes to Jorn, she saw the man she'd seen in the pub. Those dark green eyes surveying her. She saw the man whose seductive looks had captivated her across the open office, whose presence had made her lightheaded. Who had made her drop that coffee cup. She could see the man who had come to her aid at the hospital, who had taken her to see Julia. Who had bought her the rose that sat on her bedside cabinet. She could feel him igniting the fire in her, fuelling the passion as it rose from the pits of her stomach to every fingertip. Her chest heaved as she remembered him between the bed sheets, his touch, his kiss, his taste. Jorn was the man she had dreamed of as she lay in bed at night, the man she daydreamed about at work. When she had lain dying on this floor, this was the man she loved.

And yet, something was wrong. The whole room pulsed with anguish. A sadness she didn't understand. Her eyes widened as she saw his uncle holding the blade that had maimed her to her lover's throat. Was his uncle going to kill him now?

"Jorn?" her voice croaked, making her hands grasp her throat.

But Jorn just looked away, saying, "Jorun, please take her away from here. She does not need to see this."

Jorun got to his feet, after extracting himself from his father's embrace, and moving to Logan, lifting her into his arms.

"Please don't take me away," she stammered, her throat rasping.

"I must, Logan. You do not want to see this," Jorun said, not looking back at his twin.

"But I must be with him." Her lips trembled as he walked her away. "Please don't make me leave him," she stuttered, tears falling now.

"You must, Logan," Lachlan said, walking alongside them; he, too, did not want to see his cousin's sacrifice. He could not bear to witness the torture.

"I cannot let him do whatever it is that he is planning," she whispered, as they walked past the marble pillars.

"I'm afraid he has already done it," Lachlan grimaced, the sparkle absent from his eyes. "He offered his ability to him in exchange for your life. There is no going back now."

"I do not understand what you mean. I must stay with him until the end," she said, twisting in Jorun's arms.

"No. You must be taken to a place of safety, Logan. This is what Jorn would have... wanted," Jorun said, wiping tears from his eyes. "He has made his choice, and we must respect him." He sniffed and then collapsed, his emotions too hard to bear.

'Do not weep, my brother, for I shall always be a part of you.'

Jorun listened to his twin in his mind, and even though it gave him little comfort, he picked himself back up and once again attempted to escort Logan out of the room.

"Jorun, please put me down; I must be with him. I......"

The screaming then started, the gut-wrenching screaming of someone in sheer agony, making Jorun buckle again as he felt the pain his brother was experiencing. The torture of a red-hot poker scalding his body, it burrowing underneath the skin, shearing off piece by piece. Clutching his chest, Jorun fell into Lachlan, his head filling with what was a thousand wasps, them stinging every part of his brain. Bolts of lightning started popping within his skull, ricocheting about, bouncing off every surface of the bone.

'Fight him, Jorn, you must fight him, or he will kill us both.'

Jorun mind linked with his twin, pleading with him not to give it up. And for a second, the pain stopped, and Jorun looked around to see Jorn kneeling on the floor, his torso ripped to shreds, his skin slashed with claw-like marks and yet his uncle stood there as still as marble, his hands by his side, his eyes closed. He hadn't lifted a finger; Jorn was bleeding profusely from injuries induced only by words.

Randin now had hold of his father, who had sunk broken to the floor, watching his son go through such hell that no one could ever forget or envision. Oska, Lamont, and Kol sat together, their heads bent in on each other, trying to find the strength to fathom what had happened to their world, which had, only hours ago, been full of fun and happiness and was now so destroyed that there was no point of reconciliation. Ellika, Portia and Louiza sat only visually aware of what was happening. Quinn crouched to the floor, his arms around his head, for even he, a strong mammal-shifter, could not handle the anguish of what he was witnessing.

'Jorn? If you can hear me, fight him! If you are The Natural, you believe you are, then your abilities far

outweigh his. He is stealing powers from another person, far greater than he will ever be. Don't let him take you, Jorn. Please!'

Jorun leaned back into the wall, the pain to his chest so bad that he felt his lungs were folding in on themselves. They could not be filled with air, and he began to struggle with his own breathing. Lachlan sat him upright, speaking into his ear, trying to get him to steady his breaths. But he couldn't. The Emperor was killing his twin, and though they were not bonded any more by anything other than brotherly love and family, he was slowly allowing the encroaching darkness to take him. He could see Jorn writhing and turning on the floor now, his blood smearing over the white rug, his body twisting into such obscure shapes that Jorun wondered how it could do it. His arms contorted, his fingers curled like talons, each one individually tremored as Jorn fought against his uncle's ambitions, as he fought against everything his uncle held in high regard.

Jorn knew his uncle would never win against a Natural. But could he, Jorn, have enough fight in him to succeed? Could he finally beat this man who had, for centuries, haunted his nightmares? Who had haunted his father's life. Jorn knew that The Emperor must die; the torment he had caused was too much for any family to take. He needed him gone. He needed him to forgo his hold on his family, for it was he who had lied and cheated his way into their intimacies. He would not win. And yet, the pain was getting too much to bear. Surely it was just easier to let him have what he had offered? For The Emperor to take The Watcher ability from him. For him to die and know nothing of the future? But could he leave his family to their fate? Could he let them stand alone against his tyranny?

"Jorn? You were born to beat him."

Jorn knew the words spoken by his mother weren't real; they were just imaginary. An incorrect signal through his brain to assist him in his suffering. Was she perhaps calling him to the shadowlands, calling him to come to her and be at peace? No. That was not possible. He wasn't ready. He had so much more to do in his life. He didn't want to go out like this. He didn't want to die kneeling at the feet of a tyrant who was so hellbent on causing agony and chaos when there was no reason to be had. Nevertheless, the burn began to be too much. His skin was being peeled from his bones. He couldn't open his eyes to see, but he knew his skin was puckering, sizzling in a heat so hot it was melting him. How long would this go on for? He was on the edge of a desert, a sandy wasteland that stretched out for thousands of miles with no horizon to be seen. There was to be no end to it all. There was to be no finish line. The anguish would be endured for eternity.

It was then that a hand brushed over his skin, and he welcomed the relief it brought him, though he did not know whose it was, but it was a tender hand. A tender hand that filled him with light. A light that shone so bright that he was blinded, blinded by its unmitigated brilliance. The whispers in his ear were that of beauty, like a single snowflake or individual raindrop. Like the reflection of the moon on a still pool or the rising of the sun on the sea.

"Jorn, hear my voice." He could hear her, but who was she? "I am not afraid anymore, for I also feel as you do." Her arms encircled his neck as he struggled to keep the fight going. "I was scared to say it before, for I felt that once it is said, there is no going back." She inhaled deeply. "But I realise now that I wouldn't want to go back. I want to go forward and keep going forward, with your hand in mine and your love in my heart." He could hear a smile in her voice. "For I love you, Jorn, and I will love you until the end of my days, and if that is by your side right now in death, then that is what it is. But I love you now, and I always have done. I am yours, and you are mine."

Jorn felt his arms edge around her neck, smell the scent of her perfume, and feel the heat of her skin. Hear the beatings of her heart. It was her, the woman from his imaginings. The woman from the screens in his room, from across the room filled with masked people. She was his, and he was hers, and if he was to die, then this is how he wanted it to be. In her arms, in her presence. In her embrace.

Logan held Jorn as close as she could, their foreheads together, their bodies so near, their breathing in time with each other that no one could tear them apart. It was then that she felt it. The feeling that started as an ache now began to flare, a sharp stab as a knife to the back and yet, it wasn't the blade of death. It was the blade of life. A life so different that neither of these people could have conceived it. From her spine, two large black wings appeared, the feathers so soft and intricate that they shimmered with the colours of petrol on water. A glimmer of purple, green, pink and blue swirled through the vast appendage that looked, from the watching audience, to be a shelter of safety. She allowed her wings to spread wide, encasing them both with a protective shield that prevented The Emperor from touching him.

For she was special, more special than any of them had ever known or even comprehended. It had taken Jorn's sacrifice to bring her to fruition, taken the paralysing headaches she'd endured to ensure she was ready for her ability to make itself known.

For she was, and always had been, The Dark Angel and her birth had been written in the ancient scriptures. She was to change the course of his life forever.

The End

All species on this planet are but specks of dust suspended in a beam of sunlight. But for The Watcher and The Dark Angel, there is no shadow that can cast them in darkness.

Next instalment:

The Gifted Series

Book Two

The Dark Angel

About The Author

Ennis Stanley was born in Cambridgeshire, grew up in Bedfordshire, and now lives in Hertfordshire with her husband, two children and family dog. Her enthusiasm for writing comes from sitting up at night breastfeeding her second child and wishing for an easy read book, that she could pick up, read a chapter and then go back to bed; hence The Watcher and The Gifted Community was created.

Printed in Dunstable, United Kingdom